# LEGEND OF THE FIVE RINGS

The realm of Rokugan is a land of samurai, courtiers, and mystics, dragons, magic, and divine beings – a world where honor is stronger than steel.

The Seven Great Clans have defended and served the Emperor of the Emerald Empire for a thousand years, in battle and at the imperial court. While conflict and political intrigue divide the clans, the true threat awaits in the darkness of the Shadowlands, behind the vast Kaiu Wall. There, in the twisted wastelands, an evil corruption endlessly seeks the downfall of the empire.

The rules of Rokugani society are strict. Uphold your honor, lest you lose everything in pursuit of glory.

# *The* MARKET *of* 100 FORTUNES

MARIE BRENNAN

First published by Aconyte Books in 2024

ISBN 978 1 83908 259 7

Ebook ISBN 978 1 83908 260 3

Cover art by Shen Fei

Rokugan map by Francesca Baerald

Distributed in North America by Simon & Schuster Inc, New York, USA

Printed in the United States of America

9 8 7 6 5 4 3 2 1

**ACONYTE BOOKS**

*An imprint of Asmodee Entertainment Ltd*

Mercury House, Shipstones Business Centre

North Gate, Nottingham NG7 7FN, UK

*aconytebooks.com // twitter.com/aconytebooks*

Dragon Lands
SHELTERED PLAINS CITY
Phoenix Lands
Rokugan
Lion Lands
BRITTLE FLOWER CITY
Northern Crane Lands

# CHAPTER ONE

The streets of Brittle Flower City's market were narrow to begin with, and made more so by the counters lining shop-fronts, banners advertising wares, and itinerant sellers with packs and sticks of trinkets to sell. Add in hordes of customers and residents, and making one's way down the street at any speed greater than a snail's crawl became a test of agility.

A test Sayashi was entirely capable of passing. In human form, she didn't even have to worry about someone treading on her tail.

But no feline dexterity could get her past the man now coming down the street. The heavy pole balanced across his shoulders almost scraped the walls on either side, and the wrapped bundles dangling from the ends threatened to sweep all before him like the oncoming tide. Passers-by squawked in annoyance, some of them dodging into shops for safety. A potter flung her body over the rice bowls stacked on her counter to protect them, and got a solid buffet from one of the bundles for her pains. The porter with the pole shouted apologies with every step, twisting sideways in an attempt to present a narrower profile, but that nearly resulted in him braining the potter, who was straightening as she thought the storm had passed.

Sayashi hissed in annoyance. For one brief instant, she considered turning into a cat to escape. But her small form would get stepped on, her large form would still have a difficult time getting past the man, and in either case, a traveler suddenly revealing herself to be a bakeneko in the middle of a crowded street would only cause more trouble than it was worth.

There was no handy doorway to slip through. Instead Sayashi flattened herself against the nearest wall, face-first so that if something took an unfortunate hit, at least it wouldn't be her nose.

She found herself in licking distance of a tiny shrine embedded into the wall. Not surprising: this was the Market of a Hundred Fortunes, one of Brittle Flower City's most famous districts. Some of the Fortunes got big, fancy shrines with gateways and everything; the rest made do with little structures tucked in between the shops and houses, or even less than that. Sayashi doubted the Fortune of Whetstones felt very honored by its accommodations, but it wasn't any of her business. She wasn't here for any such piddling spiritual power.

The power she sought had no shrine. At least, not that she'd been able to find… so far.

The scrape of a pole-end across Sayashi's back made her snarl. The porter's cheerful apology didn't do much to soothe it. She stayed where she was, not trusting that he wouldn't accidentally hit her again, until the noise of the street returned to something more like its usual clamor. Then she peeled herself off the wall. If he'd torn the fabric of her kimono, she would follow him, wait until he returned home at the end of the day, and then–

Sayashi drew in a deep breath, held it for a count of eight, let it out slowly. No. She wouldn't get revenge. That wasn't what she was here for, either.

But it was hard to resist the temptation when she was having such an absence of luck on other fronts. Sayashi had been up and down every street in the market a dozen times, by day and by night, at dawn and at dusk, walking every path in every direction. She'd examined the gates set into the four walls that surrounded the market, the gate of every shrine that had one. She'd made offerings. She'd tried to step through into the Enchanted Country, the spiritual realm that lay just to the side of the mortal world, with no success.

She could hear her mother laughing. *Foolish kitten. Why do you bother?*

Her mother was dead, split apart like her two tails by the blade of a samurai scholar. A nekomata couldn't become a ghost like a human could – Sayashi was *fairly* certain – but she didn't need actual spiritual existence to haunt Sayashi. Memory was enough.

A man bent under the weight of a water barrel and a portable brazier for tea smacked into Sayashi's back, and she hissed a curse at him before she realized it was her own fault. She'd stopped in the middle of the street, caught by a sudden thought.

That samurai scholar. Asako Sekken – assuming he hadn't

come to his senses by now and married his all-too-honorable Dragon priest. He might be Isao Sekken at this point. Sayashi didn't know why humans made such a fuss about such matters, all the names and the rituals and holding back from people they loved because society said it wasn't allowed. But it was only a few months since she'd seen him last. If Sekken hadn't yet married Ryōtora, if he hadn't gone to Dragon lands…

She hurried onward, darting through the crowds with a grace and speed that hardly even brushed the sleeves of those she passed. To the western gate in the wall surrounding the market, leaping over the wooden sill that confined carts to a narrow path, and into the broader street beyond. Here there was space enough for her to run, and if this Crane city wasn't as abundantly supplied with stationers' shops as she'd become used to in Phoenix lands, she still didn't have to go far.

For a copper penny, she got a sheet of paper and the use of the shop's supplies. The brush was battered and the ink was watery, but Sayashi wasn't a geisha now, sending elegant letters to her clients. Still, pride made her write the opening salutation as neatly as she could.

Then she stopped. How to phrase it? How much to admit? And would Sekken even heed her letter?

Well. If he didn't, that would answer some of her questions all on its own. He wouldn't be the first human to fall victim to hypocrisy, nor even the first samurai.

Sayashi wrote and sealed her letter, then returned the brush and ink to the shopkeeper. For a bit more money – she'd even earned it honestly! – he agreed to send the letter north, to Sheltered Plains City in Phoenix lands. If Sekken wasn't there, his family could forward it on.

It would take days. Weeks even, before she received an answer. Assuming he sent one.

In the meanwhile, she would keep searching. The sword at the shrine might have proved fake, but she still had hope for the market: not the ordinary thing she'd just left behind, but the *real* Market of a Hundred Fortunes. She just had to find a way in.

Then she could buy herself some answers – and, perhaps, a new fate.

# CHAPTER TWO

Ryōtora knelt on the polished wooden floor of the little shrine behind the Dragon embassy and, closing his eyes, let out a slow breath.

He'd spent many hours meditating here since he came to Phoenix lands for winter court. First in an attempt to hold together the unstable edifice of his health; then, once he knew the truth of his affliction, to reach some kind of peace with it. To absorb the understanding that his soul was now linked with Sekken's – a link they could manage, nurture, protect, but must always, for the rest of their lives, take into account.

It didn't have to be bad. True, there were still days when they misstepped, when one or the other of them drew too deeply on their pool of shared strength without warning the other. But now that they knew that pool *was* shared, they were discovering interesting things they could do with it.

Ryōtora whispered the repetitive syllables of a mantra under his breath, barely a ghost of sound in the silence. This was one of the first techniques he'd learned, when he first began training as a priest who could speak to the elemental spirits: the basic task of *sensing* those spirits.

They were all around him, always. Everything in the world, Ryōtora included, was made up of them. But the spirits inherent in the cypress boards beneath his knees, the sturdy cotton of his spring kimono, the incense-tinged air that brushed his skin – those were tiny, all but mindless things. It took the gift of speaking to spirits, then training to use that gift, before someone could wake them and persuade them to perform some task. Other spirits were more powerful, like those of rivers and ancient trees; some of them rose to the rank of Fortune, receiving offerings from ordinary people.

Still, in the end, everything came down to this: the simple elements of Earth, Water, Air, and Fire. And Void, the element that did not exist... and yet, through its absence, defined and gave purpose to everything around it.

Ryōtora focused on that last one now. Reaching past the solidity of Earth, the delicacy of Air; past the serenity of Water and the faint warmth of Fire as the afternoon sun crept through the open door of the shrine to touch Ryōtora's back. Beneath and behind and within them all lay the emptiness of Void, in which the boundary between him and Sekken was revealed as illusion. All things were one in the Void, distance dissolved, spirits united.

Ryōtora and Sekken.

Sekken and...

There.

For a moment, Ryōtora was both in the shrine and not. Kneeling on the floor, and trotting across a flagstone courtyard. From there down the graveled channel meant to catch water dripping from the eaves, then onto a cushion of moss, softer against his paws. More flagstones, cypress steps…

Tanshu had good enough manners not to shove his nose under Ryōtora's arm. But the vertiginous sight of his own body, kneeling in meditation, tipped Ryōtora out of his trance; he opened his eyes to find Tanshu sitting a short distance away, tongue lolling out in a canine grin.

"Well *done*," Ryōtora said, giving the inugami a thorough scratch behind the ears.

From outside came Sekken's voice, wry with amusement. "Are we sure this was a real test? If I were Tanshu, this shrine is the first place I would have looked for you."

"I felt him," Ryōtora said, rising. The motion seemed briefly peculiar, as if he ought to be on four paws instead of two feet. "Then I saw through his eyes. He knew exactly where I was."

"Give it another month, and you'll be a better witch than I am."

Sekken put up one hand to shade his eyes as he said it, casting his expression into shadow. Not fast enough, though, to hide the faint disappointment and frustration there – or maybe Ryōtora just felt it. He couldn't be sure how much his growing awareness of Sekken's mood was filtering through the connection between them, and how much was him coming to understand the other man more deeply.

It was peculiar to think how short a time they'd known each other. A few chaotic weeks in Seibo Mura, two strangers struggling to rescue the village from the supernatural threat of the Night Parade; a few months at Ryōdō Temple, but much of that time spent asleep or otherwise recuperating from the aftereffects of that battle. Then winter court here in

Phoenix lands, where both of them had been trying to hide their weakened health from each other and from the rest of the world. Only in these last few months had they been able to live something like normally.

Tanshu ran down the five steps to the courtyard and planted himself loyally at Sekken's side. They were still discovering just how intelligent the inugami was – or sometimes Ryōtora wondered if the spirit's intelligence was growing as his bond with Sekken did.

And through Sekken, with Ryōtora.

"Tanshu will always be *your* familiar," Ryōtora said, following the inugami out of the shrine. "Kaimin-nushi was your ancestor, not mine, and it's your bloodline he's bound to. I only have a connection to him because you and I are connected."

"Yes, but you're able to use it so much better."

Because Ryōtora had more training in such matters. Sekken *knew* vastly more about many things than Ryōtora did – even the Spirit Realms, which ought to be Ryōtora's domain as a priest – but much of his knowledge was theoretical, not practical.

He could change that. Had already begun to do so, first in Seibo Mura, then here in Sheltered Plains City, when the influence of a baku from the Realm of Dreams overtook many of the samurai at court. In the end, though, it was true that Sekken didn't have the gift of speaking to the spirits. There would always be things Ryōtora could do that he could not.

Would that extend even to working with Tanshu?

Ryōtora was still searching for a good response when Sankan Yoichi, the chief clerk of the Dragon embassy, came along the curving path through the garden and bowed to them both. "Please forgive me for interrupting, but Lord Isao, you wished to be informed when the escort arrived."

"So soon?" Ryōtora said, blinking up at the sky as if the time of day had anything to do with it. He hadn't expected the travelers to reach the city until tomorrow at the earliest.

"The benefits of traveling in this season, I expect," Sekken said. "By now the roads have dried out. I can return home if you're busy, Ryōtora–"

"Come with me to greet them," Ryōtora said on impulse. "After all, you'll be traveling with them, too."

The truth was that he didn't want Sekken to leave yet, not with the shadow of that exchange about Tanshu still lying over them both. What he said wasn't false, though. If their two clans had been hostile to one another, Phoenix samurai would have escorted Sekken to the border between their lands, there to be handed off to a Dragon delegation. Since they weren't – and since the Dragon preferred to limit the number of travelers in their territory – instead the delegation had come here to collect him. Together they would travel to Fire Tooth Castle… and there, at last, they would marry.

The front courtyard, where Sekken had been waiting with Tanshu not long ago, had transformed into a bustling mass of ponies and riders. Mirumoto Kinmoku, the Dragon ambassador, stood at the top of the embassy steps; she was not a woman inclined toward great formality, waiting to receive the new arrivals inside. As Ryōtora and Sekken joined her, another woman in a stiff-shouldered jacket embroidered with the crest of the Mirumoto family approached Kinmoku and bowed.

As they exchanged greetings, Ryōtora's gaze drifted past the woman to the rest of the escort. A priest had joined the Mirumoto warrior; that would be Agasha Tōemon, the man usually assigned to the embassy, who'd returned to Dragon lands over the winter for the funeral of his mother. He would remain here when the rest departed. Apart from him, Ryōtora saw two more samurai, six ashigaru, and at least a few servants, though it was hard to separate those who worked at the embassy from those who'd arrived with the group.

Did this count as a large or impressive escort, honoring Sekken, or had the Dragon kept it insultingly small? Ryōtora had no idea. It was small by the standards of a daimyō's procession, but Sekken's family wasn't *that* high in rank. He hoped it wasn't an insult. The Dragon should be pleased to have a man as esteemed as Sekken joining their ranks.

Then he spotted two familiar faces in the crowd, and his heart surged with delight. Whatever political message the escort might convey, the personal one was of clear warmth and welcome. For among the ashigaru were two faces he recognized from those harrowing days in Seibo Mura: Ishi and Tarō.

Sekken was standing close enough to Ryōtora to notice the twitch when the other man spotted their old ashigaru comrades. But Ryōtora was far too courteous to ignore Kinmoku and the others so he could go greet a pair of commoners. Not until the ambassador invited her samurai guests in for tea did Ryōtora excuse himself. Sekken murmured his own apology and followed Ryōtora, with Tanshu – now incorporeal and invisible, so there was no risk of being stepped on – close at his heels.

By then some of the ponies had been led to the embassy stables, opening up space in the courtyard. Tarō saw Ryōtora and Sekken coming, and as he tapped Ishi on the shoulder, his square face broke into an unrestrained smile.

A smile Ryōtora mirrored, for once not holding himself to some higher, more aloof standard. "Tarō! Ishi! I had no idea you would be coming – will you be escorting us back home?"

"We will," Tarō confirmed.

His hands flicked in a few gestures before he spoke, and Sekken's attention sharpened. The movements weren't the ones Sekken had seen before, but he guessed at their purpose. Facing Ishi, he tapped his ear and said, "Your hearing hasn't returned?"

The shout of a yamajijii had deafened Ishi in Seibo Mura, though when they'd parted, there'd been some hope that a priest might be able to heal that injury. Ishi shook his head, and his hands moved fluidly in the air. Tarō ducked his chin in embarrassment and said, "No, and he says – well. My daughter's hearing isn't good, either; that's why I know the signs."

Presumably whatever Ishi had said about him was more flattering than that. Ryōtora raised his own hands, but their movements were far more halting as he echoed his spoken reply. "I used to know a little… I haven't had much occasion to use it, though."

Sekken bit down on the impulse to say *I'm quite good at Phoenix sign language*. First, because that wasn't strictly true, and second, because it hardly mattered if he knew the Phoenix signs. It was Dragon lands he'd be living in going forward; Dragon signs were the ones he needed to learn. He only wanted to defend his knowledge because…

Because he was feeling self-conscious about Ryōtora's success with Tanshu. And because he was used to thinking of language as one of *his* skills, a thing he knew that Ryōtora did not. Which was petty and unworthy of him.

Instead he made himself say, "I'm very glad to see you both." The two ashigaru had fought alongside Ryōtora in Seibo Mura; were it not for them, Ryōtora would have been dead long before Sekken had a chance to save him. And if Sekken watched Tarō's hands closely, marking how he translated that for Ishi... well, no harm in starting his lessons right away.

There would be plenty of time to practice on the journey west, though. And the arrival of their escort had made Sekken's impending departure suddenly, inescapably real. When he took his leave a few minutes later, Ryōtora followed him a short distance away. "Is everything all right?"

Ryōtora's voice was pitched low enough not to be overheard, and his eyes were soft with concern. Sekken made himself smile. "This has just made me realize how soon I'll be leaving. There's much to be done–"

"–and not much time to spend with your family. I understand. If there's anything I can do..."

"I'll tell you," Sekken promised.

The truth was, there was nothing Ryōtora could do. Sekken had traveled before – to Kyuden Asako, to Nikesake, through the western parts of Dragon territory – but he'd lived his entire life in Sheltered Plains City. Even his formal education had been at Yōbokutei, because why go elsewhere when there was an excellent school in town? Students lived at the compound, the better to focus on their studies, but his family had been only a short walk away.

Soon, though, he would leave all that behind – forever.

*Don't be dramatic,* he told himself as he made his way through the streets toward his family's mansion, Tanshu trotting at his side. He would still be able to travel back for visits. Though it would be a long journey, and the reclusive tendencies of the Dragon Clan meant they were reluctant to grant permission for many outsiders to enter their own territory. Sekken's mother, his father, his sisters... he'd be lucky to see them once a year.

And yet, he knew he *was* lucky. Samurai handed over in political marriages, cementing some peace treaty with their nuptials, could wind up living like virtual hostages in their new home, shackled to a spouse they barely knew. Sekken would be welcomed, would be starting the next stage of his life with the man he loved.

But reminding himself of these things did little to ease the feeling of the ground being pulled out from under him.

A feeling he was trying not to burden Ryōtora with. The Dragon couldn't afford to lose people; it had never been a question in Sekken's mind which of them would leave to join the other clan. No doubt Ryōtora had made the same calculation. It was one thing for him to know, though, and another to see Sekken visibly moping about having to leave the only home he'd ever known.

With those thoughts weighting his mind, Sekken was fully unprepared to arrive home and find Isawa Miyuki sitting with his second and third sisters, Shūkai and Ameno.

It was neither a surprise, nor unpleasant. Miyuki got along very well with Sekken's family, and she visited them often these days. But Sekken couldn't look at her without drowning in a mixture of pride, wonder, and embarrassment... because Miyuki was carrying his child.

The arrangement was a good one for all involved. Sekken knew that. Miyuki's mother, Isawa Chikayū, wanted to ensure that the *tsukimono-suji* bloodline Sekken carried, through which he'd inherited Tanshu, would not die out. Since Ryōtora could hardly bear children, that meant finding someone else. And the Dragon Clan was desperately in need of people to bolster their declining numbers; some of Miyuki's offspring would be raised as Dragon instead.

But even though Miyuki had offered this – even though Sekken had accepted – even though everybody was in agreement and all was proceeding well – every time they met in public, he felt vaguely like he was failing to be discreet in conducting an illicit affair, the way a properly trained courtier should.

*Well*, he thought wryly, *there's one benefit to relocating. You can run away from your own embarrassment.* Though it would be lying in wait for him every time he came back to Miyuki.

She greeted him and Tanshu warmly, though the warmth was tinged with dismay when he told the trio of women that the Dragon escort had arrived. "So, you'll be leaving soon?"

"Not right away," Sekken assured her. "I still have preparations to make, and they'll want some time to rest before they get back on the road. But... yes, I suppose it's not long now." He tried not to look as if the bottom dropped out of his stomach when he said that.

"Then it's a good thing the message came when it did," Shūkai said. "Otherwise we'd have to send a rider chasing after you."

Sekken frowned. "Message?" He couldn't think who would be writing to him. With all of his sisters here in town, and Ryōtora as well…

"From Crane lands," Ameno said. "I put it on the desk in your room."

"Don't stand on politeness," Miyuki said, when Sekken hesitated. "We won't be offended if you go read it now. Who knows? It might be important."

She knew him well, and Sekken smiled in gratitude as he rose.

His desk was a reminder that he hadn't lied about preparations. Sekken ought to have packed far more of his belongings by now; it was just that, faced with the daunting prospect of putting his entire life into traveling chests, he rather wanted to crawl into one of those chests and hide. Ignoring the pile of books and scrolls he needed to sort through, he found the battered packet of a well-traveled letter set in the open space Ameno must have created for it so he wouldn't overlook the new item.

The handwriting was good, the ink and paper execrable. But when Sekken saw who the letter was from, all such considerations fell out of his head.

*Sayashi* had written to him.

The last he'd seen of the bakeneko had been in the front courtyard of this mansion, not all that long ago. She'd been setting off on a journey of her own – and yes, hadn't she said she might go to Crane lands? On the pretense that she was just following her own fancy, wandering to see what she might find… but judging by the letter in his hands, that had been an unsurprising lie.

She hadn't bothered with any formulaic opening pleasantries. After the salutation, her letter got right to the point.

*I'm in Brittle Flower City, and as much as it pains*
*me to admit this, I need your help. Ryōtora's as well,*
*perhaps – it's a spiritual matter. But also a puzzle.*
*   You told me once that the benefit of being human*
*was having other people to stand at your side.*
*   I'm not human, but you are.*
*   When I call for your aid… will you come?*

# CHAPTER THREE

Ryōtora didn't expect to see Sekken again that day. They'd been spending a great deal of time together since their winter court business was concluded, but as Sekken's departure drew near, naturally the man would stay close to his family while he could.

So it came as a shock when, scarcely an hour after Sekken left the embassy, a servant came to tell Ryōtora that Lord Asako had returned.

"Is something wrong?" Ryōtora asked once Sekken had been escorted into his room. "Trouble for your family, or–"

"No, no, nothing like that." Sekken was more distracted than usual, shoving one hand into his hair before remembering he had part of it up in a topknot – a topknot that was now distinctly lopsided. "I suppose you could say it's trouble, but not for us. Unless we choose to involve ourselves. Which we shouldn't, I know that. But–"

Ryōtora put out one hand to stop his pacing. "Sekken. Tell me what's going on, then we can discuss what to do about it."

Sekken hesitated. Then, wordlessly, he dug in his sleeve and thrust a crumpled sheet of paper at Ryōtora.

Smoothing it out, Ryōtora saw it was a letter. By the time he was done reading – three times through, to make certain he understood – his eyes were dry from lack of blinking.

"I know I shouldn't go," Sekken said in a rush, as Ryōtora drew breath to respond. "I know *we* shouldn't go. The last thing we're supposed to do is put a request from a bakeneko ahead of our responsibility to your clan – not to mention the insult we'd give if we left your family daimyō waiting! It's an honor to be married at court in Shiro Agasha, and a slap in the face if we run off to Crane lands instead.

"But you weren't there, Ryōtora. When Sayashi and I were in the Enchanted Country, when she told me her story... she used to care about humanity. She saved a man's life from an ambush that would have killed him. When the Fortune of Death offered to reward her with reincarnation as a human, though, she refused, because she didn't see any benefit to it. I think maybe she's starting to see that benefit now – starting to believe what I told her about people helping each other, because she's seen what you and I have done. For each other, and for the people around us.

"And maybe, just *maybe*, that means she might be experiencing spiritual growth. At the very least she might become a marushime neko again, instead of a bakeneko. But what if it means she might reincarnate as human? I don't know if we can help her do that. I'm terribly afraid, though, that if we refuse, it certainly *won't* happen. How can I walk away from that? How can I tell Sayashi, this is what's good about humanity... and then fail to live up to that myself?"

Only a trained courtier could have spoken so eloquently, with so few gaps into which another person could slide even a single word. Partway through, Ryōtora was tempted to grab Sekken by the arms, knowing the shock of so blunt an intervention would cut short the torrent of his words. Instead, he waited until Sekken talked himself to exhaustion, and then into the silence, merely said:

"I agree."

Ryōtora had *not* been trained in the use of words like a martial art. It was rare – and peculiarly satisfying – for him to execute the verbal equivalent of a throw, leaving his partner blinking and flat on his back.

Affection and humor swelled in him as the other man gaped. "Sekken, did you think I would refuse? Clearly you *did*, if you felt I needed so much convincing."

"I…" Sekken glanced around, as if fearing someone else might be in the room to see, then dropped gracelessly onto the tatami. "Ryōtora, more than anyone I know, you believe in the importance of proper behavior."

Ryōtora tucked his kimono beneath him as he sat, his knees less than a handspan from Sekken's. "Yes, but there are many kinds of propriety. Sayashi has helped us many times; without her assistance, we might both be dead, and the Night Parade rampaging freely across Rokugan. We owe her a debt of gratitude for that. The *Empire* owes her a debt."

Sekken puffed a silent laugh. "Don't tell her that. She'll be insufferable. *More* insufferable."

Smiling in rueful agreement, Ryōtora went on, "Furthermore, as you said, it's a matter of personal integrity. You made her an implicit promise. How could I ask you to break that now?"

"Aren't we supposed to put the good of our families and our clans ahead of our personal concerns?"

"Yes – but what will this cost my clan? Only a little inconvenience. Weighed against that, we have the chance to help a soul rise in the Celestial Order. Sekken, I'm a *priest*. Of course I'll try to help her."

Ryōtora hoped he was displaying more serenity than he felt. Every word he'd spoken was both true and sincere... but that didn't mean others would agree with him. Many samurai would say that as a mere yōkai, Sayashi and her needs mattered far less than those of any human, let alone the daimyō of the Agasha family. For all Ryōtora knew, his daimyō would be one of them. And while his deeds in Seibo Mura had earned him a higher rank – with all the social protection that brought – with status also came a heavier weight of expectation. He and Sekken might return from Crane lands to find themselves in disgrace.

But he meant every word he'd said. This mattered more.

Sekken reached up to his head again and further ruined his topknot. "Damn it."

Ryōtora fetched a comb from his dressing stand. "May I?"

There was simple pleasure in removing the pin and the band that held Sekken's topknot and combing his hair straight, working the tangles out of the silky black strands. By the standards of many courtiers, Sekken's hair was still on the short side; it would be months more before it returned to the length it had been prior to him sacrificing it against the ōmukade. That made it easier to comb, though, and separate into two parts so Ryōtora could coil the upper half into a fresh topknot.

Sekken talked as he worked. "We'll have to arrange for travel papers."

"I can ask Mirumoto Otoyu," Ryōtora said. "She's

leading our escort. Though… I'm afraid she won't be very understanding." From what he'd seen of the woman, she lacked Kinmoku's political flexibility. Having been given orders, she would want to carry them out with no deviation.

After a brief silence, Sekken asked, "What if she forbids you to go? Will you still want to follow through?"

Ryōtora paused in the middle of pinning his hair. Sekken was talking about outright disobedience: not just accepting some inconvenience to his clan, but defying Otoyu directly.

*Sekken will go regardless.* And that decided for him. Not only did their bond require cooperation, but Ryōtora knew his own presence would help shield Sekken from the consequences. A Phoenix on his own, running away from his wedding to help a yōkai, was a diplomatic insult; a Dragon running away from his wedding with his Phoenix betrothed was a matter to be handled quietly within the clan.

"Yes," he said softly, and finished the topknot. "But what do we do if we don't have papers? Sneak through Crane lands like criminals?"

Sekken twisted slightly to grin at him. "We ask my mother for help."

By the time Ryōtora showed up at the mansion the next morning, Sekken had shoved everything in his own room to the walls so he could cover the mats with maps and books.

He'd been crawling around on the floor for a good hour, comparing one map to another, looking up information about the various locations marked on them. There were maps that showed the entirety of a clan's territory – even the whole Empire – but they tended to be artistic images, rather than anything of practical use. Smaller maps had more detail, but those details didn't always agree. Cartography was an imprecise art at best, and the most precise examples weren't made available to the world, lest a clan's enemies take advantage of them.

Then there were decisions to make. No road led directly from Sheltered Plains City to Brittle Flower City; Sekken and Ryōtora would have to take a winding path. But which one? As near as Sekken could tell, it would be fastest to go west from Nikesake to Toshi Ranbo, cutting through the northeastern corner of Lion territory before crossing their border with the Crane. That, however, would mean getting permission to travel through the lands of not one but two other Great Clans – and the Lion weren't exactly fond of either the Phoenix or the Dragon.

Or they could go east from Nikesake to the City of Remembrance, then turn south. That still took them through another clan's territory, but the Centipede rather than the Lion. A minor clan was much less likely to refuse permission, and the Centipede got along well with their Phoenix neighbors. Unfortunately, that road would require Sekken and Ryōtora to travel through the Mountains of Regret: a potentially slower journey, and certainly more arduous.

When Sekken outlined this to Ryōtora, the other man's eyes all but crossed. "I... could not begin to tell you which route is better."

"Either would work; we'll just need to pick our poison. How did your own conversation go?"

Ryōtora sighed. "Not well. I phrased it like you suggested, but Mirumoto Otoyu cut the idea apart without hesitation."

Sekken had feared that. He had coached Ryōtora on how to

float the idea, feeling Otoyu out without presenting a request she could unequivocally refuse; they weren't *quite* disobeying orders if they'd never been given any. But it would have made life easier if she'd been more cooperative. "Well, I went ahead and asked Mother about travel papers, and she said she'd try." Sekken stood, his back popping as he straightened it. "She got a speculative look in her eye; I'm half afraid she has some clever scheme in mind."

He'd been a little surprised by how willingly his mother accepted the task. Then again, she was *Phoenix*. The spiritual advancement of any soul was the kind of thing they were supposed to encourage. Or perhaps she just relished the political challenge.

Ryōtora had his own contribution to the planning, a list of supplies he thought they might need. Now it was Sekken's turn to feel his eyes crossing. "Isn't this a bit much?"

"Not if we're traveling on our own," Ryōtora said firmly. "And if we go through the Mountains of Regret, I'll want to add to that."

Of the two of them, Ryōtora would know. His prior duties had meant constant travel through the harsh terrain of the Dragon hinterlands – and not the sort of travel Sekken was used to, but the sort he'd endured on the way to Seibo Mura, with only his servant Jun in tow. Although this journey wouldn't be quite that bad, Sekken had to admit he'd been thinking in different terms.

Then his mother spoke through the closed screen. "Son, I have good news."

Sekken slid the door open to find her looking entirely too pleased with herself. "You've managed travel papers for us?"

"More than that," she said, after giving a proper greeting to

Ryōtora. All prior coolness toward the man was long gone; her warmth was more than mere courtesy. She directed her smile at them both equally as she said, "There's an Emerald Magistrate in town."

At least by the time they arrived at the inn where the Emerald Magistrate was staying, Sekken had more than enough opportunity to get his reaction under control.

It wasn't that he believed all the stories about the Scorpion Clan. If they really did lie constantly and stab everyone in the back, then no one would ever interact with them. True, their divine founder Bayushi had promised to serve as "the Emperor's underhand," carrying out duties more virtuous samurai would find distasteful or repellent. But they did so in service to the Empire.

*Or to their clan,* Sekken thought as he disembarked from his litter outside the inn, a moment before his mother and Ryōtora climbed out of theirs. *Or to their families. Or sometimes to their own desires, under the cloak of some greater cause.* Just because the Scorpion weren't always untrustworthy didn't mean they were never so. In a way, that made it worse: one could never be certain what to expect.

If *he* had such reservations, he could only imagine what Ryōtora was thinking. The other man had gone silent the moment Sekken's mother disclosed who the magistrate was, and he'd said very little except to agree to this meeting. Sekken wished he could have drawn Ryōtora aside for a private conversation. Odds were far too high that Ryōtora had swallowed his objections so as not to offend Sekken's mother, after she'd moved so swiftly to help them.

"Shall we?" she said, then led them both inside.

The inn was one of the nicest in the city, as befit an official of the imperial bureaucracy. It boasted three rooms overlooking a small but lovely garden, starred with the buds of cherry blossoms on the verge of bursting. Two of the three were empty, their screens slid wide to show that no one was hiding inside to eavesdrop. The Emerald Magistrate awaited them in the third, amid several low tables that already held delicacies to nibble and a steaming pot of tea.

Bayushi Meirō was somewhat older than Sekken, perhaps in her early thirties, but still with the bright, cheerful face of a younger woman – what he could see of it, anyway. Like all members of her clan, she wore a mask; like many courtiers, hers was more ornament than concealment. A narrow band of sculpted silk enveloped her eyes, with strands of glittering green beads dangling from its lower edge to brush her cheeks. Even imagining that sensation, the beads dancing against his skin, was enough to make Sekken twitch. He could only assume long familiarity had taught Meirō to ignore it.

He would have to learn to ignore the distraction it posed for the observer. As Meirō greeted them, his eye kept being drawn to the shining, swinging beads, rather than her eyes or her mouth or her body language. Which was, no doubt, the point.

Meirō's voice was as cheerful as her face, and laced with conspiratorial excitement. Once the pleasantries were out of the way, she said, "I understand from Lady Asako that the two of you need to travel to Brittle Flower City. Yes?"

"Yes," Sekken said, knowing Ryōtora wouldn't want to lead this conversation. The other man had accepted a cup of tea without so much as a blink of suspicion – not that even a

Scorpion would randomly poison a guest, though Sekken had seen people have stupider fears – but he sat silent, watching Meirō. Left to carry the meeting, Sekken said, "And we should ideally leave quite soon. You are willing to write out travel papers for us?"

"I *could*," Meirō said, drawing the word out. Sekken hoped he didn't visibly stiffen. Magistrates like her served the Emerald Champion and the Emperor, not any one clan; they had the authority to issue such papers at will. But an Emerald Magistrate drawn from any clan would expect some favor in return, and Sekken could only wait to see what a Scorpion would ask for.

Rather than ending the suspense, Meirō leaned forward, bracing one hand on her knee. *She's a courtier and a warrior both,* Sekken's mother had said as their litters were being prepared. *Capable in a fight, but don't mistake her for a blunt instrument.* Was she deliberately using a warrior's posture to seem straightforward and plain-dealing? Sekken hoped this meeting wouldn't take long, or he'd second-guess himself into oblivion by the time they left.

Unaware of his thoughts – Sekken hoped – Meirō said, "But if you'll forgive me for a bit of speculation, I'd like to see if I'm reading the situation right. The two of you are moderately famous; I know about the Night Parade, and while nobody will discuss the strange events this past winter, it's clear that some kind of spiritual affliction went through the lord governor's court, and you were instrumental in resolving it. You're headed back to Dragon lands to be married – congratulations, by the way!"

She sounded absolutely sincere, and yet Sekken's own bow of acknowledgment felt as wooden as Ryōtora's looked.

Meirō went on, "But now you want to go to Crane lands, and you need my help getting travel papers. Which suggests – I apologize for speaking so directly – that you're doing this without permission from your clans."

"Our business is our affair, and I promise it will bring no difficulties to you."

Her eyes widened. "Oh, no! You misunderstand me! I'm not worried that I'll get in trouble. Just that it sounds like this will get *you* into trouble. And I have an idea for how to deal with that."

The disarmingly frank air with which she spoke only wound Sekken's muscles tighter. "We would be grateful to hear your thoughts, magistrate."

"What if," Meirō said, "you weren't going to Brittle Flower City for purposes of your own? What if you had a perfectly respectable reason for delaying your return to the Dragon?"

For the first time since greeting Meirō, Ryōtora spoke. "I have no intention of lying to my clan, magistrate."

It was blunt enough to make Sekken wince inwardly. Meirō shook her head so hard the beads must have struck like whips. "Not a lie! I'm traveling in that direction myself – well, more or less; it's not absurd for me to go to Kyuden Bayushi by way of Brittle Flower City. And if an Emerald Magistrate were to conscript the two of you to serve as *yoriki* for a time, it would be very discourteous of your daimyō to complain."

"For how long?" Sekken asked. If she wanted to be direct in her speech, he'd return the favor and see how she reacted. "And for what purpose? We may be some time in Brittle Flower City; if we're required to accompany you to Scorpion lands, that might create difficulties."

Meirō dismissed this concern. "Oh, you won't have to travel onward with me. I'll leave you in the city with travel papers to get you home. As for purpose… well, what is it that takes you south? Is it something that could plausibly be the business of an Emerald Magistrate?"

Sekken should have had a good answer prepared. All of this had happened too fast, though; it was less than a day since Sayashi's letter had arrived, and scarcely an hour since his mother suggested this meeting. In truth, he couldn't give her a real answer even if he'd wanted to. Sayashi hadn't shared any details other than "a spiritual matter" and "a puzzle." Likely to test them – to make sure it was loyalty and friendship, not the nature of the problem, that motivated them to aid her.

*So let that be your answer.* "A personal matter, I'm afraid," Sekken said, bowing in apology. "Nothing that would concern someone of your status and responsibilities."

Meirō's lips pursed in disappointment, but only for a moment. "Well, I'll think of something. There will be plenty of time on the road to find a reason suited to your skills – even if it's something beneath the notice of heroes like yourselves. Then I can be the one blamed for wanting you in my entourage, when you were needed elsewhere."

She didn't sound distressed at the prospect. Cautiously, Sekken asked, "Is there anything we might do for you in return, Lady Bayushi?" The answer would be *yes*, of course. Nothing came without a price, and especially not from a Scorpion.

"Tell me stories on the road," Meirō said lightly. "It's a long way to go, and I'd love to hear about your adventures."

# CHAPTER FOUR

With the rush to prepare for their departure with Bayushi Meirō, Sekken had almost no time to think about what he was doing. It wasn't until their group assembled in the street in front of Meirō's inn that it truly registered on him: *I'm leaving.*

Would he come back here after their business was done in Brittle Flower City, or would he and Ryōtora proceed straight to Shiro Agasha? He didn't know. But his belongings were being sent west; his sisters had promised to finish the packing he'd scarcely begun, so the chests could accompany the entourage that was supposed to escort him. Even if Sekken returned here, he wouldn't be returning *home*. Not anymore. That ended today.

He wasn't the only one who realized it, either. His family were all too well-behaved to embarrass themselves with tears in a public street, but Ginshō had given him a bone-cracking hug just before they left the mansion, and Ameno had that peculiarly distracted look that said she was working very hard to maintain her composure. Sekken's father kept pacing around and asking questions or checking the loading of the pack horses, annoying Meirō's own attendants. Just looking at them all made Sekken want to fling propriety to the wind and cling to his mother, never to let go.

Ryōtora, unfortunately, could not do much to help. A cluster of people from the Dragon embassy had shown up just a few minutes earlier: Mirumoto Kinmoku, Sankan Yoichi, and a servant Sekken didn't recognize, followed by Ishi and Tarō. One glance at the packs carried by that latter pair had told Sekken what they were here to do.

"Yoriki," Kinmoku said dryly, raising an eyebrow at the bustle in the street. "And some unspecified business that was *so important*, Lady Bayushi had no choice but to commandeer the two of you on the eve of your departure. All of which, I'm sure, had nothing to do with your conveniently vague conversation with Otoyu, or the letter Lord Asako received three days ago."

Sekken didn't hear what Ryōtora said in response; his sister Shūkai was too busy handing him letters to carry to friends in Nikesake and advising him on where to find the best dumplings there. By the time he could spare some attention, Ryōtora was introducing Ishi and Tarō to Meirō. "Two constables, volunteering for my service?" the Emerald Magistrate said. It was hard to tell over the noise, but Sekken thought she sounded amused rather than irritated. "And I'm sure they're not here to keep an eye on you and Lord Asako, at Lady Mirumoto's orders. Oh, don't glare at me; they're welcome to come. Men of your rank ought to have a few attendants anyway."

So their traveling party grew by two more. A whole cavalcade of people and noise, Tanshu invisible and incorporeal to avoid being stepped on, and in the controlled chaos of getting everyone ready, Sekken could almost ignore what this signified.

Almost.

"May the Fortunes watch over you," his mother said, as his family bowed deeply in farewell.

Sekken's throat closed up. His voice thick with unshed tears, he said, "And over all of you. I- I will miss you all."

There was no time for more. Meirō was on her horse and whistling for them to depart; and, that abruptly, Sekken left his home behind.

Ryōtora's horse felt unnaturally tall.

He was accustomed to riding, but only on the sturdy ponies better suited to the steep terrain and harsh winters of the Dragon provinces. Proper horses were reserved for samurai of greater wealth and higher status than even his new rank. He could have taken the pony he'd ridden on the way to winter court, but Sekken was riding a fine mare, and Meirō had declared that Ryōtora couldn't possibly trot along on a "stumpy little thing" with his husband-to-be towering above him. Instead she'd loaned him one of her own horses. The mechanics were the same, but the ground felt *very* far away.

He didn't actually have to ride at all. Their entourage was carrying three litters, currently empty. According to imperial law, samurai of their status were permitted the use of such conveyances along the roads between cities. "I'll get in mine if the weather turns foul," Meirō had said, "and when etiquette calls for it, but the rest of the time – feh. I can't stand being cooped up in a little box all day."

Etiquette was not Ryōtora's chief concern. As the houses and vegetable gardens on the fringes of Sheltered Plains City began giving way to rice fields, green with growing crops, Ryōtora guided his horse up to Sekken's and spoke in a low voice. "What are you and I going to do? What should we tell Lady Bayushi about…"

Sekken nodded, not waiting for the end of that sentence. "Good question. I don't have a good answer."

They were both stronger than they'd been a few months ago. Recognizing that they were now linked on an elemental level had reduced the frequency with which exertion on the part of one led to unexpected weakness on the part of another, and the treatments they'd attempted separately proved more efficacious when performed together. But those things remained treatments, not cures; they still shared the strength of one man between two.

And maintaining the balance between them took special effort. How were they supposed to explain to Bayushi Meirō that they needed to make room in their travel plans for Sekken and Ryōtora to sit down and perform a tea ceremony?

It would help if they simply got into the litters. That was hardly the pinnacle of comfort – hours in a stuffy box, swaying from side to side as the bearers walked down the road – but it was less tiring than riding. More dignified, too; plenty of elite samurai traveled that way all the time, especially those who weren't warriors. Still, Ryōtora's pride balked at it. He'd tramped up and down the Dragon mountains, on a pony and on his own two feet, in vastly worse weather than he expected the south could throw at him. Now he was supposed to sit in a padded box, like some reedy bureaucrat or–

*Or an invalid.* Ryōtora suppressed a sigh. He might not be bedridden, but he was also no longer the man who'd hiked through snowstorms to reach remote villages. Hard as it was to accept, perhaps he *should* use the litter.

Sekken was eyeing Meirō, riding at the front of their column. "It's possible she already knows, at least in part. There have been rumors about my health going around court for months, despite my mother's best efforts. We could blame it on me, and not tell her the situation includes you, too."

Ishi and Tarō were walking not far from Ryōtora's knee. They must have overheard snatches of the conversation between the two samurai, because Ishi signed to Tarō, who nodded thoughtfully. "Lord Isao… Lady Mirumoto told us to look after you. And we – your escort, I mean – were briefed at the embassy that you might travel at a slower pace. If you want, we can arrange reasons to stop when you need it. Problems with the horses, maybe."

Ryōtora fixed his gaze on the upright figure of Meirō, chatting with her senior yoriki as she rode. Something made her laugh, and the wind carried that bright, carefree sound to him. He gritted his teeth and said, "No. We tell her the truth."

A stifled noise came from Sekken. "Ryōtora, that's not a good idea. I know she seems friendly and helpful, but you'd be handing her an advantage over you. Over both of us. That's a bad idea with *anyone* of political influence, and triply so when it's a Scorpion. They feed on the weaknesses of those around them."

"So instead we should compromise ourselves?" It took effort for Ryōtora to keep his voice low. "Secrets, deception, shielding ourselves at the expense of what's right. If it were a matter of protecting our clans, I would consider it – but that's not what we're talking about, is it? We just don't want her to know that we're less than fully hale. It's the truth, though, and hiding from it might do more harm than good."

He could see Sekken reaching for counter-arguments. Nothing came from the other man's mouth, though, until finally a rueful laugh escaped. Shaking his head, Sekken said, "Oh, ancestors give me patience. Honestly, I'm a fool for not seeing this coming."

"Seeing what?"

"You," Sekken answered, and if there was aggravation in his tone, there was also affection. "Put you in the company of a Scorpion, and of course you'll plant your feet more firmly on the ground you know."

It didn't feel like Ryōtora knew any of the ground beneath him. If traveling east for winter court had been edging out on the limb of a tree, not sure whether it would hold his weight, this journey was akin to flinging himself out of the tree entirely.

But… yes. When everything else was so uncertain, there was comfort in the solidity of the principles that had guided him all his life.

Maybe he was letting that comfort override common sense. After Ryōtora voiced that possibility, though, Sekken shook his head again. "No, I think in this instance you're right. And who knows? We might put her off-balance with our honesty. It's always good to keep a Scorpion on her toes."

With the weather good and their pace kept to one the unmounted constables could maintain, the first day wasn't so grueling that Ryōtora and Sekken were in any particular danger. But delaying would serve no purpose, and so once they arrived at the first post station, Ryōtora steeled himself to talk to Bayushi Meirō.

The post station was one of many built by imperial command and maintained at clan expense for the use of traveling officials. Since officials passed through only occasionally, and in small numbers, the clans also granted the right to use the stations to high-ranking samurai, lesser samurai on clan business – even the occasional wealthy merchant, when connections or political favors earned them that honor.

And where a station inn was built, other things followed. Not just other inns for those without special approval but baths, physicians, blacksmiths and farriers, shops selling clothing, sandals, hats and cloaks to keep the rain off... everything that might be of use to those passing through.

For a price. Ryōtora had stayed at post stations twice on his way to winter court, and both times he'd winced at what the proprietors charged for their goods and services. Samurai weren't supposed to grub after money like merchants, but he'd lived too much of his life as a poor vassal to abandon the habit of frugality.

Traveling with an Emerald Magistrate, though, he didn't have to concern himself with such things. Meirō paid for nothing; one stamp of her official seal, and the cost of their lodgings, food, and other requirements would be added to the tally sent to the clerks serving the Emerald Champion. For the sake of the innkeeper and others, Ryōtora hoped those clerks were prompt in paying the bills.

"I'm for a bath," Meirō said, dismounting and handing the reins of her gelding to an ostler. "Join me for dinner afterward?"

"A moment, if you please, magistrate," Ryōtora said as she turned to go inside. "There is one thing we should discuss first."

Something in his tone made her attention snap to him. While on the road, Meirō had chosen to forgo her elaborate, beaded mask; the strip across her eyes, while still of stiffened silk, was only faintly patterned with hydrangea blossoms. Even without the distraction of the beads, Ryōtora hated how difficult it made her expression to read.

Which was, of course, the point. Ryōtora knew the story: at the dawn of the Empire, the divine ancestor Bayushi, like all his siblings, had spoken with the Little Teacher, Shinsei. When Bayushi claimed to understand the meaning of a parable Shinsei related to him, the Little Teacher struck him across the face, saying that while his mouth said one thing, his eyes said another. Bayushi immediately took a scrap of silk and tied it below his eyes, concealing most of his face. Though another version of the story said that Shinsei had not struck Bayushi at all; instead the divine ancestor *did* understand the message of Shinsei's parable, which was to keep one's full capabilities hidden. Whatever the truth of it – an ironic consideration, when dealing with the Scorpion – all his subsequent followers and their descendants had made a practice of masking their faces, so that those around them could never quite be sure of their intent.

Meirō tilted her head toward the inn. "Come inside. Everyone will thank us if we're not underfoot while they deal with the horses."

Sekken and Tanshu followed Ryōtora inside. That Meirō knew about the inugami was a given; Tanshu featured too much in the story of why Sekken had gone to Seibo Mura for her to be ignorant of that connection. But the dog spirit had largely been staying invisible around her, which made Ryōtora feel uncomfortably like either Tanshu or Sekken had decided it was better to keep their full capabilities hidden. That Ryōtora himself could see Tanshu at all times now was a result of the stabilization of the bond between himself and Sekken.

The innkeeper likely wouldn't have objected to the inugami even if she'd known Tanshu was there; judging by her obsequious bows to Meirō, an Emerald Magistrate could bring anything she liked into the building, from a dog to an elephant. The best chamber being currently unoccupied, she immediately led Meirō and the other two samurai to it, and only with difficulty was convinced to stop offering them tea, snacks, the assistance of maids, and the services of a masseur if the esteemed guests were feeling stiff from the road.

"Phew," Meirō said once the door was finally closed. "All right – what was it you wished to speak of?"

This time Ryōtora wouldn't hide behind Sekken's superior conversational skills. "Magistrate, there is something I should have told you sooner. I have no excuse for my silence; it was simple discourtesy. And since it may affect our journey, that discourtesy is particularly inexcusable."

Meirō had shrugged out of her traveling jacket; now she draped it over the stand at the side of the room, not looking at him. "Does this have to do with your reasons for going to Brittle Flower City in the first place?"

"No, magistrate. A health matter only, for myself and Lord Asako."

Ryōtora didn't go into full detail as he explained. There was a distinction between honesty and burdening someone with personal minutiae they might not want to hear. As he'd feared, Meirō was upset… but to his surprise, she wasn't angry.

"If I'd known" – she said, her voice rising to almost a squawk –"we could have stopped five miles back! There's another post station there, smaller than this one, but it would have served our needs. Lord Isao, Lord Asako, you must let me know what is reasonable to ask of you. If the litters aren't comfortable enough to ride in – hmmm, I don't think we can replace them here, but once we get to Nikesake–"

"That won't be necessary," Ryōtora said hastily. "We are perfectly capable of managing, so long as we take appropriate measures. I know it is peculiar to ask you to make time for us to conduct a tea ceremony–"

Meirō snorted. "It would hardly be the strangest thing I've had to deal with. I once escorted an Otomo lord who insisted on stopping every hour, on the hour, to stretch his legs – no matter where we were, be it in the middle of a bridge or halfway up a hill. And if you think it's easy to tell precisely when the new hour begins while in the middle of nowhere, you have a much better eye for the angle of the sun than I do. Or there was the Crane priestess who… never mind. The point is, yes, we can do this."

Ryōtora fought the urge to turn and exchange a baffled stare with Sekken. Or maybe the other man wasn't baffled; maybe he, with his greater understanding of politics, could explain why Meirō was so accommodating. Not merely of this request, but of the entire affair, helping them get to Brittle Flower City in exchange for nothing more than an offhanded suggestion of storytelling. Sekken had found that incomprehensible before, but perhaps in the interim he'd come up with a sensible answer.

Once away from Meirō, though, Sekken shook his head. "I have no idea. Will she spring some demand on us when we least expect it, leaning on our sense of obligation to make us agree? Does this serve some hidden Scorpion agenda I can't see? Is she secretly a shapeshifting kawauso, or–"

"What?" Ryōtora asked, when Sekken's eyes went wide and his voice went silent. Alarm built in him. "What have you thought of?"

"Sayashi," Sekken said, half laughing. "I honestly wouldn't put it past that cat to deliver her own letter to my house, then take up residence in the inn to wait for my mother to come ask a favor from one of the few people who might be willing and able to grant it. Though I *think* Mother would have noticed if 'Bayushi Meirō' had appeared out of nowhere… assuming the real magistrate isn't tied up somewhere back in the city."

Ryōtora's alarm hadn't subsided. Sayashi was certainly capable of such deception. She'd masqueraded as a village girl for days in Seibo Mura – and hadn't she demanded storytelling from them during the Game of a Hundred Candles?

"I can try to find out," he said uncertainly. "Though if I go flinging a charm at an Emerald Magistrate, demanding she reveal her true form…"

The consequences didn't bear thinking about. Sekken's pained laugh said he agreed. "No, not without far better reason. If that *is* Sayashi, she'll be annoyed at us for ruining her test. And it's just as possible that this is some cunning Scorpion plot. But we can both keep our eyes open for evidence one way or another."

"Then for now," Ryōtora said, "we should make sure we're in good shape for whatever happens. Come, let's enjoy tea together."

# CHAPTER FIVE

When a baku possessed the lord governor during winter court, Ryōtora had journeyed briefly into the Realm of Dreams.

Part of him felt like that experience, however peculiar, had been less alien than the journey he undertook now.

The Lion might not like the Scorpion any better than they liked the Dragon or the Phoenix – the stories Ryōtora heard sometimes made him wonder if they liked *any* of the other clans – but shielded by her status as an Emerald Magistrate, Meirō felt no compunction about taking the western route Sekken had outlined, into Lion territory.

Before they even left the Phoenix provinces, the mountains receded into the distance behind them, giving way to flat and fertile land. Once across the border, the peaks vanished entirely, leaving Ryōtora in a world that seemed to go on forever, an endless brocade of dry fields and flooded paddies.

He'd known, intellectually, that the Dragon traded much of their mineral wealth for the rice and wheat their inhospitable territory could barely support. In his studies he had looked at maps of the Empire, the blank expanse of the southerly regions broken up only by rivers, forests, labels marking major cities and castles, instead of the shaded contours of mountains. But it was a different matter entirely to travel through those blank areas, to see the farmland stretching out beyond the limits of his vision. To have the sky arching above him like a porcelain bowl, so broad and empty that he found himself profoundly homesick for the Great Wall of the North before they'd journeyed more than a few days south.

Sekken was very little help. As Ryōtora might have expected, he was devoting himself to mastering the sign language of the Dragon, finding the similarities to and differences from the signs the Phoenix used. Ishi was delighted to have someone else to talk to, and Tarō to have a second interpreter, so they eagerly gave Sekken all the lessons he might want.

Ryōtora joined in sometimes, but despite having more starting familiarity, he was less adept than Sekken. And the silent conversations somehow made the vast expanses of Lion lands feel even emptier than before. It was easier for him to simply ride, and try to meditate, and close out the world around him.

Until they reached Brittle Flower City.

It stood hard by the border with the Lion, close enough that Sekken said control of the city had changed hands more than once. But despite those conflicts, it was a thriving center of trade between the Crane and the Lion, and even beyond: not far to the southwest lay Beiden Pass, one of the few routes through the Spine of the World, granting access to the lands of the Scorpion, the Crab, and the southern minor clans. Ryōtora squinted in that direction, but clouds lay heavy on the horizon, blotting out any glimpse of Rokugan's other great mountain range.

Instead he turned his attention to the city. As befit a place that so often saw battle, it was surrounded by a high wall, with towers looming over the gates. Relatively few fields stood outside the walls; Ryōtora presumed that after having them repeatedly trampled by armies, the city's governor had decided to use the wealth from trade to have grain shipped in from more peaceable areas. It gave the land a somewhat vacant feeling – until Meirō finished registering them with the guards at the gate and he rode into the city beyond.

Then he found himself in utter pandemonium. Hemmed inside their walls for safety, the population of Brittle Flower City lived shoulder to shoulder, in buildings nearly as tall as pagodas. And what a population! If someone had told him the equivalent of the entire Dragon Clan had been poured into this space, Ryōtora might have almost believed it. Even Sheltered Plains City had not been this crowded – but then, the Phoenix were one of the smallest of the Great Clans, even without the troubles that plagued Ryōtora's people.

This was decidedly not a Phoenix city, nor a Dragon one. Its mercantile character showed everywhere Ryōtora looked, from the wagons trundling along its broad streets to the vendors hawking their wares off shopfront counters, mobile stalls, and their own backs. Signs everywhere boasted of medicines from the Coastal Isles, indigo cotton at bargain prices, the best buckwheat noodles in town. For those who couldn't read, shopkeepers cried out the same information in sing-song counterpoint, each seemingly trying to outdo their neighbor in volume, if not enthusiasm.

Just this morning, Ryōtora had been wishing for something to break up the endless rush of the wind over the plains besides the jangling of horse tack and the tramp of the constables' feet. Now he almost wanted the silence back.

Sekken grinned at him. "Not what you're accustomed to, eh?"

Ryōtora bit down on the urge to snap back. He'd known his whole life that he was a provincial samurai, not cosmopolitan even by the limited standards of the Dragon, but the way life seemed determined to rub his face in that fact was not Sekken's fault. Ryōtora had survived the genteel warfare of winter court; he could survive a little noise and bustle.

Meirō adroitly turned her horse in the street without trampling anyone and rode back along the column of her constables to join Sekken and Ryōtora. "Brittle Flower City, as promised! If you already know where you intend to stay, then go with my blessing. But if you'd like, you're welcome to come to my inn. I'll be stopping here for a day or two, at least."

Ryōtora would have preferred to separate from her as soon as possible, before any unseen traps could spring shut. Their attempts to investigate the possibility that she might be Sayashi in disguise had been ineffective, proving nothing one way or another. Sekken had made a point of telling a story about Seibo Mura in a way that downplayed Sayashi's role, which had provoked her in the past, but Meirō made no comment. Because she wasn't a bakeneko, or because she'd learned more self-control? Neither of them could say.

When it came to inns, though, they had little choice. The only inn either of them could name was the one marked on Sayashi's letter – the one she'd presumably been staying at.

They still hadn't told Meirō about their bakeneko friend and her request, so Ryōtora wasn't surprised when Sekken, after a brief glance at him to confirm, said, "We wouldn't want to be a burden on your hospitality any longer, magistrate."

His polite demurral was the sort that invited a renewed offer, and Meirō obliged. "Not a burden at all! It's covered by the allocation for my duties, and I hardly ever make real demands on that. Come on. I always stay at the Eisuitei when I pass through here; I think you'll like the place. It even has a proper tearoom in its garden!"

Feeling a bit like a duckling, Ryōtora followed her through the streets. Brittle Flower City was laid out along classical lines, with its streets meeting at right angles in a neat grid – a pattern few Dragon settlements could follow, as their layouts bowed to the demands of the terrain. At least it meant Ryōtora couldn't truly become lost. If at any point he needed to escape the city, all he had to do was keep heading in a straight line until he hit a wall, then turn and follow that until he found a gate.

The fact that he was already thinking in terms of escape was not reassuring.

The Eisuitei wasn't an official post station, but the innkeeper there still readily accepted Meirō's seal as payment. It was far more luxurious than the post stations; like Sekken's family mansion, a low wall separated the grounds of the inn from the street outside. It did little to muffle the noise, but at least in the courtyard Ryōtora felt like he could breathe without bumping into someone. The inn itself rose three elegant stories, the ends of the roof posts capped with ceramic roundels showing a flower he didn't recognize.

Sekken, following his gaze, said, "Morobana. The flower this city is named after. Very beautiful and useful for medicine, but short-lived and difficult to grow; it's found in the Aokami Forest, just west of here." Meirō was still speaking with the innkeeper; Sekken lowered his voice so none of the constables would overhear. "There are… interesting legends about the forest. I wonder if that's why Sayashi asked us here."

A forest sounded very nice right about then. Green silence, the enclosing canopy of trees, and if spirits indeed dwelt there, at least Ryōtora might have some notion of what to do with them.

Meirō strode back across the courtyard, brushing her hands off. "I've arranged for a meal as well. If this is our last night together, I want it to be a pleasant memory! And it would be a very great pity if you finished your business in this city without trying the local specialties. Their chestnut rice is divine. But first, of course, a bath!"

They'd arrived too late in the day for Sekken and Ryōtora to go looking for Sayashi right away. Sekken hoped the bakeneko would forgive their delay – always assuming, of course, that she wasn't the Emerald Magistrate who'd traveled with them from the north. He'd seen nothing to confirm that wild theory… but also nothing to disprove it.

He wished they had time for a tea ceremony, even if it were only a small rite conducted in the chamber they shared. By now both of them were used to carrying out the process in a variety of locations that would make a tea master clutch his kettle in horror; Sekken was even thinking of writing a small book about it. The essence of the way of tea was supposed to be simplicity and unpretentiousness, yet samurai had found ways to dress it up with all kinds of expensive requirements. The famous bowl used by the historical teacher Asahina Heiko was said to be nothing more than a vessel she'd acquired from a roadside seller of miso broth; three hundred years later, two Kakita lords had gone to war over who should inherit it. Perhaps, in rededicating themselves to the principle of harmony over the trappings of ritual, he and Ryōtora were returning to a more authentic experience.

Sekken shook his head. His thoughts were wandering – a worrisome sign. Not that they never did that of their own accord, but these days it tended to be a hint that Ryōtora was particularly exerting himself to stay focused. The other man didn't seem inclined to talk, though, and Sekken knew him well enough by now not to press. There would be time enough for it tomorrow, after they'd found Sayashi.

A process that might be easier than he expected. The next morning, not long after Sekken rose, a servant's knock came at the door to their room.

He slipped out onto the veranda and slid the door shut behind him. Ryōtora was still asleep – with Tanshu curled against his side – and although he would complain about not being woken, Sekken saw no reason the man should be forced out of bed when there was no immediate demand on their time. Let him rest; Fortunes knew they both needed it after that long journey.

The servant bowed and presented him with a tray bearing two items: a thread-bound book, rather cheaply made by the looks of it, and a large sheet of paper folded up small enough to go into a sleeve or a sash. "Lady Bayushi Meirō asked me to convey these to you, my lord."

Mystified, Sekken took them and waved the servant away. He'd barely had a chance to glance at his new acquisitions when the door slid open again.

"Damn," he said at the sight of Ryōtora. "I was hoping I'd been quiet enough not to wake you."

Ryōtora looked as he always did on waking, which was to say charmingly rumpled. He tried so hard to maintain a stoic, dignified manner that mornings were Sekken's treasured opportunity to see his more unguarded side.

Now he rubbed at his eyes, squinting in the bright light of the morning. "You were quiet. It was your absence from my side that woke me."

Guilt and warmth alike rose in Sekken's heart. "I hope you'll learn to sleep through that, or I shall be like the poet who remained in the garden all day because he couldn't bear to disturb the cat dozing on his sleeve."

"No, I should–"

"Get up; yes, so you always say. We can debate the virtues of early rising later, when you're properly awake. In the meanwhile, look at this." Sekken handed over the book.

Ryōtora blinked blearily at it. "The *Brittle Flower... Pigeon*?"

He sounded like he was sure he must have misread the last character of the title. "You read that correctly," Sekken said. "Why they call them 'pigeons,' I'll never know. It's a Crane custom: in many of their larger cities, booksellers offer printed guides for travelers. Famous places to see, esteemed delicacies to try, the best prostitutes to hire, that sort of thing. I'm not making this up!" he added hastily, seeing Ryōtora's stare.

Rather than question Sekken's probity, Ryōtora handed the book back. "Where did you get it?"

"From Rokugan's most helpful Emerald Magistrate, by way of a servant. Along with this," Sekken said, holding up the folded paper. "A map of the city. According to the first section of the pigeon – well, after the bit extolling the great history of this *Crane* city; periods of Lion control quietly elided almost out of existence – there are two main areas where travelers can find accommodation. Now if we unfold this..."

He knelt on the veranda and spread out the western part of the map, where most of the travelers' accommodations lay. A moment of scanning the densely packed labels brought his searching finger to its target. "The–"

Ryōtora's hand came down on his shoulder before he could speak the name. Of course: they were out in the open, where anyone could overhear. And for all Ryōtora's dedication to honesty, he'd agreed there was nothing wrong with keeping what truly was their own private business from Meirō. Especially when her motives for prying were a worrisome unknown.

But Sekken didn't have to say it. Ryōtora could read as well as he could. The Reiya, Sayashi's inn, lay not far away, in a ward – the map helpfully informed them – owned and administered by the Hakusho Temple.

Now the only question was whether they could go visit Sayashi without some Scorpion-sent agent tailing them there.

"I'll get dressed," Ryōtora said, and shambled back inside.

Even Sekken found the streets of Brittle Flower City a bit of a shock.

It wasn't just the density of the crowds, though for two men accustomed to the smaller populations of the north, those were breathtaking enough. No, it was the sheer commercial *exuberance* that threatened to leave Sekken gaping like a country bumpkin.

This wasn't like the city he'd grown up in. The primary concern of the people here was not learning, religion, or catering to those concerned with such things; the lifeblood of this place was trade. Sekken had read a bit about Brittle Flower City before leaving home, and so he knew about the enormous warehouses that lined the city's main canal, about the famous Market of White Fortune where nearly anything could be bought and sold.

But nothing he'd read had prepared him for the entertainers staking out nearly every street corner, spinning tops or doing animal impressions or lying on their backs with their feet in the air, large barrels turning and leaping with every twist of their ankles. Signboards jutting out from what seemed like every fifth building advertised more diversions within: comic monologues, sutra satires, mechanical wonders from the provinces of the Kaiu. Less frivolous services, too, like dentistry, parasol repair, and eyebrow plucking – but why on earth were those being *advertised*?

It was Ryōtora who arrived at the answer, not because he had any more experience with such a place, but because he was still better than Sekken at seeing the lower classes in a clear light. "Can the common folk here truly afford such things?"

An adolescent girl on the corner up ahead gathered herself, then leapt headfirst through a basket-woven tube into which someone had thrust – were those *burning candles*? Tanshu barked in alarm, but the girl emerged uncharred on the far side, and applauding spectators tossed bronze coins into the sack held by her younger assistant. All of those watching were townspeople, not a samurai among them. "Apparently they can," Sekken said, shaking his head in disbelief.

Ryōtora's jaw set in a hard line. Almost too quiet for Sekken to hear, he said, "While my clan struggles to keep its people fed."

Despite the masking noise, his shame came through. Sekken drifted closer and lowered his own voice. "Don't assume what you see here means that every commoner lives an easy life. Crane wealth grows in their rice paddies, and the more they squeeze the peasants who work the fields, the more there is to spare for the lords – and the townsfolk. Your people value a farmer's life far more than anyone here is likely to."

He heard what Ryōtora didn't say: *Because we have so few of them.* So few of anyone, their population declining generation by generation. But that meant the Dragon, more than perhaps anyone in Rokugan, believed what all the classical philosophers said, that the peasantry were the legs upon which the body stood. Without them, everything else would collapse.

Those same philosophers had very little good to say about the merchants who dominated Brittle Flower City. Unlike the samurai who guided and protected, the peasants who kept the world fed, the artisans who produced useful goods, merchants were nothing more than leeches, feeding off the labor of others. They created nothing, only profited from moving other people's creations here and there. There was a reason the Celestial Order placed them at the bottom of the human hierarchy, scarcely above outcasts.

Of course, without those same leeches, the Dragon and even the Phoenix would go short of rice. And if no one could profit from trading grain and other goods, who would undertake the effort and risk of transporting them?

A headache was forming between Sekken's brows, and not just from the clamor of the streets. He'd never liked that corner of philosophy, and he was irrationally annoyed at Brittle Flower City for dragging it so prominently to mind.

It was a relief to see the sign up ahead proclaiming the Reiya. This inn was far less refined than the Eisuitei; it lacked a retaining wall or front courtyard, its door opening directly onto the street. When Sekken and Ryōtora stepped out of their sandals and went inside, Tanshu following invisibly, the interior was dim and smelled more than a little musty. Why would Sayashi choose to lodge in a place like this when she could trick her way into something better?

*Perhaps because she's choosing not to use trickery.* Sekken hoped that was the case.

The innkeeper who hurried forward to greet them was full of bows for her unexpected samurai visitors. When Ryōtora queried her about a guest named Sayashi, though, she shook her head. "Or Teishi?" he asked, trying another name the bakeneko might have used. "Aoi?"

That last one was a long shot, being the name of the dead peasant girl whose identity Sayashi had assumed in Seibo Mura. Sekken was relieved when the innkeeper shook her head again – but they were out of possibilities. Why, for the love of all the Fortunes, couldn't Sayashi have given them more useful information?

He glanced down at Tanshu. The inugami had gone sniffing

around as soon as they entered, without being instructed. In the past, Tanshu's sensitive nose had been able to track the bakeneko; could he do that again?

It seemed he could. Tanshu barked once: inaudible to the innkeeper, but definitely affirmative. Sayashi had been here.

In a sudden burst of inspiration, Sekken said, "Any young women traveling alone, carrying themselves with an air that suggests even a governor's palace might not be good enough accommodations for them?"

*That* struck home. "You mean Marushime," the innkeeper said, her demeanor cooling.

Delight rose in Sekken. If Sayashi was using that as her name... "Yes, her! Forgive our confusion; she's used a number of names in her – er – trade. Where could we find her?"

The innkeeper sniffed. "Not here. She left the city last month."

"Left!" Sekken's delight curdled back into annoyance, and then into suspicion. What kind of game was Sayashi playing? Was she just toying with their sympathies, using those to lure them into a trick for her own amusement?

Ryōtora's brow furrowed. "But Lord Asako received a letter, asking him to come here."

"That's very generous of the lord, traveling all this way." The woman's tone made it clear she assumed some kind of ill-advised love affair was involved. "But I'm afraid she isn't here – and before you ask, no, I don't know where she's gone. Kuzu!"

Her abrupt bark baffled Sekken until he saw the smudged face of a girl peeking around the edge of a door that, by the looks of it, led to the inn's earthen-floored kitchen area. "Get back to work!" the innkeeper snapped. "Samurai don't need the likes of you poking around! My apologies, my lords, but there's nothing more I can do to help. Unless you need a room…"

Sekken and Ryōtora escaped with Tanshu back to the noise of the street, then stared at each other. "If she's playing with us," Sekken muttered, then didn't know how to finish that sentence. What was he going to do? Go back north and try to explain their absence?

"Surely not," Ryōtora said. "But if she had to leave the city, why not also leave a message telling us where to go next?"

The answer came from Sekken's elbow, in a timid voice heavily tinged with the local accent. "'Cause she didn't go nowhere. Not like the mistress said. She went to the market, and she ain't come back."

# CHAPTER SIX

It was the girl from inside, the one the innkeeper had called Kuzu. Ryōtora couldn't immediately parse what she'd said; he had thought himself coping fairly well with the dialect of this city, but venturing into the streets had made it clear that the servants at the Eisuitei, and the woman they'd just conversed with, were all taking care to speak in something closer to the dialect generally used by samurai. The rest of the commoners in Brittle Flower City had a rapid, staccato way of talking, like pebbles rattling down a cliff face, and he had to race to keep up.

Then the meaning registered. "Sayashi – Marushime – went to buy something?" Ryōtora asked, frowning.

The girl shook her head. "No, not the market. The *market*."

If there was some difference in the way she pronounced those two words, Ryōtora couldn't hear it. Only a heavy emphasis on the second version. Sekken apparently couldn't follow the distinction, either, because he said, "Why don't you start at the beginning? Do you know what Marushime was here for?"

A shout from inside the inn made Kuzu glance fearfully over her shoulder. "If the mistress catches me out here–" A second shout broke her nerve; with a gasped apology, she bolted around the corner and out of sight.

Sekken groaned in frustration. "We'll have to come back later. When she has more time to talk."

Eyeing the inn, Ryōtora said, "I think you overestimate her freedom. Grubby face, patched clothes… that isn't a servant whose mistress treats her well. I'll bet you anything she works from the moment she wakes until long after the innkeeper has gone to bed." This was no servant of a wealthy samurai household. And even if she were… Sekken might think the Dragon treated their peasants better than other clans, but that didn't mean no one in Ryōtora's lands exploited those below them.

Sekken grimaced. "Then how are we supposed to talk to her? Convince Bayushi Meirō to intervene?"

It would certainly get results. If an Emerald Magistrate showed up to interrogate Kuzu, the innkeeper would hardly have grounds to object. But once that was over… "Leaving aside the fact that we've been trying not to involve her in this business, what do you think would happen to Kuzu afterward? The innkeeper claimed Sayashi has left Brittle Flower City; now her servant has called her a liar."

"I know, I know." Sekken pressed the heel of his hand into his brow. "But I'm not going to take a room here just so we can sneak around and question that girl on the sly – and if we're caught, that will cause the exact same problem."

They both fell silent and, by unspoken accord, drifted away from the inn, lest the woman inside should notice them lingering. They didn't go far, though, just a short distance down the street. "I suppose she might have meant the Market of White Fortune," Sekken said, looking around until he settled on what was presumably the correct direction. "The book I consulted before we left didn't say much about Brittle Flower City's layout – just its history between the Lion and the Crane – but I've got that map Meirō gave me. We could go look there?"

Ryōtora nodded, but his heart wasn't in it. The city already felt like barely controlled chaos, so full of people and activity that trying to find one disguised bakeneko seemed as futile as looking for one grain of rice in a bushel – when the grain might well be on the move. Without more guidance than "she went to the market," they could search for days and accomplish nothing. Unless… "Do you think Tanshu could track her there?"

They both looked at the inugami. He'd been sticking close to their heels since arriving in the city, seemingly as overwhelmed as the humans by the sheer tumult. In a market district, where trails would cross and overwrite one another – and if the rain that caught the travelers two days ago had fallen on the city as well…

Tanshu whined faintly, head dropping. "So much for that," Ryōtora said, defeated. There were limits to what even an inugami's sensitive nose could achieve.

But something else had lit a fire in Sekken, because abruptly his chin rose and his shoulders went back. "No. I know a way to solve this – and do some good in the process. Follow me."

Sekken knew he ought to at least lay his idea out for Ryōtora before following through on it. But one of the downsides to being a witch, bound to an animal familiar, was that it tended to erode one's self-control. Distressing for a samurai, bordering on disgraceful – but since right now there was no fellow samurai to witness it save Ryōtora, Sekken didn't bother trying to rein himself in. He just pivoted and strode back up the street, then through the front door of the Reiya.

The innkeeper looked alarmed to have him back, which as good as confirmed what that girl had said about her lies. "Please pardon the intrusion again," Sekken said, not meaning it at all, "but our business is urgent enough that we really can't wait. You see, my companion and I are yoriki in the service of an Emerald Magistrate, Lady Bayushi Meirō, and it's imperative that we find Marushime as soon as possible."

That was only stretching the truth a little. Meirō had said she would release them from her service once they arrived in Brittle Flower City – but she hadn't yet reclaimed the seals marking them as yoriki. Until she did so, Sekken was free to flash the carved jade… and to pray that word of this didn't get back to her.

"Furthermore," he went on before the innkeeper could find her tongue, "the haste that led us here in search of Marushime unfortunately meant we had to depart without a proper entourage. I find myself in need of a maid to see to my belongings. So as an apology for inconveniencing you, I'd like to hire away that servant girl we saw before – Kuzu, I think her name was?"

Several emotions flickered across the innkeeper's face, wariness and greed and anger. They settled into crafty, eager lines as she said, "The girl's no more than ten, my lord, but that means she'll give you years of service. If you'd like to buy her–"

Fury flared up in him, and Tanshu snarled. Sekken only realized the dog had manifested visibly when the innkeeper recoiled, yelping in shock.

He'd meant to be more subtle than this. But her insinuation that the maid could be sold like chattel pushed Sekken over an edge he hadn't known was there. Two strides put him up in the innkeeper's face, Ryōtora's sudden grab for his sleeve not enough to hold him back. With the woman trapped between him and the wall, Sekken growled, "You should be aware, mistress, that we know you lied to us before. My dog spirit can smell Marushime's trail; we know she hasn't left the city." Also strictly true, even if those two statements weren't connected the way he implied. "So you will tell us the truth, or–"

A sound from Ryōtora stopped him. When Sekken looked away from the innkeeper, he found Kuzu on the stairs, wide-eyed with shock… and with fear.

Guilt crashed onto him. *What am I doing?*

His resonant voice gentle, Ryōtora addressed the girl. "Please forgive us, Kuzu. We're only trying to help – not just Marushime, who is our friend, but you as well. We don't want to get you in trouble with your mistress here, hence the suggestion of employment. But you needn't stay with us, either, if you do not wish to. The Emerald Magistrate we serve, Lady Bayushi Meirō, will take you in, or make arrangements for you to be settled somewhere else."

A clumsy offer, and one that might well get them in trouble with Meirō, but Sekken was grateful to Ryōtora for trying to retrieve the situation. And it seemed to be working, because the girl's gaze flicked toward the innkeeper.

"*Kuzu!*" the woman snarled.

Sekken had assumed the maid was named for the arrowroot plant – and maybe she was, originally. The way the woman said it, though, turned the word into the one for *garbage*. And in that moment, Sekken wanted nothing more than to set Tanshu on her.

But he held himself back. Ryōtora was right: his sudden inspiration, that they could hire Kuzu away from the inn and thereby keep her safe, had somehow turned into a bullying display of intimidation. No sense making that any worse.

Instead he wiped his brow and offered the girl an apologetic smile. "Yes, please forgive me. I suppose I'm not making myself look like a better employer than the one you currently have."

The dull hate that flashed in Kuzu's eyes said he'd have to do far worse before he sank to the level of the innkeeper, which made Sekken very much not want to know what her life here had been like. Gaze jittering between him, Ryōtora, Tanshu, and her mistress, she whispered, "You serve an Emerald Magistrate?"

Ryōtora produced his own seal. "We do."

"And you ain't from here."

"I am Agasha no Isao Ryōtora of the Dragon Clan," Ryōtora said. "My friend is Asako Sekken of the Phoenix. And the dog there is Asako's spirit companion, Tanshu."

Sekken's hand had dropped reflexively to Tanshu's head, to the soft comfort of his fur. Now he nudged the dog with his fingers, and Tanshu paced slowly over toward Kuzu, the very picture of canine friendliness.

Kuzu timidly held out her fingers for the dog to sniff. Then, abruptly, she said, "Mistress – Adae, that is – she still has Marushime's things. They're in the storeroom out back."

The innkeeper spat what Sekken thought was a curse on all ungrateful girls who betrayed those who'd so generously taken them in, but he found himself uninterested in asking her to repeat it, this time in less thick dialect. Stepping back from the innkeeper, he smiled and said, "If you would be so kind as to show us where this storehouse is?"

Like many houses and shops in Rokugan, the inn had a thick-walled storehouse set behind the main building, sheltered from the risk of fire. A heavy padlock sealed the doors against thieves, but the innkeeper had clearly given up on obstructing her samurai visitors; with a glower, she unlocked it for them. "Skipped off without a word to me, and no money paid for her next week of lodging," she complained, referring to her guest. "I had a right to keep her things."

Ryōtora didn't care enough to debate that point. Sayashi had left little enough regardless; just a small bundle that Sekken reached for with a sound of recognition and a few papers that Kuzu pointed out, lying atop a coil of unused reed screens. "Is this everything?" Ryōtora asked.

"Take it and be satisfied, *my lords*," the innkeeper snapped. "And if that friend of yours comes back, tell her she ain't welcome here no more."

If there had been anything valuable, the woman had probably sold it already. Kuzu merely ducked her head when Ryōtora glanced at her. Very well: this would have to do. "Let's be gone," Ryōtora said.

Kuzu trailed at a shy, respectful distance as they returned to the street. "Are we bringing her back to the Eisuitei?" Ryōtora asked quietly, leaning toward Sekken.

The other man glanced back at Kuzu. "Unless you want to get a room for her somewhere else. But I think that would attract... other kinds of attention."

He hadn't thought of that. Yes, the Eisuitei would be better, even with Meirō's questions. "But first," Ryōtora said, "let's see if she wants a bath."

She could have cleaned up at the inn, of course. However, Ryōtora suspected the atmosphere there would have been overwhelming to her; the Eisuitei was the sort of establishment where servants stood ready to bathe the guests. Instead he took a few coins from the string in his sleeve and dispatched Kuzu into one of the public bathhouses they'd passed on their way to the Reiya, promising her they would be at a tea shop across the street.

Sekken at least waited to question his decision until after Kuzu was gone. "Is that a good idea? What if she takes the money and runs out the back door?"

Ryōtora shrugged. "Then we don't see her again. Our goal was to free her from one trap, Sekken; we can't snare her in another one, even if our intentions are good."

"I suppose you're right," Sekken said grudgingly. "But since I'd prefer not to wait here until sunset to find out if she's abandoned us..." He took Tanshu's head between his hands and closed his eyes, concentrating. After a moment, the dog whuffed and trotted off, slipping through the narrow gap between the bathhouse and the shop next to it, whose sign boasted of wooden and ceramic spoons at very reasonable prices.

While they waited, they browsed through the papers from the storehouse. Unfortunately, these appeared to be Sayashi's notes for herself, not letters or any kind of documentation meant to be read by other people. As a result, they were as cryptic as a koan: one scribbled comment read *Fukiau Chiyo 716*, another *chirizuka kaiō?* "The first is presumably a woman's name," Sekken said, peering at it, "though Fukiau must be a vassal family, and not one I recognize. If 716 is a date, that might explain why I don't know them. The second… 'strange king of the garbage heap'? Are we looking for a rubbish collector now?"

"Maybe," Ryōtora said, spreading out a folded paper. "Look at this map."

It was a rectangular sketch with characters on the four sides to indicate north, south, east, and west. The lines hatched across it would therefore be streets, but the spots marked along them baffled Ryōtora. Each was labeled with something like *silk* or *wagon wheels* or *rope*, and there were dozens.

"This might be the Market of White Fortune," Sekken said. "In which case I suppose those are places where you can buy the indicated products. But why? What's Sayashi's interest in this?"

Ryōtora had no answer to that. But someone else might: Kuzu had emerged from the bathhouse, scrubbed clean and her hair still dripping as she twisted it into a knot behind her head. She darted through the traffic of the street and skidded to a halt near their table, dropping to her knees in the dirt of the road. "I'm sorry to keep you waiting, my lords."

At least, that was what Ryōtora presumed she'd said. Her breathlessness made her staccato speech even harder to follow than before. She'd clearly hurried through her bath as fast as humanly possible, fearing the impatience of her new masters.

"You didn't need to rush," he said, hoping his gentle reply sounded sincere. "And please, get up. We'll get fresh clothing for you, but in the meanwhile, don't make your kimono any dirtier than it already is."

"I'm sorry, my lord," Kuzu repeated, rising with her gaze still downcast. This time the apology seemed to be for the state of her patched and threadbare clothing – or perhaps simply for the fact of her own existence and the way it inconvenienced others. Ryōtora had the uncomfortable feeling that she'd spent much of her life apologizing, while that woman shouted at or beat her.

He wasn't going to be able to undo that damage today. But there was one thing he could do: attend to Kuzu's needs first, and interrogate her about Sayashi later. Before Sekken could brandish the map and his litany of questions, Ryōtora rose and glanced around. "Tell me, Kuzu – where should we go to buy you a new kimono?"

Impatient though Sekken was, he bit back his protests as he followed Ryōtora and Kuzu through the streets. The girl reminded him of a dog Shiba Mitsusada had once owned, a creature so cowed by words and blows that the spark of life within it seemed almost extinguished. Warning them about her mistress' lies must have taken tremendous courage – and he suspected that Sayashi had done something to earn the loyalty of that courage. Hopefully the bakeneko would forgive them a small delay in the hunt for her.

Unsurprisingly, Kuzu led them to a modest secondhand shop. Ryōtora didn't dispute her choice, but he did pick out the nicest, sturdiest child's kimono available, over Kuzu's protests. Then a sash to tie it closed, and socks and sandals for her bare feet. Kuzu was half in tears by the time he finished, and without prompting, Tanshu – whom Sekken had called back from sentry duty with a simple thought, a fact that pleased him immensely – sat close to comfort her.

"Food," Ryōtora said when that was done. "Sekken, you have that bird book–"

"The pigeon?"

"Yes, that. We don't have many restaurants in Dragon lands, apart from noodle shops. Can you suggest a place we might go?"

He didn't bother to lower his voice at that admission of inexperience the way he usually would have. So he wanted Kuzu to overhear him: a way of making himself seem less intimidatingly fancy, Sekken presumed. Ryōtora might insist he was less adept at social matters than Sekken, but that was only because he insisted on discounting interactions with anyone who wasn't samurai.

In keeping with Ryōtora's intent, Sekken ignored the most prestigious establishments mentioned in the *Brittle Flower Pigeon*, seeking out a more comfortable option. "Let's see… we're in the Old Willow ward, yes? Then it looks like we're very near to some shops that specialize in broiled eel."

By the time they were ensconced at a shared table with an array of bowls containing rice, eel, and soy broth with tofu cubes, he judged that the delay had gone on long enough. Much more of this, and Kuzu would begin to wonder if their interest in Marushime had been some kind of pretense – and to fear what their actual demands of her would be.

"Do go on eating," Sekken said, suspecting that otherwise,

the rest of the meal would be left untouched. "We're not worried about manners here. But what can you tell us about Marushime? You said she went to the market and didn't come back – which market is that?"

Surprise flashed in Kuzu's eyes, quickly tamped down. "My lord… it was the Market of a Hundred Fortunes."

# CHAPTER SEVEN

Sekken forgot to eat his own soup. "The Market of – do you mean the Market of White Fortune?"

"Maybe, my lord," Kuzu whispered to her bowl. "I ain't familiar with that one."

"You have to be. The big walled market just east of here; I'm told the city is famous for it."

Her shoulders hunched up toward her ears. "I only ever heard it called the Market of a Hundred Fortunes. But my lord is right, I'm sure."

Sekken dug the *Brittle Flower Pigeon* out of his sleeve and flipped to a section he hadn't looked at yet. There, in large characters along the right margin, was the name: *The Market of a Hundred Fortunes*. And the map Meirō had sent – when he unfolded it fully, instead of just the western part – announced the same thing.

He was a scholar. He knew his memory was good, and his reading skills above reproach. Through his teeth, Sekken said, "Are you telling me that all this time I've had the name wrong, because whoever printed the book I read back at home *left the top stroke off the character for 'hundred'*?"

"No, my lord, I'm not–"

Ryōtora put out one hand to stop Kuzu's tearful retraction. "He isn't angry at you. Only at the person who printed the wrong name. And now we know the truth, so thank you."

Yes, they knew the truth – and it sent spiders crawling down Sekken's back. Staring at Ryōtora, hearing the wild edge creeping into his own voice, he said, "That's it. From now on, you and I are going *nowhere near* the number one hundred."

The Night Parade of a Hundred Demons. The Game of a Hundred Candles. Now a market that apparently had something to do with a Hundred Fortunes. It could be simple coincidence; many things in Rokugan were named with that number, just as they referenced eight for auspiciousness, or a thousand or ten thousand to imply a countless quantity. Those other hundreds hadn't caused any trouble for him and Ryōtora.

*Yet,* Sekken thought mordantly. Was there some Fortune whose attention they'd attracted, that they kept finding themselves in the path of such troubles?

Ryōtora might have been thinking along similar lines. To Kuzu he said, "Tell us about this market – and its Fortunes."

Despite Sekken's earlier admonition, Kuzu put down her spoon at once. "To the east of here, as my lord said. A walled market. All kinds of things get sold there."

"But why the name?"

"Shrines," Kuzu said. "All over the place. Some are big, some really small, all along the streets."

Sekken folded the printed map over until he could look at the market without the rest of the paper flapping in the wind. Three shrines were flagged on it: one to the Fortune of Wealth along the eastern side, and two in the west flanking the gate, one to the Fortune of Rice, the other to the Fortune of Roads. But Sekken supposed the little ones wouldn't be marked. "All right. Why did Sayashi have an interest in it? That's the name we know her by," he said when Kuzu frowned. "And remember, eat! We don't mind if you talk with your mouth full."

She obediently took a bite of broiled eel, but only one. "Because the market on your map ain't the only one, my lord. There's another market, people say – a hidden one."

*That* sounded more like the kind of thing Sayashi would have dragged them south for. "A supernatural place?" Ryōtora asked.

Kuzu nodded. "There's different stories. Some say it's ghosts. Others say there's all kinds of living objects there, the things we buy and sell. Or the Fortunes themselves come to trade. And when people go missing…"

She trailed off. Sekken nudged the bowl of eel toward her with a fingertip, and she picked up another bite, but didn't put it in her mouth. Gently, he said, "Someone you know went missing?"

"Amo," she whispered, fingers tightening until the eel squished apart. "Years ago. That's how I wound up at the inn."

Sekken recognized the word from a play – one that mocked the Crane and their quirks of speech, though he didn't need to mention that part. "'Amo' means 'mother,' yes? Your mother vanished into the market?"

Kuzu answered with a tight nod. After a moment, she drew in a ragged breath and said, "That's why Marushime – Sayashi – was at the inn. She came to ask me about amo. And she said… she said she'd help me find her."

"Then we'll do the same," Ryōtora said without hesitation. "How does one get into this hidden market?"

For a moment Sekken thought the girl would scramble off her bench to kneel on the ground again. He put out a hand before she could move, and so Kuzu only bobbed something like a seated bow, narrowly avoiding the dishes in front of her. "That's the problem, my lords. I- I dunno. Nobody really knows. Your friend tried all kinds of things, but they didn't work. Until they did, I guess."

"Then how do you know Sayashi's in the hidden market?" Sekken asked. "Couldn't she have gone somewhere else? Maybe to look for answers, or for help? Oh, don't duck your head like that – I *want* you to disagree with me, if you think I'm wrong. If I get nothing but 'I'm sure you're right, my lord,' then I'll do more stupid things like calling it the Market of White Fortune, and I'll wind up wasting everyone's time. You can save me some embarrassment by just arguing back from the start."

He got a brief glimpse of eyes as wide and round as eggs before Kuzu jerked her chin back down. Good; it meant he'd actually broken through the defensive layers of humility and abjection. Maybe she would believe that he meant every word he'd said.

Her underfed shoulders tensed in sudden determination, and she said, "I suppose I dunno for sure, my lord. But I- I don't think she'd've gone without telling me. You're the friends she wrote a letter to, right? My lords. She told me when she sent that. So why would she try something else that might help, and keep it secret?"

Sekken could think of potential reasons, starting with *she's a cat* and proceeding from there. But Kuzu clearly wasn't ready yet for him to argue back at her; she would only take it as a sign that she'd misstepped. Instead he mused, "That's fair. But if you're right about her being there, it means she found the way in, and didn't share it with you."

"She may not have had the time or opportunity," Ryōtora said.

"Also fair," Sekken acknowledged. He was beginning to enjoy himself. "Kuzu, these people who go missing – is there a pattern? Are they trying to get into the hidden market, or does it happen to people with no interest in it? Do they go to the market, the regular one, at a certain time of day? Are they taken by force? Does anyone see it happen – their disappearance, I mean? Are they ever seen again, and if so, what do they say? If there are returned individuals we could go question..."

He trailed off as Ryōtora cleared his throat meaningfully. Kuzu's eyes had gone wide again, and belatedly, Sekken realized that might have been a bit much to fling at her all at once. "My apologies," he said. "That's another thing to know about me; sometimes my curiosity carries me away."

"Let's take this one step at a time," Ryōtora said. "It's fairly obvious that we need a local guide. Kuzu, are you willing to do that for us? I'd like to go look at the ordinary market first, if you don't think that's too dangerous."

By way of response, she shot to her feet. Smiling, Ryōtora gestured for her to sit back down. "We don't need to go right now. Sit and finish your meal first."

If Ryōtora had found Brittle Flower City overwhelmingly busy, it had nothing on the Market of a Hundred Fortunes.

The walls of the district, like the walls of the city, penned the inhabitants into a limited space. They'd made up for it by building both upward and inward, encroaching on the broad streets that ran between the gates and branched off to subdivide the area into smaller blocks. But while Sayashi's hastily sketched map had suggested a regular grid, that turned out to be only part of the story: alleys so narrow one could easily overlook them led deep into those blocks, zigging and zagging until debouching into tiny courtyards from which there was no escape except back the way one came.

In this warren, it seemed that absolutely everything was for sale. Not in bulk; the great warehouses of rice, soybeans, and other staples occupied other parts of the city, where there was more room and easier access to the canals. But every kind of product, from the mundane to the luxurious, seemed to be available in the market. Brooms, flutes, straw hats, lacquered boxes inlaid with mother-of-pearl, secondhand tea kettles – it seemed impossible there could be enough people and enough money to buy all those things, yet the bustle of the market said otherwise.

Ryōtora didn't understand how shrines to a hundred Fortunes could fit into this space until they arrived at the point Sayashi had marked with the label "oak." To get there, he and Sekken had passed between a pair of shrines, one to the Fortune of Roads, the other to the Fortune of Rice, which faced each other across the entrance on the western side of the market. Both were modest in size, occupying no more space than a commoner's house might. But it turned out that was what Kuzu considered a "big" shrine for the district, because Ryōtora could have walked right past the one for the Fortune of Oak without even realizing.

He supposed it might be classed as a hokora. It wasn't uncommon to see that kind of miniature shrine along a street: essentially a cabinet atop a pedestal, with a projecting roof to shelter the contents and offerings from the rain. In this case, though, the shrine was set right into the side of a joiner's workshop, the sheltering roof reduced to a token lintel beneath the workshop eaves. The whole thing could easily have been mistaken for a window, if he hadn't looked closely enough to see the flowers wilting in a tiny vase next to a bowl of sand dusted with incense ash.

"Are they all this small?" he asked Kuzu, after paying his respects at the shrine, minor and makeshift though it was. "Other than the three marked on Sekken's map?"

"Not all, my lord. There's one around the corner here..."

*Around the corner* involved ducking into one of the alleys, so narrow that an old man coming the other way had to press himself against the wall to let Ryōtora and Sekken pass. In a gap between two shops that likely only saw the sun at high noon, someone had crammed a structure like a full building shrunk down for dolls. The air here was damp and faintly rank, a far cry from the clean, natural environment Ryōtora was accustomed to for shrines, but once again, offerings lay on the stone before it.

Sekken peered at Sayashi's map in the dim light. "This is dedicated to the Fortune of... Buckets? I can't be reading that right. Rafters? Fermentation? Her handwriting here is shockingly messy."

"You had it right the first time," Ryōtora said, picking some moss out of the crevices of the inscription carved above the shrine's hand-high entrance. Tanshu sniffed at them and sneezed. "This names the Fortune of Buckets."

He turned to find Sekken's eyebrows climbing in disbelieving hilarity. "There isn't any such Fortune," Sekken said. "Is there?"

Not that Ryōtora had ever heard of. In his peripheral vision, though, he saw Kuzu shrink back into the shadows, biting her lips together so hard they vanished into a flat line.

For the common people especially, uneducated in the refined principles of theology, the Fortunes were the bedrock of their lives, the powers watching over their daily challenges and concerns. Hearing a lordly samurai question their existence must cut deep. But to contradict that samurai would be worse, even if Sekken had openly invited argument back at the restaurant.

"Few people had heard of Kaimin-nushi, either, until we went to Seibo Mura," Ryōtora said, choosing his words carefully. "Who knows what other divine powers exist in corners of the Empire you and I haven't seen?"

Sekken spread the map against the wall, heedless of the damp wood. "Then if what she's marked here are all shrines… you're telling me there's a Fortune of Thresholds, too? Of Handcarts? Of *Secondhand Clothing*?"

"This is an unusual place," Ryōtora pointed out. "Even if people disagree on the exact nature of the hidden market, it's clear *something* is going on here. The presence of shrines to such unexpected Fortunes may relate to that."

By the pinch of Sekken's brows, he still wasn't picking up Ryōtora's hints to stop doubting the local faith. It was unlike him to miss them – though given the subject, perhaps not entirely surprising. Hoping to forestall his next objection without embarrassing him, Ryōtora added, "Besides, just think, you have the opportunity to do so much more than correct a misprint when you return home!"

He knew it for a mistake the moment the words came out of his mouth. Ryōtora had been thinking of Sekken's home among the Phoenix, where scholarship on spiritual matters was highly valued. Not that the Dragon disdained such things, of course – but it wasn't the same.

Would never *be* the same, not with Sekken coming to live among the Dragon. They still didn't even know what their life there would look like; they were supposed to discuss that with Ryōtora's family daimyō after the wedding. Running away to Brittle Flower City had left that unanswered question hanging over their heads like a blade.

He wanted to apologize as Sekken closed up the map and his own expression along with it, but a woman was edging past them with a bucket of something that smelled strongly of vinegar balanced on her head, and Kuzu was there, too. Discussing personal matters in public wouldn't make anything better.

All Sekken said was, "Let's explore some more."

For all that the Market of a Hundred Fortunes was geographically small, it felt like they could walk forever and still not see the whole place. With Kuzu to reorient them when they got turned around, they crossed it from west to east and south to north, seeking out shrines to Fortunes both familiar and not, on street corners, in dark alleys, and in one instance – dedicated to the Fortune of the West Wind – perched atop a teahouse like it was meant for a congregation of birds.

They were at that one, up in the fresh air, when Sekken spread the map out again and knelt in silence for a moment, tracing the lines. Then he said, "I only count ninety-nine shrines marked here. What's missing?"

Kuzu had loosened up a little as the hours went by and her new samurai masters neither struck nor abandoned her. She sounded less timid than before as she said, "Nothing's missing, my lord. The hundredth Fortune – it's the market itself, the good fortune this place brings us."

Sekken sat back on his heels. "Fortune in the pragmatic sense, rather than the metaphysical one. That... doesn't sound very plausible to me."

Nor to Ryōtora, and he was glad to see Kuzu nodding in agreement. "That's the reason people give, my lord, whenever somebody talks about building another shrine. That one place has got to be left empty for the market's fortune, or it'll go away. But..."

"But you think there's another answer," Ryōtora said.

Kuzu cast a swift glance around. She couldn't possibly be looking for someone eavesdropping on them; the only path to this rooftop shrine was a rickety staircase that had creaked alarmingly under Ryōtora's weight. Tanshu would warn them if someone approached, and they had a clear view across the rooftops of the market. In the east the gilded caps of roof beams marked the shrine to the Fortune of Wealth, gleaming in the afternoon light.

But depending on what really lived in the hidden market, there might be eavesdroppers Ryōtora couldn't see.

"We've been walking a long time, and it's getting late," he said. "I think we should head back to the Eisuitei and consider what we've found. Especially since we may need to find a new inn, Sekken, once Lady Bayushi moves on tomorrow."

Kuzu looked alarmed, and too late, Ryōtora realized what that would sound like to her. "We won't be leaving, Kuzu, or taking you away from Brittle Flower City. We – ah–"

"Lady Bayushi intends to leave us here to investigate this matter, while she carries out some business of her own elsewhere," Sekken said, with the smooth ease of a courtier presenting true but incomplete information. If they told Kuzu they were about to leave the Emerald Magistrate's service, she might fear she'd be sent back to the Reiya. Or just abandoned on the street.

Returning to the Eisuitei with a new servant in tow might arouse Meirō's curiosity. But they couldn't delay that forever.

The staircase survived long enough for them to return safely to street level. It wasn't until they passed back through the western gate and crossed the canal just outside the district wall, though, that Kuzu let out a breath of relief. Taking that as his cue, Ryōtora said, "Are you willing to talk now? It seemed like you had something to say about the hundredth Fortune."

She guided them to the side, out of the stream of people and handcarts. There wasn't much room, and they had to stand awkwardly close, but Kuzu seemed more comfortable being able to speak quietly instead of raising her voice above the din. "It's what Sayashi was looking for, my lord. In some of the stories of the hidden market, there's a hundredth Fortune there – one that ain't got a shrine out in the normal market."

"Why not?"

"I dunno, my lord. But Sayashi said this one could buy and sell *anything.*"

Ryōtora exchanged a worried glance with Sekken. "Anything? As in…"

"Stuff you can't touch. Talents or fate or some such."

He'd never heard of anything of the sort. Then again, he'd also never heard of the Fortune of Braziers or the Fortune of Chopsticks, and he'd made brief prayers at shrines to both today.

But braziers and chopsticks were both less alarming prospects than someone who could trade in the kind of intangibles Kuzu was talking about.

And he could read the unspoken question in Sekken's eyes. Why was Sayashi trying so hard to find such a thing? What did she want to buy or sell, that she needed the assistance of such a Fortune?

Assuming it existed, and local tales hadn't spun an interesting story around something else entirely. Which might be even *more* worrisome, depending on what that thing was.

Ryōtora chewed on that question the whole way back to the Eisuitei, forgetting to think about what they would do when they got there. Fortunately, as they entered the front courtyard, he heard a familiar voice around the side of the building used by the inn's staff. Gesturing for Sekken and Kuzu to wait, Ryōtora rounded the corner and found a trio of people in the open, graveled area there.

Ishi and Tarō held spear-forks, polearms used to catch and trap the limbs of criminals. Kakeguchi Botan, Meirō's senior yoriki, was instructing them in the weapons' use, though she halted the practice as Ryōtora approached.

Seeing the grins Ishi and Tarō exchanged with each other before they noticed his presence made Ryōtora wonder. For him and Sekken, working with Meirō was nothing more than a convenient arrangement, sheltering them from the consequences of running off to help Sayashi. But the other two, for all they'd been dispatched by Kinmoku to keep an eye on the samurai, seemed to be truly enjoying their role as constables. Not that they'd had any opportunity yet to act in that role, but still, it made him feel faintly envious and guilty at the same time. Meirō would be leaving tomorrow and yet here they were, learning to use a constable's weapon.

He could do nothing about that right now. Ryōtora bowed to Botan, a stocky woman who was surprisingly short for a Crab, and said, "I apologize for interrupting, but Asako and I have need of these two."

Without hesitation, the ashigaru handed over their spear-forks, and Botan waved them off. Ryōtora led them back around the corner, explaining, "We've hired a girl to act as our guide here – in part to get her away from an abusive mistress, but also because she knows and was working with Sayashi. Can I ask the two of you to look after her?"

As he'd suspected, Tarō warmed immediately to the notion. Ishi took a moment longer, because Ryōtora's patchy attempt to convey his point in sign hadn't been comprehensible enough; once Tarō repeated it, Ishi laughed and flicked his hands in a reply too small and quick for Ryōtora to follow. "We'll take care of it, Lord Isao," Tarō promised.

Kuzu looked a little relieved to be given into the care of the ashigaru. They might be strangers, but at least they weren't samurai lords. Ryōtora, sending the three of them off, felt some relief himself. Tarō had children; he would know what to do with her.

"Did you catch what Ishi said?" Sekken asked, once the trio were gone.

Ryōtora hadn't realized he was watching that closely. "No, what?"

"I think he said, 'Didn't take them long to adopt, did it?' I suppose he assumed you wouldn't be able to read it."

Sekken was grinning. Ryōtora felt simultaneously offended, surprised, and embarrassed. Adopt? He intended nothing of the sort. They were going to help Kuzu find her mother.

But it reminded him of his misstep before, his thoughtless comment about home. "Sekken… I'm sorry for what I said earlier."

The other man tilted his head in confusion. "Earlier?"

"At the shrine to the Fortune of Buckets. I just wanted you to stop saying things that upset Kuzu, but instead I upset you." Ryōtora glanced around to make sure they were still alone, then said, no less passionate for being quiet, "I am *sure* that whatever duties we're assigned won't preclude you from being able to keep up your scholarship. No – I will *make* sure of it. I don't want our marriage to cost you something else you care about." Something in addition to his family and his home.

Sekken's expression softened into its own medley of feelings: affection, wry amusement, sorrow. "Ryōtora, don't worry. Yes, I'll miss what I'm leaving behind. That doesn't mean I have any regrets about choosing to marry you and join your clan. You poked a sore spot, it's true, but I wasn't upset for long – and I'm glad you intervened, for Kuzu's sake. It was rude of me to repay her help with mockery of her Fortunes."

Ryōtora drew in what felt like his first deep breath in ages. "I do mean it. About our duties."

"I know you do." Grinning, Sekken slung an arm across

his shoulders, as if they were making their way home after an evening of drinking. "With the greatest of respect for your clan, I'd like to see them try to *stop* a Phoenix boy from writing about the wonderful new things he's learned!"

# CHAPTER EIGHT

The next morning Sekken roused Ryōtora from bed, even though he would have preferred to let the man sleep later than the Hour of the Hare. Meirō was scheduled to leave today, and although she wasn't an especially early riser, she would want to get a good start toward the mountains, not laze away half the morning before departing.

But when they arrived at Meirō's chambers, with the intention of returning their jade seals and presenting the thank-you gift Ishi had bought the previous evening, they found Kakeguchi Botan in the outer room and the inner door still firmly closed. There was no sign of preparation for departure.

"We're not leaving today," Botan said when Sekken explained their business in a quiet murmur.

Unease trickled down his spine. "Oh? Has something come up?"

Botan shrugged. "That's for the magistrate to say. I'll let you know once she wakes, and you can return the seals to her then."

Ryōtora and Sekken exchanged glances as they left. "Why don't I trust this?" Sekken muttered.

Neither of them said the obvious: *Because Meirō is a Scorpion.* They'd known all along that she must have some secret purpose behind her helpful behavior. Now she was changing her plans without warning... and they were no closer to figuring out why.

"At this point I doubt our previous theory," Ryōtora said as they straggled to a halt on the veranda.

The theory that Meirō was Sayashi in disguise. "Given what Kuzu said, it does seem unlikely," Sekken agreed. To the best of his knowledge, even a bakeneko couldn't be in two places at once, and Sayashi had remained in Brittle Flower City long after she would need to have departed north to masquerade as Meirō.

He was almost disappointed. As irritating as it would have been to find out Sayashi was playing an elaborate game, it would have meant they didn't need to retrieve her from some supernatural realm of unknown nature, nor did they need to untangle the hidden schemes of a Scorpion magistrate. Of the two, Sekken preferred the first challenge by far.

Botan didn't send a servant to bring them to Meirō until nearly the end of the Hour of the Dragon. By then Sekken and Ryōtora had thoroughly discussed their options for pursuing Sayashi, ranging from possible ways to get into the hidden market to the likelihood that they could gain any assistance from the samurai governor of Brittle Flower City, without arriving at any decision. Reluctantly leaving off that conversation, they gathered up their seals and gift and went to see Meirō.

True to Botan's word, they found the magistrate in a comfortable robe, not traveling clothes. She was back in her beaded mask, and even though Sekken knew that was probably because she wasn't on the road, he couldn't help but take the distracting sway of the beads as a bad sign.

But underneath the mask, Meirō wore a smile. "Lord Asako, Lord Isao. How did you find your first day in Brittle Flower City? What do you think of the place?"

"It's..." Sekken began, then trailed off. He ought to be able to manage a politic response in his sleep, but nothing was coming to mind.

Ryōtora did better. "I have never seen any place like it."

Meirō had a full-throated laugh, rich and inviting. "Invigorating, isn't it? Or as an Ikoma once put it to me, 'as invigorating as accidentally snorting shochu out of your nostrils.'"

Despite himself, a tiny laugh burst from Sekken. If he was being honest, he *liked* Meirō. She had an easygoing manner, a frank sense of humor – at least, it seemed frank. And that was what he hated the most: this apprehension that the woman he liked might just be a performance put on for some unseen purpose.

"Sit, sit!" Meirō waved them toward cushions and gestured for Botan to pour tea. Sekken wondered if the Crab resented being made to act like a junior right now. Sekken and Ryōtora held higher status than she did, but theoretically they were *her* juniors, as the newest pair of yoriki – however much of a pretense that assignment might be. If she did resent it, her expression and posture betrayed no sign. Maybe she'd been warned in advance, as a part of... whatever Meirō was trying to do.

He accepted the tea from Botan and was in the middle of taking a sip when Meirō asked, "Have you visited the Market of a Hundred Fortunes yet?"

The question might have been innocuous, but Sekken assumed Meirō had set someone to track their movements the day before. Botan, or one of the constables? In the chaos of the city, it would be almost impossible for him to spot someone following them, even if he knew which person to look for. Sekken finished drinking and said, "One can hardly come here and not visit the city's most famous district. Do you have a favorite artisan or tea house there to recommend to us, magistrate?"

"I always stop in at the shrine to the Fortune of Roads before I depart," she said, with evident sincerity. "I've been an itinerant magistrate since being assigned to the Emerald Champion, so it's best to make sure I'm in the Fortune's good graces!"

"We'd be delighted to go there with you today," Sekken said. "I always enjoy visiting a place with someone who knows it well."

The beads swung like toys to tempt a cat as Meirō shook her head. "Oh, not today. I'm not leaving just yet."

*Of course you aren't.* Sekken hoped his complete lack of surprise didn't show. "Has something gone wrong? I recall you saying you were needed in Kyuden Bayushi."

"I'm *headed* there, not *needed* there," Meirō said, with a meticulous precision Sekken found ironic, coming from a Scorpion. "But that plan may be changing anyway. It's the hassle of being itinerant: while you're on the road from one place to another, the conditions that sent you in that direction might change. We have a whole division of couriers whose entire purpose is to chase after traveling magistrates and update them on what they need to be doing now."

Which all sounded very plausible and very unreliable. Sekken said, "I'm surprised they don't have priests beseech the spirits to carry messages to you instead."

"The spirits aren't meant to act as our servants for every minor matter," Ryōtora said sharply.

Sekken lifted his teacup in acknowledgment and apology while Meirō said, "That does happen occasionally, but it's as Lord Isao says. If the Emerald Magistrates were demanding such service from them on a regular basis, the spirits might well become impatient. Though between you and me, I think our restraint has less to do with piety and more to do with too few priests capable of invoking them for that purpose. Also the fact that they will only carry extremely brief messages." She laughed again. "I'm just as glad it's this way. Otherwise I'd have swarms of spirit couriers coming after me at all hours of the day – never a moment of peace and quiet."

Sekken put down his tea and reached into his sash, drawing out the jade seal she'd given him. "Well, even if you're staying in Brittle Flower City for the time being, we should return these to you. We greatly appreciate your assistance, but it wouldn't be right for us to go on carrying these when they aren't necessary anymore."

Ryōtora set his own seal next to Sekken's on the mat. As Sekken was reaching for the gift he'd brought, though, Meirō leaned over and pushed the seals back toward them. "No, no – keep them for now. You never know when they might be useful."

As they'd been the day before. Did Meirō know about that?

Sekken slid the seal forward again. "That's very generous of you, magistrate, but truly, I don't want to presume. It's an insult to hard-working yoriki like Lady Botan for us to present ourselves as your subordinates when we've done nothing to earn that status."

I shouldn't have said that.

But as in their first meeting, even though he'd left the door wide open for Meirō to now present some kind of demand, she shook her head. "Given the services you and Lord Isao have rendered in the past, I don't think it's inappropriate at all for you to armor yourselves with some authority. I've seen situations where matters become more difficult than they had to be because the people most capable of addressing the problem lacked the official status to do so, and the people with the status were absent or unwilling. I trust you not to abuse what you hold."

It was clear that no matter what Sekken and Ryōtora did, Meirō wasn't going to pick the seals up. With reluctance, Sekken put his back inside his sash, and after a long hesitation, Ryōtora did likewise. Sekken said, "Your trust honors us, Lady Bayushi."

*And worries me.* There were proverbs about how trusting a Scorpion wasn't a good idea… and being trusted by one wasn't much better.

Sekken's suggestion of an early lunch after they left Meirō's company wasn't born of real hunger. They went out to a nearby restaurant, and he paid extra up front to have a pair of merchants evicted from their table in a corner so the two samurai could use it. From there, they had a view of the entire dining area, the door included. No one working for Meirō could listen in without them noticing.

*Unless they're in disguise,* he thought grimly. It was the sort of thing people said the Scorpion did, though he had no idea how often that actually happened, versus being a rumor the Scorpion liked to spread around. Or Meirō could have agents here in the city that he didn't recognize. After all, she traveled through here often.

He could drive himself mad imagining the possibilities.

"So we're not getting rid of her any time soon," he muttered, once they'd been served tea. Tanshu lay at his side, an invisible and watchful presence. "I wish I were surprised. What do we do next?"

Ryōtora toyed with his cup, before stilling his hands with a visible effort. "She clearly wants to know what we're up to. What if we simply told her?"

An inarticulate noise burst from Sekken. "Ryōtora–"

"I know. She's untrustworthy; any information is a weapon in her hands. But we're also tying ourselves in knots over what she may or may not already know. We can't devote ourselves wholeheartedly to helping our friend if we're constantly looking over our shoulders."

"And you think telling her would mean not having to do that anymore? You're more optimistic than I am."

"No, I'm just more tired," Ryōtora snapped, with uncharacteristic impatience. "Tired of – of all of this. We're not even using names right now because – why? We think someone's listening in? You said it yourself, when we first set out: maybe honesty will put her off-balance."

There was the honesty of telling her about their personal

health, and then there was the honesty of telling her about their purpose here. About Sayashi. Who had never even met Meirō, and likely wouldn't welcome a Scorpion meddling in her business.

Shaking his head, Sekken said, "That's a piece we can't take off the board after we've played it. I'm not saying it's impossible…"

Ryōtora crossed his arms over his chest. "All right, then. If you were at h–"

Despite their mutual frustration, Sekken gave him a wry smile. "You can use the word 'home.' It's all right."

"If you were at court," Ryōtora said, "how would you handle her?"

"Learn more about her," Sekken said promptly. "Ask questions of the people I know; see if there are records I can access about her family or what she's done as a magistrate. But I don't have those resources here."

They had almost no resources at all. He'd brought money, very little of which they'd used so far, since Meirō had been paying for most things. They had Ishi and Tarō. "Can you ask the spirits to help?" Sekken asked, thinking of the conversation about couriers. "Some kind of divination, or–"

"No," Ryōtora said curtly. Then he let out a slow breath, his hands tightening briefly into fists before releasing. "That is – there are divinatory rituals. But they won't deliver the kinds of precise answers we need. And while I'm sure there are invocations an unscrupulous priest could use to spy on someone else…"

He would never use them, or even learn them. And Sekken would never ask him to.

Ryōtora almost never slumped, and he wasn't slumping

now. Still, Sekken wanted to reach across the table and grip his shoulder, to bolster the thing inside him bent and wearied by the situation they'd wound up in. They were both far from home, with too little to guide them, and too many potential threats in the shadows.

As if he'd felt the touch Sekken hadn't given, Ryōtora firmed up. "I'd rather devote my attention to finding Sayashi, and worry about Meirō if and when she becomes a problem. The sooner we finish our business here, the sooner we can go home and stop being concerned with such things."

Sekken began to nod in agreement – then stopped.

And cursed.

Ryōtora stiffened in alarm. "What's wrong?"

Sekken tapped his sash, where the seal was tucked safely away. "She left these with us; fine. But did you notice what else didn't happen during that meeting?" He smiled mirthlessly. "Neither did I, until just now. She didn't give us papers for traveling back home."

The papers she'd promised to supply once they reached Brittle Flower City and she parted company with them to continue on toward Kyuden Bayushi. Without those, Sekken and Ryōtora couldn't go anywhere.

It might have been a simple oversight. But Sekken didn't believe that for a heartbeat.

Tension flattened the resonance from Ryōtora's voice. "What do we do if she withholds those?"

That, at least, Sekken had an answer to. "Send messages to our clans. I don't know if they have representatives here, but Kyuden Kakita isn't too far, and there will certainly be ambassadors there who can give us papers. But…"

He didn't bother finishing that sentence. Going to their clans for help would open the door to the exact trouble they'd been hoping to avoid by traveling with Meirō.

A servant brought food to their table. It was really too early for lunch, and Sekken's realization had killed his appetite; he merely picked at the grilled bream and boiled burdock root. Ryōtora ate mechanically, gaze distant.

When his food was gone, he put his chopsticks down. "I stand by what I said before. We worry about Sayashi first, everything else later."

He spoke with the air of someone with a plan. "What do you intend to do?" Sekken asked.

"Go talk to a priest," Ryōtora said.

Most of the shrines in the Market of a Hundred Fortunes clearly had no formal priesthood looking after them, just the local inhabitants. But there were exceptions, most notably the three most significant shrines, to the Fortunes of Roads, Rice, and Wealth. Ryōtora avoided the first of those because Meirō had said she favored it – then wondered if she'd said that precisely so he would go elsewhere, thinking that elsewhere was safe.

He loathed the ease with which his mind was starting to come up with such deceptive twists. It felt too much like *he* was the underhanded one.

The Fortune of Wealth had the largest shrine, and seemed like the best place to start. Leaving Sekken to pursue other paths of investigation, Ryōtora circled the outside of the market district rather than trying to force his way through the crowds within. The shrine itself was ornate, even gaudy, with many details painted or plated in gold. In Dragon lands, they favored a more naturalistic look for their holy sites, often leaving even the torii arches along the sacred path as bare wood, rather than painting them vermilion. But nothing could be naturalistic, crammed into a teeming city like this.

The atmosphere within was far from serene. Two men were chatting as they purified themselves at the fountain by the entrance, one of them bragging about the profits he'd made through some kind of trade maneuver Ryōtora couldn't follow and didn't want to. He tried not to feel too judgmental, and failed. Yes, the Fortune of Wealth favored merchants and their cleverness… but those men spoke as if the money they earned was the prize in a game, rather than a blessing to be shared.

*That's not your concern,* he told himself, and tried to block out their conversation as he poured the water over his hands and head.

Moving onward, he tossed coins into the offering box, lit incense, and prayed to the Fortune. For his clan, struggling as it was, and for people like Kuzu, cast up on the shores of the river of gold while others sailed freely onward.

Once his respects had been paid, standing near a statue of the rat that served the Fortune he found a junior priestess. She pointed him toward the office, tucked behind a stone wall, where the head priest sat smoking a long pipe.

As Ryōtora had expected, the priest was a Crane samurai, Daidoji no Hōgo Nihei. He welcomed Ryōtora warmly enough, pouring him tea, offering him a pipe, remarking on the rarity of Dragon samurai in Brittle Flower City and marveling at the long distance his guest must have traveled.

Stifling his impatience, Ryōtora endured the pleasantries, and tried not to raise his question so early as to be rude.

But when he finally did so, Nihei scoffed. "A hidden market? Oh, yes, I've heard the stories. That's all they are, Lord Isao – stories. A way to explain one's son eloping with an unsuitable bride, or a woman fleeing her debts. Or someone 'went to the market,' and a few days later we find his body in a canal. This is a busy city, Lord Isao; people go missing all the time. I've never seen any evidence that such a place exists."

He sounded supremely confident, yet Ryōtora didn't find that reassuring. "How long have you served at this shrine?"

"Six years, so long enough to have noticed if anything peculiar were happening." Nihei brought his pipe to his mouth, then stopped short. "You're not the first person to ask me about this recently, though."

Hope flared. "Oh?"

"Yes, a young peasant woman got in here somehow. She was *most* rude when I told her to stop pestering me about local folklore."

"I'm here because of her," Ryōtora said, eagerness straightening his spine. "She's gone missing–"

"Ah, and you think this hidden market is to blame?" Nihei leaned forward. "Lord Isao, I can give you a list as long as my arm of more likely places to look. Starting with the brothels; she was pretty enough for one of them to have snapped her up."

Did *everyone* in this city see people as commodities to be bought and sold? Ryōtora leaned forward, too, and bared his teeth at the other priest in something like a smile. "I very much doubt that, Sir Nihei, as the 'peasant woman' you spoke to was, in fact, a bakeneko."

Nihei jerked back. "Nonsense."

"I assure you it's true. And if she believes the hidden market exists, I'm inclined to agree. Have you ever attempted to search for such a place, or have you simply waited for the evidence to present itself to you?"

Ryōtora's irritation seeped through into the question, and the hearty, insincere friendliness of the other man's demeanor fell away. "Have you seen how busy this shrine is, Lord Isao? We are constantly being asked to bless new canal boats and carts, write out protective charms–"

"I take it the answer is 'no,' then."

"This shrine has stood here for over five hundred years!" The head priest was reddening around the neck and ears. "The entire market was laid out according to geomantic divinations to be as auspicious as possible. I think that if some foul influence had crept in, one of my predecessors would have noticed."

One of his predecessors – not him. An unpleasant suspicion formed in Ryōtora's heart. "Sir Nihei, I imagine you're accustomed to being paid for your services. In that case, I would like to hire you to commune with the spirits throughout the market district and perform whatever invocations you know that might be of use in finding my missing friend."

"You think we have those kinds of capabilities?" Nihei snapped. "Priests who can speak directly to the spirits have better uses for their gift than investigating silly rumors."

Ryōtora put down his tea, set his hands against the mat, and bowed with all the cool, dismissive precision he could muster. "So you lack the gift yourself. As I thought. In that case, Sir Nihei, I apologize for wasting your time. This particular priest will have to consult with the spirits himself – for unlike you, I *do* consider investigating this matter to be a worthwhile undertaking. May the Fortunes bless you."

He was shaking as he left. Partly with anger, and partly with apprehension. That rash declaration to Nihei had been sincere, and having said it, he didn't feel like he could back down. But it would mean going well beyond the simple communion he'd engaged in for the experiments with Tanshu.

*And what,* he thought grimly as he strode out of the market, *will that do to Sekken?*

# CHAPTER NINE

While Ryōtora pursued the avenue he was best suited to, Sekken figured he might as well pursue the one most suitable for *him*.

"Kuzu," he said, "where in this city could I find a bookseller?"

She was unsurprisingly illiterate, but she still knew where books were sold. It turned out to be a street not far north of the market – just *one* street, and Sekken bit back the urge to make smug comparisons to his own home. *It's not your home anymore,* he reminded himself. And depending on what the Dragon chose to do with him and Ryōtora, he might wind up in a place with no booksellers at all.

Pushing that thought down, he followed Kuzu north.

There were six shops there, and he visited them all. Queries at the first one made it clear that Brittle Flower City had no libraries apart from collections in private hands, which Sekken had expected. This was not a place that would foster anything like the Kanjiro Library. He might still look into those private collectors, but he wasn't optimistic; from the sound of it, they were more likely to have works of poetry or military history than anything related to his present needs.

But if libraries were a dead end, he met with slightly more success on the shelves of the shops. Brittle Flower City might be a hill of money-minded ants, but those variety halls he'd seen on the way to the Reiya had made it clear that people here liked to spend their money on entertainment. Mostly performances of assorted kinds, but enough people were literate that their hunger extended to written works, too. And Sekken doubted there was a settlement in Rokugan that didn't have its share of local folklore.

Everything he could find on the lore of the hidden market, he bought. A volume of spooky kaidan, one of which concerned a wit-wandering man said to have escaped the market's clutches. An illustrated, yellow-covered chapbook about a woman who went into the market in search of her missing husband, had strange adventures, and ended up deciding she was better off without him. Woodcuts purporting to depict lively scenes of the market, no two of which agreed on just what could be found there. He even purchased books that had clearly been plagiarized from someone else's work, cringing at the thought of rewarding such theft, but unwilling to pass up the chance that they might contain some useful detail.

The load grew much too heavy for skinny Kuzu to bear, so Sekken hired a porter to carry it all back to the Eisuitei. Then he was winded enough that he found a teahouse for himself and Kuzu to rest in, while Tanshu sat at his feet and let loose a whine no one else could hear.

*We've been pushing too hard,* Sekken thought, imagining what Ryōtora might be up to. They were getting better at managing their joint condition, but that had largely been in the context of idling around, not engaging with challenges like this one. Even the journey south hadn't felt quite so taxing; Sekken suspected the strain was less when he and Ryōtora were together, doing the same thing at the same time.

But they couldn't live the same life for the rest of their days. They needed to be able to separate, too, pursuing their own aims. Doing that successfully, it seemed, would take more work.

Kuzu hadn't asked why Sekken wanted to pause. She was sitting very quietly, sipping from her teacup at regular enough intervals that he suspected she was counting in her head: fast enough not to seem ungrateful, slow enough not to seem greedy. Hoping to break her from that obsessive caution, Sekken said the first thing that came into his head. "How did your mother vanish?"

He timed it poorly; she aborted the sip she was about to take. Seeing her hesitate, Sekken amended his question. "No, my apologies. Tell me about your mother in general. What kind of woman is she?" *Is, or was?* he thought. Some of the tales he'd glanced at during his shopping were of the opinion that people who "went to the market" didn't survive for very long.

"Hard-working," Kuzu said, with the stout loyalty of a loving daughter. "She worked for Gobachi – a vinegar wholesaler."

"What about your father?"

Kuzu shook her head. "Dead, my lord. Rice water sickness, when I was just a babe. He worked for Gobachi, too."

Sekken had only the vaguest awareness of that sort of thing. The financial and domestic affairs of the larger merchants almost fused into a single mass, their employees marrying and raising families within the confines of the business. "And you?

How did you come to be at the Reiya, instead of staying with this vinegar wholesaler?"

She took a steadying breath. "I was a maid in Gobachi's kitchen. When amo was still there, that was enough. But she went missing, and then maybe a month later, Gobachi died and his son took over. He said there were too many people not doing enough. So..."

Kuzu didn't have to say the rest: this son of Gobachi had tossed an orphaned girl out onto the street. Sekken remembered Kuzu saying her mother had gone missing years ago; if she wasn't more than ten now, then she might have been only five or six at the time. Old enough to do light work in the kitchen, but not more than that. Too many years before she would be useful enough to earn her keep.

Sekken breathed down his simmering rage. He hoped it wasn't visible to Kuzu, and that it was only the memory of his original question that made her say, "It was the son who sent her out on the errand. I don't think he meant anything bad by it, just... he had bad lungs, my lord, and he smoked moonflower to treat them. But the box got spilled, and he needed fresh. So he sent amo to the apothecary he liked in the market."

The intervening years clearly hadn't dulled the memory. Sekken felt guilty for asking... but this could help them save Sayashi, and maybe Kuzu's mother, too. "What time of day was it?"

"Night," Kuzu said. "I dunno when exactly. After midnight. I heard amo get up, but I- I went back to sleep."

Of course she had. She was a little girl, and a servant being woken to run an errand would hardly be unusual. No reason to think anything of it, not until morning came and her mother was nowhere to be found.

But it was a tiny piece of useful information. After midnight: it could have been the Hour of the Ox. A time more associated with the performance of curses at shrines than supernatural transitions, but Sekken couldn't discount the possibility of a link.

"Thank you for telling me," he said quietly. "Fortunes willing, this will help us find your amo."

When he shared what he'd learned with Ryōtora, the other man blanched. "If action at that hour is the key to entering the market, it doesn't bode well for the nature of what lies on the other side."

"I'm not convinced it is," Sekken admitted. "Kuzu says Sayashi went to the market late at night – repeatedly – with no success. And from what I've seen in the books I bought, they don't show any clear pattern. One I think has things happening at the Hour of the Ox, but in another one it's sunset, and in a third it's the middle of the day."

The two of them were in the gardens of the Eisuitei, theoretically preparing to share tea after a long, tiring afternoon. They would do that soon enough, though this conversation was hardly conducive to the kind of tranquil mind one should bring to the event. In the meanwhile, the stand of bamboo around them prevented anyone from coming close enough to eavesdrop except via the path, the far end of which was guarded by Tanshu.

At least Meirō might not think much of it if she heard that Sekken would spend tomorrow lounging around reading. That was just an ordinary day for him. "Any luck with the priest?" he asked.

Ryōtora's scowl took him aback, but the news about Hōgo Nihei was what Sekken might have expected. Not all priests were like Ryōtora, capable of invoking the spirits for miraculous effects. Too many, especially at postings like this one, weren't even especially religious; their appointments were more political than spiritual, a nice little sinecure for someone with family connections. And in a city like this one, the odds of finding any pious monk or priest of great mystical power who might aid them were... not good.

But they didn't need that. They had Ryōtora. When Sekken said as much, though, he was surprised to see Ryōtora's mouth press into a thin line.

He recognized that line; he just didn't know why it was appearing now. "What's wrong? This isn't like it was during winter court, when you had to worry about flattening me or yourself. I haven't had any bad reaction to you invoking the spirits since we began practicing the way of tea together."

Ryōtora's breath hissed out between his teeth. "You haven't had any bad reaction because... I haven't done it."

Despite knowing perfectly well that he'd heard correctly, Sekken had the urge to ask Ryōtora to repeat himself. "You – but – our experiments with Tanshu."

"Simple communion," Ryōtora said. "Putting myself in a state to sense the spirits, to reach out to Tanshu. And I still make offerings. But... I haven't *invoked* them. Not outright, not in the sense of asking them to perform any actions on my behalf."

His chin dipped low while he spoke – as well it might.

Sekken wasn't merely surprised; he was *angry*. "And you never thought to *tell me*?"

"I did think of it. But I- I didn't."

Ryōtora's despairing reply only fanned the flame. They'd kept secrets from each other before – Sekken had kept secrets from Ryōtora, in Seibo Mura, at winter court – but weren't they supposed to be past that? Different bodies, same heart, like the scroll said the day they discovered how to bring themselves into balance? How could they have any kind of harmony, when Ryōtora held back something this vital?

The other man passed a hand over his eyes. "At first it was sensible caution – we'd only just begun to get ourselves into balance, and I thought that adding the weight of the spirits to one side of the scale so soon was a bad idea. Then there simply weren't many reasons for me to invoke them, and the few times a reason came up, I always had an alternative. Then..."

Sekken could guess the rest. *Then you were afraid.* When he was a boy, he'd once tried to climb the garden wall. The subsequent fall had broken a bone in his lower leg, and Sekken's father opted not to ask a priest to beseech the spirits to mend it, so that Sekken would learn from his own foolishness. The break healed well enough, but after weeks of using a crutch, he'd had to fight to convince himself that the leg could support his weight without pain.

It wasn't the fear that angered Sekken, even though he knew Ryōtora would be flagellating himself over it. "Fine. That's why you haven't invoked any spirits. But what's your reason for not telling me?"

The muscles in Ryōtora's neck tensed, but his voice was soft as he said, "I don't have one."

He had a reason. There were always reasons, even if they were poor ones. "Did you think it would damage my opinion of you, knowing you were afraid to try? I thought we knew each other better than–"

"I knew you would tell me to go ahead and do it!"

Ryōtora so rarely interrupted anyone that it left Sekken briefly speechless, an opening through which the other man's words charged without hesitation. "Can you tell me I'm wrong? That your immediate response wouldn't have been, *well, let's try it and see what happens? I can take notes!*"

Admittedly, that did sound like something Sekken would say, though he fancied he would have phrased it differently. "What would be so bad about that?"

"The possibility where it leaves you unconscious on the ground, and it's *my fault!*"

The bamboo around them rustled in the breeze as Ryōtora dragged his voice down from that shout. He was winter-pale, but red spots stood out on his cheeks. He stared at Sekken, desperate, then looked away.

They were still alone. Sekken breathed in, held it, exhaled. Then again. Breathing out his anger, one cycle at a time. *Of course that's his reason.* The same reason both he and Ryōtora had avoided admitting their illnesses to each other: because the last thing in the world either of them wanted was to hurt the other.

But in keeping those secrets, they'd caused each other harm instead.

When he'd regained a semblance of equanimity, Sekken laid his hand on Ryōtora's, then took the other man's hand between his own, against the slight resistance. Quietly, he said,

"This is an argument we were always going to have, I think. We should have had it sooner."

Ryōtora's shoulders hunched. "I don't *want* to argue."

"Too bad," Sekken said, more lightly than he felt. "I'm told it's traditional for married couples. The only way we can spend the rest of our lives together without arguing is if we tie ourselves in knots to avoid it... which, in the long run, will be worse."

The resistance drained out of Ryōtora's hand, leaving it slack between Sekken's. "I know. But..."

"But you don't want to hurt me. I'm glad of that. In the end, though, shouldn't it be my choice what risks to take? And better to take them now, when we're safe, than when we're in the middle of the hidden market and – I don't know – beset by ghosts or whatever is there."

It would have been better still to take such risks back in Phoenix lands, when they were surrounded by friends and knowledgeable physicians instead of a Scorpion magistrate, an illiterate peasant girl, and a city full of people more interested in money than metaphysics. But that was past, and he didn't have to shove it in Ryōtora's face.

After a moment, Sekken said, "What did you want to try?"

Ryōtora let out an unsteady breath. "*Want?* Nothing. But... something akin to what I did when I warded Seibo Mura. Everything we've heard gives us reason to think the hidden market occupies the same ground as the Market of a Hundred Fortunes – that it's bounded by the walls. If I place prayer strips at suitable intervals along those walls, I might be able to get a sense of the spiritual terrain within."

Sekken could see a few challenges with that plan, starting

with navigating the market to gain access to those suitable intervals and continuing on to what the residents might think of his actions. But apart from that, the plan was sensible. "All right. Will the moment of greatest strain be the creation of the prayer strips?"

"More likely after they're placed, when I activate them."

"I'll plan to be ready for both. If I meditate while you work, it might help. Or it might turn out that we've got nothing to be worried about."

Ryōtora's look said he wasn't optimistic. But when Sekken rose to get started, the other man caught his sleeve. "I'll do it tomorrow. I promise, I'm not delaying out of fear. But we should go into this properly prepared."

The tea they were supposedly out in the garden for. An argument was hardly a good prelude... but the honesty it had brought was. They couldn't attain harmony with each other while holding things back.

Sekken bowed with a touch of impudence. "Then by all means, lead the way."

If Ryōtora didn't go into the Eisuitei's teahouse with the serene spirit considered ideal for the process, he at least came out with something closer to it.

Those quiet moments inside didn't erase the apprehension he felt about testing the effects of an invocation on Sekken. They did, however, ease his shame over having hidden that apprehension. Not because he felt more right about what he'd done – quite the contrary – but because it reassured him that he hadn't done irreparable damage to their relationship. And even if their next step went awry...

He tried not to think about that.

Afterward they had a quiet dinner together and worked out a plan. One of the first questions was timing: Ryōtora steadfastly refused to try investigating the market at night, not as a first resort. "It feels too much like curse magic," he said, thinking of the number of shrines crowded within the market's walls.

"But if you do it during the day," Sekken pointed out, "there are more people around to notice what you're doing. Word of it may even get back to Sir Nihei."

"I told him I was going to consult the spirits." Ryōtora shook his head before Sekken could say anything. "I know; it's one thing to say that, and another to hang up prayer strips all around a place he considers his territory. But people live in the market, so even at night, I'm likely to be noticed. And I would look like I have something to hide."

The place was going to be crowded no matter what time of day he went. Ryōtora wasn't even certain he could hang all the prayer strips without some curious passer-by spotting one of them and pulling it down. If he could claim some kind of authority for his actions... but they'd already leaned on their association with Meirō once, and doing it for this seemed even more hazardous. Pursuing that thought, Ryōtora asked, "Who's the governor of Brittle Flower City, again?"

"Daidoji Tadahiro, and unfortunately, I doubt that will work. I asked around; at this time of year he's out of the city, at his country estate. Which isn't far from here, and we can pay him a visit if it becomes necessary, but I doubt he'll be all that sympathetic to our search for our bakeneko friend."

It was more than just Sayashi; it was Kuzu's mother and

everyone else who might have been lost to the hidden market. But if the governor hadn't shown much concern for that before now, Ryōtora doubted he and Sekken would convince the man. They would simply have to take their chances.

Together they plotted out the best arrangement for the prayer strips, four of them equally spaced along each wall. "Or as close to equal spacing as we can manage," Sekken said ruefully. "I'd wager my best calligraphy brush that there used to be a law prohibiting structures within a certain distance of the wall – to keep fires from spreading – but either it got rescinded, or nobody's bothered to enforce it in years."

"We'll do our best," Ryōtora said, folding up the map. "And that also means getting some sleep. I'll make the prayer strips in the morning."

For lack of a better location, Ryōtora did the preparatory work at a shrine to the Fortune of Wisdom and Mercy, outside the Market of a Hundred Fortunes, while Sekken meditated and prayed. "I feel fine," Sekken said once it was done, and smiled when Ryōtora peered at him as if in doubt. "Would I mar our study of our condition by putting a good face on how I actually feel? I *hope* you don't think I'm so poor a scholar as that."

"Never," Ryōtora said, much reassured.

They met up with the rest of their group at the market's northern gate. Ryōtora didn't much like these clandestine arrangements, designed to avoid Meirō's curiosity about where he, Sekken, Tanshu, Ishi, Tarō, and Kuzu were all going together, but he and Sekken had agreed it would be better to have assistance. Kuzu knew her way around the market and could talk to locals who grew suspicious about Ryōtora's actions; Ishi and Tarō could keep any of those locals from causing trouble.

Tanshu's assistance proved invaluable. Invisible and incorporeal, he could dart through the crowds at a speed none of the humans could manage, up and down alleys and into the narrow gaps between buildings, scouting until he found a path to the next spot on the wall Ryōtora wanted to access. In one case there *was* no such path – the owner of the adjoining tatami workshop had tacked a shed on by the simple expedient of extending his building straight up to the wall itself – but Ryōtora declined to enter the workshop and ask the owner for permission to go inside his shed. "This will be close enough," he said, pasting the prayer strip onto the wall next to the shed.

It took quite a while, but by early afternoon they were done. "Where now?" Sekken asked.

"The center," Ryōtora said. "That will be easiest."

In some senses of the word, at least. The center of the market was easy to reach; it was where the relatively broad streets between the gates crossed. But that also meant it was thronged with handcarts, porters, and all the other traffic that filled the district.

Ishi tried to bull a path forward and nearly got run over. Instead the group had to time their passage carefully, darting through gaps and then pausing, ignoring the curses from passers-by who cared more about their destinations than the status of the men in their way. When they finally reached the center of the crossroads, the others set themselves up in a ring around Ryōtora: Ishi and Tarō to his left and right, Sekken in front of him, Kuzu and the manifested Tanshu a more fragile shield behind.

A shudder chased across Ryōtora's skin as he remembered the last time others had ringed him defensively like this. Seibo Mura, battling hordes of malevolent yōkai.

The sheer need to finish his work quickly and get out of everyone's way helped ground him. Ignoring the mercantile clamor, as he'd once ignored a battle, Ryōtora drew a deep breath and exhaled it as a prayer.

From the feel of it, one of his prayer strips had indeed been torn down, or maybe he simply hadn't pasted it firmly enough. There was a weaker area to the southeast, as if one of the strands of his net was missing. But a net could hold with one strand gone, and through the remainder, Ryōtora felt the Market of a Hundred Fortunes.

Earth, Water, Air, Fire. All were present, of course – but each element encompassed more than one concept, and Ryōtora could learn much from its particular cast. Earth here was the patient work of craftsmanship, shaping raw materials into their final forms, while Fire was the passion of the artist seeking to do more than simply produce the same thing again and again. Air was the cunning trickery of the merchant in search of a bargain; Water was the ceaseless flow of goods and money.

That was the surface. Ryōtora needed to look deeper.

He'd already made offerings while creating the prayer strips, but now he placed a cat's-eye stone on the ground and poured a little sake over it. Kuzu had taught him the song performed during the market's yearly festival in the fall; Ryōtora sang it quietly as he took out a bamboo tube and opened it to reveal an ash-covered coal inside. In between lyrics he puffed the coal to life, until it could light the final slip of paper, on which he'd written his prayer to the spirits.

As the paper flared and died, he closed his eyes – and his sense of the market *shifted*.

It was like a painting, where the near figure of a traveler and the distant outline of a mountain lay along the same plane. Hōgo Nihei was an ignorant fool; there absolutely *was* something else here. Ryōtora felt it, in the echoing space bounded by the walls – for however much the residents of Brittle Flower City packed into that space, the space itself was what defined the market, as the hollow interior defined a bowl. Void: represented in Ryōtora's ceremony by the gates, gaping open between the markers of his prayer strips.

And the Void was the element of the strange, the untouchable, the unknowable. The element of that which went beyond.

He'd imagined many things beneath the ordinary market... but he hadn't expected something elementally almost identical to what lay above. This wasn't a realm of ghosts; it had no scent of the underworld about it, and the Realm of the Dead was nearly devoid of Fire. Nor did it have the airy lightness associated with the celestial realms above, where the Fortunes dwelt. *The hidden market*, people called it, and that was exactly what it felt like: another market, full of buying and selling, just... not here. And not quite the same.

If it was another market, then where was its gate? How did people pass in and out of it? And was Sayashi truly in there?

Ryōtora linked his hands into a mudra, fingers precisely tucked and bent, and began chanting anew. He was going beyond the bounds of his knowledge now: his Agasha instructors had taught him a variety of traditional invocations, prayers used for centuries in the confidence that the spirits would correctly understand what was desired. Extemporizing was less reliable, with far more risk of the spirits misunderstanding or simply declining to cooperate. But Ryōtora had a fingertip on the edge of what he sought to grasp, and he knew without opening his eyes what look Sekken would give him if he asked whether he should continue.

*Show me the way,* he said, reaching out to the Water of the ordinary market and the hidden one alike. *Water always finds a way. Flow toward our friend, and make a path we can follow.*

He heard Tanshu bark behind him, once, sharp and urgent.

Then something *kicked* Ryōtora, right at the center of his soul. Knocking him backward, spiritually and physically; he stumbled into Kuzu, his eyes flying open.

Sekken stared at him, one hand reaching out – and then Sekken, not Ryōtora, collapsed to the ground.

# CHAPTER TEN

Sayashi tried to convince herself that scrubbing a floor wasn't much different from grooming her own fur.

She failed.

Grooming was a soothing, satisfying process. It stretched the body; it brought order to the world. She'd never seen much utility in some of the types of meditation humans practiced – chanting certain words, or trying to hold certain thoughts in their minds – but two kinds, all cats understood: the drifting serenity of just sitting, and the mindfulness of absorbing oneself in a task.

Scrubbing a floor made her back hurt. Her knees ached from the hard wooden boards beneath them; her hands cramped from gripping the brush; her skin wrinkled in unpleasant ways. And if she was bringing order to a world, it wasn't *hers*. All of this was being done for someone else's sake, and she loathed that.

*Stupid kitten,* she imagined her mother sneering. *This is what you get for caring what anyone else thinks.*

Sayashi let go of the brush and sat back on her heels, trying in vain to stretch the stiffness away. She couldn't even take satisfaction in being nearly done, because Tōji would just find something else for her to do. More scrubbing, or maybe sewing. Or maybe this would be one of the nights when the song changed and Tōji wanted her to dance for entertainment. Which wasn't any better, even though Sayashi had been a skilled geisha back at the House of Infinite Petals. That had been by her own choice, and this…

This was by her own choice, too, after a fashion. Though the choice had been far from freely made.

How many nights had she gotten through? How many more remained?

Questions like that were foolish, human-style thinking. If she let herself start keeping count, she would go mad.

Sayashi wanted to shift to cat form and clean herself, lick away the bitter soap that stained her forepaws and the ache that ran all down her back. It would be even worse, though, to give herself that relief, then take human shape again and resume scrubbing. She was on the ground floor of the palace now, a back corner where Tōji likely never came; would anyone notice if Sayashi left the job incomplete?

Rattling footsteps sounded nearby, and with a flinch, Sayashi reached for her brush again. Tōji wouldn't come here, but the general very well might. And the last thing she wanted was a second altercation with *him*. Even after the rattling noise receded upstairs, Sayashi kept scrubbing.

"Oh, my – so *very* hard at work. Like something out of a tale."

Sayashi's mouth pinched tight. "Leave me alone, old woman."

"Now, is that any way to speak to an elder?" A squeak of wood against an ungreased axle as the old woman rolled her little cart closer. Sayashi was certain the cart only made noise when the old woman wanted it to. Otherwise, why hadn't she heard their approach?

The old woman stepped past Sayashi, her clawed feet leaving damp prints as she crossed from the scrubbed part to the dirty. When she went back, she would track dirt with her, and Sayashi would have to clean it away again. "Almost done!" the woman said cheerfully, as if there wouldn't be some new task to follow. "When you're finished, would you like to write a letter for my cart?"

"No," Sayashi snapped, leaning on her brush as if she could scrub the old woman herself away.

"Are you sure? It might strengthen your spirit for your long toil. A reminder of why you're enduring all of this."

Sayashi was enduring all of this because she'd been *stupid*. If she hadn't gotten caught, she wouldn't have been forced into this bargain; she could have been away from here, her quarry maybe even found by now. But no, that damned shrine bell had spotted her and started ringing, and the general had been close enough to intervene, and now here she was, soap-wrinkled and aching and *bored*.

Maybe she should write *that* for the old woman. Feelings like annoyance and frustration weren't the yōkai's usual diet, but didn't they say variety provided spice?

The old woman leaned closer. "Come, now, it would make a delightful tale. The faithful little cat, seeking her long-lost–"

Sayashi couldn't take any more. She whipped her brush in a short, sharp arc, spattering the old woman with grey-tinged suds. "Leave me be. I won't dance for your entertainment."

"You'll dance for Tōji's, though! Again and again, until you hardly even remember why you began." The old woman cackled, not bothering to wipe the suds away. "Like all the rest of us. Dancing for so long that most have forgotten we're even doing it. But I remember, oh, yes."

She stepped back to her little wooden cart and patted the sides of its box fondly. "It's all safe and sound in here."

"Then take it somewhere safely away from here," Sayashi said rudely. "Before I 'accidentally' spill my bucket over your cart."

That did the trick. Snarling, the old woman rolled the cart away, its wheels squeaking with every turn. And Sayashi, snarling, went back to her work.

Sayashi was used to sleeping lightly, waking up every so often to groom or shift position or make sure an unfamiliar noise posed no threat before lapsing back into a doze. These days, though, she was so tired at every dawn that she fell asleep like a human, hardly rousing until dusk.

When a cool, wet nose shoved itself into her face, it took her completely by surprise. She yowled and shot into the air, landing in her larger form and looking for some safe path to escape.

The dog that had woken her immediately lay down, looking contrite.

Not just *a* dog. Sayashi recognized that slobbering mutt. It was Asako Sekken's inugami.

Sayashi would never have admitted it, but the racing of her heart switched from alarm to hope. Were the samurai here?

But the swift rake of her gaze showed her only what passed for the palace garden, a sad little place with a handful of trees and rocks, bathing in the sunlight. No humans in sight.

"Where's your master?" she demanded of the inugami.

The dog's head drooped low. She was never quite sure why he didn't talk; she grudgingly had to admit he was intelligent enough for it, and certainly more than old enough. Maybe something to do with how he'd become a witch's familiar in the first place, instead of awakening on his own as Sayashi had.

Whatever the reason, he could still more or less communicate, just without words. Asako Sekken was here, and Isao Ryōtora, too – no surprise there – but not *here*. They were still on the wrong side of the gate.

"Then get them here!" she snapped. "They're a pair of cleverpaws; maybe they can find some way to get me out of this – this–"

She stopped short of putting it into words. She couldn't admit to the inugami just how bad a mess she'd made of what was supposed to be a quiet, personal quest, a bit of foolish vulnerability no one was ever meant to know about. Sooner or later the humans would learn of it; she could hardly expect them to help her without finding out what had happened. But Sayashi would put that off for as long as she could.

The inugami stood and whuffed softly. He was loyal, she had to grant him that. Loyal and helpful, even when the person asking for help was a cat.

He came forward and presented his face, not invading her space the way he had a moment before, but offering. After a moment's hesitation, Sayashi padded closer and stretched out her neck, sniffing delicately at his nose. She surprised even herself when that turned into a rub, dragging her cheek along the side of his muzzle and deep into his doggy-smelling fur. Damn it, she'd reached such a nadir that this mutt felt like a comfort.

The inugami nuzzled her back. Then he was gone, and Sayashi lay down again in the sun, feeling warmer than she had in days.

# CHAPTER ELEVEN

Kuzu was pressed into a corner of the room as if she didn't know whether to hide or flee, but Ryōtora couldn't spare much attention for her, because Sekken was still unconscious.

If it hadn't been for Ishi and Tarō, he and Sekken would still be in the middle of that intersection. Ryōtora knew an invocation that would help him lift Sekken's weight, but he wasn't about to use it – not when his previous efforts had caused the other man's collapse. Ishi had quite literally stood over Sekken, to keep him from being trampled, while Tarō went running for assistance and came back with a handcart. Then the two of them had loaded him into it and brought him back to the Eisuitei, with Ryōtora scarcely retaining enough presence of mind to make sure Kuzu wasn't lost in the chaos.

Now he didn't know what to do. Summon a physician? From what he'd seen on the streets of Brittle Flower City, there were countless people ready to sell him elixirs, powders, and pills. All of dubious merit, and besides, their shared condition was no ordinary affliction. While medical help had become slightly more useful once Sekken and Ryōtora realized the true nature of the problem, Ryōtora doubted anyone here was qualified to assist. Or if there was any such person, how to find them.

That left him with this: Sekken laid out on a futon, twitching periodically like a man caught in a dream, and not waking up.

Guilty, angry tears stung Ryōtora's eyes, held in only by the awareness that letting his self-control slip would do Sekken no good. This happened to them *too often*. Not just since their souls became linked, but before that and apart from it: Sekken collapsing after Ryōtora inadvertently called the spirit of Kaimin-nushi into his body, Sekken unconscious after he gave Ryōtora half his life. Sekken falling victim to the sleeping curse of the baku. Ridiculous as it sounded, even in his own head, Ryōtora would have felt better if they could at least share such burdens more equally.

Except that was tantamount to wishing Sekken suffer through this experience instead, kneeling helplessly at the side of the man he loved.

Ryōtora had tried to do what he'd done when his investigation at the Komoriyome Pavilion laid Sekken low, after he realized they suffered from the same affliction. But this time there was no echoing emptiness within Sekken, no lack Ryōtora could remedy by pouring a bit of himself into the other man. He tried to take comfort in the knowledge that their careful management had at least achieved that much, but without success. *I should have tried invocations sooner, when we were still in Phoenix lands. Then I would have known not to try here.*

"Lord Isao?" Tarō said, leaning forward to get Ryōtora's attention. "Do you want us to go look for a doctor?"

He opened his mouth to say yes, and the door to their room slid open with an unceremonious clack.

"Lord Isao," Hōgo Nihei said icily. "I received word of a disturbance in the Market of a Hundred Fortunes – a group of peasants and two samurai blocking the central intersection, disrupting traffic and carrying out some kind of unauthorized ritual. From the looks of it, your foolishness has already brought some appropriate consequences down upon your companion's head, but–"

If he hadn't mentioned Sekken's collapse, Ryōtora might have been able to keep his temper. As it was, he shot to his feet. "If you paid half a shred of attention to something besides profit, Sir Nihei, you would know that something supernatural lurks under your very nose."

The acolyte accompanying Nihei stepped forward – a young man burly enough that he was probably a warrior monk. Ryōtora thought at first the acolyte was just stepping forward to protect Nihei, but the man kept advancing, reaching for Ryōtora. "Such actions can't be allowed to pass," Nihei said. "I'm taking you to the city magistrate, where you will answer for your presumption."

Leaving Sekken alone. Ryōtora jerked away from the acolyte, and then Ishi was there, interposing himself; he might not be able to hear their words, but the situation was plain enough to read. Tarō joined him, the two ashigaru making a human wall between Ryōtora and the Crane.

"I told you I was going to consult the spirits," Ryōtora said to Nihei. "You said nothing about needing authorization."

"And *you* said nothing about festooning the market with talismans of unknown purpose. Placed there by a group of outsiders from other clans, no less! A suspicious man might see threat in that, Lord Isao."

A priest with any real spiritual power would be able to tell the prayer strips posed no such threat. But that wasn't the point. The real issue was that Nihei felt insulted, and he'd found a way to take that insult out on Ryōtora. And he was right; they were outsiders here. Ryōtora had no authority to hide behind, no grounds to refuse being taken into custody.

From the doorway came another voice, a light veil of amusement over a core of implacable steel. "And an intelligent man might inquire further into the identity of those outsiders before he takes action. If you have an issue with how my yoriki conduct themselves, Sir Nihei, you should come to me."

There was no relief in seeing Meirō appear behind Nihei. Her gaze didn't even flick to Ryōtora, but the pit of his stomach dropped out all the same. *How much does she know?*

Nihei's chin rose as he pivoted to look at her. "I don't believe we're acquainted."

Meirō feigned disappointment. "Oh, how awkward – so many people in possession of so much information you lack. I am Bayushi Meirō. Emerald Magistrate."

He was disciplined enough not to recoil. There was even a hint of a sneer as he said, "This Dragon is your yoriki?"

"The Phoenix, too. The pair preventing your acolyte from laying impertinent hands on Lord Isao are my constables. What a good thing I arrived in time to prevent your man from doing something he might regret."

"Did you give them orders to disrupt the market with their ritual?"

Whether she said yes or no, Meirō would be held

responsible. Either she'd chosen to cause trouble, or she'd failed to control her underlings. This was why Sekken and Ryōtora had tried to return their seals, to avoid such entanglements.

Meirō leaned forward slightly. She wasn't any taller than Nihei, but somehow her posture combined the sharing of a secret with intimidation. Voice sinking to a conspiratorial purr, she said, "Sir Nihei, word of the... *situation* here... has made it all the way up to Phoenix lands. Now, it's not common gossip yet; count yourself lucky for that. But we had to come down here personally to deal with matters. Lord Isao and Lord Asako are specialists in addressing all kinds of unusual problems – most famously, the Night Parade of a Hundred Demons? Ah, *that* at least you've heard of. Well, that should give you a scale for imagining what might happen if you interfere with their work. I think a brief disruption in traffic is a small price to pay, don't you?"

It was a good thing nobody was looking at Ryōtora, because his jaw was almost on the floor. Nothing Meirō had said was an outright lie, but it all added up to a completely false picture of what he and Sekken were doing in Brittle Flower City.

He ought to say something. Ought to disavow Meirō's words, admit the truth and accept the consequences. But he couldn't bring himself to do it.

Nihei's shoulders had gone rigid, and he tried twice to speak, both times cutting himself short before more than half a sound came out. Meirō straightened and smiled. "I'm glad we could settle this so amicably. Thank you for your concern, Sir Nihei, and if we need any further assistance, I will be sure to let you know."

As if he'd given any assistance at all – but what was Nihei

supposed to do, argue against her courteous dismissal? With a growl, he snapped his fingers to summon his acolyte and headed for the door, not even bowing to anyone as he left. Meirō glided out of his path, and smiled as she watched him go.

The tension in the room didn't lessen at all with Nihei's departure. Ryōtora curled his hands into fists while Meirō stepped inside and slid the door gently shut behind herself.

Then she glanced down at Sekken. "I presume this is the sort of trouble you and Lord Asako warned me could happen. Is there anything I can do to help?"

"I don't know," Ryōtora forced himself to say. "This particular situation is... new."

"And brought about by whatever you did in the market." Meirō's head came up. Her voice remained soft, but the steel beneath it was back. "Since I just took responsibility for your actions, why don't you tell me what exactly it is that I'm now on the hook for?"

Ishi and Tarō hadn't moved, still guarding Ryōtora against any threat. He tapped their shoulders gently, and with reluctance, they retreated to guard Sekken instead. Trying to sound courteous, Ryōtora said, "I am grateful for your intervention, Lady Bayushi... but I didn't ask for it."

"That doesn't matter, and we both know it. Since you're my yoriki–"

"A position we have already tried to relinquish. But *you* wouldn't let us."

"Because there's no need for you to give it up!" The beads of Meirō's mask swung. "Whatever it is you're here to do, Lord Isao, having some amount of authority behind you can only make it easier. Authority, and allies."

Ryōtora's whole body ached with stiffness. "And why are you so eager to be our ally, Lady Bayushi? Why help us travel to Brittle Flower City, asking nothing in return save some entertainment on the road? Why give us the authority of yoriki, yet require no duties of us to go with the title?"

"Would you *rather* I extort some kind of payment out of you?"

"Yes!" Ryōtora said, startled into pure honesty. "Hardly anyone in this world acts wholly out of altruism. The inferior obeys the superior out of duty, or from fear of the consequences. The courtier grants a favor in the expectation of a favor in return. Merchants seek profit; the ambitious seek advantage; even those who seem noble often hope to burnish their reputations. Why should *you* be different?"

He needed Sekken. He needed someone with a hope of reading past those swaying beads, past the impassive line of Meirō's mouth, to whatever lay behind. If there was an invocation that would persuade the spirits to show him the truth of her heart, like the hidden market past the ordinary one, Ryōtora didn't know it.

Meirō exhaled a soft laugh. "Why should I be different, indeed? Seeing as how I am a Scorpion."

Ryōtora gestured at where Nihei had stood a moment before. "Lady Bayushi, I just watched you spin that priest around until he couldn't tell which way was up, all without saying an untrue word. You can't behave like that in front of me and then expect me not to be suspicious. I have no idea what you do and don't know about our purpose here in Brittle Flower City, or what you hope to gain out of this situation. And even if you told me, how could I be sure that was the entire truth?

"I am no courtier; I have very little skill at crafting elegant phrases. I can only ask that you forgive my bluntness when I say, *I cannot trust you.* If that lack of trust offends you, then I will happily surrender our seals right now, and we will no longer be your problem. We will deal with Sir Nihei ourselves."

He was breathing hard by the time he finished. Meirō, by contrast, hardly seemed to be breathing at all; even the beads were still, lying against her cheeks and framing the sides of her jaw.

Then they swung, hard, as she nodded with the crisp precision of a superior to an inferior. "How can I be offended by the reaction every member of my clan experiences from birth? And since my words will not convince you otherwise, Lord Isao, let my actions do so – if they can. Keep the seals, and I will continue to defend you against Sir Nihei and anyone else who questions your actions – *without* asking you further about your business. Whatever consequences come from that will fall upon my head. Perhaps, when you see my sincerity of intent, you will come to trust me. If not… then so be it."

She glanced down again at Sekken. "I know a good physician. If you wish her name, ask Botan. But I will understand if you do not."

Meirō bowed herself curtly out of the room, leaving Ryōtora with Ishi, Tarō, Kuzu, and the unconscious, trembling Sekken. Ryōtora slid to a graceless heap on the tatami, hands shaking. If he were Sekken, he would have been reaching out to bury them in Tanshu's ruff.

Then he looked around, frowning. Linked his hands into a mudra and prayed – to no effect.

Only his human companions were in the room. Tanshu was nowhere to be seen.

Nothing smelled quite right.

He was trotting through streets and alleys, dodging brooms, shoes, a book cart rumbling down the middle of the lane. The market was waking up, its residents starting to go about their business, but all the scents of before were gone. He could follow his own trail back to its starting point, but that didn't help. No matter how he cast about, he couldn't smell the others anywhere.

Except at the wall. Faint traces here and there, but no more than that. Someone had gone around and torn down the papers. Maybe if they were still there…

What was that?

A little flutter of breeze tickled his nose with a familiar array of odors. Different from everything else here. He set off at a run, pausing now and again to make sure he was headed the right way, until at last it led him to–

No, where had it gone? The source ought to be *here*, but when he came around the corner it vanished. Back he went, and there it was: around the corner again, and gone.

He growled. No. Not acceptable.

The building had a fenced-in area at the back. He managed to scramble up and over the fence, and yes, the scent was here, very strong. The sliding door into the building was open a crack; he nosed it farther, until he could slip inside. And there was the front door, open to the street, familiar smells pouring through it – smells that *weren't there* on the street itself, when he came at it around the corner. He didn't know what that meant, but it hardly mattered. He launched himself at the exit–

And bounced back, hard. The door was open, but the door wasn't open. Frustrated, he planted his paws foursquare and began to bark. If he barked loud enough and long enough, the others would hear, and they would come.

"What's that racket? Hey, now, you're not supposed to be here! Quit making so much noise! I step away for one minute and some inugami just strolls inside like he owns the place…"

A broom whacked his nose, driving him back from the open-but-closed door. Hands grabbed him around the barrel. He barked louder. Then, with nobody touching it, the door slammed shut–

–and Sekken jerked awake.

For a good ten heartbeats, he couldn't make sense of anything. Where he was, who he was, what was going on. His head was full of muddled dreams. Was he out in the market? No, because there was a ceiling over his head. Their inn – the Eisuitei, that was the name. It must be morning. Except he was fully clothed, and the light was wrong: dim, but not like dawn. Sunset. Why had he fallen asleep in the afternoon?

"M'lord?"

Sekken's twitch of surprise rolled him onto his side, facing Kuzu. She rose hastily from her cross-legged seat to more properly kneeling and jerked into something like a bow, except she was still trying to look at him while she did it. "You're awake? Of course you're awake. Your eyes wouldn't be open, otherwise. Though the mistress, she sleepwalks sometimes." Kuzu shook her head violently, dismissing her former employer, her own babbling, or both. "I'm sorry, m'lord. I- I should get the other lord." Before Sekken could protest, she shot to her feet and out the door.

Ryōtora appeared fast enough that Sekken knew he couldn't have been far away. By then Sekken had made it to a sitting position – which shouldn't have been a challenge, except his body didn't feel like it fit quite right. Memory was starting to push its way through the fading wisps of dream. The market, and the ritual with the prayer strips. "How long was I out?"

With a thud that made Sekken wince, Ryōtora fell to his knees at the side of his futon. "I knew this would happen," he said, guilt lacerating his voice.

His hands were grasping empty air like he felt he didn't deserve to touch Sekken, not when matters had gone so wrong. Sekken took hold of them and said, "We both knew it *could* happen. There's a difference." A difference in what had happened, too. This wasn't like it used to be, back before they knew how they could drain each other. Sekken didn't feel cored out; he felt like he wasn't quite here. Normally he woke cleanly, unlike Ryōtora, who often seemed to leave half his wits abed until he'd been up for a while. But for the first time in his life, Sekken understood what that was like.

His own wits weren't the ones that mattered right now. "What did you learn?"

Ryōtora's mouth thinned, but his fingers curled around Sekken's. "Not much… but one thing that's useful. And alarming. Whatever is in the market, it very much did not appreciate my prying."

Sekken listened with growing concern to his description of what had happened and tried to match it to his own confused memories. "I think I felt that 'kick', yes. It took me by surprise.

I was trying to meditate while you prayed; I hoped it would help keep us balanced. And I was communing with Tanshu, too – I don't really know what I hoped that would do, except that a witch's familiar ought to be good for *something*, even if the witch himself isn't. But–"

Then Sekken stopped, taken aback by Ryōtora's sudden indrawn breath. "What?"

The other man looked around the room. "Is Tanshu here? I couldn't see him before, even when I tried."

How badly was his own brain scrambled that he hadn't noticed the dog's absence? Since Seibo Mura, Sekken had grown accustomed to always having Tanshu there, warm fur and a questing nose, a solid presence ever ready to lend comfort. Not having him there felt almost like missing a limb.

Except that, just like a limb, Sekken knew where Tanshu was without having to look.

"He's not here," Sekken breathed. "I think… I think he's in the hidden market."

# CHAPTER TWELVE

By the time they were done talking, the sun had well and truly set, and Sekken was hungry enough to eat the futon he was sitting on.

Ryōtora sent Kuzu to have some food brought up to their room, and while they were waiting, Sekken tried to figure out what they should do now. He wished very much that he'd woken up sooner; maybe then they could have handled Sir Nihei without Meirō needing to intervene. Or, if not that, he could have prevented Ryōtora from laying into her like that.

"I should have handled Lady Bayushi better," Ryōtora said glumly, even though Sekken hadn't commented on it. "Just held my tongue, or…"

The way he trailed off said it all. *Or what?* Sekken had met people worse suited to dealing with Meirō than Ryōtora – Kuzu, for example. But the list was short, and mostly consisted of peasants so disadvantaged by status, they had no choice but to knuckle under.

Sekken would smooth that over, just as soon as he thought

of a way to do so. Which was hard when he had the persistent feeling that part of him was somewhere else. It wasn't like the link between him and Ryōtora, draining energy from him if he wasn't careful; instead it was more like a persistent feeling of distraction. As if there were sights, sounds, *scents* demanding his attention – but when he tried to give them that attention, they weren't there. He could barely even remember what he'd seen in his dreams. Had Tanshu genuinely found Sayashi? Or was that wishful thinking?

Their dinner arrived, and they ate in silence. Finally, Ryōtora put down his chopsticks and said, with a heaviness that made it clear he'd been ruminating the whole time, "We should try to figure out what blocked me from investigating the market. But I don't know how to do that, except through more invocations. And no matter how much you assure me that you don't mind the consequences for you, *I* mind them."

Sekken jerked his awareness back to the present moment. "You know," he said slowly, "the more I think about it..."

After several heartbeats, the corners of Ryōtora's mouth compressed – the first touch of humor he'd shown since Sekken woke up. "How long must I wait for the rest of that thought?"

"Sorry." Sekken laughed ruefully. "I actually think I was in the middle of proving my own unspoken point. I keep being distracted by what I'm fairly certain is my link to Tanshu. And didn't you say that while I was unconscious, I kept twitching? Like I was having some kind of dream?"

Ryōtora nodded. Sekken said, "I think my 'dream' was actually me experiencing what Tanshu is doing. I was twitching because my body was reacting to his movement. Maybe your invocation did drain me a bit... but maybe the reason I passed out was because my spirit went into Tanshu instead."

There were stories of witches doing that, but Sekken had never tried. If he was being honest with himself, some part of him had assumed he'd never be *able* to. After all, he wasn't a real witch, was he? Just a scholar who inherited a dog spirit from his ancestor, and in due course would pass it on to some more worthy descendent.

But maybe he was – could be – more than that.

The tension of guilt began to melt from Ryōtora's eyes. "The day we had Tanshu come find me in the shrine... I felt for a moment like I was seeing through his eyes."

"And smelling through his nose," Sekken said dryly. "It's hard to know for sure what tsukimono-suji witches can do; they're so rare these days, and illness kept me from experimenting the way Isawa Chikayū wanted. But there are tales of them entering their familiars like that. And I *was* trying to commune with Tanshu as I meditated."

"While I prayed for a path to open for us." Ryōtora rubbed the back of his neck and eased his head in a circle, as if to release more tension there. "So between the two of us, we managed... *something*."

If only they could figure out how to make use of it. But Sekken didn't remember how Tanshu had crossed over, and even if he did, was it a path two ordinary humans could walk?

When he voiced that question, Ryōtora said, "We can try to find out. Before that, however, there's something else I want to do."

He sounded surprisingly grim. At Sekken's quizzical look,

he reached into the pouch dangling from his sash and drew out his yoriki's seal. "I want to give this back."

"How, by hiding it in her room when she's not there? From the sound of your conversation with her, I doubt she's changed her mind."

"She may not have. But won't there be another Emerald Magistrate in town?"

For a city this size – and so close to a contested border – that was very likely. "You mean to circumvent Meirō? That will look…" Eloquence deserted Sekken. He honestly couldn't imagine *how* another magistrate would react.

"I don't care how it will look," Ryōtora said, his tone unyielding. "The more determined she is to leave these in our possession, the less I trust it."

"But without the protection of her authority, Sir Nihei could easily come after you again."

"*I don't care,*" Ryōtora snapped. "We'll find a way to deal with Sir Nihei – some way that doesn't involve biting a Scorpion hook."

At least he kept his voice low. Etiquette said that people should disregard private conversations they happened to overhear, but when had etiquette ever stopped a Scorpion?

Might as well ask when pragmatism had ever stopped Ryōtora from doing what he felt was right. His stubbornness was endearing and aggravating by turns.

Fighting the urge to rub his brow, Sekken said, "May I suggest a compromise? We go to the local Emerald Magistrate and ask their opinion. For all we know, Lady Bayushi's actions are in accordance with her official duty, and we simply haven't been privileged to share that information.

If the one here says to keep our seals of office, we can take that as a good sign."

Ryōtora's expression said he doubted any such thing would happen, but he nodded.

Eagerness to slip free of Meirō's net helped Ryōtora get out of bed the next morning, without the usual dragging feeling of sloth. An inquiry at the gate through which they'd entered Brittle Flower City supplied them with directions to the local Emerald Magistrate; the office was on the other side of the city, but Ryōtora set off with a swift, ground-devouring stride.

Swift enough that after a while, Sekken caught his sleeve and begged him to slow down. "We don't need to run ourselves into the ground for *this*."

No, they didn't. It was guilt as much as eagerness that propelled Ryōtora forward. Was he doing the right thing, shedding Meirō's assistance like this? Attempting to quit her service by going to a fellow magistrate could be taken as a grave insult. For all Ryōtora knew, she might demand to settle the offense with a duel, and neither he nor Sekken was equipped to face her with a blade in hand.

It was hard to imagine her reacting that way after all her generosity and tolerance. But that was exactly why Ryōtora wanted out from under her authority.

The office of the Emerald Magistrate was a modest building, fenced off with a low wall. A guard stood at the gate; with a wry quirk of his mouth, Sekken produced his unwanted seal to explain why they were requesting a moment of the magistrate's time. "We are in service to Lady Bayushi Meirō," he said.

Mercifully, the magistrate stationed here was not a fellow Scorpion. Ryōtora knew the imperial bureaucracy made an effort to assign samurai away from their own clans' lands; given the tensions around Brittle Flower City, that ruled out both a Crane and a Lion. The current resident was a Unicorn, Lord Utaku Teruo, a man of no little seniority. Considering Teruo's rank, Ryōtora settled into the visitors' chamber for a long wait.

The servants hadn't even brought tea yet when the Emerald Magistrate appeared, a young woman at his heels.

His bow was perfunctory. "Is it true? You're Lord Asako Sekken and Lord Agasha no Isao Ryōtora? Yoriki under Bayushi Meirō?"

"We are," Sekken replied, his usual polished tone suddenly cautious. "Has something gone amiss?"

Teruo's jaw hardened. "Very much so. Why are you here in Brittle Flower City?"

Either Sekken heard Ryōtora's silent urgings, or his own sense of honesty prompted him to be candid. "Lord Utaku, Isao and I came here on personal business. It was as a favor to us that Lady Bayushi offered to make us yoriki and travel through this city on her way to Kyuden Bayushi."

"Kyuden Bayushi!" That outburst came from the woman at Teruo's side. She was slender and short, dressed in practical traveling clothes, her hakama bound tight around the calf.

Teruo's gaze flicked from her to Sekken. "And why did she say she was headed to Scorpion lands?"

"She didn't, my lord."

The unease that had been coiling inside Ryōtora for days – that had only begun to loosen when they came here to return the seals – suddenly twisted tight. "Lord Utaku," he said, trying not to sound as unsteady as he felt, "if we have unwittingly interfered with Lady Bayushi's proper duties, we offer our most sincere apologies."

"*If.*" Teruo's exhalation came just shy of being a snort. "Lord Isao, after leaving Sheltered Plains City, Bayushi Meirō was supposed to travel west to Shiro Moto. She had no instructions sending her to Kyuden Bayushi. One way or another, she is pursuing some private agenda... and in the absence of another reason, I must assume that agenda has something to do with *you.*"

His words struck with the icy shock of a snowmelt stream. Appalled, Ryōtora turned to Sekken; the other man was already bowing low. "I wish I could say this came as a surprise, but the truth is, we've feared for some time that Lady Bayushi had a secret motive for offering her help. Isao insisted we come here today to give you our seals, so that we would no longer be beholden to her. In light of what you've said, if there is anything we can do to assist in setting this matter right, you have only to instruct us."

Teruo glanced at the young woman again. She said, "You can tell us where Bayushi Meirō *is.* The place of residence she recorded with the gate guards when you entered Brittle Flower City claims they have no such guest. Did the staff at the Tsutsujiden lie to me, or are you lodging somewhere else?"

"The Eisuitei," Ryōtora said immediately. "Please believe, we had no idea she'd entered false information–"

"I don't blame you for that," Teruo said. His curt tone, though, implied that his understanding might end there. Meirō abandoning her orders and bringing them south... that might yet be laid at their feet. After all, they'd asked her to help them.

Part of Ryōtora quailed at the thought of what that might mean. Perversely, though, he felt more at peace now than he had since the Scorpion first agreed to help them.

Because whatever consequences might fall on their heads, he knew now that he was right. They should never have trusted Bayushi Meirō.

The journey back across the city at least gave them the opportunity for introductions. As Sekken had surmised from her accent, the young woman with Teruo was a fellow Phoenix, Shiba no Koganshi Haizumi. She worked in the courier division of the Emerald Magistrates, and Sekken thought sourly of the conversation with Meirō about how traveling magistrates were notified of changes in their duties. *No, she wouldn't want people tracking her with the aid of the spirits, would she?*

Haizumi had been sent after Meirō as soon as they realized she'd ignored her orders. "If you hadn't come to visit Lord Utaku," Haizumi said as they hurried through the streets behind Teruo's horse, "it might have taken us days to track down Lady Bayushi. I'll be sure to thank the Fortunes for their favor."

"And I should thank them for Ryōtora's stubbornness," Sekken muttered under his breath, too quiet for Haizumi to hear. But for Ryōtora's insistence that they resign their seals, how long would it have taken for them to discover Meirō's deception? And what would she have achieved in the meanwhile?

But Sekken's own stubbornness was vindicated, too. *If we'd told Meirō the truth…*

When they arrived at the Eisuitei, Teruo dismounted and strode straight past the servants, gesturing peremptorily for Sekken and Ryōtora to lead him to Meirō's chambers. Despite all their haste, when Teruo threw the doors wide, they found only one person waiting for them.

Kakeguchi Botan.

Who bowed low in the empty room and remained bent, her face just above the mat. "For my actions, I have no excuse. I willingly accept whatever punishment you choose to mete out."

Sekken's breath hissed through his teeth. Teruo snapped, "Where is Bayushi Meirō?"

"My lord, I do not know."

"You are relieved of your duties to her. Whatever commands she has given you, your obligation now is to assist me and not conceal her whereabouts."

"My lord, I genuinely do not know. Last night, Lady Bayushi confessed to me that she had lied about her orders having changed. She offered no explanation, but said only that I was free from her service. She–"

For the first time, Botan's level voice wavered. "A servant came from the Tsutsujiden last night, and I…" She swallowed, then went on, "I overheard her saying to Lady Bayushi that someone had come to find her at the inn. After the servant left, Lady Bayushi called me in and gave me a letter for the Emerald Magistracy. She said it absolves me of complicity in her misdeeds, but my lord, I am not innocent. I suspected all was not as it should be."

She lifted from her bow just enough to look at Ryōtora, then at Sekken. "And it has to do with these two."

Hearing Botan confirm his suspicions sent a chill skittering across Sekken's back. Then it came back and took up residence as he thought, *What's worse than having a Scorpion hovering over you?*

Not knowing where she is now.

It made his voice curt as he said, "Do you have any idea why she took such an interest in us?"

"No, my lord." Loosed from her duty to Meirō, it seemed Botan felt free to let her resentment stain that polite address. "But I don't think she planned this. We were all set to depart for Shiro Moto, until she met with you."

Yet they'd told her nothing of their business in Brittle Flower City – nothing to justify that change of plans. Unless... "Where had you been before then?"

"The Monastery of the Northern Sky. She was given special dispensation to go there after we finished our duties in a village near Morning Frost Castle."

That latter lay in Dragon lands. Sekken didn't look at Ryōtora, but he heard the other man's indrawn breath. It was inevitable that Emerald Magistrates came and went from Dragon territory; the clan had no authority to deny passage to imperial officials. Yet that had to make them nervous, given how much they strove to hide the decline in their population from outsiders. The Monastery of the Northern Sky, by contrast, was a Phoenix site, isolated from the world in the Isawa Mori. They were known primarily for their study of esoteric subjects.

Meirō's actions were a puzzle box, and try though he might,

Sekken couldn't figure out which pieces to slide to make it open. In pairs, perhaps: Meirō could have become aware of the Dragon Clan's problems, and for some reason went to the monastery to get the opinions of the monks there. Or she learned something about Ryōtora while in Dragon lands, and that was why she took an interest when he showed up at her inn. Or something she'd discovered at the monastery had to do with Ryōtora, or Sekken, or the Market of a Hundred Fortunes – even though Ryōtora and Sekken themselves hadn't known about that when they went to ask for her help.

Truth be told, he'd wanted Botan to say "yes, we'd just come from Brittle Flower City." It would have made everything so much more comprehensible.

Teruo looked like a headache was building between his brows. "Koganshi, please take Lady Botan back to my office. Lady Botan, you are not under arrest, but I must ask you to stay close until we have resolved this matter."

Sekken had no authority to contradict Teruo's order, and Botan likely knew nothing else of use anyway, but Sekken still had to bite down on his desire to object as Koganshi Haizumi dipped a quick bow and led Botan away. Once they were gone, Ryōtora asked, "What of the people at the Tsutsujiden?"

Some people gained appointments to the magistracy through nepotism and favors, but Teruo was quick-witted enough to hear what Ryōtora meant. "You mean, will they be punished? No. They were given instructions by an Emerald Magistrate; they had no reason to think those instructions were inappropriate. I'll talk to them, but I doubt they have any notion where she's gone."

Sekken doubted it, too. They'd already done their job, alerting Meirō that someone had been sent to recall her to her duty. But that didn't mean they were without ways of finding Meirō – even if he could have wished for a better option. "Lord Utaku, given that Lady Bayushi's interest seems to be specifically in us and our business, I doubt she'll have left the city."

"No," Teruo agreed. "She'll be keeping an eye on you."

Ryōtora's mouth flattened. "And we can keep an eye out for her... but how much good will that do? Forgive me for asking this, Lord Utaku, but what do you know of Meirō's skills and methods? Do you think she is likely to disguise herself?"

*Definitely,* Sekken thought, not saying it only because it would be bad manners when the question was directed at Teruo. The Emerald Magistrate nodded. "I must ask you to keep a close watch out. And tell me – just what is this business of yours, that she's taken such an interest in it?"

The dip of Ryōtora's chin left responsibility for answering in Sekken's hands. For once, he felt no desire to rely on courtly caution and misdirection; the Unicorn were generally a plain-spoken clan, and at this point, hiding details could only do them more harm than good. After bringing Teruo to their own chambers, where they could at least sit in comfort while they talked, Sekken explained everything, from Sayashi's true nature to the recent interference of Sir Nihei.

"That's quite a tale," Teruo said when they were done. "By which I don't mean that I doubt you; only that I have no more notion than you do what to make of it. To be honest, the entire situation baffles me: Scorpion or not, before today I would have said that Bayushi Meirō was a loyal servant of the

Empire. Sometimes by less than admirable means, yes... but a woman of integrity nonetheless."

Sekken remembered how much he'd enjoyed Meirō's company. He wanted to agree – and he hated feeling like he couldn't trust that reaction.

Teruo frowned, tapping his fingers against one knee. Abruptly, he asked, "Is there any chance she could be tracking this bakeneko of yours? That she attached herself to you in pursuit of Sayashi?"

Sekken hadn't considered that possibility. Ryōtora looked equally startled as he said, "It could be, my lord. I don't know why or how, but if word got out about Sayashi..."

"Lady Bayushi would have needed to access private reports about either Seibo Mura or the problems at winter court," Sekken said thoughtfully, turning the puzzle box over in his mind. "To know of our connection to Sayashi, I mean – why she should be in pursuit of a bakeneko is a separate matter. But I presume that for an Emerald Magistrate, access like that is not out of the question."

He knew even before Ryōtora finished reaching into the pouch dangling from his sash what the other man was doing. "Speaking of Emerald Magistrates and their authority. Lord Utaku, as Asako said earlier, we visited you today so we could offer our resignations. In light of what we've learned about Lady Bayushi's actions, I no longer have any doubt that what status we have held as yoriki is deceptive and unjust. Please accept this, with my humblest apologies." With a deep bow, he slid his seal across the mat to Teruo, and Sekken echoed him a heartbeat later.

Teruo took the seals and held them for a moment, as if

weighing them. Then he set them on the mat again, this time facing toward Sekken and Ryōtora. "I accept your resignations. And, having done that, I ask you to enter into *my* service instead."

Sekken wasn't really surprised. "You want us to find Lady Bayushi for you."

"If you can. I will not fault you if you fail; Meirō is experienced and clever. But any information you can gain on her whereabouts, or why she abandoned her duties to come here, you will pass along to me." Teruo huffed a short laugh. "Meanwhile, if Sir Nihei gives you trouble again, you may refer him to my office. I expect that will make a quick end to his complaints."

From the sound of it, he'd had dealings with Nihei before, and not congenial ones. Sekken almost expected Ryōtora to argue, but the other man took his seal back with something that looked a good deal like relief. "Lord Utaku," Ryōtora said, "we will do our best to serve you well."

# CHAPTER THIRTEEN

The thought that Meirō was likely to be watching them made the hairs on the back of Ryōtora's neck prickle. Still, he preferred that to the false pretense of working for her. At least now he was *allowed* to treat her as a threat.

Really, though, what right did he have to condemn her? After all, he and Sekken had disregarded their own orders in favor of coming to help Sayashi. For reasons Ryōtora still believed worthy... but the thin veneer of justification they'd painted over the whole affair by entering Meirō's service didn't change the underlying act. They, too, were in dereliction of their assigned duty.

With that reminder sharp in his thoughts, he was all the more determined to finish their work here and return home. "Let's go back to the market," he said to Sekken.

The other man perked up. "Ah, clever – you're thinking we can lure Meirō out by looking as if we're making progress in finding Sayashi?" Then he deflated. "No. You weren't thinking that at all."

Ryōtora was glad of the laugh that bloomed in his chest. "I was hoping we might make *actual* progress. If that indeed lures Meirō out, so much the better."

Knowing that a Scorpion magistrate might be watching them in secret, they didn't quite dare venture out alone. Kuzu remained at the inn, but they brought Ishi and Tarō along. Unfortunately, the crowds in the market thwarted any hope of having the ashigaru tail them discreetly – not if they wanted to be of use, should Meirō make some kind of move. "Discretion was probably a lost cause anyway," Sekken said as the four of them clumped together. "I don't think you two could look more like Dragon if you tried."

He signed it for Ishi as he spoke, and the ashigaru both shrugged. "Don't know what you mean, my lord," Tarō said.

Ryōtora did, though. Winter court in Phoenix lands had sharpened his eye for the subtleties of dress and demeanor, and when he paused to consider the people in the street, Ishi and Tarō indeed stood out. The people in Brittle Flower City were a mixed assortment, not just Crane residents but Lion, Scorpion, Crab, and others, but there were few if any Dragon apart from Ryōtora and the ashigaru. And in half a dozen subtle ways, from the fabric of their kimono to their accents as they spoke, they marked themselves as different. Meirō would hardly be fooled by them hanging back.

He tried to put her from his mind. Let others worry about Scorpion schemes; he wasn't likely to be the one who untangled those. The metaphysical enigma of the hidden market was his concern. "Are you able to sense Tanshu now?" he asked Sekken.

The other man stopped and closed his eyes, got jostled by

an irritated passer-by, and opened them again with a grimace. "Maybe if we go somewhere quieter."

Quiet was hard to come by, even at the larger shrines. Ryōtora was able to sense that one of his prayer strips remained in place, though; it turned out to be the one pasted to the side of the shed, slightly out of ideal alignment. "Will this help?" he asked.

By dint of having closed off the pathway along the inside of the wall, the shed had created a pocket of relative peace. Sekken hesitantly laid his hand atop the calligraphed paper and closed his eyes again. After a moment, he shook his head. "I… I'm not sure. Maybe it would be better if you tried."

It echoed his bitter words back home, about how Ryōtora would soon be a better witch than he was. Foolish self-doubt – but saying that outright wouldn't help.

Here in this sheltered corner, with Ishi and Tarō standing watch, Ryōtora didn't mind a touch of impropriety. He placed his hands on Sekken's shoulders, standing close enough to feel the warmth of his back. "You're the one with the connection to Tanshu. Settle your mind. Breathe. Think of what that connection feels like."

The tension under his palms began to ease. Sekken murmured, "He doesn't see things like we do, does he? It's more about scents – so many scents! Perfumers and incense admirers don't have a tenth of his discernment. As if he views the world through his nose first, everything else second."

Ryōtora had caught only the faintest hints of that when he briefly experienced Tanshu's perception. "What is he smelling now?"

"I don't know."

"Relax. Meditate like you did before, at the crossroads.

You know how to do this, if you don't get in your own way."

Sekken's breathing smoothed out. Ryōtora risked a soft prayer – hardly even a formal invocation, just a greeting to the earth beneath their feet, the water of the ink he'd used on the paper, asking them to lend Sekken some of their stability and peace. To lend those things to them *both*.

"Can you feel him?" Ryōtora asked very softly.

The other man's voice grew more distant. "No words for it. We can't describe what we're incapable of sensing. It's almost like color, isn't it? Ten shades of brown, twelve of gray… dirt, wood, stone, some damp, some dry. No light, but he can still see with his nose. Indoors somewhere."

Without warning, Sekken stiffened and turned to face Ryōtora. His pupils had dilated, black overtaking the rich brown as if he, too, stood in a lightless place. "He found something before. When I dreamed I was him. A doorway – he smelled this place, *this* market, through a door from the other one. If we can find that door…"

"Do you know where?"

Sekken blinked and shook his head. His pupils contracted back to their proper size. "Not exactly. But I might recognize it if I saw it."

Ryōtora smiled. *That* was more like the confidence he was used to hearing from Sekken. "Then we'll search."

The market was such a crowded place, with countless streets and alleys. Still, Ryōtora was prepared to walk every inch of it if necessary. As he led Sekken away from the shed, the other man thought out loud. "Not one of the central streets, the ones running from gate to gate. And not a tiny back way either; there were people going past."

"That narrows it down," Ryōtora said. "Did you see any signs?"

"Did *Tanshu* see any, you mean? I think so… but he's a dog. It's all just scribbles to him. He's clever, though; do you think I could teach him to read? Later, I mean." Sekken shook his head again, as if to shed his own distraction. "Sorry. It's that self-control thing, I think. It's worse when I reach out to Tanshu."

Ryōtora laughed quietly. "Babble all you like. I don't mind."

They began to trace the streets, as systematically as they could, with Tarō in front and Ishi behind. Ryōtora wished they'd brought Kuzu along after all. She might have been able to make something of the shreds Sekken dragged up from his memory: an awning next to an opening too narrow to even be called an alley, possibly a stack of baskets put out for sale? Sekken's brow knitted tight in thought. "And I think someone was shouting–"

A shout came from directly behind them, and Ryōtora turned in time to see Ishi sprinting away.

Down the side street they'd just passed, nimbly dodging through the crowd, pursuing – Ryōtora couldn't even see what. "Go!" Sekken said, and Ryōtora didn't know if that was directed at him or at Tarō, but the other ashigaru hardly even needed the order. The samurai followed, slowed by their unwillingness to risk slamming into people, but they could track Ishi and Tarō by the outraged protests left in their wake.

And they didn't have to go far. The side street dead-ended at a teahouse, and from the looks of it, the man at the door had refused entry to the peasant woman who'd tried to bull her way past. By the time Sekken and Ryōtora caught up, she'd turned like an animal at bay to find her retreat blocked by the ashigaru.

Ryōtora didn't recognize her. She wore a simple kimono and hakama, clean and new, and her face looked like it was more accustomed to smiling than the scowl it held as they approached. Without taking his eyes off her, Ishi signed something. Sekken translated it out loud: "He recognized the way you walk."

The woman's scowl collapsed into a look of aggrieved resignation. "Oh, for the way I *walk*? Really?"

It was her voice that did it for Ryōtora, though he had no doubt she could have altered it, had she not simply abandoned her pretense altogether. But her face... he had no idea how much of the unfamiliarity was actual disguise, and how much was the fact that he'd never seen Bayushi Meirō unmasked before.

His voice heavy with irony, Sekken said, "Isn't it a disowning offense or something for a member of your clan to go without a mask?"

"What you don't know about my clan would fill an entire Phoenix library," Meirō shot back.

"And what we don't know about your recent actions is going to fill an entire report to the Emerald Magistracy," Sekken replied, his tone cuttingly urbane. "Given that you fled the Eisuitei, you've presumably realized that your insubordination has been exposed. Lord Utaku Teruo has Kakeguchi Botan and your constables in custody. We've been re-deputized to bring you to him."

Meirō sighed heavily. "Of course you have."

They were gathering an audience: the man at the door to the teahouse, various customers and shopkeepers and pedestrians. Many looked like they were hoping for a brawl.

Softly, Ryōtora said to Sekken, "It might be better to bring her to Lord Utaku right away."

Either Meirō could read lips, or she was simply able to guess at his words. "Before you do something irrevocable," she said, "will you give me a chance to explain?"

Ryōtora turned a cold gaze upon her. "You mean a chance to mislead us further?"

Without the mask to hide the minute shifts of the muscles around her eyes, the beads to distract him with their swaying and their glinting light, her expression was much easier to read. She looked guilty, frustrated – and bitter. "This is the trap I've been in from the start. Whatever I tell you, you're going to doubt, because of who I am."

A Scorpion. They didn't lie *all* the time… but that made it worse. Because one could never be certain where the hooks and the poisoned barbs lay, hidden among the innocent truths.

Desperation edged into Meirō's voice. "I've already thrown everything away, and I know it. You want to tell me I've been stupid? Go right ahead. Search me, tie me up if that's what it takes to give you peace of mind – just let me talk. Then after that, if you want to hand me over to Teruo and ignore everything I've said, at least I'll know I tried."

She sounded utterly sincere. Ryōtora hated the part of himself that said, *that's exactly why you shouldn't trust it.*

When he looked at Sekken, the other man shrugged minutely. *He* was willing to listen… but he was leaving the choice to Ryōtora. Because he knew that Ryōtora would be less able to live with himself, if he went against his instincts and it turned out they'd chosen wrongly.

They'd pledged themselves into Teruo's service, with an

explicit duty to find Meirō. Delaying in carrying out that duty just created more opportunity for her to somehow slip away. Ryōtora had no doubt of her cunning. At the same time – yes, damn her. He wanted to hear what she had to say. And he needed to trust *himself* to sort through her words for merit, not toss them aside, unheard or unheeded, simply because she was a Scorpion. Letting his judgment of her end there would be rank foolishness.

Where could they go? Not the Eisuitei. Not anywhere out in the street, with the growing crowd of onlookers, so eager for a new bit of entertainment.

Ryōtora looked past Meirō to the man at the door of the teahouse. "Is there a private room we might hire for a while?"

Ishi sat inside the door. Tarō sat in front of the room's only window. Meirō was unarmed except for the dagger she handed over freely; Ryōtora had, after visibly steeling himself, searched her for any other weapons or tricks. Meirō submitted to the search without any offense Sekken could detect, even to the point of telling Ryōtora not to let propriety hold him back from reaching between her legs. "I'd strip naked if that would make you more comfortable," she said dryly, "but somehow I doubt it would."

They were as certain as they could be that she posed no physical threat. Mentally… that was a different matter.

Search complete, Ryōtora settled himself on the mat with a stony demeanor that said he would leave the actual questioning to Sekken. Which worked out well, because the search had given Sekken time to decide on his approach.

"You wanted to explain," he said to Meirō. "So start talking."

Was it tension that made her look so different, or had she done something subtle with cosmetics to disguise herself? Certainly the amusement that darted across her expression did little to make her more recognizable; it was too sour for that. "Concealing what you know, in order to see if anything I say fails to match up. Good choice. Since I'm a Scorpion, you probably assume I'm skilled at controlling my reactions, and therefore attempting to surprise me into giving something away by dropping an unexpected revelation is unlikely to work. I'd recommend you for an actual appointment as an Emerald Magistrate, but somehow I doubt my opinion will carry any positive weight."

"You're trying to distract me with irrelevant chatter," he said coolly. "It won't work."

"Actually, I'm babbling because I'm on edge – but as with everything else, I don't expect you to believe that." Meirō let out a wavering breath and rubbed her face. "Somewhere, clan-mates of mine are hanging their heads in shame at how bad I am at this sort of thing. We're not all masterful liars, any more than every Crane is artistically talented or every Lion is a military genius."

Sekken didn't respond to that, just let the silence stretch out.

Meirō seemed to be using the time to gather her thoughts. Then she said, "All right. It starts with me being sent to a village near Morning Frost Castle, in Dragon lands."

That matched with what Kakeguchi Botan had said, but Meirō was exactly right about the tactics Sekken intended to use. Rather than acknowledging anything, he waited for her to go on.

"I was sent there because bandits had been raiding across the border into Unicorn territory," Meirō said. "A fairly routine duty, as all things go; we dealt with the bandits and settled matters between the local Dragon and Unicorn lords. But I dug a little deeper.

"It turned out the leader of the bandits had started on his career of pillaging after a visit to a local shrine. People said he'd received an oracle from the priestess there." Meirō laid her fingers gently against the mat, spreading them as if mapping out the terrain in her mind. "You'll be familiar with this kind of thing, I imagine, after your experiences in Seibo Mura. Rural area, local spirit – they called it a Fortune. I'm not qualified to say whether that's the right word or not."

She paused and glanced up at Ryōtora, but he didn't so much as shift where he knelt.

Shaking her head in unsurprised acceptance, Meirō went on, "The shrine was in a cave. The priestess was a young woman – dirty, half-feral, not what I'd consider a reliable source of spiritual guidance. I'm not even sure she understood the questions I was asking her. But then…"

Meirō shivered, and despite himself, Sekken didn't think it was staged. "She went into the cave and started chanting. I was just about to give up and leave when she came out again and grabbed hold of me. Her voice was completely different. Maybe just an act, but people had said this was how she delivered her oracles. Given that her last one had nearly started a border skirmish between two Great Clans, I figured it was worth investigating further. I was supposed to continue on to Shiro Moto after I left the village, but I got permission to go to Phoenix lands instead, to the Monastery of the Northern Sky."

Again, just as Botan had said. The congruence of their stories didn't guarantee anything; it was entirely possible Meirō had coordinated with her yoriki ahead of time. Samurai had lied in the service of their lords before, and not just Scorpion. But Sekken imagined he could at least verify Meirō's movements with the Emerald Magistracy, if not necessarily what happened in each place.

"I wanted to know if it was true," Meirō said. "If this priestess of some Fortune I'd never heard of might be speaking genuine oracles, channeling insight from the local spirit. It seemed impossible, and yet ..."

To Sekken's surprise, Ryōtora answered. "It's not uncommon in rural areas, bringing a spirit into the body of some medium. Usually children, but not always."

Sekken suppressed a shiver, remembering how Kaiminnushi had possessed him in Seibo Mura. Meirō said, "Channeling spirits, I'd seen before. It was the oracle part I doubted. Especially because when she came out of that cave, she spoke one to *me*."

He could see where she was going, and even though Sekken had intended to remain silent and stony throughout, he couldn't help speaking, dry with disbelief. "Let me guess. You're going to claim this priestess' words are the reason you attached yourself to us."

Meirō shot him an angry look. "Yes. And that response is exactly why I didn't tell you sooner."

Ryōtora growled low in his throat. "You think hiding it from us made anything better?"

"I think *nothing* could make the situation better. Tell me truthfully: if a Scorpion came up and said to you, I know I'm a stranger, but I think your business is somehow my business because a half-feral girl in a cave said so, what would your response have been?"

"At least then you would have been honest."

"A great satisfaction to me, I'm sure," Meirō said bitterly, "as I watched you walk out the door."

Virtue at odds with pragmatism: the eternal debate, and one where the Scorpion all too often sided with the latter. Sekken said, "Could you not have obtained backing from the Emerald Magistracy? We would have trusted that."

Meirō's mouth thinned in displeasure. "Oh, I tried. The monks I consulted said that yes, oracles were possible, and yes, it was possible the one I'd heard was true. But that carried very little weight with my superiors. Going to the monastery had already delayed me enormously; they wanted me in Shiro Moto as soon as possible. Sooner, even. If I'd had a clear sense of what the oracle meant, maybe I could have convinced them, but I didn't – not until the two of you came to speak with me."

"What *was* it?" Ryōtora's tone was wary, but carried the same fascination Sekken felt. If he hadn't asked, Sekken would have.

Meirō drew a deep breath, straightened, and spoke.

*"Bodies sharing one pure heart – dragon and phoenix*
*Echoes of a soul long gone – a cat on the hunt*
*Love that's withered to a ghost – shadow of a crane*
*Flowers hiding fortunes lost – a scorpion's fate."*

# CHAPTER FOURTEEN

The first words out of Ryōtora's mouth weren't the most important ones, but they beat the rest out the door: "That priestess delivered her oracles in *poetry?*"

"Archaic poetry, at that," Sekken said, a little unsteadily. "That's what they used to call 'modern style'... which is ironic, seeing as how it hasn't been in fashion since the fifth century. I briefly served a courtier who was working on annotations of – never mind. Lady Bayushi, either you're a scholar of outdated poetic forms, that half-feral girl in a cave is, or that genuinely came from a spirit."

Satisfaction warred with relief in Meirō's expression. "So you believe that, at least. And now you see why I was so unnerved when I met you."

*You still should have told us.* And yet, Ryōtora understood why she'd been hesitant. It would indeed have sounded like some convoluted lie, a mystical explanation designed to pique their interest: Ryōtora as a priest, Sekken as a scholar of language and history.

It could still be that. But such explanations seemed far less likely now, with Meirō hunted by the Emerald Magistrates, hiding out in the Market of a Hundred Fortunes disguised as a peasant. That she might sacrifice her entire career and standing in service to her clan, Ryōtora could well imagine; even he, relatively unfamiliar with literature and drama, knew there were plenty of stories about Scorpion samurai doing exactly that. But it would require him to invent an entire framework whereby there was some profit for her clan in doing all of this, and Ryōtora couldn't conceive of what that might be.

Neither, it seemed, could Sekken. "All right," he said. "Let's say for the moment that all of this is true: you received this oracle, it means what you think it does, and you kept it hidden from us because you feared – with justification – that we wouldn't believe you. You're even so dedicated to this that you're throwing away your future in the Emerald Magistracy to follow through. What I don't understand is, what under heaven does this have to do with the business that brought me and Ryōtora to Brittle Flower City?"

Meirō's smile was as sharp-edged as the dagger she'd surrendered. "Only you can tell me that, Lord Asako, Lord Isao. If you are willing."

The two men looked at each other. Days on the road, days here in the city, trying to hide their purpose in Crane lands. *What might have happened,* Ryōtora wondered, *if we ourselves had been honest sooner?*

Like he'd urged, more than once. But there was no pleasure in that thought; he knew why Sekken had been reluctant. The important question was, how did Sekken feel about it now?

No conversation was necessary. Ryōtora nodded, Sekken smiled – and then they told Meirō the full story.

When they were done, Meirō glanced toward Ishi, as

unmoving as the stone of his namesake in front of the door. "I don't suppose we could have some sake brought up to lubricate our thinking – no? All right." Her cheeks puffed as she blew out a pensive breath. "A bakeneko. This hidden market. Your town girl's missing mother. That's ... not a lot to go on."

Her posture had shifted, taking on the decisive air of the Emerald Magistrate she would probably never be again. As if this were the duty she'd been assigned, and she meant to see it through to the best of her ability.

Part of Ryōtora would welcome her help. Unfortunately, he and Sekken had a duty of their own.

Ryōtora cleared his throat. "Lady Bayushi, while I appreciate your intent ..."

"Oh, bother." Meirō's shoulders sagged from their upright line. "I'd honestly forgotten. You're supposed to bring me to Utaku Teruo."

"We gave him our word."

Her expression turned speculative. "What *exactly* did you promise him?"

"To tell him anything we learned about–" Sekken stopped mid-reply, looking at Ryōtora. "No, I know what you'll say. Lady Bayushi, you may be comfortable with wriggling through loopholes in your promises, but Ryōtora isn't. And frankly, neither am I. Lord Utaku is not someone I want to antagonize."

Meirō groaned in frustration. "I see why you placed yourselves under his authority, but I wish you hadn't. To be clear, I meant what I said before, about why I wanted you to remain yoriki ... though I suppose at this point the value of being *my* yoriki has dropped to nil."

She'd been sitting cross-legged; now she rose to a kneeling position and bowed slightly to them both. "Well, I can hardly expect anything else, given your reputations. And I shouldn't have asked. Take me to Lord Utaku; I'll simply have to hope he's willing to listen to me as you have done."

Ryōtora held up one hand. "A moment, Lady Bayushi. I think we can consider another possibility, without being dishonest."

He still wasn't entirely convinced of his own logic. Or rather, he was suspicious of that logic – for wasn't this exactly how people justified their bad behavior? They wanted to do a thing, so they found a way to rationalize it. But rigidity was a fool's path, and his priority must be the greater good.

Ryōtora said, "We should inform Lord Utaku of what we've learned, yes. And if he asks us to bring you to him, we will do so. But Lord Utaku knows what Sekken and I are seeking in Brittle Flower City; he's given his tacit approval to our work. I think that, so long as you remain in our custody, he will allow you to assist us while we await his command."

Sekken made a thoughtful sound. "Yes, that will be faster than the two of us wandering the streets on our own. Especially since she knows this city better than we do."

Warmth flowered inside Ryōtora's chest. To have someone like Sekken, who could guess at his plans without being told… it wouldn't always be that smooth, he knew. Even the best-matched partners had gaps, misunderstandings, disagreements. But moments like this were to be treasured.

He nodded at Sekken. "Then I will leave Lady Bayushi in your keeping, while I go back to the Eisuitei and write a message for Lord Utaku."

Confusion had etched a crease between Meirō's brows, but she didn't ask what the two of them hadn't said. She merely offered, "There are places closer by where you can borrow a brush and send a message."

Sekken huffed in mock offense. "You think I don't carry such things with me? What kind of a Phoenix do you take me for?"

"I know," Ryōtora said, smiling at him. "But I'm also going to fetch Kuzu. If we're trying to find one doorway in a market full of them, we might need her help, too."

Ishi went with Ryōtora; Sekken kept Tarō at his side. Or perhaps it would be more accurate to say Tarō kept himself there: whatever arrangement the samurai had made amongst themselves, the two ashigaru plainly felt it was their duty to remain suspicious and alert.

Sekken didn't mind. He didn't think Meirō was playing him false, but if he was wrong, he might be very glad of Tarō's strong arm to protect him.

"All right," he said once they were back out on the street. "How long were you following us?"

"I caught sight of you coming around the corner by the sandal-seller," Meirō said. At his blank look, she added, "On Makomo Street?" Sekken shook his head. Meirō looked like she was just barely not rolling her eyes. "Half an hour, at least, before your ashigaru spotted me. I see now why you need my help, if you're trying to find anything here."

Nettled, Sekken said, "My mind was on other things."

Unfortunately, that tenuous sense of connection he'd built up to Tanshu was long gone. He could backtrack to the remaining prayer strip – maybe, assuming he could find it – and try again, but it seemed better to go on looking for the place he'd seen in his dream, the doorway that seemingly led from the hidden market to the real one.

He gave Meirō what description he could, and she shook her head. "You do like to take on challenging tasks, don't you? If you'd been able to read the sign your inugami saw, I'd give myself good odds of finding the place. As it stands… well, at least I know some places *not* to look. Let's get started."

She led the way; Tarō followed; Sekken brought up the rear, safely distant from Meirō should she try anything. Or, viewed differently, out of Tarō's way if Meirō tried to bolt – Sekken had no illusions about where he'd place in a footrace among the three of them. Together they worked their way up and down the streets, far more systematically and efficiently than he and Ryōtora together could have done. Meirō paused every so often to point out a possible door, showing no impatience every time Sekken said, "No, not that one," or, "I don't think there was a sweet shop visible from where Tanshu stood."

*It's a pity that she's likely destroyed her career forever,* Sekken thought as they looped back toward the market's center. *If this is any sample of her usual behavior, she's a very meticulous investigator.*

"Here?" Meirō said, gesturing at a shop that sold umbrellas. "There aren't any posts supporting the awning, I know, but…"

But Sekken could have misremembered. The dream had been hazy and filtered through a dog's perception. "I'd rather you suggest possibilities that are probably wrong than rule out the one that might be right," he told her. "Having said that, no, this wasn't it."

Rather than moving on, Meirō stood very still, gaze going distant with thought. Sekken waited, not disturbing her. His patience bore fruit when she said, "How certain are you that it was a doorway?"

"Very," he said immediately. Then: "Ah. Where *Tanshu* was, he saw a doorway. But can I be certain it looked the same from the other side? No, I cannot. Does that suggest anything to you?"

"Maybe," Meirō said. But the way she pivoted and headed down a side street was a good deal more confident than her reply.

The moment they drew near, Sekken knew she'd led him right. There was the awning, the alley – even the stack of baskets. The only thing missing was the door.

In its place, a window pierced the wall. Or rather, one of the market's many little shrines; Sekken even remembered passing this one, when Kuzu had led him and Ryōtora on their first tour of the market. He pulled out Sayashi's map and unfolded it, squinting at her scrawled notes. "That's – *hah*. That's the shrine to the Fortune of Thresholds."

Meirō was lounging against the wall, not looking directly at the shrine. She even pulled off one sandal and poked at its straps, as if that were her reason for stopping. Tarō just crossed his arms and looked patient. "It can't be that simple, though. There's no door, and your bakeneko friend knew this was here. I can't imagine she didn't try praying at the shrine as one of her first acts."

"Yes, Kuzu said she prayed at all of them." As Sekken put the map away, he glimpsed movement through the window. The shrine's shutters had been closed when he and Ryōtora passed before, but now they were open, and it looked like the window let into a tiny room. Again, not what Tanshu had seen. If it was indeed an entrance to the market, how did that work?

Sekken shook his sleeves out. "There's someone in there. I'm going to go talk to them."

Meirō discreetly hooked one foot in front of his ankle before he could move, so that Sekken had to either stop or trip. "You don't know what will happen when you do. Let me try."

It brought his suspicions back, not quite at full strength, but enough that this time Meirō did roll her eyes. "You think I want to be left standing here with your ashigaru if you disappear? That I want to be the one explaining to Lord Isao that I lost you to this supernatural market? If I vanish, you'll have learned something very valuable, and I'll be stuck Fortunes know where. This is the better way to test it, Lord Asako."

She was right, and yet... "You do the talking," Sekken said. "But Tarō and I are coming with you."

"Fine." Meirō pushed off the wall. "Makes more sense anyway. I'm your servant, conducting my lord's affairs so he doesn't have to sully himself with them."

She proposed the deception far too readily for Sekken's peace of mind, but he and Tarō followed her down the narrow street to the shrine window.

The person inside was a curled little shrimp of a man, his back hunched, his hands knobbled, his eyebrows aspiring to droop low enough to join his wispy mustache. By the way his head suddenly rose in elevation, Sekken could only assume he had a box or stool he stood on to greet people at the window. "Can I help you?" he said to Meirō, in a voice so thin and reedy it could hardly be heard above the noise of the market. Then, noticing Sekken behind her, he added, "M'lord."

Meirō squinted up at the carved plaque above the window as if she couldn't read it. "This is the shrine to the Fortune of Thresholds, yes?"

"Yes, of course. Have you come to pray?"

Sekken tried to avoid craning his neck too obviously as Meirō agreed and made her offering. What did he think he was going to see, anyway? Supernatural creatures running about inside? Tanshu tied up in the corner? This wasn't the dark room he'd sensed before. It was just a little shrine set back from the window, with barely enough space for even so tiny a man to fit. There was a burner for incense, a miniature jug that might hold sake. Nothing like what Tanshu had seen.

And nothing happened while Meirō prayed – though in truth, he hadn't expected it to. The proof, if any, would come later, when she either vanished or didn't. But with the shrine open and the keeper right there, Sekken couldn't resist investigating deeper. "Thresholds," he said, in a musing tone. "Just in the sense of literal, physical doorways? Or does your Fortune oversee the concept in a broader sense – borders, transitions from one state to another, and so forth?"

"M'lord is very learned," the shrine-keeper said. "Many things are thresholds, when seen in the right light."

"Like the boundaries between Spirit Realms," Sekken suggested.

Meirō's bland expression said she would be glaring at him if it wouldn't ruin her pose of being his servant. Sekken wasn't doing a very good job of standing back and letting her handle the matter. But being this close to where Tanshu had stood –

perhaps – meant he couldn't just stop at a quick glance around the tiny closet of the shrine.

Was the keeper peering at Sekken in a shrewd, evaluating way, or was his sight simply clouded by old age? With his eyebrows drooping like a reed screen over his eyes, it was hard to be sure. "M'lord has an interest in the Spirit Realms?"

*And personal experience of them, too.* Sekken said, "I'm surprised I've never heard of your Fortune elsewhere in the Empire. Others here – the Fortune of Buckets, for example – I can see why they don't attract widespread worship. But if thresholds include clan borders, or the boundaries between here and places of spirit, perhaps even abstractions like funerals as the threshold between life and death... one would think many would want to honor such a power."

"I could not say, m'lord," the shrine-keeper answered stiffly. "I have never seen the rest of the Empire. Duty has long bound me to this place."

Sekken was accomplishing nothing except offending this poor, ancient man. "Well, since I'm here, I might as well offer up my own prayers. Fortunes know I could use some help getting to where I want to be."

Meirō twitched as if she wanted to intervene, but Sekken ignored her. He'd report all of this to Ryōtora, and then if he vanished later, at least someone would know what had happened. He lit the incense, clapped his hands, and prayed briefly. *If you do exist, and are not simply a quaint local custom, then help me and my companions find a way to the people we seek.*

When he finished, he found the shrine-keeper eyeing him, one age-withered hand tentatively raised. "May I ask – is m'lord a priest?"

"No," Sekken said. "Just a scholar of esoteric things."

"And have you any priest with you in your travels?"

"No one in our group is a priest," Meirō said, without hesitation. "Just me, my lord, two ashigaru, and a peasant girl."

It was Sekken's turn to clamp down on the impulse to glare. So far they'd been only a little deceptive, but that was an outright lie. "Why do you ask?" he said to the keeper, a little more harshly than he intended.

"Forgive me, m'lord," the shrine-keeper said, twitching in what might have been a bow, if his back weren't permanently hunched. "From time to time a priest takes offense at our ways here, the Fortunes we worship. I don't want any trouble. But if you have none with you, then I feel safe offering you this."

He opened a little drawer, revealing a small stock of tiny cloth bags, embroidered with the word *threshold*. Protective charms, such as many shrines sold – but Sekken wouldn't have expected to find them in a makeshift place such as this one, staffed by a single old man worshipping an unorthodox Fortune. From what he'd seen of Brittle Flower City, it was entirely possible that these were nothing more than bags stuffed with blank paper, made to scrape a few coins off the gullible.

But it was also possible they were a great deal more than that.

Keeping his voice level, Sekken said, "A little good luck never hurt, did it? I'll take five, one for each member of my group." Not that he had intention of involving Kuzu, if these did indeed prove to be supernatural in nature. But Meirō had claimed five people.

"No priest?" the shrine-keeper asked again, sounding anxious. "I don't want any trouble, m'lord."

Hide this from Ryōtora, or lie to the priest's face. Either way, Sekken would be acting deceptively.

Ryōtora had once lied to protect Sekken. This was nothing like so noble a cause – but Sekken wasn't as noble as Ryōtora, either. And this was, somehow, the place where Tanshu had looked through into the mortal world.

Sekken shook his head. "No priests."

The shrine-keeper creaked into a deeper bow. "I will wrap them up for you."

Tarō, it seemed, was something of a gossip – or maybe it was only that Kuzu reminded him of his own daughter. Whatever the reason, Ryōtora soon discovered that Kuzu heard about Meirō's disappearance from the ashigaru, because she looked shocked when Ryōtora said they would be returning to the market to meet up with Sekken and the disgraced magistrate.

She didn't ask questions, though, no doubt feeling that it wasn't her place. Ryōtora dashed off a message to Utaku Teruo, caring more for speed than the quality of his handwriting, and sent Ishi across town with it. Then, en route back to the market, he questioned Kuzu about what Sekken had seen.

"I dunno the spot, m'lord," she said, once she was done being awed at Sekken's ability to connect with Tanshu like that. "But I know who to ask. The market, it's got tons of hares, and they know the place like nobody else."

"Hares?" Ryōtora stepped aside to evade a porter and frowned down at Kuzu. "As in, the minor clan?"

She laughed, then clapped an apologetic hand over her mouth. When she saw Ryōtora wasn't angry, she said, "No, messengers. Errand boys. That kind of thing. They'll know if there's a spot like you described."

The hares proved unnecessary, though. Ryōtora had arranged to meet the others just across the canal that edged the western side of the market, where it was marginally less crowded. He and Kuzu had to wait a while, but when he saw Sekken coming across the low bridge, Meirō and Tarō not far behind, he knew from the other man's stride that they'd met with success.

After a fashion, at least. Sekken shared what they'd found, but put out a hand to stop Meirō before she could hand over the charms. "A question first. What we said to the shrine-keeper doesn't have to be a lie. If the deception makes you uncomfortable, Ryōtora, we can make it true instead and leave you out of this part."

His consideration was simultaneously charming and vexing, as it dangled the secret in front of Ryōtora's face even while offering to keep it hidden. Meirō looked carefully neutral. Did she scorn him for caring about such things, scorn Sekken for holding back?

Whether she did or not, it didn't change Ryōtora's answer. "If the shrine-keeper's concern is that a priest will cause him trouble, then he has no reason to fear me. Let me see them."

The charm Meirō gave him was a little bag sewn out of a scrap of azalea-patterned silk, likely left over from a bolt used for other purposes. Cupping it between his hands and closing his eyes, Ryōtora concentrated, praying softly under his breath. After a moment he opened his eyes and shook his head. "There's nothing noteworthy about it. No awakened spirit within, or anything like that."

Sekken wrinkled his nose in disappointment. "I'll admit, I was hoping to discover a great– what are you doing?"

By then Ryōtora had already broken the stitching and was opening the bag. "It won't curse us," he said, amused. "But if it makes you happier, I'll burn it properly once we're…"

Then he stopped, because he'd unfolded the slip of paper tucked inside.

It wasn't the usual red-stamped prayer. Instead someone had inked a brief message onto it, in tiny, precise characters:

> *The bearer of this permit, having disavowed any*
> *connection to the spirits, will be traveling into*
> *the market. Please grant them safe passage.*
>    *From Enjiki, Keeper of the Threshold*
>    *To Tōji of the Market of a Hundred Fortunes*

He looked up to find the others waiting impatiently. "It's not a charm," Ryōtora said, puzzled, holding it out for Sekken to examine. "It's a *travel permit.*"

Sekken didn't so much pass it to Meirō as let it dangle loosely enough from his fingers that she took it before it could blow away. "Tōji?" he echoed in confusion. "That's a title, not a name. The Lady of the Market. Who under heaven is that?"

Ryōtora looked to Kuzu, but she shook her head, eyes wide. He let out a slow breath, regretting his blithe declaration just moments ago. "I fear I'll need to talk to this charm-seller after all."

"Or one of us will, anyway. But first things first," Sekken said, collecting the paper from Meirō and the bag from Ryōtora. "This is *definitely* something Lord Utaku should know about – especially if we're about to cause trouble. Tarō–"

The ashigaru's brows snapped together into a scowl. "Begging your pardon, my lord, but if you're going to cause trouble, you should have someone there to protect you." His gaze flicked to Meirō. "Someone you trust."

If they sent Meirō to the Emerald Magistrates, Teruo was unlikely to let her come back. Ryōtora said, "We also need this message to be carried by someone we trust – someone Lord Utaku will listen to. If you go now, you'll be back soon. Look for us here, or else at the shrine to the Fortune of Thresholds. Do you think you can find it again?"

Tarō's nod didn't allow for any doubt. He took the paper and the bag from Sekken, then set off as if he meant to run the whole way there and back.

By now the sun was nearly down. Would the shrine-keeper still be there? He hadn't been when Ryōtora and Sekken passed by the first time. One of his neighbors might know where to find him, though… or if they didn't, that might be informative in a different fashion. The quartet of them set off across the bridge to the market gate, Sekken leading the way. "If these are travel papers," he said over his shoulder as they stepped over the gate's lower beam, "then that suggests there's some kind of checkpoint where you have to present them in order to enter the hidden market. I doubt it's the shrine to the Fortune of Thresholds."

"No," Ryōtora said, staring past Sekken into the market. "No, it's right here."

The market stretched out before them – but not like it had been a moment ago, full of humans and ordinary commerce.

They had found the hidden market at last.

# CHAPTER FIFTEEN

Sekken stopped dead.

In the warm, fading light, the market was every bit as busy as it had been – but not with people. Not with *humans*, anyway, for all that a great many of the creatures in front of him had human forms.

For sufficiently flexible definitions of that term, at least. The nearest fellow might have simply been an eccentric who chose to wear a boot on his head in place of a hat. Nearby was another who could have been mistaken for an ordinary man, albeit an extremely short one, were it not for the scissor blades rising from his forehead like the ornament on a warrior's helmet. But next to the man wearing the boot... that one looked utterly normal from the neck down. From the neck up, he didn't so much *wear* a hat as he *was* a hat – complete with teeth along the brim and eyes poking up from the top of the cap.

And past them...

A kimono without an occupant, except for the hands emerging from the sleeves. A trio of sandals scurrying through the crowd as if playing a chase game, running on tiny legs and waving tiny arms. An umbrella hopping along on its handle, which seemed comparatively fine until it turned and revealed a single huge eye blinking in the middle of its folded canopy. The lanterns overhead began to light in the growing dusk, fire springing up within as their own single eyes opened and their paper sides split in gaping yawns.

"*Tsukumogami*," Sekken whispered under his breath. So of all the stories told of the hidden market – ghosts, Fortunes, and so forth – this was the correct one: yōkai born from objects. He'd heard of creatures like this, seen them depicted in art many times. But as with the Night Parade of a Hundred Demons, it was one thing to read about such things, another matter entirely to see them in the ceramic, silken, and metal flesh.

At least none of them were trying to kill him, Ryōtora, or any of his companions. That was an improvement over the Night Parade, and Sekken hoped devoutly it would stay that way.

In fact, none of the yōkai immediately noticed the four people standing just inside the gate, between the two larger shrines. Sekken was torn between the urge to dart into one of those shrines so he could see what else might be there – fox spirits for the Fortune of Rice? What creatures, if any, might serve the Fortune of Roads? – and wanting to dart inside to get out of sight. He felt horribly conspicuous, the only human present apart from the three he'd brought with him.

When he turned to his companions, he found that Kuzu had ducked behind Ryōtora for safety, and Meirō was standing in the loose, alert stance of a warrior ready to draw the blade she wasn't carrying. Judging by the hard set of her jaw, she sorely regretted that lack. When Ryōtora sent Tarō away, none of them had realized they were about to leave the ashigaru and the entire world of normal humanity behind.

How had they even *done* that?

For a question of that sort, he looked instinctively to Ryōtora. The other man met his gaze, eyes wide, and shook his head. The charms had no spiritual power; Ryōtora had examined them, and Sekken trusted his judgment. Yet here they were. Meanwhile, just outside the market–

With no visible hand on them, the heavy gates of the market swung shut. The strike of those weighted, iron-studded panels against the stone of the gateway boomed like a drum, and somewhere in the distance, a bell rang out. Like a city closing for the night... except this one looked to be just now waking up.

Something shoved itself into Sekken's hands and he yelped, jerking away, before he realized it was only Meirō distributing the charms. "Just because we didn't have to present them to get in here doesn't mean no one will ask," she said in a curt undertone, shoving one at Kuzu. "With that gate closed, do we have a way out?"

"How can I answer that when I don't know how we got *in*?" Sekken muttered back. "If just having the charms were enough, surely Brittle Flower City would have lost more than a handful of inhabitants to this place before now." And even somebody like Sir Nihei would have noticed the pattern.

Ryōtora gripped his charm, white-knuckled. "We may be here until dawn, unless I try something unsubtle. And if I do–"

"Look! Over there!"

The shout came from behind Sekken. A tide of murmurs rose as he turned, dreading what he might see.

Yes, they'd been spotted. By a beaten-up old pottery jug with arms and legs, cracks in its battered side serving to mark eyes, nose, and a mouth. It was pointing at the four of them, and one by one, the other inhabitants of the market were taking notice.

They sounded more surprised and confused than hostile; Sekken took what comfort he could from that. Which wasn't much, when a creature with a flaming kettle in place of a head came closer to peer at them. "Humans!" it said in a disbelieving voice that crackled like fire. "Mortals! Four of them at once, here, in our market!"

Kuzu shrieked and recoiled. A barrel next to her had suddenly popped its lid up, eyes sprouting from the top, the opening rising and falling as it spoke. "Humans? No, surely not. Wait – yes, it's true!"

From all around came awed responses. "Four at once!" "How did they get in here?" "It's been so long…"

The jug came closer, sloshing and reeking of sake as its ceramic body rocked from side to side. "Welcome, welcome! Someone go tell Elder Sister Noren; she'll want to make ready for our guests. Hello! Welcome to the Market of a Hundred Fortunes. I am Kameosa. Might I have the pleasure of knowing your names?"

"Er…" Nothing in Sekken's extensive training had prepared him for a conversation with an animate jug. Courtesy, however, was reflexive. "I am Asako Sekken of the Phoenix Clan. My companions are Agasha no Isao Ryōtora of the Dragon Clan, Bayushi Meirō of the Scorpion Clan, and Kuzu of, ah, Brittle Flower City."

By the time he was done with the introductions, enough of a crowd had gathered to make him uncomfortable. An undulating piece of cloth with a tanuki's head and limbs tried to poke at Sekken's leg, until Meirō interposed herself. "Please," Sekken said with a forced laugh, "we didn't mean to make such a disturbance. In fact, we didn't even know we would be coming here. Is it – ah – I noticed the gates have closed. By that, am I right in thinking we can't depart right now?"

Laughter came from all around, but it was more friendly than cruel. "The market's doors only open at dawn and dusk!" the jug, Kameosa, said with boisterous good cheer. Then it sobered – as much as anything could be called sober which contained sake. "But passage in and out isn't that simple anyway."

Sekken raised up his charm. "We have these, from the shrine to the Fortune of Thresholds."

"Of course you do," Kameosa said, almost pityingly. "But I'm afraid it's the rule of the market. No one is allowed to leave without Tōji's permission."

That was the name, or rather the title, that had been on the scrap of paper Ryōtora found inside the charm he opened. And at the sound of it, the crowd abruptly became subdued. At the fringes of the group, Sekken noted more than a few creatures slinking or bustling away, as if they suddenly recalled the business they should be about. Whoever this Lady of the Market was, her subjects clearly held her in great reverence.

*Interesting that Enjiki had the authority to let us in, but only Tōji has the authority to let us out.* That wasn't how travel permits ordinarily worked… but Sekken had only to glance around to remember he wasn't in an ordinary place.

Worse than that. From the sound if it, they were trapped here – at least until Tōji let them go.

"In that case," he said to Kameosa, "I suppose we should present ourselves to Tōji and offer greetings."

The jug recoiled hard enough that a wave of sake slopped onto the ground. "What, approach the lady in person? Are you mad?"

Maybe her subjects held her less in reverence than in fear. "Forgive us," Sekken said hastily, as more of the tsukumogami dispersed. *What have we bumbled into?* "We know very little of this market. Could we prevail upon you, or someone else here, to be our guide?"

"I think I'd better," Kameosa said, rather severely. "Come on. I'll bring you to Elder Sister Noren."

As they followed the jug-creature through the streets of the market, Ryōtora had to remind himself that holding his breath would do no good whatsoever.

*The bearer of this permit, having disavowed any connection to the spirits...* Yet here he was, a priest with just such a connection. Not even one hour ago, he'd dismissed that as unimportant, thinking it was enough that he had no intention of causing trouble for the priest at the shrine. But that was before he'd realized the charms were travel permits – and before he had, all unwitting, crossed the boundary into the hidden market.

Why were priests not permitted in? Their whole purpose was to honor the Fortunes and the little elemental spirits of the world. Some, like Sir Nihei, were more bureaucrats than clergy, but that wasn't what the laws of this place were concerned with. Did they fear Ryōtora would somehow disrupt the spiritual balance of the market?

Until he knew the answer to that, one thing was certain: he should not attempt any invocations, nor even try to commune with the local spirits. He'd violated the law once by coming here, and he had no idea what the consequences might be. Since he couldn't take back that mistake, he could only do his best to avoid compounding it.

And learn what he could about this market, so he and his companions might avoid further missteps. Did its layout mirror that of its mundane counterpart? The two shrines at the gate had been the same, and it looked like there were still two major boulevards through the district, one running east-west, the other north-south. Ryōtora hadn't memorized the locations of the other shrines well enough, though, to look for those as they passed.

The market itself had something of a festival air, with its streets so busy after sunset. Lanterns hung from the eaves of buildings and in strings across the streets, though the narrower alleys were often dark, and music, laughter, and the clatter of dishes and dice came from inside many buildings.

It was almost charming, except for one thing: nowhere did Ryōtora see other humans. Every time he thought he spotted one, it would turn and prove itself a tsukumogami instead. *It's been so long,* the creatures at the gate had said. How often did visitors cross over?

A shiver danced across his skin. *And how does time pass here? Is it the same as back home, or is each day here a year?*

He put that question firmly out of his mind. Whatever the answer, he could do nothing about it until after he returned. And that required them to get out of here safely first.

The building Kameosa led them to was a multi-story inn,

less dingy than the Reiya, but nothing so fancy as the Eisuitei. Ryōtora didn't remember seeing any such establishment in the ordinary market. When they passed under the curtain marking the entrance, he found the interior as deserted as the Reiya.

"Hey, Elder Sister!" Kameosa bellowed. "I have some guests for you!"

Ryōtora was hardly surprised to find that Elder Sister Noren was exactly what her name implied: the spirit of a split curtain, like the one that hung at the entrance. She had the appearance of a pretty young woman wrapped in nothing more than a few panels of fluttering cloth, and Ryōtora was startled to notice two spots of color appearing high on Meirō's cheeks. He would have expected a practiced liar like her to be better at controlling such reactions.

"Guests!" Elder Sister Noren clapped her hands together and then bowed repeatedly, like a bamboo deer-scarer catching water and pouring it out. "Oh, my, four of you – not the best number, is it? – but no matter; one of you is so small, anyway! Please, come in, be welcome, let me fetch some tea…"

Ryōtora was grateful for the warmth of the cup in his hand and the pleasantly astringent taste of the tea, familiar touchstones in a world gone strange. If this was unsettling for him, though – a man who'd faced the Night Parade and traveled, albeit briefly, into the Realm of Dreams – how much worse was it for Kuzu? He managed to coax her to join them at the low table, but she sat with her thin arms wrapped tight around her knees, face white and mouth shut. Meirō seemed composed, but Ryōtora noticed that the liquid in her teacup remained at the same level after each sip. Did her suspicious Scorpion mind fear poison? Or some spiritual danger?

Sekken, fortunately, was managing with admirable aplomb. He exchanged pleasantries with Kameosa and Elder Sister Noren as if his courtly teachers had trained him in making small talk with curtains and sake jugs. Ryōtora thought he might be the only one at the table who could recognize the wild edge of nerves and hilarity that made Sekken's smiles a little too broad, his laughter a little too bright.

For his own part, Ryōtora could only bear small talk for so long. At the first available opportunity, he said, "Please forgive my rudeness, but we came here – however unexpectedly – with a purpose in mind. Two friends of ours are here in the hidden market, and we were hoping to…"

He trailed off, not sure what words to put there. *Find them* was insufficient. *Free them* sounded too much like he was accusing the market's denizens of imprisoning their visitors. Which might be true, but it was impolitic to say.

Sekken rescued him, skipping neatly over the gap. "Yes, and I'm afraid one of the intrusions is my fault. I have a familiar of sorts, an inugami named Tanshu. I didn't intend to send him through into the market the other day, but I'm afraid that's exactly what I did."

"An inugami?" The cracks that marked Kameosa's brows dove inward in thought as the creature turned to Noren. *He, or it?* Ryōtora wondered, trying to decide how he should think of the animated jug. Elder Sister Noren's honorific settled that question for herself, but Kameosa was a different matter. The jug's voice sounded masculine, but then, so did Mirumoto Kinmoku's when she dropped into her lower range.

Did such questions even have meaning, when considering tsukumogami?

*"He" for now,* Ryōtora decided. *It* might be suitable for objects, but that felt too impersonal when the object in question could walk and talk.

Noren pondered for a moment, then shook her head. "An inugami would occasion less gossip here than a human. But I don't recall hearing anyone talking about such a thing."

"No?" Sekken looked surprised. "He made a terrible racket, I thought. At the – well, on our side it's a shrine to the Fortune of Thresholds. It might be different here. But he was barking very loudly, to the point where he disturbed whoever was there. Now he's somewhere else, some kind of windowless room."

"That could be many places," Noren said diplomatically. Her hands fiddled with the edge of one of the curtains wrapping her body, twisting the corner tight. "Your other friend... that wouldn't by any chance be a bakeneko, would it?"

Ryōtora leaned forward eagerly. "Sayashi, yes. You've seen her?"

"Noooo," Noren said, drawing the word out. "But that one, I have indeed heard about."

Kameosa's snort made the sake inside his body bubble. "*Everyone* has."

His tone wasn't reassuring. Sekken asked, "Where is she?"

"Wherever Tōji decided to put her," Kameosa said. "Your bakeneko friend got in here a while back. Wasn't three nights before she tried to rob a shrine."

"Rob a–" Ryōtora choked on the question. What could drive Sayashi to commit that kind of blasphemy?

Sekken asked for him. Noren shrugged gracefully. "I can't say. But General Uebe caught her and dragged her to Tōji."

Dread weighted Ryōtora's tongue, making him stumble over his words. "This Tōji you speak of – would the Lady of the Market *execute* someone for such a crime?"

"Oh, no," Noren said hastily. "She's not a *cruel* lady, our Tōji. I'm sure your friend is… quite fine."

Ryōtora didn't miss her hesitation before finishing that sentence – or the way Kameosa looked decidedly less certain. Guilt joined the dread. It was no good thinking that Sayashi had attempted to rob the shrine before he and Sekken even arrived in Brittle Flower City, much less found their way into the market; it still felt like they'd failed her. He could only pray the failure was not beyond all redemption.

Sekken spoke with brisk determination. "Is there any course we can follow to aid Sayashi? I understand from our good Kameosa here that we can't expect to arrange a meeting with Tōji. But perhaps this General Uebe instead, if that's who arrested our friend?"

Kameosa sloshed again in alarm. Noren's curtains fluttered. "No, no. The general is – I should say – no, I don't think you'd want to speak with him."

*Is there* anyone *of authority here we can safely approach?* Ryōtora was still searching for a polite way to phrase that when Noren said, "But you might be able to arrange something with Chirizuka Kaiō."

Sekken came alert like Tanshu picking up a scent trail. A beat later, Ryōtora remembered: that phrase had been written in Sayashi's notes. *Strange king of the garbage heap*, it translated to. What manner of creature might that be?

They would find out soon enough. Sekken shifted back from the table so he could bow low, his bony, long-fingered hands poised beautifully on the mat. "We would be most grateful for your assistance in meeting this strange king."

# CHAPTER SIXTEEN

While Kameosa went to see about arranging a meeting, Elder Sister Noren bustled up and down the stairs, preparing rooms for her guests. Sekken turned to Kuzu and nodded an apology. "Kuzu, if I'd known we were about to end up here... of course we hoped to find a way into the market, but I didn't intend to bring you along. There could be dangers we're not prepared for, and I meant to spare you those."

Ryōtora agreed wholeheartedly, for all the good that did now. It worried him that Kuzu didn't respond. From the moment she'd sat down, she hadn't unclamped from her curled-up posture. A glance at Sekken showed only helpless uncertainty in the other man's eyes; he had even less notion of how to handle a frightened young girl than Ryōtora did. And Meirō was–

Meirō wasn't there. Ryōtora bit back a curse. Where had she gone?

"I think we're the only ones here," Meirō said from behind him, and this time it was a yelp Ryōtora bit back. She knelt on her cushion and poured her tea back into the pot. "The question is, does this place normally have more custom? Or is this usual? There's a great deal here I have questions about, actually. Like, where did this tea come from? Do they trade with the regular market somehow, or steal their supplies? Or is all of this..." She waved an inarticulate hand. "Spirit stuff?"

Ryōtora huffed a quiet laugh, and her mouth soured. "Or whatever you would call it," she said.

He was grateful to her for not specifying *you as a priest*. Meirō's deceptive habits might make him uncomfortable, but he couldn't fault her discretion. They all knew he was where he shouldn't be, and none of them could talk about it.

Uncomfortable silence reigned until Noren showed them to their rooms, then renewed itself until Kameosa returned. "Success!" the jug said, sloshing happily. "Not only is Kaiō willing to meet with you, he'll do so tonight. Follow me!"

Mindful of Sekken's apology a little while before, Ryōtora said, "It might be best if only some of us go. Lady Bayushi, can we leave Kuzu in your keeping?"

She stared at him. "You want to leave a ten year-old girl with *me*?"

"Is there some reason I should not?" he said evenly. "Whatever opinion people commonly hold of your clan, I can't imagine you would fail to care for her to the best of your ability."

Kuzu was still sitting by the table; they were close enough to the entrance for their conversation not to be easily overheard. Still, Meirō lowered her voice as she said, "I don't give a bent nail for your opinion of my integrity right now. *I don't know what to do with a child.*"

That made three of them. Ryōtora knew he and Sekken

would eventually have one to raise, but an infant under the care of a wet nurse was a far cry from a ten year-old girl. Especially a traumatized girl suddenly caught in a place of untold supernatural danger – though truth be told, he would have felt unprepared regardless. He desperately wished they'd managed to bring Ishi or Tarō with them, or better yet, both.

In the absence of the ashigaru, the samurai would simply have to do their best. "We know Sayashi," Ryōtora said, equally quietly. "You don't. It makes the most sense to leave you here."

She resisted two heartbeats more, then her shoulders sagged. "Don't be gone long."

Nowhere in the market could be very far away, given the small space enclosed by the walls. Kameosa led Ryōtora and Sekken by back routes, muttering about the spectacle they'd become if he let too many market denizens spot them, and before long they'd arrived at a building in what Ryōtora thought might be the northeastern quadrant of the district.

It was not what he expected.

*Strange king*, this creature was called. But he didn't live in anything resembling a castle or palace. Instead his home appeared to be a junkmonger's shop, with rakes and incense burners and iron hooks leaning up against the walls outside or dangling in baskets from the eaves. "Here?" Sekken said dubiously, peering inside. The interior looked even more crowded, with things piled into precarious towers.

"Go on," Kameosa urged him. "Don't keep Kaiō waiting!"

Sekken led the way, his sleeves held close so they wouldn't catch against anything and pull a tower down upon his head. Ryōtora, broader in the shoulders, turned sideways and shuffled in his wake. He didn't dare look back to see how Kameosa might fit through this narrow passage.

It opened up a little once they were well into the store. And because Ryōtora had faced down the Night Parade, when he saw who awaited them there, he *didn't* stumble backward into the mess behind him.

Under other circumstances, he might have thought the creature was an oni. It was human in form, but there the resemblance ended; its hide was blood-red and covered in sparse, wiry fur. Its ears were almost as long as a rabbit's, but stuck out sideways from its head; its teeth ended in points as sharp as the claws on its two-toed feet. Ryōtora got all too clear a view of those teeth as the creature grinned at them both and gave a mockery of a bow. "Welcome, visitors!"

A gold crown sat incongruously atop its head, glinting in the light of the few candles scattered about the heaps. "Chirizuka Kaiō, I presume?" Sekken said, with all the smooth grace of a man at court. "Please pardon us for inconveniencing you like this. We are grateful you could make time for us."

"Oh, I have plenty of time," the yōkai said, with cheerful bitterness.

Ryōtora wondered what manner of creature this strange king was. The tsukumogami of that crown? But it was said that such creatures were born out of objects that saw long use, and Ryōtora didn't know of any place where crowns like that were commonly worn. Could it date all the way back to the time before the divine siblings fell to earth and founded the Empire of Rokugan? Or was it a foreign creature, somehow wandered deep into Crane lands?

Judging by the avid curiosity in Sekken's eye, he didn't

know and very much wanted to. He was too polite, though, to launch into such questions – and Chirizuka Kaiō didn't give them much chance, either. Bypassing the courtesies, the yōkai said, "So you're friends with that thieving cat."

"She has done us many favors in the past," Sekken said, neatly sidestepping the word *friend.* "We owe her a great debt. If we can somehow make amends for the offense she's given…"

The strange king cackled. "Offense, oh, that's a word for it, sure."

"We heard she tried to rob a shrine," Ryōtora said.

"Not just rob!" Kaiō's expansive gesture somehow avoided knocking anything over. "She tried to steal *a sacred artifact.*"

*Worse and worse. What under heaven was Sayashi thinking?* "Tried," Ryōtora said, hoping to take comfort in that. "She failed?"

When Kaiō nodded, Sekken asked delicately, "Might we know what she aimed to steal? It might go some way toward shedding light on her behavior."

The yōkai ran the tip of his tongue over his pointed teeth, eyeing Sekken, then Ryōtora. They apparently looked innocent enough, for he said, "A sword. Something one of you people gave to the Fortune of Roads."

The donation itself made sense. Samurai often presented objects to shrines as a devotional act; swords and other weapons were a common choice. But what would Sayashi want with a *sword*?

Ryōtora saw no harm in asking out loud. "I have no idea," Sekken said. "To the best of my knowledge, she doesn't know how to use one. And even if she did, she'd rather get other people to do the fighting for her."

"We'll just have to ask her." Turning back to Kaiō, Ryōtora said, "Is there any way to make that happen? We're told she was taken to Tōji for sentencing, but we don't know what kind of punishments are levied here for such crimes."

"It depends," the yōkai said, with another unnervingly toothy grin. "Tōji, she likes to *negotiate*. Not much sense in taking things people don't value, is there? One man is happy to give up his memories, his status, his skill at his craft; another clings desperately to those same things. Whether the deal is fair or not… well, that depends on who you ask."

Ryōtora's breath shallowed. Kuzu had said it before, hadn't she? Sayashi believed that whatever dwelt here could buy and sell talents, fate, and other intangible things. If this strange king was telling the truth…

It ought to be impossible. Surely only the Heavens themselves had such power.

But the market supposedly held a hundredth Fortune. That was what Sayashi had come here seeking – a heavenly power reputed to have control over such matters. Maybe she'd found it.

Yet she'd also tried to steal a sacred blade. Why? Did she hope to *kill* this Fortune, rather than to bargain with it?

Those were all questions for Sayashi, not for the strange king. And first they had to find her – if she could even still be found. Voice low and tight, Sekken asked, "So what did Sayashi give up?"

The lights in the shop seemed to dim around them as the king of the garbage heap laughed. "Her freedom. Your friend is now Tōji's slave."

•••

After news like that, Sekken shouldn't have been able to sleep.

Sayashi, enslaved to the Lady of the Market! Never mind that Chirizuka Kaiō claimed she had agreed to it – that supposedly Sayashi would earn some reward when her service was complete. She'd written to Sekken for help, and he'd come too late, and now she was bound here for the next hundred years. Even for a bakeneko, who needn't fear death from old age, it was a terrible fate.

They had to free her. He and Ryōtora were in agreement, without even needing to do more than exchange glances. But it wasn't going to happen that night.

Because Sekken, to his everlasting embarrassment, couldn't stop yawning. He was a creature of the dawn, not the night, and by the time they returned from meeting with the king of the garbage heap, midnight had come and gone. Ryōtora, blast him, looked as fresh as a lily – a very worried and tense lily, perhaps, but no hint of sleep hung about his eyes. In a more just world, he would be a courtier instead of a priest, where his ability to stay up late was an asset rather than a source of shame.

"You should rest," Ryōtora said, the fifth time Sekken failed to stifle his sleepiness. "Whatever we do, it will go better if you've slept."

The mere suggestion triggered another jaw-cracking yawn. "You'll wake me if something happens?" Sekken said, giving up. "Or if you and Meirō form a plan?" So far the Scorpion had offered nothing more than a pensive look, but Sekken held out hope.

"Of course," Ryōtora said. Five minutes later, Sekken was dead to the world.

At least, to the world around *him*. Whether it was proximity at work – Sekken having crossed over the boundary that separated him from his familiar – or simply his own worries drawing his mind in that direction, he dreamed of Tanshu.

Still in that dark, enclosed room. Hungry, but starving only in the sense that every dog in existence, mortal or otherwise, was perpetually starving. Patient. Waiting for his chance. The door opened for a bowl of food and another of fresh water to be placed on the floor, but that wasn't his chance. They were too alert, too ready. He had to wait. Opportunity would come.

Sekken would come.

Sekken woke early the next morning to an unsettlingly quiet world. He'd known cities that remained boisterous after dark, especially during festivals, but daylight should have been the market's busiest time. When he peeked out a window, though, he found the streets deserted. It matched with his vague recollection from the last time he'd connected with Tanshu: the hidden market came alive only at sunset.

Literally, or figuratively? If he found the tsukumogami now, would they be inert objects, their animating spirits fled until dusk?

Ryōtora certainly resembled an inert object, curled neatly on his side like a cat. If the market was active at night, better to let him sleep now. Sekken himself might be better off going back to sleep, if he could.

Except that memory lingered – maybe not even a memory. Sekken's awareness of Tanshu felt dreamlike, but that didn't make it any less immediate. Like when Ryōtora had helped him commune with the inugami before, he had a sense of connection now. When he turned his head, a lodestone pull drew his attention to the west.

Someone was holding Tanshu captive.

Someone who might be asleep right now.

Moving as quietly as he could, Sekken dressed and slipped out the door.

No sign of Elder Sister Noren in the inn. No sound other than the wind in the streets. That was good; it helped Sekken concentrate. He drifted along as if in a dream, letting instinct guide his steps. That was intermittently a mistake, as instinct led him into dead-end alleys he had to backtrack out of, but he persisted.

Finally, it brought him into another alley and up against a fence. Sekken mouthed a voiceless curse, unwilling to break the silence. The fence wasn't tall; his sister Ginshō could probably haul herself over it without even disturbing her breathing. But Sekken had spent over a year as an invalid, and was a courtier to boot.

In the street around the corner he found a crate. Sekken sidled toward it warily, not sure how he could even tell if it was a sleeping tsukumogami or an ordinary box. Nothing happened when he poked it with an exploratory finger, so he hauled it around to the fence, not quite able to suppress a few grunts of exertion. Whatever the crate held was *heavy*.

But it was tall enough to help him drag himself over the fence into a small, weed-choked yard. There he found a sliding wooden door into the building, but it didn't yield to his gentle tug, nor even to a firmer one. *Latched from within*, Sekken thought. *Damn.*

He stepped back and cast a glance around. Nothing else

useful in the yard… but on the floor above, a window stood open to the breeze.

Sekken eyed the wall. The eave overhanging the lower floor wasn't *that* high up; if he got a running start, could he grab hold of it? Then he had only to pull himself onto the bit of roof below the window and climb on through. It would be easier with the crate, of course, but no way he was getting that over the fence.

Just a jump, a pull, and on through the window. He'd made it over the fence, hadn't he? Really, this was no harder than the garden wall he'd climbed as a boy.

*The wall you fell off? The one that ended with you breaking your leg?*

*I'm taller now,* Sekken told himself, as if that would make all the difference.

Before he could talk himself out of it, he backed up to the fence, ran, and leapt.

He was indeed taller, and got his hands on the eave without trouble. It even held his weight. The hard part was the pulling. Sekken couldn't remember the last time he'd tried to drag his own body weight up using nothing more than his arms, but a lot had changed since then. He twitched, swung, and finally, after great effort, managed to hook one heel over the eave. Then an elbow and a knee, and with the last of what he was sure had been an unholy amount of noise, he dragged himself onto the narrow, sloping roof of the ground floor.

When he looked through the window, he nearly fell off that roof. Because a man was sleeping inside.

Well, something that looked like a man: in his thirties, perhaps, and careworn. Sekken couldn't see any obviously supernatural features, though the kimono draped over him for bedclothes might hide any number of oddities. The important thing was, either the yōkai of the market were incapable of waking during the day, or this one slept as soundly as Ryōtora. He didn't so much as stir.

Once Sekken's heart had resumed its proper place in his chest instead of his mouth, he eased himself through the window, touching down on the floor one cautious toe at a time. The sleeper kept sleeping. Was he the one who'd taken Tanshu prisoner? Why?

The only way to find out was to wake him and question him, and Sekken wasn't ready to be that profoundly stupid. Instead he crept past, slid the door open as silently as he could, shut it the same way. No outcry from within the room, and Sekken took what felt like his first breath in a year.

His sense of Tanshu had brought him to this building, but that tenuous connection had been thoroughly lost somewhere in all his athletic exertions. On the principle that a fully-enclosed room was more likely to be on the ground floor than the upper, Sekken found the stairs and went down.

He recognized the room at the foot of the stairs. This was where Tanshu had stood and barked: on one side was the sliding door the inugami had come through, the one Sekken had found barred, and on the other was the door that led to the ordinary market. This, too, was barred, and Sekken couldn't figure out how. There was no visible lock or latch, but it wouldn't open no matter how hard he pulled. *The market's doors only open at dawn and dusk,* Kameosa had said; it seemed that applied to this one as well as the gates. And no brute mortal force could change that.

Abandoning the door, Sekken resumed his search. A curtained opening led deeper into the building. Not knowing if anyone else was there, he stepped carefully... and that was when he heard the sudden, low *whuff* from behind one of the doors.

It was latched, but not locked. Heart pounding, Sekken flung it open, and Tanshu slammed into his legs.

The dog was quiet in his enthusiasm, but his tail whipped back and forth with unbridled joy. Heedless of his surroundings, Sekken knelt and scratched Tanshu all over, behind the ears, along the ribs, whispering idiotic pet names, while the inugami's head further disarranged the disaster he'd made of his kimono with all his escapades outside.

"Let's get you out of here," Sekken murmured when the first rush of reunion was past. They might not be able to go out the front door, but he could unlatch the back, the one that led into the little yard. As for the fence... well, he'd manage.

A broom was leaning against the back door. Sekken lifted it away–

–and the broom came alive in his hands, shrieking an alarm.

Sheer fright made him fling the broom into the opposite wall. It clattered to the floor and then flipped upright, balancing on its handle end. "*Intruder!*" it roared, with a mouth that appeared amid its splintered bristles. "Enjiki, someone is taking the dog!"

For once, even Sekken's mind didn't pause to contemplate the nature of the yōkai yelling at him. He yanked the door open and bolted into the yard, hurling himself at the fence. Somehow he was up and over it in a trice, one sandal lost, kimono yanked all askew; when he turned back he found Tanshu had already followed him, claws scrabbling for purchase until the inugami was able to leap down into the alley.

The broom was still yelling. Sekken yanked off his other sandal and started running. Belatedly, his memory offered up, *Hahakigami. That's what a broom spirit is called.*

Laughing madly, he escaped with Tanshu through the empty streets.

# CHAPTER SEVENTEEN

"Good morning, sleepyhead! I should almost say, good afternoon."

Ryōtora pried one eye open. Sunlight laid a golden stripe across the tatami; on the far side of that line, Sekken lounged with an expression of great satisfaction. One bony hand ostentatiously reached out to scratch Tanshu behind the ears.

The sight prodded Ryōtora upright, though not as fast as it should have. "He found you?"

"I found *him*," Sekken replied proudly. "I dreamed about him while I was asleep, and when I woke and realized the whole market goes quiet during the day, it seemed the ideal time to look for him. But when I got there, I realized I had to climb a fence…"

Ryōtora only half paid attention as Sekken related the tale. He wanted to be excited and pleased, truly he did, but despite sleeping half the day away, he felt like somebody had carved him out of an old and rotten log. His joints ached, and if he'd lain back down, he was sure he could have been asleep again within three breaths.

"–not even sure *how* I got back over the fence, to be honest, and I don't think I stopped running until–"

Cold settled into the hollow within Ryōtora where his vitality should be.

Sekken's narrative limped to a close as he noticed Ryōtora's lack of enthusiasm. "Are you angry?" he asked, a little plaintively. "I suppose I should have waited for you to wake up, so we could at least discuss it first. But I didn't want to lose that sense of connection to Tanshu. I know I may have made an enemy here in the market, but…"

"No, I'm not angry."

Instinct and habit made Ryōtora want to swallow down the rest. But he couldn't do that, not anymore; Sekken had to know. Yet he also didn't know how to put it into words.

He didn't have to. A heartbeat later, Sekken's hand curled inward, as if grasping his sudden realization. A soft curse escaped him. "You're tired. Because of me."

How many days had it been since they shared tea? Not an ordinary cup, but the ritual and companionship that kept them balanced. Too long, he feared. Even with that, Ryōtora might have been a little tired; as it was, he recognized this empty feeling all too well. Sekken's escapades had drawn too hard on their shared strength, with too little warning, at a time when the harmony between them was beginning to wear thin.

Guilt crumpled Sekken's face like a discarded letter. "Ryōtora, I'm so sorry. I- I didn't think. And I should have. Things have been good enough for us that- that I–"

He wasn't close enough for Ryōtora to touch. Words would have to do instead. "I know. I forget, too. We'll manage." Though how, he didn't know. They hadn't brought any supplies with them.

Sekken began to scramble to his feet, caught himself, and moved with more decorous care. "We can do a tea ceremony here, can't we? It might not be ideal, just whatever cups and kettle and so forth we can scrape together... but after all, that's supposed to be the essence of the way of tea. Simplicity, not a tea caddy that belonged to some great master and a whisk worth more than a provincial lord's domain. This inn might have what we need. Or if it doesn't, I'll send Meirō out to pillage the market. What a tale *that* would make for our heirs: here, my grandson, this scoop is now yours. Our Scorpion friend stole it from a tsukumogami."

Clearly *all* the Fire they had between the two of them had gone to Sekken for the time being. The other man hastily excused himself. In his wake, Ryōtora rubbed his eyes. *Drained or not, I still need to get up.*

He shambled his way into clothing and went into the upper-floor corridor. Meirō and Kuzu had been given the room across the way; not quite ready yet to face the stairs, Ryōtora knocked gently and called out, "Is anyone in there?"

No answer. Ryōtora was about to turn away when something – instinct; a whisper of sound from inside – made him tug the door open.

Meirō was gone, but Kuzu was there. Sitting in the far corner of the room, her knees wedged up in front of her again and her chin propped atop them. Ryōtora might have thought her asleep were it not for the wet gleam of her eyes.

"Kuzu?" he said softly.

She sniffled, wiped her nose with one sleeve, and turned to face the wall.

He came in and eased the door shut behind him. "I won't

ask if you're all right. It's a foolish question. We never should have brought you to a place like this."

"I wanted to come."

Her voice came out thick with snot. Sekken would have had a scrap of soft paper to offer her; Ryōtora did not. He knelt a little distance away. "You *wanted* to…" Memory stirred. "Ah. Your mother."

Whom they hadn't discussed at all last night, too distracted by the questions of Tanshu and Sayashi. "We haven't forgotten her, Kuzu," Ryōtora said. "Or our promise to you. We won't leave here until we've found her."

Kuzu's thin shoulders shook. For a moment Ryōtora thought her fresh tears brought on by his renewed vow. Then she forced words out through her sobs: "*She ain't here.*"

"She isn't…" Ryōtora's mind was moving through thick mud, too slow and dull for this conversation. "How can you tell? We've hardly begun to look around the market–"

"Look at how they're acting!" Kuzu uncurled with explosive force, slapping her hands against the tatami. Tears streamed unchecked down her face. "All the creatures here – they ain't seen anything like us in a long time, they said so!"

He dimly remembered those whispers, when they were spotted at the gate. Even so… "What's a long time, to creatures like this? You told us your mother vanished years ago. That's a long time, isn't it? Those comments don't mean we won't find her."

"We won't," Kuzu said, breaking further into sobs. "She went to the market at night, not sunset or sunrise. She ain't here. I know it."

Ryōtora wavered. He had scarcely any more experience

with children than Sekken did, and less gift for social graces.

But he remembered the time when his adoptive father, Sir Keijun, had admitted that Ryōtora was born into a peasant family. Ryōtora had fled to hide underneath the house and stayed for the rest of the day, even sleeping there overnight. The next morning he'd gone to his father and insisted that he should be sent back to his village of birth. When his father refused, saying that Ryōtora was a samurai now, he'd broken down crying... and Sir Keijun, a stiff and proper man whose self-control Ryōtora had always striven to emulate, had gathered his son into his arms and held him tight, whispering encouragement, promises that Ryōtora was good and strong and would always have a home with him.

Ryōtora was not Sir Keijun. But when he touched Kuzu's shuddering back, she flung herself against him, her voice breaking in a wail. And he did his best.

"Is he going to die?" Meirō asked.

Sekken gaped at her. "What? No! It's not *that* bad; he's just tired and slow-witted, is all."

"Then no, I'm not going to go poking around in search of tea utensils." Meirō settled back onto her cushion in the downstairs room where Sekken had found her. "If it's not life-threatening, then it can wait until Elder Sister Noren wakes up or... whatever it is these creatures do. No sense antagonizing them any more than you already have."

He swallowed the urge to point out that she'd gone poking around enough to find herself that sake she was drinking. When Sekken returned from freeing Tanshu, Meirō hadn't been at the inn; she claimed she'd gone to the market gate at dawn, only to find the prohibition against leaving without permission was an outright barrier. She'd come back before Ryōtora woke up, though, and Sekken had related his tale.

*Meirō's right*, he admitted grudgingly. It was only guilt at his own thoughtlessness that made him so eager to mend things with Ryōtora. Well, not *only* guilt; he could muster a very reasonable argument that they didn't know what would happen at sunset, when the market woke up again, and it would be better if he and Ryōtora were back on a more stable metaphysical footing before then. But it wasn't worth possibly waking and angering any more broom spirits.

"I wonder about them," Sekken said, dragging a cushion over to Meirō's table. Tanshu flopped down at his side, as if unwilling to be more than arm's reach away. "The tsukumogami, I mean. I've heard about such things, but never so many in one place. Usually it's just a bell here, a biwa there. In ways that make it hard to separate tsukumogami from nemuranai." Such objects were prized by samurai, as the awakening of the spirits within them often conferred strange benefits on the user. Some awakened through the sheer skill of the artisans who made them, others through the performance of great deeds, but for some, it was simply long years of use. The same thing that was said to create tsukumogami.

When he shared this with Meirō, she didn't respond right away. Then she said, "I wonder if that's what your bakeneko friend was trying to steal. I'm not sure if the sword at the Shrine of Roads is a nemuranai, but it might be."

"You know about it?" Sekken asked, startled.

"I've never seen it, but I know the story, yes. I told you, I visit that shrine every time I pass through Brittle Flower City."

Meirō eased her legs straight and leaned back on her palms. "It was donated by the last surviving member of a Crane vassal family, since she had no one to inherit it from her."

Having met Chirizuka Kaiō the night before, Sekken was primed to remember other details. "Was that the Fukiau family?"

Meirō eyed him with surprise. "Even for a Phoenix scholar, that's fairly obscure."

"It was in Sayashi's notes." Which were back at the Eisuitei, which might as well be the Burning Sands for all he could get to it now. "Fukiau... Chiyo, I believe. Some eighth-century date."

"Yes, that's when the sword was given to the shrine. I don't suppose her notes said why Sayashi was interested?"

Sekken snorted. "She wasn't writing a pillow book some friend could swipe and have printed 'without her knowledge.' There are no explanations of *anything* in there." If there had been, he and Ryōtora might have managed something other than this stumbling disaster of an investigation.

"Pity." Meirō brooded, letting her back sag until her shoulders pushed up toward her ears.

A sound from upstairs gave Sekken a fresh thought. "Kuzu might know, though. She and Sayashi were working together; maybe Sayashi dropped a hint or two? I'll go ask her."

But Meirō lunged across and caught his sleeve before he could do more than rise halfway. "Are you an *idiot*?"

She seemed to have shed half her samurai decorum along with her Scorpion mask, and Sekken was not at all sure he liked it. "What?"

"Listen."

He did as she bade. And after a moment, he realized what Meirō meant. "Is she crying?"

"Rather loudly." Meirō released his sleeve. "The girl is a wreck. But I can't spend all my time here watching over her."

None of them could, and the three of them together still didn't add up to even half an experienced parent. Sekken had expected years to pass before he was responsible for someone like Kuzu. They could share the burden of caring for her – from the sound of it, Ryōtora was upstairs with her – but they needed to find Sayashi, find Kuzu's mother…

*Oh.*

"While you were out," Sekken asked, "did you see sign of any other humans in the market? People in the streets, or noises that imply someone at work indoors?" Meirō shook her head. "Me neither. They might be asleep; maybe they've all adjusted to being up at night. I did see one fellow who might have been human – I can't be sure. But… we promised Kuzu we would find her mother."

He explained, and Meirō shook her head. "By the way that jug and that curtain were acting, I don't rate your odds very highly."

Neither did Sekken. And so they sat in uncomfortable silence, sharing the jug of sake, listening to Kuzu weep and Ryōtora's deep voice, trying in vain to comfort her.

There was nothing Ryōtora could do for Kuzu other than let her cry herself out. Once she'd done so, Sekken brought in a bowl of miso soup that he and Meirō had managed to scrounge up, which Kuzu obediently drank. Then it was simply a long wait for the sun to set, as none of them particularly wanted to venture out more into the eerily silent streets.

"What manner of creature do you think that man was – the one who had Tanshu?" Ryōtora asked after a while.

Sekken shook his head. "I don't know. And I don't know *why*. They weren't mistreating him, just keeping him closed into that room. I think…" When Ryōtora looked at him inquisitively, Sekken hesitated, then shook his head again. "A wisp of memory, but I can't really get a grip on it."

"Do you want to try connecting with Tanshu?"

Like they'd experimented with before. Tanshu perked up as if willing and eager, but Sekken said, "I don't think I'd be able to get the memory without your help."

Which was the one thing Ryōtora shouldn't give. They lapsed back into silence, and waited for the sun to set.

It was like watching an ordinary town wake up, except with the light dimming instead of growing. The cheerful greeting cries from the street even said "good evening" instead of "good morning." Shutters opened; wares were set out; the smells of cooking began to rise. If the carts rumbling down the street were doing so of their own accord, with neither human nor beast to pull them, Ryōtora simply tried not to think too hard about that.

They were braced for someone to come looking for Tanshu or demanding consequences for Sekken's intrusion, but either they didn't know where the new humans in the market were hiding out, or they didn't care to pursue the matter. Sekken himself wasted no time in asking Elder Sister Noren about tools and a place to practice the way of tea – not to mention some sandals to replace the ones he'd lost. She hurried out into the streets and came back some time afterward, bearing non-animated sandals and looking very pleased with herself.

"It's been so terribly long since anyone had an interest in this! I wasn't sure if – but no sense fretting over troubles that didn't happen. Come with me!"

Meirō sighed before either Ryōtora or Sekken could even look at her. "Yes, I'll watch Kuzu. But we can't hide in this inn forever."

Unlike Kameosa, Elder Sister Noren made no particular effort to keep her guests out of the public eye. Ryōtora felt his shoulders tightening under the stares and whispers of the tsukumogami around him, hearing them murmur confirmations of last night's incredible rumors.

To distract himself from that, he lengthened his stride until he drew even with Noren. "Elder Sister, how long has it been since mortals like us were here?"

Her curtains fluttered in uncertainty. "Oh, that's hard to say."

"Within the last year?" Ryōtora asked, not willing to let the matter drop. "Five years?"

Sekken bracketed her on the other side. "What we're really wondering about is a peasant woman – the mother of the girl with us. She vanished four or five years ago, and Kuzu says it was because she wound up here, in your market. But…"

Ryōtora picked up what he'd been about to say. "But she went missing late at night. And Kameosa told us the gates only open at dawn and dusk. Can people cross over at other times?"

"I don't think so," Elder Sister Noren said dubiously. "That is to say, they *used* to – but Tōji has become much stricter over the years. It's for our own safety, you see. Humans, they break their belongings, tear them, toss them away. We're safer here, sheltered from their abuse." Then she seemed to remember who she was talking to and bobbed an apologetic bow.

*It still isn't proof,* Ryōtora told himself. But what *would* be proof? They couldn't search every corner of the market for Kuzu's mother. And the balance of reason said she likely wasn't there.

He set his jaw. *One thing at a time.* His own state had improved a little since he awoke – Sekken had spent much of the intervening time meditating, trying to help him – but his wits would be sharper once they shared tea.

Noren led them to a shop crammed with all manner of tea implements, some of them illustrating her point about human abuse. There was no room among the teeming shelves to do anything, but they passed through to a small room at the back, which Ryōtora suspected had been hastily cleared of debris for their use. It wasn't a properly structured tearoom, with the four mats laid around a half-mat space for the hearth, an alcove for the decorations. There was a scroll on the wall and a vase set below it, but the scroll was a landscape painting neither of them had chosen and the vase was empty.

But to complain would be rude. Ryōtora bowed his thanks as Noren slid open the door on the far side to reveal a lantern-lit space hardly larger than the tearoom itself, laid out as a tiny dry garden. "Thank you, Elder Sister."

She fluttered nervously. "Is it all right? Do you have everything you need? There's water there, and here's the tea, and I'll be just outside–"

Sekken reassured her and ushered her out of the room. When the door was closed, with Tanshu on the other side as a guard, he let out a soft laugh. "Simplicity indeed. Well, just as one can meditate under the battering flow of an icy waterfall, we can contemplate the Void here. Would you like to play host, or shall I?"

Given how leaden Ryōtora felt, he didn't trust himself to do a good job of it. He didn't say that, though. Instead he retreated to the door, knelt, and bowed. "Please, lead the way."

# CHAPTER EIGHTEEN

Even under such less-than-ideal circumstances, it was a pleasure to watch Sekken prepare the tea. His hands, too bony for proper courtly elegance, flowed with grace from one movement to the next, each pause like an indrawn breath before the next step began.

Here, in this hushed space, it hardly seemed to matter that Sekken had used so much of their shared strength that morning. How could he take anything away from Ryōtora when the division between them was an illusion? What was Ryōtora's was Sekken's. What was Sekken's was Ryōtora's. Though they were not yet wed, already they shared their lives. And yet that illusion of division was what gave them their separate identities, as the emptiness of a bowl gave it purpose. They were both two and one, a paradox he felt at peace with. Just so long as they had this, the quiet communion of tea.

They sipped from the same bowl, and warmth welled up in Ryōtora's heart. The Fire whose decisive energy Sekken had borrowed that morning returned to him now as the comforting glow of the embers in the little portable brazier.

"Ahhhh... thank you," a voice said. "It has been too long."

Had the ritual not instilled a sense of peace in Ryōtora, he might have shattered the moment by yelping. As it was, he felt only mild surprise as the lacquered box that held the powdered tea rose, stretched, and settled back into a kneeling position atop a pair of glossy black legs.

With a tiny shiver, the whisk Sekken had used shed its droplets of tea. "Yes, thank you. Your balanced style is lovely. The Five Elements school, if I don't miss my guess."

One by one, the tea implements around them roused and expressed their gratitude. It should have unnerved Ryōtora, discovering that everything they'd used here was in truth a yōkai. It *did* unnerve him, just a little, when the bowl rolled up onto its lip to form a body, with two eyes peeping from the top rim – right where his own mouth had touched to drink. But these tsukumogami were born from the way of tea, with its serenity and simplicity, and they carried some of that aura with them.

Sekken bowed to them all. "I feel as if I should have suspected. For your assistance, we are in your debt."

"No, no," the whisk said earnestly. Two bubbles of green froth formed its eyes, poised delicately between the thin bamboo strands. "It's been so long since we had the chance to play our roles. Things were very different in the heyday of the market, but now…"

Ryōtora remembered what Noren had said about Tōji restricting access to the market. "It used to be different?"

"Oh, yes." The square of hemp cloth Sekken had used to wipe the bowl clean had folded itself into a doll-like shape. "People came and went all the time. But these days, no one cares."

"It isn't that they don't care," the tea scoop began.

"Yes, it is," the incense box said. "Everyone wants new things in the latest style. As soon as something becomes a little bit worn, they toss it out. To them, heirlooms are old-fashioned and stuffy. They hardly give anything a chance to grow its own spirit."

Quiet murmurs of agreement rose all around. Sekken said, "This is why Tōji seeks to protect you all?"

Silence fell. Had the tsukumogami been ordinary people, Ryōtora suspected they would have been shuffling their feet and looking away. A puff of ash rose from the brazier.

Finally the hemp cloth dared a reply. "How can we come alive, without people to make use of us?"

All the creatures in the room were already alive, of course, but Ryōtora heard the plaintive note in that question. These spirits were *lonely*. Cut off from the interaction that made them, that gave them purpose. And though no one would say it, their very silence implied they blamed the Lady of the Market for their isolation.

But like the loyal retainers of a samurai lord – or perhaps like that lord's peasants – they dared not criticize her. Ryōtora wanted very much to ask further questions, to learn how these creatures came to be here, whether any of them ever left. To hear more about this Tōji who ran a market with no customers, who bought and sold things that should never be for sale. To find out whether there was a way to free Sayashi from her hundred years of servitude.

Doing so, however, would break the beautiful atmosphere of this room – the very atmosphere these tsukumogami existed to create. Having just given them their first taste of it in untold ages, he didn't want to ruin that.

When he glanced at Sekken, the other man nodded. Instead of asking more, they let the silence stretch out, gazing at the flickering lantern-light of the garden.

They hardly spoke on their way back to Elder Sister Noren's inn. Thoughts were turning over in the depths of Sekken's mind, too submerged for him to identify them yet, but he was content to leave them in peace. Once a revelation or conclusion had formed, it would rise to the surface. Until then, he would enjoy the serenity he'd attained.

A serenity that cracked and threatened to break when they got back to the inn… and found it deserted.

"Where did they go?" he demanded of Elder Sister Noren, as if she could answer that when she'd been with them at the tea shop. "Did someone come here? Are Meirō and Kuzu in trouble?"

"I don't know!" she said, wringing the edge of her curtain. "Let me go ask questions – stay here; if there's a problem, better not to catch you in it, too."

She fled out the door. In her wake, Ryōtora said, in a carefully neutral tone, "I might be able to find them."

By calling on the spirits. "Not yet," Sekken said grimly, fighting the sense that the market was determined to steal away his friends every time his back was turned. First Sayashi, then Tanshu; now, when he'd just gotten Tanshu out of captivity, Meirō and Kuzu had vanished.

*Tanshu.* Sekken knelt and took the dog's head between his hands. "Can you find Lady Bayushi and Kuzu? Can you track their scent, as you once did with Sayashi?"

The dog headed for the stairs. Understanding, Sekken

followed and slid open the door to the women's room. Tanshu cast about, sniffing the futon where they'd slept, then went back downstairs. Ryōtora, who'd stayed by the door, said, "Should we be risking it? Elder Sister Noren seemed to think it was better for us to stay here."

*She's a curtain – what does she know?* But Sekken recognized that was unfair. She might have started her existence as a piece of fabric, but now she was an intelligent spirit, and one that knew the market a good deal better than he did.

Still… "I can't just sit here," he said, unable to keep the frantic edge out of his voice. "I should never have brought Kuzu to this place. She's a child, she lost her mother – oh, no. Do you think they went looking for *her*?"

Ryōtora bit his lips together in doubt. "Kuzu herself was the one who said her mother probably wasn't here. But if Meirō was optimistic–"

"She wasn't when I spoke to her. I can only see her taking Kuzu out to hunt if something happened to change her mind." Which it very well might have. And sitting around the inn wouldn't answer that question for them. "Look, I–"

He didn't need to finish that sentence. As if he could read Sekken's mind, Ryōtora shook his head. "No, I'm not sending you and Tanshu out to search on your own. Not right after we shared tea."

The whole point of that ritual being to join them together. "Well, we can't leave this place empty," Sekken said. "What if Meirō and Kuzu come back and think *we've* vanished? Just give me a moment to write a note." Fortunately, he had a few scraps of paper and a portable writing kit with him. At that moment, he didn't think he could have borne the prospect of picking up a brush that talked back to him. Though after what the tea implements had said, he took comfort in the fact that his kit was a proper heirloom, owned by a Shiba courtier before Sekken's uncle acquired it and gifted it to him.

*It would be a great wonder if it awakens. Just… I'd prefer it not to do so now.*

He left the note on the table, a quick message saying they'd gone out to search, and that Meirō and Kuzu should absolutely stay put until they returned. That done, he turned and nodded decisively at Tanshu, waiting patiently by the door. "All right, my friend. Let's go."

"Look, is that the humans?"

"So it's true…"

"How long has it been?"

Even Tanshu's supernatural senses couldn't follow the trail from the safety of a back alley, and Sekken probably would have gotten lost if he'd tried to guide their little group into such places. Since Meirō and Kuzu had apparently gone down larger, more trafficked streets, he and Ryōtora and Tanshu had to do the same.

And they attracted a *lot* of attention.

It seemed that word of their presence had spread. A tattered old fan spirit sashayed up to proposition them, which wouldn't have been effective even if the creature the fan was attached to hadn't been a squat, clawed thing with blue skin and rabbity ears. Two doors down they encountered an animated kitchen grater, apparently the proprietor of some restaurant, who followed them halfway down the street when they declined to come in and sample his grated daikon specialty. The proprietor's pleas became increasingly desperate, and only ended when Tanshu took them around a corner and out of sight.

"Ryōtora," Sekken muttered, "does this place seem... odd to you?"

Even as he asked that, an umbrella tried to lick Ryōtora with a long, red tongue that emerged from a tear in its oiled paper. True to form, the priest rattled out a polite apology even as he recoiled. Eyes a little wild, he looked at Sekken. "Does it seem *odd*?"

"Not like that," Sekken said, gesturing back at the umbrella. "I mean the market as a whole. The way it's run. The things those tea implements said, and the way everyone reacts to us, like they're starving and somebody's just put a bowl of rice on the table. It feels... off. Like this place isn't working the way it should."

"And how *should* it work?"

Sekken thought back to the books he'd bought, the day he went out with Kuzu. They were of limited use at best, being largely works of fiction written for entertainment, not scholarly accounts of history. "I don't know. Aren't the Spirit Realms supposed to be in balance with the mortal world? And this is a Spirit Realm of sorts, though not the canonical ones you and I both learned about."

A brazier trundled by, leaking smoke and light from its sides. Watching it pass, Ryōtora said, "The ordinary market is full of shrines, but nothing here seems to have the status of a Fortune – nothing except this Tōji. Where are they, if not here?"

"Maybe they don't actually exist. Or maybe they're in

the Heavenly Realm, where the orthodox Fortunes are. Or," Sekken said, "their absence is one of the things that's wrong."

"We could try asking."

"I don't think that's a good idea." Sekken drew closer and lowered his voice. "Did you notice how the tea tsukumogami all went quiet when I asked about Tōji protecting them? And the way Kameosa and Elder Sister Noren have reacted when she comes up in conversation? I think everything here is afraid of her." Except possibly Chirizuka Kaiō, who seemed more bitter than anything else. But Sekken had seen that dynamic among humans, the person who'd given up on fear and was just waiting for the inevitable doom to crush him.

Instead of answering, Ryōtora stopped abruptly in the middle of the street. "I don't remember *that* being in the market."

Sekken had gotten so caught up in his thoughts, he'd lost track of where Tanshu was leading them. Their path had gone down some of the smaller side streets, though not into any of the tiny alleys, but now they were back out on a main street, in the northern part of the market – and they were facing a palace.

There were definitely no palaces in the ordinary market.

This one looked like it was trying to be a miniature castle, rising in three stepped tiers, each a touch smaller than the one below. A wall surrounded it, shoving into the territory that should have been occupied by shops. The whole effect was extremely inelegant: even by the market's crowded, chaotic standards, the structure had no respect for the harmony of space and proportion.

And incongruously, two massive komainu guarded the gate,

as if the palace were instead a shrine or temple. The leonine creatures stood taller than a human – which Sekken knew because one of them was currently looming over Meirō.

Tanshu barked, once, as if Sekken hadn't noticed their quarry in sight.

He hurried forward, Ryōtora at his heels. Kuzu, thank all the Fortunes, was next to Meirō, her hands balled into tight fists as if she was steeling herself, or maybe holding herself back from punching the komainu. Meirō's voice rose. "... take a message inside, then, or just tell me who to speak to in order–"

Kuzu noticed the men coming up the street and tugged at Meirō's sleeve, interrupting her. Meirō, when she turned, didn't look particularly surprised or perturbed. "Maybe you'll do better than I have," she said to Sekken.

"Better at *what*?" he demanded. "Why did you two leave the inn? I told you to stay!"

"You did no such thing, and even if you had, I would have ignored you. Young Kuzu here came to me not long after you left and said we should be trying harder to rescue Sayashi. So we've been out looking."

One glance at Kuzu's red-rimmed, determined eyes filled in everything Meirō hadn't said. If Kuzu couldn't find her mother – if her mother wasn't here to be found – then the girl had a choice: crumple up in despair, or find something else to keep her going.

He applauded her resolve, but they could have *waited*. "Tanshu can find her," Sekken said impatiently. "The only reason I hadn't tried yet was that Ryōtora and I had to take care of our health first."

Meirō shrugged. "That may be, but I still see no reason we shouldn't begin our own investigation."

"The fact that these streets are filled with yōkai isn't enough?"

Ryōtora stepped past Sekken and bowed respectfully to the komainu Meirō had been arguing with, then to its counterpart on the other side of the gate. "Please allow me to apologize for my companion's rudeness in ignoring you. He is Sekken, and I am Ryōtora, and we are in search of a friend of ours."

Why had he spoken so casually, omitting their family names? *Komainu,* Sekken realized. Guardians of sacred sites... and of all the creatures in this market, perhaps the ones most likely to recognize the name of a family with a strong priestly tradition like the Agasha.

As Sekken followed Ryōtora's introduction with a belated bow, the komainu rumbled, "You may search the market as you please, but not the palace."

"Of course," Ryōtora said at once. "I presume this is the residence of the Lady of the Market? Our understanding is that we will need her permission to leave, so at some point it will be necessary for us to communicate with her. What is the appropriate means by which to do that?"

"You may not enter the palace," the komainu repeated.

Was it just not that bright, or did its duties somehow constrain it from offering more than prohibitions of entry? Sekken glanced at the other one, but it was watching this exchange silently. Possibly that one *couldn't* speak, since komainu traditionally came in pairs: one with an open mouth, the other one closed.

"Should we make offerings?" Sekken asked, uncertain

how to proceed with a creature this unhelpful. "If this is the residence of Tōji, and she is the Fortune of the Market—"

"*There* you are," said a familiar voice. "I've been expecting you ever since that mutt of yours showed up."

The voice's sharp exasperation didn't quite hide the relief underneath. A similar mix of emotions washed over Sekken as he pivoted – not toward the palace, but toward the street he and Ryōtora had just come up.

Where Sayashi stood, basket on one hip, fist on the other, and a look of hope and dread in her eyes.

# CHAPTER NINETEEN

The humans had come at last... and part of Sayashi wished they hadn't.

Writing to Sekken had made sense at the time. That was before she found her way into the market, when it was just a puzzle to be solved, and didn't he like that sort of thing? She could have curled up and waited for him and his Dragon priest to arrive. Let them deal with the problem.

But no, she'd kept searching. Poking her whiskers where they didn't belong, until something tried to snap them off. When Tanshu had found her that day, she'd been glad of it, but after the inugami left she'd had time to think. To imagine what could go wrong if two humans came blundering in.

Instead of two, she'd gotten *four*.

Kuzu bolted forward and flung her arms around Sayashi's waist. Dislodging the basket Sayashi had propped there, and Sayashi had to scramble to keep it from tipping, because she didn't want to find out what Tōji would do if the things she'd been sent to buy fell into the street. She was left holding the basket awkwardly above Kuzu's head, until Ryōtora stepped forward and took it from her.

"We thought you were being held captive as a slave!" Sekken blurted.

That bond with the mutt had definitely scraped some of the polish off his manners. Sayashi sniffed. "And who told you that?"

"Chirizuka Kaiō," Ryōtora said.

It was very uncomfortable, feeling her hackles rise when she was in a form that had no actual hackles. Sayashi grabbed Kuzu by the scruff of her collar and dragged the girl off to the side, away from the watching komainu. As she'd hoped, Sekken and Ryōtora followed –and with them, the fourth member of their group, a woman who dressed like a peasant and held herself like a swordswoman.

"Keep your voice down," Sayashi hissed. "Don't go mentioning him right in front of the palace!"

Sekken at least had enough brains left not to look over his shoulder at the komainu. "Why not? Is he a criminal?"

She curled her lip at him. "Of course not. He's Tōji's minion – but not a loyal one, I don't think. She's constantly worried he's plotting against her. Maybe he is, I don't know."

"But you're not enslaved," Ryōtora said.

His palpable relief made her squirm. Pure reflex had driven her reaction a moment ago, but continuing to dodge the truth was a level of folly she couldn't stomach. "Yes. I am."

The stranger spoke up. "Tōji lets her slaves wander the market?"

"Who are you?" Sayashi snapped.

"Bayushi Meirō," the woman said, unfazed by her hostility. "Do you always avoid answering questions by asking your own?"

Of course a Scorpion would be rude enough to both notice *and* point it out. But Sayashi very much did not want to admit that Tōji had her running errands like some kind of trained pet – especially not with Kuzu there, when the girl had admired her so much before. What had possessed the samurai, dragging an innocent like that into this place? Sayashi was almost grateful for the diversion when Sekken asked, "Is it true that you tried to steal a sword from one of the shrines?"

At Sayashi's stiff nod, Ryōtora said, "But *why*? What use do you have for a sword?"

With what little dignity Sayashi could muster under the circumstances, she said, "It belonged to someone I used to know."

"Fukiau Chiyo?" Sekken said. Then: "No, she was merely the one who donated it to the shrine. Someone before her, I'm guessing. Coming all the way to Brittle Flower City and entering the market just so you could obtain this sword…"

"The one at the real shrine was fake," Kuzu said. Annoyed, Sayashi pried the girl off her side, but that didn't stop Kuzu from adding, "She tried to steal that one first."

"I *did* steal that one first," Sayashi said, offended by the implication that she'd failed. "I put it back when I realized it was the wrong sword. And I didn't come into the market *for* the sword. But once I got in and realized it was here – never mind. You know what happened."

Unfortunately, Sekken wasn't so easily deterred. "Still, you must have some strong reason for doing all of this. And the one you'd prefer me not to mention by name implied you'd made a bargain with Tōji – that you'd *agreed* to be enslaved for a hundred years. Why? Was the alternative execution?"

Ryōtora was watching her far too closely. Sayashi felt hemmed in by her own rescuers, their presence long desired, and rejected now they were here. Ryōtora said, "Or is it that you were bargaining for something? Kuzu told us that the Fortune of the Market can buy and sell anything. Did you give up a hundred years of servitude for the sword, or for something less tangible?"

*Fortune of the Market.* Sayashi couldn't suppress the noise rising in her throat, one part growl, one part hiss. "She's no Fortune. I thought so, yes, before I got here – but Tōji's nothing more than a common ghost."

It set them all back a step. Ryōtora repeated, "A ghost? But… this isn't how ghosts behave. How did one wind up overseeing the hidden market? How did she get such power, to conduct deals of that kind?"

"Assuming she actually *can*," Sekken interjected.

"Oh, she can," Sayashi said, skin crawling. "And she's going to notice soon that I haven't returned. I can't stay here talking to you forever." Maybe by the time they met again, she'd have come up with a plausible-sounding answer for why she wanted the sword, what Tōji had promised in exchange for a hundred years of servitude. Something less humiliating than the truth.

Ryōtora still had her basket, and he maintained his grip when she reached for it. "Sayashi. I was willing, *barely*, to honor your deal with Tōji when I thought it was made with a Fortune. But if she's a ghost…" His gaze flicked around, at the street, the shops, the ugly bulk of the palace. No one came near the gates if they could avoid it, but there were tsukumogami casting uneasy glances their way. "Something is wrong here.

We came here to find you, but having done that, maybe it would be better for all of us to simply leave. Retreat to safer territory and learn more before we decide what else to do."

Kuzu lit up at this suggestion, nodding vigorously as if this were a village council deciding things by vote. Then she shrank back down when Sekken said, "We can't get out, though. Tanshu couldn't get through the door. Without Tōji's permission, I'm not sure anyone can."

The priest's face settled into uncompromising lines Sayashi had seen before. "I believe I can open the way. Against a Fortune's will, likely not, but against a ghost? With a bakeneko and an inugami to help? I doubt Tōji can hold us."

Sekken pressed his lips together, then turned to the Scorpion, who'd been watching silently. "What do you think?"

"You know what fate waits for me out there," Meirō said cryptically. "I'd still rather be there than here."

Sayashi wished she were in proper form, so she could lash her tail. "So you just make these plans, without consulting me?"

"Do you *want* to stay and be a slave?" Sekken asked, disbelieving.

Ryōtora had more sense than that – but not enough. "Whatever Tōji has pledged in return, I promise you, we'll find some other way to achieve it. Sekken and I can help."

It was all very touching and all very pointless, and the hope it sparked in Sayashi's heart anyway only made her angrier. "Do you think I simply gave Tōji my word, and that's it? I told you, she has real power. I *can't* just leave. I run her errands and I dance when she wants entertainment and I scrub her floors when she wants to make me crawl, and that's how it will be for the next hundred years, even if I die. I'm *trapped*, and you came too late to save me."

She could have clawed their faces and they would have looked less hurt. There was no way they could have come in time; she'd been a stupid cat and gone sniffing in the wrong places, and that was entirely her fault. But she couldn't admit that. Couldn't admit anything. And if she offended them enough, maybe they would leave – leave this street, leave the hidden market, leave Brittle Flower City – and then she wouldn't have to worry her stupidity was going to end with them trapped, too.

*That* hope was even more foolish than the other. She knew this pair far too well for that.

Ryōtora put the basket down. Before Sayashi could reclaim it, he drew a deep breath, interlaced his fingers into a complex shape, and chanted under his breath.

Sekken yelped in protest, but his hands stopped short of grabbing Ryōtora's and yanking them apart. Dread slinked down Sayashi's spine. Tōji didn't want priests in the market – probably because she was afraid one of them would figure out her true nature and exorcize her. Whatever Ryōtora had just done, would Tōji be able to sense it?

He lowered his hands, jaw set and hard. "What Sayashi said is true. And the binding on her…"

His silence lasted long enough to break the Scorpion's patience. "What about it?"

Ryōtora looked back to Sayashi. "Are you *sure* she's a ghost?"

"You think I can't smell the difference?"

"I have great faith in your senses. But I also don't know how a ghost could possibly wield such power. What binds your spirit… if I didn't know better, I would say it *was* created by a Fortune."

"Mortal souls can ascend," Sekken replied, but he didn't sound convinced. "My own ancestor–"

Ryōtora shook his head. "Not like this."

Kuzu left Sayashi's side. Apparently someone had succeeded at teaching her boldness where Sayashi had failed, because she shoved Ryōtora without hesitation and said, "Whatever it is, break it! Break it and let's take her away from here!"

The priest knelt, putting his face a little below Kuzu's. Regret weighted his voice as he said, "I'm not sure I can."

Sayashi hadn't realized just how bright that spark of hope was until it guttered out. Ryōtora had imprisoned *the Night Parade*. Sure, at the cost of his life, but then Sekken had saved him. These two could do the impossible. Couldn't they free one little cat?

She should never have contacted them. It was worse to hope and be disappointed, than never to hope at all.

Tanshu whined a soft warning. From inside the palace gate, Sayashi heard the sound she dreaded most in the world, more even than Tōji's voice: the rattling that heralded General Uebe's approach.

"Get out of here," she snarled, pushing Ryōtora herself. She snatched up the basket. "Leave the market, or at least go *hide*, you stupid–"

If the general had been heading out on some task for Tōji, she might have been able to get them away. But no sooner had he passed through the gates than he pivoted and headed straight toward them, lackeys at his heels, a creature clearly on a mission.

A strangled laugh burst from Meirō.

Sayashi could understand why. At her first glimpse of General Uebe, she'd thought him ridiculous, too. Unlike some of the tsukumogami, he was neither a human-like creature with a few odd features, nor a single object endowed with limbs and eyes. Instead he was a rattling assemblage of crockery, dozens of smaller pieces strung together: bowls stacked to make articulated limbs, flat plates encasing his torso, ceramic ladles for feet. His head was a sake bottle whose painted design had rearranged itself to form features.

The birds that served him for eyebrows dove inward to form a scowl. "INTRUDER!" he thundered, brandishing the razor-edged shards of his hand.

At Ryōtora.

If only he'd had the sense not to pray. Or had done it further from the palace. Or at least not so close to the komainu. Sayashi didn't know how General Uebe had discovered the priest so quickly, but she clutched her basket, dreading what would come next.

Sekken interposed himself smoothly. "We have travel papers," he said, offering up a charm Sayashi recognized.

The general slapped it aside, his attention all on Ryōtora. "A priest! Here, in violation of Tōji's edict!"

Bayushi Meirō had shifted over by Ryōtora, as if she was prepared to defend him bare-handed. Kuzu was hiding behind Sayashi. Sekken kept talking, defending Ryōtora in his own way. "We trespassed by accident. We did not realize we were about to enter Tōji's territory; had we known, my companion would never have accompanied us. For our ignorance, I most sincerely apologize. The fault is entirely mine."

"No," Ryōtora said, his resonant voice firm. "I was aware of what the charm's contents said, and yet I took one anyway, even after entering your market. The offense is mine."

Sayashi barely kept her curse behind her teeth. Stupid humans and their stupid moral codes! But she knew Ryōtora; he would sooner die than give up on his precious virtue.

And besides, what else could they do – fight their way out? Sayashi had tried that, with humiliating and painful results. Unless Ryōtora called on the spirits like he had in Seibo Mura, they would fail. And if he did… what were the limits to Tōji's power?

The Bayushi woman said, "If Isao is not permitted to be here, then let him simply depart. We will, of course, be glad to compensate you for the inconvenience we've caused."

Why had they spent so much time babbling about unimportant things, when Sayashi could have been giving them warnings about General Uebe? "BRIBERY!" he roared, rattling his ceramic body at the Scorpion. Sayashi couldn't contain her flinch "Do you think me so easily corrupted?"

Ryōtora bowed low. "Please, how should we address you?"

One of the smaller ceramic followers piped up indignantly. "You have the honor of speaking with General Uebe!"

"General," Ryōtora said, bowing even lower. "We would be grateful to know how we can rectify our error."

The sake bottle's painted face rearranged itself into a sneer. "Rectify? You are under *arrest*, intruder. It is for Tōji to judge what should be done with you."

Sekken yelped a protest. Sayashi would have stepped on his foot if she could have done so without drawing the general's attention. Instead it was left to Ryōtora to calm the other man.

With a touch on Sekken's arm, he said, "I'm sure you'll be able to smooth this over. In the meanwhile, let's not make any more difficulties than we have to."

He had more faith in Sekken than Sayashi did. Or he was just less of a fool, and knew it was better for only one of them to be imprisoned than all. Sekken gripped his hand and whispered, so quietly Sayashi almost couldn't hear it, *"Don't make any deals."*

Ryōtora's hand tightened on his, then let go. One of the general's minions produced a rope and bound his wrists behind his back, cruelly tight, then the general himself stuffed a wad of cloth into Ryōtora's mouth and tied it into place. He hadn't done that to Sayashi, but then, she wasn't capable of talking the elemental spirits into doing her favors. Meirō had a firm grip on Sekken, holding him back as the assembled followers marched Ryōtora away.

Only then did the general's painted, dead-eyed gaze fall on Sayashi. "You're late, cat," he snapped. "Tōji will be angry."

Sekken was looking desperately at her, all the questions he hadn't had a chance to ask brimming in his eyes. Questions whose answers he believed would help Ryōtora.

She was just a little cat, not capable of helping anyone. Not even herself.

"I'm sorry," Sayashi whispered, and ran back into the palace.

# CHAPTER TWENTY

The cloth shoved into Ryōtora's mouth absorbed all his saliva and left his mouth feeling as barren as a stone. He knew why General Uebe had gagged him; it prevented him from offering any prayers out loud. Rumor said there were priests in Rokugan who knew how to invoke the spirits without words – particularly among the Scorpion – but for most, Ryōtora included, it was an effective way to render him harmless.

Every time he let himself think about that too closely, panic tried to rise. He'd gone a long time without using that gift much, first when he didn't understand his own illness, then when he did understand, yet feared he might harm Sekken. All that time, though, the option had still been there: not without risk or cost, but he could invoke the spirits if he had to, and accept the consequences after. Now, he didn't even have that.

Ryōtora breathed slowly through his nose, timing the rise and fall of his chest to his strides as he followed the ceramic tsukumogami into the palace. It kept the panic at bay. It didn't banish it.

He couldn't spare much attention for the world around him, even though he knew he should be studying it. Sekken would have been noting everything, the layout of the palace, what hints he might glean about its inhabitants and its ruler. Ryōtora couldn't even try. He'd willingly submitted to arrest because he believed they stood a better chance if they cooperated than if they fought, but in the back of his mind, there had been the assumption that he could defend himself if necessary. He'd been thinking like a samurai, where a man's pledge that he wouldn't resist arrest carried weight. But these creatures had no such trust.

As hard as he clung to his belief in the benefits of cooperation – it was true; it *had* to be true – a cold, insistent voice whispered, *Did you just make a terrible mistake?*

The creak of a door jolted him to heart-pounding awareness. Inside the palace compound, he'd been led around the outside of the building, its lowest floor faced with stones like a castle keep. Now they'd arrived at a side door, and General Uebe shouted at the guards, "We have captured a priest! Put him downstairs!"

Ryōtora forced himself not to fight as a new creature approached him. This one appeared to be a warrior's saddle, draped in bloodstained silk as if its owner had fallen in battle. The straps of the saddle held a pair of iron manacles, which the creature clamped around his wrists in place of the rope before the latter was removed. The gag, unsurprisingly, stayed in place.

For a time. But after they marched Ryōtora down a narrow spiral staircase and shoved him into a cell, the fact that they'd removed his gag before slamming the door hardly mattered. If he could have made a sound, it would have been not a prayer, but a scream.

There were no spirits in the cell.

He didn't have to pray to know that. He felt the absence like an open wound. Everything in the world had a spirit, however tiny; the stones that made up the floor and walls and ceiling would be less than a grain of sand laid against the mountain god he'd once transferred to a new shrine, but they still should have *been there*. It was these spirits that priests often called on in their invocations, begging them to rouse from their slumber.

Yet the stones of this cell were empty. As was the air. As was everything around him.

Ryōtora shuddered uncontrollably. He'd heard of this happening before, down in the lands of the Crab Clan. After the monstrous forces of the Shadowlands overran the provinces of the Kuni family, the entire landscape had become Tainted, its soil and waters corrupted by malevolent spirits. The Crab had managed to drive out those Tainted forces, but at great cost: the landscape was left utterly barren. Not simply devoid of plant and animal life, but devoid of spiritual life, too. What material things existed there were like corpses, hollow bodies bereft of what once made them vital.

Had that happened here? Had the hidden market, wherever it lay in the metaphysical geography of the cosmos, been touched and twisted by the Realm of Evil, until the only way to purge the infection was to destroy its spiritual life?

Or had someone *chosen* to make the cell this way, so they would have somewhere safe to imprison priests?

His breath was coming faster and faster. Ryōtora couldn't

bring himself to kneel on the dead floor; instead he stood and closed his eyes, fighting for control. His hands clenched and released spasmodically, wrists straining against the iron of his bonds. *I should never have come here. I should never have submitted to their demands.*

Breath by breath, a modicum of stability returned to him. *I'm alive. The mistake is not yet irrevocable.*

Ryōtora opened his eyes again. He was alive. Which meant this cell was *not* completely devoid of spirits; there were the ones he'd brought in with him. His clothing, his few possessions, and above all, his own body. Earth, Water, Air, Fire. The Void that was there and not. If he had no other tools, he still had those. His captors could not take them away, short of killing him outright. And if they tried to do that, he had absolutely nothing to lose by fighting back.

He would have prayed for it not to come to that, if there were anyone other than himself to pray to.

Of course, he did wind up praying, because there was little else to do.

Not invocations to the spirits, meant to achieve some immediate effect. But could even a cell like this keep the Fortunes from hearing his words? Ryōtora didn't know, and unlike Sekken, he didn't find that theological puzzle soothing. He begged for kindness from the Fortune of Justice, the Fortune of Mercy, the Fortune of Patience. The Fortune of Roads, whose holy sword Sayashi wanted for some unknown reason – he would seek ways to help her make amends for that. The Fortune of Thresholds, to whom he'd given offense by crossing a forbidden boundary. "I have no excuse," he whispered, knowing that talking would only dry his mouth out more… but that was a form of offering, a show of respect and penitence that might win him forgiveness.

He stopped short of praying to the Fortune of this hidden market. *Nothing more than a common ghost,* Sayashi had said, but that couldn't be entirely true. If Tōji was indeed a ghost, she must be far from common. Still, even if she was like Kaimin-nushi, a human whose soul had ascended to a greater status, Ryōtora refused to offer her worship. Not when all he knew of her was that she enslaved criminals and forbade priests in her domain. *If she wanted prayers and offerings,* he thought grimly, *she wouldn't keep us out.*

In this windowless, dead cell, it was impossible for him to track the passage of time. What was Sekken doing? Something to help him, Ryōtora had no doubt… but what form could that take, when Tōji was so unwilling to grant an audience? *Please, Sekken, don't do anything too rash.* The only thing worse than Ryōtora being held captive here would be knowing Sekken was a prisoner, too.

Hoping to banish such thoughts, he forced himself to sit on the spiritless floor and crossed his legs, assuming the best meditative position he could with his arms still shackled behind his back. Eyes closed, mouth closed, he communed with the spirits of his own flesh and clothing. Not asking anything of them, not yet… but in Seibo Mura he'd made preparations like this, offerings given in advance so that he could call upon the spirits more swiftly once the battle began. If a confrontation happened here, it would come fast. Ryōtora needed to be ready.

The iron shackles first. To break them would require the

cooperation of Earth; his hair would suffice as an offering. Ryōtora pledged it in advance, not with shears or a knife, but with the simple willingness to give it up. He mentally drafted and re-drafted a poem, hoping to find words the spirits of Air would accept to conceal him from watching eyes or knock his opponents down. He could find little to offer the spirits of Fire, though – unless he gave up something more intrinsic to himself.

He'd done that in Seibo Mura, too. Sacrificed everything within his body and soul, so the Night Parade and its leader might be contained again. But the point here was to escape; no use killing himself in pursuit of that goal.

And what of Sekken?

Ryōtora's focus wavered. His elemental strength was Sekken's, shared to save his life in Seibo Mura. How much could he offer to the spirits without draining the other man? He knew Sekken would tell him to try anyway and damn the consequences... but Ryōtora had no idea where the others were right now, what challenges they might be facing. If he called too much upon their shared strength and brought Sekken low at a bad moment, they might both wind up in greater danger.

There was no way of knowing. He could only prepare, and pray for all to be well.

Even sound couldn't penetrate the cell, as if that, too, required the aid of the spirits. Ryōtora heard nothing until the bolt on the door shot back and the heavy panels creaked open.

By then he felt nightmarishly detached from the world around him, his body the only real thing. Was it still the same night? Or had a whole day passed? His dried-out tongue didn't want to move to ask.

At the sight of the saddle-creature, gag in hand, Ryōtora's heart thumped like a drum. If he was to be gagged again, then it was likely they were about to take him out of the cell. For all he knew, his next destination would be the execution ground. This might be his last chance to fight for freedom.

Or it might not. And fighting now might wreck any hope that Sekken could find a more diplomatic solution.

Ryōtora remained silent as the saddle-creature marched inside, shoved the cloth into his mouth, and dragged him into the palace.

Up the stairs and up again, away from the stone foundation and into lighter, airier rooms of tatami mats and paneled walls. If he was to be killed, he doubted it would be in a place like this; Ryōtora's heart slowed its thundering pace. No, this suggested he might be about to meet with someone with authority: General Uebe, perhaps, or Tōji, or someone else in whatever passed for the government of the hidden market.

A steady squeaking announced the approach of something around the corner. It proved to be a yōkai pushing a closed-sided box on wheels. She was as wrinkled as an old woman, but with clawed feet and pointed teeth, and she cackled at the sight of Ryōtora. "Oh, my, that's quite the prize you have there!"

*Tōji?* Ryōtora wondered. Judging by the contemptuous noise the saddle-creature made, no. "Out of the way, old woman."

"Now, now – didn't anyone ever tell you to show respect to your elders?"

"Age means nothing. You have no authority here."

Ignoring the saddle, the old woman peered around Ryōtora, noting his manacled hands. "Well, this is no good. How is he supposed to write something for my cart if you lock him up like that?"

"He isn't," the saddle said rudely. "Nobody needs the worthless trash in your cart."

Ryōtora caught the flash of resentment in the old woman's eyes as she drew back. "You say that… and yet, aren't the things I collect half of what keeps this place going? Not that anyone will admit it."

The saddle stepped forward, straps flapping in threat. "Out of the way. I'm taking him to Tōji."

This neither intimidated nor impressed the old woman. "Of course you are, dear. Given what lives in this one's heart, I'll be *fascinated* to hear how that goes." She patted Ryōtora on the cheek, smiling a sharp-toothed smile that somehow managed to both reassure and unnerve him.

Ryōtora fought the urge to twist around and look back at her as the saddle marched him on. What was the old woman? A tsukumogami of that book cart, perhaps, but she had nothing to do with scholarship. *What lives in this one's heart* – did she mean his feelings for Sekken? And was there any truth to what she'd said about her collection sustaining the market?

Sekken's argument that something was wrong here echoed in his mind.

The saddle-creature took Ryōtora into a large chamber partially walled off by folding screens. Like the palace as a whole, it felt like it reached for grandeur and fell short. The screens themselves were painted in a motley assortment of motifs and styles, none of them harmonizing, a sharp contrast with the elegant chambers Ryōtora had visited during winter court.

His jailer forced him to his knees, with no cushion provided. No surprise there. But Ryōtora flinched at an unpleasant laugh in a new voice. Glancing to the side, he saw an unnaturally tall figure looming over one of the screens. It leered at him suggestively, tongue licking the air as if desperate for a taste of something. "Is this Tōji's next plaything?" it asked. "It's been so long."

The same thing creatures all over the market kept saying – but *plaything* was less than reassuring. Ryōtora was almost glad when the saddle-creature sneered and said, "Idiot. Can't you see he's gagged? Somehow Enjiki let a priest into the market."

"Prayers aren't the only reason for gags," the other tsukumogami said, giggling.

The crash of a gong sent it diving back below the folding screen. A moment later, a small retinue swept into the room, and Ryōtora straightened up: here, at last, was Tōji.

She didn't look like the classic ghost of paintings and the theatre. Her hair wasn't wild, her robe was layers of gaudy purple and red and gold instead of white, and if her body faded to mist before it reached her feet, the sweeping hems of those robes hid that lack. She even wore her clothing as the living did, the left side wrapped over the right, instead of right-over-left as corpses were dressed. Lacking Sayashi's yōkai instincts, and unable to pray for hints from the spirits, Ryōtora could have mistaken her for an ordinary woman.

Several tsukumogami accompanied her: a pair of tall, silk-covered sandals; a biwa with its stringed body wrapped in a priest's robe, tapping along with a blind person's cane; a doll-sized boy carrying a beautifully lacquered box; a sash that slithered along the mats behind Tōji like an obedient pet snake. After Tōji seated herself on a sumptuous cushion laid out by the sandals, a flick of her pale hand sent the sash toward Ryōtora. He fought the urge to shudder as it slithered around his body and bound his arms tight to his sides.

"Remove his gag," Tōji said to the saddle-creature. Her voice was high and thin.

The sash's near end reared up by Ryōtora's face as the saddle untied the band holding the cloth in his mouth. "If you attempt any prayers," Tōji said, "my jatai will choke you before you finish your first word. Do you understand?"

Ryōtora's own voice came out paper-dry, his tongue sticking to the roof of his mouth as he spoke. "Yes. I would bow to show you the proper respect, but I cannot."

"I don't want your respect," Tōji snapped. "I want to know why you trespassed in my market."

"An accident, for which I most sincerely apologize."

"Apologies do nothing!" she said shrilly. "You should not be here!"

He dipped his head forward, the closest approximation of a bow he could manage. "I will gladly leave, Tōji, if you allow me to go."

"No!" She leaned forward, slapping one hand against the mat. "No, you will not insult me like this and then *leave*. Not without paying a price for your error."

*Don't make any deals,* Sekken had said. But Sekken hadn't known where they would imprison Ryōtora. If this was his only way out of that cell...

"What price," he forced himself to ask, "would you consider suitable?"

Tōji tapped one long fingernail against her lower lip. Even Ryōtora could tell it was a theatrical gesture; she'd made up her mind long before she came into this room. But she enjoyed playing the part of the market's ruler, swinging between anger and a pretense of mercy. Much like the baku that had briefly reigned over Asako Katahiro's winter court.

The tsukumogami of the folding screen poked its head back up again. "Tōji, this one has a lover. If you had them both here–"

"Silence!" she shrieked, and the creature dove for cover. "I will not entertain your disgusting desires!"

Memory whispered, deep in Ryōtora's mind. The oracle spoken to Meirō – hadn't it said something about a ghost, and love? Was there more to Tōji's fury than just anger at that creature breaking the mood she was trying to build?

Regardless of the answer, Ryōtora could tell her patience had suffered. "Your connection to the spirits makes you a trespasser, priest," she said, rattling the words off with much less drama. "Give it to me – trade it for your freedom – and I will let you go."

If it weren't for the tight grip of the jatai around his body, he would have sagged in shock. "What? You – how could you possibly take such a thing?"

Her lip curled in a sneer. "I'm the Lady of the Market. I can buy and sell anything I want."

*Not that. Surely not that.* It was the prerogative of the Heavens alone to decide who was born with the gift of speaking to and hearing the spirits. Even if Tōji was capable of binding Sayashi to a hundred years of servitude, she couldn't possibly take away Ryōtora's spiritual connection.

Yet she seemed utterly certain she could.

The jatai glided with teasing threat against his neck, a reminder of what would happen if Ryōtora did anything untoward. He wasn't even tempted to try; with this many tsukumogami around, this deep into a hostile palace, any such bid for freedom would be suicide.

But if he gave Tōji what she asked for…

He would be like a warrior who returned from battle too wounded to ever fight again. There were still ways such people could serve – or dignified retirement to a monastery – but he wouldn't have suffered this loss in battle; it would be the result of his own folly, running off on the thinnest of pretexts to aid a friend instead of returning to his clan as commanded. And even though Sir Keijun had adopted him from his peasant family long before anyone knew he could speak to the spirits, it still felt like the core of his identity as a samurai, the thing that justified his elevation in rank. With that gone, what would he be?

*This isn't about you,* said the quiet, steadfast voice deep in his heart. *It isn't about what you'd lose. It's about what Tōji would gain.*

She hadn't said, "give it up." She'd said, "give it to *me*." Tōji, he was mortally certain, had no such gift. Did she know that learning to use it well ordinarily took years of training? The years she might have, but where would she find a teacher, if she never allowed priests into this place? Or perhaps she meant to take all his knowledge, too. If she could take his gift, surely that would be a trivial addition.

And then the market's ruler would have a new way to control the creatures around her. Or maybe even more than that.

Ryōtora couldn't give her such a prize, not for his own freedom. But another voice in his heart whispered, *What about the others? What if you could free Sekken? And Kuzu, and Meirō, and even Sayashi?*

He bowed his head again, careful not to alarm the jatai. "Tōji... what you ask is a great sacrifice. If- if I may presume upon your mercy, I need some time to consider it. Please."

Tōji's gaze searched his, looking for any trick. Then she smiled, slow and cruel.

"Put him back in the cell," she said. "Perhaps that will encourage him to decide quickly."

# CHAPTER TWENTY-ONE

Sayashi was gone. *Ryōtora* was gone. Sekken was left standing in the street with only Tanshu, Kuzu... and Bayushi Meirō.

She'd let go of him after Ryōtora vanished through the gate with that pottery creature, General Uebe. Now Sekken rounded on her with a snarl. "Some use you are. Why did you just stand there?"

Meirō's nostrils flared. "What would you have me do? I've got no weapons, no constables–"

"You're a Scorpion, aren't you? You're supposed to have tricks up your sleeve! Ways to get us out of this, to see it coming and take steps to prevent it before anything ever happens. But you just stood there like a stump as that *thing* walked up and arrested Ryōtora!"

"I see," she said icily. "My presumed lack of honor is a problem when it comes to telling me anything about your plans... but the moment it becomes useful, you're angry I didn't pull the underhanded tricks you would have condemned me for an hour ago."

Kuzu had knelt and flung her arms around Tanshu for

comfort, burying her face in the dog's fur. Sekken still felt the print of Meirō's hands on his arms, holding him back the moment the yōkai began to bind Ryōtora and Sekken realized that cooperation had been a mistake. The sight of the other man being marched away like a criminal…

*He* hadn't done anything, either. Just stood there and let them take Ryōtora. Because for all his vaunted intelligence and education, he hadn't been ready for this. He'd walked carelessly into the hidden market, and now they couldn't get out.

Sekken couldn't just stand there now. And he didn't know what he could do. But he would find something. There had to be something.

"Get Kuzu back to the inn," he snapped at Meirō. The solid figure of the Scorpion was warping and blurring through the tears he could not, *would* not shed in front of her. "Tanshu, with me." He spun and headed across the street, not caring where he was going, so long as it was somewhere he could break down in private.

The night was further gone than he'd realized. By the time he pulled himself back together and wiped his face dry with his sleeve, the tsukumogami of the market were beginning to pack away their work.

That should have been good. The market was deserted in the daytime; surely the same would be true of the palace. If Tōji was a ghost instead of a Fortune, it became even more likely that she wouldn't be active. So long as he was careful and didn't accidentally grab any sentient brooms, this would be an ideal time to break in and find Ryōtora.

But the thing that finally put an end to his breakdown was a jaw-cracking yawn. Ryōtora was the one made for such hours, not Sekken; under normal circumstances he'd be about to wake up, not dragging himself through the tail end of an excessively long night. As obscene as it felt to think about sleeping when Ryōtora was imprisoned, Sekken knew he wouldn't be much use if he didn't get any rest… and besides, it wasn't only his own state he had to consider.

Whatever I do will affect Ryōtora.

He thanked all the Fortunes that they'd shared tea just before things went awry. The balance between them was as solid as it could get, their joint strength at its peak right when they might both need to draw upon it. But that didn't mean Sekken could afford to be profligate. Wherever they'd put Ryōtora, he doubted the man was sleeping well; therefore, it was Sekken's duty to get as much rest as he could, for both their sakes.

Assuming he could find his way back to the inn. "Tanshu," he said, taking the dog's head between his hands. "Can you lead me?" He closed his eyes and pictured Elder Sister Noren's establishment, wishing he could present it the way Tanshu perceived it, with all the relevant scents.

Tanshu wiggled free, licked his hand in reassurance, and trotted away.

Whether the inugami's confidence was justified or not, Sekken never got the chance to find out. Kameosa came running up before they'd gone more than two blocks, sloshing sake onto the ground as the animated jug lumbered to a halt. "There you are!" he said, the cracks of his face gaping wide in relief. "Elder Sister Noren has been in an absolute state – she says Kuzu and Lady Bayushi went missing, so she went to search for them, and while she was gone you and Lord Isao went missing, and now Kuzu is back but *she* says Lord Isao has been arrested–"

"He has," Sekken said dully. Was the dead feeling in his chest just from shock, or was it a sign that Ryōtora was drinking more deeply than usual from their shared energy? At least Sekken retained enough wit not to say outright that Ryōtora was a priest; there weren't many yōkai left in the street, but he knew that would cause a stir. Instead he said, "Is there *anyone* we can appeal to? No one seems to want to let us talk to Tōji."

All the answer Kameosa gave was, "Let's get you back to the inn."

To Sekken's surprise, there were other visitors there when he and Kameosa arrived. Not other humans: the tsukumogami he and Ryōtora had met – and used – for the way of tea earlier that night. Elder Sister Noren was with them, and Kuzu, but not Meirō. Sekken was just as glad. He was still angry with her, but he'd also calmed enough to feel guilty about the way he'd lashed out. She might have failed, but so had he.

The tea utensil tsukumogami offered him grave little nods when he came in. The bowl said, "Lord Asako. We are here to do what we can to help you and Lord Isao."

Hope sparked in that cold pit. "Do you have connections at the palace? Can you help us convince Tōji to let us all leave the market?"

The bowl shuffled its feet. Had it been human, that would have signaled discomfort; Sekken assumed it was the same here. "Not like that. I meant the bond between the two of you. We can feel it, you know – and we know it's going to be bad for him if we don't help."

The spark snuffed out instantly. "Bad? Why? What's happening to him?"

"We don't know," the whisk said. "We can't see. But..."

Elder Sister Noren wrung a corner of her curtain. "This isn't the first time a priest has found their way into the market. It's been a *very* long time, but that one went, um. Poorly. And afterward–" she crumpled the fabric in her fist "– Tōji announced that she was going to make a special cell to imprison any future trespassers of that sort."

A special cell? Wasn't it enough that they'd gagged Ryōtora, tied his hands behind his back until Sekken could see the rope biting into his skin – what else would they need? All the possibilities Sekken's imagination could spin were horrifying. *It's going to be bad for him if we don't help*, the tsukumogami had said.

"I have to get him out," he said. His voice had lost all its smooth elegance; the words were a harsh croak. "Out of that cell, out of the market. There has to be a way."

"Of course," Noren said, letting go of her curtain corner and fluttering a bow at him.

But Sekken couldn't shake the feeling she'd said it only to be polite.

He slept dreadfully, waking up again and again from suffocating nightmares to the all-too-real emptiness of the other half of the futon. Just his own fears troubling his mind, or spillover from Ryōtora? Sekken was deeply afraid it might be the latter.

Waking in the middle of the afternoon left him feeling logy and thick. He went to the well outside the inn's kitchen and splashed water on his face, then called softly to Tanshu.

Together they went out and found their way back to the palace.

The gates were closed. The eyes of the komainu weren't, but they looked like ordinary statues now, no different from the ones he'd seen at a hundred shrines. Sekken knew better than to trust it, though, after his experience with that broom. He didn't approach closely, just loitered behind the corner of a closed-up shop and studied the palace wall.

It was a good deal higher than the one he'd climbed to rescue Tanshu. No mere crate would be enough to get him over that edge. And once he was inside, what then?

"Can you get in?" he whispered to Tanshu. The inugami had a cat-like ability to wind up in the oddest places, though Sekken still hadn't proved whether Tanshu walked through walls. The way he'd been shut into that room suggested not, but then again, the building had some connection to the Fortune of Thresholds. If anything could block that ability, such a Fortune could.

Tanshu whined softly. It sounded less like refusal than reluctance. Sekken scratched behind the dog's ears. "I understand. I don't want to put you at risk."

But there wasn't likely to be any way out of this that didn't involve *some* risk. Sekken was perishingly short on allies – useful ones, anyway. Kuzu was a child, Meirō was missing, and none of the friendly tsukumogami seemed willing to take any action against Tōji.

Standing here, so close to where they'd met Sayashi, made that thought echo in his memory. *He's Tōji's minion,* Sayashi had said, *but not a loyal one.*

She's constantly worried he's plotting against her.

Tanshu hadn't been with Sekken and Ryōtora when they visited the strange king of the garbage heap; the dog would be no use in leading him back to that cluttered shop. Sekken could wait for nightfall and ask for directions... but was that a good idea? If Kameosa and Elder Sister Noren really were afraid of opposing Tōji, and they guessed why he wanted to speak to Chirizuka Kaiō, they might not help him. For all he knew, they might even report him.

But the sun hadn't set yet. He could search on his own first.

Sekken had paid reasonably close attention when Kameosa led them there before, but everything looked different in daylight, without awnings spread and tables of goods set out in the streets. He knew which quadrant of the market to look in, though, and patient, methodical tracing of every lane and alley finally brought him to a familiar door. The clutter outside it had been cleared away, but he was fairly certain this was the junkmonger's shop they'd visited – had it only been two days ago? Two nights, rather.

By then sunset wasn't far off, and Sekken elected to wait outside rather than try to go in. He'd done enough trespassing already, and might have more in his future. Instead he looked for the cleanest patch of ground he could find, sat cross-legged, and closed his eyes to meditate, hoping that might do Ryōtora some good.

That dead pit in the center of his chest ached, an emptiness that was not the deep mystery of the Void. He was more sure than ever that it had to do with that special cell the yōkai had mentioned, the one for priests. And Ryōtora... he seemed to be draining all the Water from their shared strength, until Sekken's own mouth burned with thirst.

He abandoned his meditation and searched until he found a well. There he drank ladle after ladle, as if the physical liquid could somehow flow through him to the imprisoned man. *Hold on, Ryōtora. I'll find a way to help you.*

Noise down the alley made him drop the ladle and bolt back to the junkmonger's shop. The market was beginning to wake up.

Sekken tried the door and found it unlatched. Poking his head inside, he called out politely, "Forgive me for intruding. I am looking for Chirizuka Kaiō?"

An unfamiliar voice laughed from somewhere among the piles of junk. "Come in, come in!"

Any number of stories told Sekken he was an idiot for doing as the voice suggested. He slipped inside, but didn't shut the door behind him – for all the good that would do.

Threading his way through the piles with Tanshu at his heels, he found an old woman sitting where Chirizuka Kaiō had been. She might have been human, but the length of her fingernails and the scabrous appearance of her skin argued against it. Sekken bowed anyway and said, "I'm afraid we haven't been introduced."

She laughed again. "Oh, everyone knows who you are! You and the man you love, so cruelly torn from your side. Yes, yes, I know all about it."

She didn't sound particularly sympathetic. Controlling his anger, Sekken said, "You may know who *I* am, but I cannot say the same of you. What is your name?"

"She's Fuguruma Yōhi." That came from further back in the shop, and a moment later, Chirizuka Kaiō appeared around a precarious stack of trivets and baskets. Despite the cramped nature of the shop, he moved without fear, as if he knew nothing there would dare to fall on him.

At his words, Sekken noticed what the old woman was sitting atop: a small, enclosed cart of the sort used by wandering booksellers. No, she wasn't human; she must be the spirit of that fuguruma.

Now that he was here, how to broach the subject? Sekken said delicately, "If you have heard of Isao Ryōtora's arrest, then it will come as no surprise to you that I hope to have him freed. But the Lady of the Market seems particularly difficult to approach. You were very well-informed about my friend Sayashi's crime and her subsequent deal, Kaiō; I was hoping you might advise me now on this matter."

The strange king's eyes glittered as gold as his crown beneath his wild brows. "No, you weren't."

Sekken said defensively, "I–"

"You were hoping I might help you against Tōji."

*Yes – but no!* Cautious now, Sekken asked, "Is it inevitable that freeing Ryōtora means going against the Lady? Is there no way to placate her and win his release?"

Fuguruma Yōhi inhaled deeply and loudly, as if appreciating a fine incense or perfume. Kaiō said, "What reason does Tōji have to let him go? What reason could you give her?"

"I know she doesn't want a priest here," Sekken said. "Even if she has him locked up somewhere safe for now, wouldn't it be better to have him out of the market entirely?"

"Would it?"

Sekken had the maddening feeling that there was plenty Kaiō wasn't saying. It wasn't even the subtle wordplay of a courtier, implying without ever openly committing; it was more like...

More like he can't.

Ryōtora, praying to the spirits as they stood outside the palace, discovering the binding that held Sayashi to her servitude. But why should the bakeneko be the only creature in this place beholden in some fashion to Tōji?

Sayashi had said Chirizuka Kaiō might be disloyal. If he was bound against his will, that could explain a great deal.

Thinking out loud – and watching Chirizuka Kaiō the whole time, alert for any sign that he was approaching a line he shouldn't cross – Sekken said, "I suppose she might not want that, no. A priest outside the market could bear tales of what's going on in here."

Kaiō's lips peeled back from his pointed teeth.

"And outside the market, outside her power," Sekken went on, "he could take action against her. Maybe even lay her ghost to rest."

The incipient smile looked more like a snarl, now. As if that wasn't quite right – as if getting rid of Tōji wouldn't be that easy. Tentatively, he added, "Of course, from *within* the market – but outside the prison – he might do even more."

Now the snarl became bloodthirsty and fierce. Chirizuka Kaiō hadn't been reading his mind before, when he suggested Sekken wanted help against Tōji; he'd been leaning on that to plant the idea, without ever claiming it as his own. Not so unlike a courtier after all.

Sekken wasn't a fool. He knew perfectly well that just because Kaiō wanted Tōji gone, it didn't make removing the Lady of the Market a good idea. However ominous a ruler she seemed, making these deals that bound others with more than words, any successor – for example, the strange king himself – might be worse. Her power might pass to that creature, and then nothing would change except who was making the deals.

Fuguruma Yōhi got up and sidled closer to Sekken, humming unnervingly. "Would you like to write something for my cart? A love letter to your imprisoned beloved, perhaps, pouring out your grief over his captivity?"

Tanshu growled in warning. Sekken shuddered and fought the urge to flinch away. "No, thank you. Any attempt to communicate directly with Ryōtora stands too much risk of being intercepted."

"Oh, I didn't say I would deliver it to him." Her smile was as toothy as Kaiō's. "But you could still write it."

*And what would happen to me if I did?* Sekken didn't want to find out – not with the old woman smiling at him like that. *Love that's withered to a ghost*; that was what the oracle had said. Had Tōji written something for Fuguruma Yōhi's cart? Was that part of how things had gone wrong in the market?

Redirecting his attention to Kaiō, Sekken said, "I imagine Tōji's closest followers and servants are all very loyal."

"Just like your friend Sayashi is," the strange king said encouragingly.

Meaning *quite possibly not at all*, except insofar as they were bound. But since they *were* bound, Sekken wasn't sure how well he could get around that. "And I imagine they're quite vigilant."

"From dusk until dawn!" he agreed.

Implying, not in the daytime. Sekken ground his teeth. He wanted very profoundly not to wait that long; every time he thought of Ryōtora, that dead feeling in his chest seemed to grow thicker. What would a second night in captivity do to the other man?

But it was better to endure and strike at the best moment than to rush and lose all.

Casting about for something else useful he could ask that might not brush up against the limitations on Kaiō, Sekken struck on a possible inspiration. "You know," he said, "in the mortal city, they have a guide for visitors that talks about all the points of interest: famous temples, the best place to get broiled eel, the architecture of the palace, that sort of thing. Fuguruma Yōhi, I don't suppose you sell any such thing from your cart?"

It was, of course, a bit much to hope that she would have a map showing him exactly where to go in the palace. But Sekken was taken aback by her thundering scowl. "I don't hand out my treasures to beggars!" she snapped, flouncing away and dropping herself protectively atop the cart again. "If you won't give me anything, then I won't give you anything!"

*So much for that,* Sekken thought with an inward sigh. He would simply have to wait for dawn.

# CHAPTER TWENTY-TWO

It was like a wound in his side, slowly seeping blood.

Ryōtora had never given much consideration before to how spirits moved. In a broad, philosophical sense, certainly: Air was very active, Earth far less so. He'd learned that in his earliest lessons, then studied invocations that might persuade the spirits to change their usual course.

But he'd never thought about how each breath in and out shifted the air, how the perspiration on his skin and the scant moisture in his mouth dissipated away. These things were not the spirits, not precisely; he wasn't inhaling and exhaling entities the way a koi, rising to the surface of the water, gulped down crumbs of food. His internal Air was not the air he breathed.

And yet, it was not *not* the same. Which he understood now, in a very visceral way, every time he breathed in the dead air of the cell without spirits.

The room was a sucking abyss, hungry for what it lacked. It was wrong to say Ryōtora's surroundings *wanted* to draw out his spiritual essence, because there was no mind to have any such desire; instead it was like a roof collapsing when the supports below were gone. He had to fight to stay aloft, to keep himself whole.

Bit by bit, he was losing that battle.

He might have lost altogether if it weren't for Sekken. Ryōtora couldn't feel the other man's presence, not the way he could share in Tanshu's senses, but he knew that the bond between them was keeping him fed. What the dead cell stole away, Ryōtora could replace, drawing what he needed from Sekken.

For now. But how long would that last? How long could Sekken live, breathe, endure for them both?

And how long would Tōji leave him here?

She wanted his connection to the spirits. If he stayed in the dead cell too long, he wasn't at all sure he would *have* such a connection anymore. But that risk might be a lever he could use in bargaining: counter her offer of his freedom with his own demand, freedom for all the others as well. If she refused...

Would he have the strength to follow through on his own threat? To come back in here and wait to die?

*You did it once before,* he thought. Giving up everything he had to stop the Night Parade. To save not only the lives of those fighting with him in Seibo Mura but others elsewhere in the Empire – those who would be threatened if Nurarihyon escaped to wreak havoc once more.

And what will Tōji do, if she has your gift? Can you accept that risk in exchange for Sekken, for Sayashi, for Kuzu and Meirō?

Tōji was just a ghost. Not as dangerous as Nurarihyon, surely.

A ghost who could trade intangibles – and he still didn't know *how*. Nor what harm she might do with that ability.

He couldn't do it. The realization coalesced within him, hardening into a stone of conviction. Making that deal would ultimately be selfish, even if it wasn't only his own life and freedom he was bargaining for. He couldn't give more power to a creature who already exercised too much, just for the sake of those he cared about. Not when every instinct told him Tōji would use his surrendered gift for foul ends. If that meant his death, then so be it.

But he would not go down easily.

Sekken went back to the inn, in the slim hope that someone there might have a better plan than "wait for dawn, break into the palace, and pray for the best."

Tanshu padded up the stairs to check on Kuzu. In the main room, Sekken found the tea tsukumogami had returned to their inanimate state, laid out as if for a performance. When he touched the kettle, he felt a deep, soundless hum, like the kettle was chanting the primordial syllable *om*.

Two people in perfect synchrony were said to be sharing the breath of *om*. This, it seemed, was the assistance the tsukumogami had offered: the careful management of the connection between him and Ryōtora, so that he could sustain the other man without draining himself beyond the point of use. "Thank you," Sekken whispered, kneeling so he could bow fully to the tea implements.

When he rose and turned around, Meirō was there.

Sekken yelped and leapt back. A moment later he felt foolish – but Meirō had moved like a ghost, utterly soundless.

Surely a bit of alarm was an excusable reaction to finding an armed woman standing behind oneself.

Armed?

She was still dressed in her peasant disguise, still unmasked. In her left hand, though, she held a sheathed sword, which she most *definitely* had not been carrying the last time he'd seen her. Meirō had claimed her own weapons were back out in the normal world, and Sekken hadn't noticed any swordsmiths in either version of the market. Either she'd found a cooperative sword tsukumogami, or–

*Or,* he thought with gut-dropping shock, *a nemuranai*. Like they'd talked about right here in this inn, discussing whether the sacred sword at the shrine to the Fortune of Roads might be an awakened blade.

His mouth very dry, he said, "Please don't tell me you just stole that from the shrine."

Meirō offered him a shallow bow. "As you wish."

Which meant she *had*. Sekken swore, using all the creative vocabulary he could remember from his eldest sister. "After what happened to Sayashi?"

"The bakeneko got caught," Meirō said, with perfect equanimity. "I didn't."

When that reduced Sekken to wordless sputtering, she sighed, losing some of her polished calm. "Look, everything we've seen so far says we can't approach this problem politically. Tōji doesn't hold audiences and trade favors in exchange for releasing prisoners. That pile of crockery calling itself a general nearly skewered me when I offered a bribe. Since you're not going to leave Ryōtora to rot in prison, that means we're pretty much down to breaking him out by stealth or force.

"And you were right: I *am* a Scorpion. Which doesn't mean I scorn the law, or always lie and keep secrets, or cheat everybody simply because I can. It just means that I don't let lofty ideals or concern for my own reputation get in the way of doing what needs to be done. Given a choice between storming that palace unarmed, with a high likelihood of all of us being captured or dying, and stealing a sword so that we have something like a better chance…" Meirō shrugged and held up the blade. The rest didn't need to be said.

It was criminal, blasphemous, and reckless. And Sekken was also shamefully grateful she'd done it.

He exhaled slowly, then bowed to her. "For my words earlier, I apologize. I…"

"You were upset about the man you love being hauled away as a prisoner, and I was an available target. I'd rather you take it out on me than on Kuzu." Meirō paused, then added grudgingly, "And I *wasn't* prepared. Not for him being arrested, not for us entering the hidden market – not for any of it. The last point where I actually had my feet under me was when I arranged to be warned if someone showed up to reprimand me for ignoring my orders."

It seemed like a lifetime ago: Utaku Teruo, Koganshi Haizumi, Kakeguchi Botan sitting alone in the inn after Meirō fled. Ryōtora had sent one of the threshold charms to Teruo; what, if anything, had the man done with it? Did he have a priest on his staff – somebody more effective than Sir Nihei – who might investigate? Sekken entertained a brief vision of the cavalry riding in to save them all, no absurd heroics required on their part. Maybe literal cavalry, given that Teruo was from the Unicorn Clan.

But they couldn't wait around for that. He nodded at the sword Meirō held and said, "So, is it a nemuranai?"

She drew the blade. To Sekken's surprise, it wasn't a katana; instead it was a much older style, a straight-bladed chokutō. The grip was plain wood, much newer-looking than the blade itself, and the pommel was capped with a flat, openwork ring of metal surrounding a primitively shaped crane.

"Having never held a nemuranai," Meirō said, "I don't know whether this is one or not. It doesn't feel any different? More comfortable in my hand than it should be, given that I'm not used to swords like this, but that's all."

"May I?" Sekken asked, reaching out.

She hesitated almost imperceptibly before presenting it to him, hilt-first. Did she think he was still angry and might stab her? Sekken tilted the blade, as if the light reflecting off it might tell him anything. No sign of rust anywhere, but that might just be because the shrine's staff took good care of it, and the Fukiau family before them. "It certainly doesn't feel comfortable in *my* hand," he said, giving it back to Meirō.

"Spent a lot of time with swords, have you?" she asked dryly, sliding it back into its sheath.

"I prefer to fight my battles by other means," he replied. "But since you're right and I don't think we can get Ryōtora out of prison by negotiation or, shall we say, *courteous gifts* to the right people, I'll just have to accept that we're doing things your way."

That brief trace of levity bled out of her. "Then let's go scout the terrain," Meirō said. "Bring your dog."

•••

When the bolt holding the cell door shut thunked open, Ryōtora tensed and opened his eyes.

He'd been holding himself ready ever since he made his decision to resist. Mapping out the battlefield in his mind. They might take him to Tōji to give his answer. They might demand it here, and close the door or kill him if he refused. If removed from the cell, he would presumably be gagged again, then menaced by that jatai around his throat. Better to stall if he could, in the hope of some useful maneuver from Sekken… but if that failed, then he must make his stand here, while he still had the use of his voice.

He was prepared for every plausible eventuality.

Which did not include Sayashi being the one to open his cell door.

"Don't get your hopes up," she snapped. "I'm not here to rescue you."

She wasn't alone. The saddle creature was with her, and it laughed meanly. Sayashi gave it a sour look and added, "Tōji's given me orders not to let you out. I can't disobey. Not that this jumped-up horse cushion trusts me."

"Basic security," the saddle replied. "Two guards are better than one. If you try anything against me, priest, your *friend* here will be forced to stop you. And you won't try anything against her, will you? Not after all you've been through together."

Sayashi had admitted they knew each other? Ryōtora supposed that being caught standing with him outside the palace must have raised questions, but he would have expected her to offer no more information than she had to. She tended to be uncommunicative even with people she theoretically liked.

*Maybe Tōji didn't give her a choice,* he thought, sick at heart.

A sickness that grew when Sayashi raised a small clay bottle that sloshed as she waggled it at him. "Water. If you agree to Tōji's deal, I'm allowed to give this to you. If not…"

"Maybe I'll drink it in front of him," the tsukumogami said, grinning.

She glared at him, raising the bottle like a weapon. "Maybe I'll throw it at your head. Nothing stops me from hurting *you.*"

Everything in Ryōtora yearned toward the tantalizing splash of the water. He'd never known such raging thirst in his life. If he could have the bottle – even one sip–

The saddle warned him, "Don't try anything. In your state, you don't stand a chance of taking us both down at once."

He hadn't even been thinking about attack. Just the water, flooding his mouth, cascading down his throat – *oh, Fortunes, if I don't get something to drink…*

Could he agree to the deal, drink the water, then make his move? But the tsukumogami was right; he couldn't defeat them both at once, not weakened as he was. Certainly not without resorting to measures that would hurt Sayashi. He could be gentle or he could be quick, but both at once was beyond his capability. And Tōji had been right to send Sayashi. Any other creature, Ryōtora would have attacked without hesitation. But not someone he considered a friend.

Nor could he pretend to accept Tōji's offered trade. Not simply for reasons of integrity, but because he had no way of knowing whether that would bind him on the spot.

"I can't," he whispered. The words were halting, thick, his dry tongue sticking to the roof of his mouth. "No deal."

The saddle seemed unperturbed. "We'll see how you feel after a few more hours in there. Give me that water, cat."

Sayashi's lips peeled back in a snarl, but this time it wasn't directed at the tsukumogami. "You really are a soft-hearted fool," she growled at Ryōtora. "Too caught up in the net of your own ideals to do what needs to be done."

Did she really expect him to hand over the gift he'd received from the Heavens, just for his own safety? To a creature he didn't trust at all?

Ryōtora stared at Sayashi, and she stared back. Eyes wide and burning, as if by sheer force of will she could shoot a message out of them and into his brain. Biting off each word, she said, "I would be better off without friends."

Soft-hearted fool.

What needs to be done.

Without friends.

Did she really mean … ?

Yes, she did. And though Ryōtora didn't know how she expected this to succeed, he was desperate, and he trusted her. He gave a tiny, infinitesimal nod.

Without hesitation, Sayashi spun and flung the clay bottle at the tsukumogami, just like she'd threatened to do. But that was only the distraction; what followed was a whirlwind of black fur and teeth and claws, ripping and tearing so fast the saddle had no chance to react. It came apart with a shriek – and then, driven by her orders, Sayashi turned against Ryōtora.

He was ready for her. He'd risen to his feet and lurched toward the door, close enough to call on the Water spilled by the shattered bottle, on the little Water that remained in him, and the Air and the Fire and the Earth. They rose to his aid and struck out–

–and Sayashi dropped.

Ryōtora sagged against the far wall of the corridor, panting as if he'd climbed a mountain. The stone against his shoulder felt warm and alive by comparison with the dead cell. He mustered enough strength to hook the door's edge with one heel, shuddering from head to foot with relief when it swung shut.

But only for a moment. There was still a whole palace to escape. He was exhausted, his hands were manacled behind his back, and he had a friend the size of a leopard he somehow had to drag out of here.

It would be easier if he left Sayashi behind.

But she was right: he was a soft-hearted fool. She'd exploited a loophole in her orders to attack the other guard on his behalf, then trusted him to fight her for his escape. It was long past time someone stood at *her* side, in her moment of need.

Ryōtora knelt alongside Sayashi, facing away, and leaned backward until he could grab hold of her forepaws. By dint of falling forward into the wall, he managed to steady himself enough to rise to his feet, dragging the bakeneko's limp body behind him like a broken-wheeled cart.

Then, praying she wouldn't wake up too soon, praying he hadn't hurt her so badly she wouldn't wake up at all, he began staggering in search of escape.

"What happened?" Meirō demanded.

Sekken peeled himself off the wall outside the palace, feeling like someone had punched the wind out of him. "Ryōtora. He just – I don't know what he did. Used most of the strength he had left. But–"

When Sekken drew a deep breath, for the first time in many hours it felt clean and vital in his lungs. The dead, empty spot was gone. "I think he's out of that cell they put him in."

Out of the cell, and using what little reserves he had. Meirō made the same calculation Sekken did. "Damn it. He's trying to break out on his own."

They'd been circling the perimeter of the palace, seeking the best approach for breaking in. But all their plans had been built on the assumption that they'd make their move after dawn, when the yōkai were largely inert or asleep or whatever they became during the day. *Couldn't Ryōtora have waited a few more hours?*

It was a stupid question. Meirō had already backed up, studying the wall. "If I give you a boost–"

"I don't stand a chance," Sekken answered. "Tanshu–"

The inugami was already gone. Over the wall or through it; the difference hardly mattered. He was inside the palace, headed for Ryōtora, like a bead sliding along the string that joined the two men. "He'll lead him toward us," Sekken said.

Meirō's lips flattened in a grim line. "If Ryōtora's as weak as you say, he'll need more than a dog to help. Can I leave you here?"

"You have to."

She moved before he was done speaking, running at the wall and flinging herself up it in a fashion Sekken would have thought impossible. In a flash, she was over. The last thing he saw was the stolen sword, its sheath tied to her hip, scraping over the tiles that lined the top of the wall.

Sekken put his back to a neighboring building and slid cross-legged to the ground. Closing his eyes, he thought, *Go on, Ryōtora. Take whatever strength you need.*

Just come back to me.

# CHAPTER TWENTY-THREE

It was one hallucination after another.

He wasn't really stumbling through a badly built palace with his hands chained behind him, dragging a bakeneko that grew heavier with each step – why couldn't she have shrunk to housecat size after defeating the other yōkai? – while trying desperately to listen for sounds of other guards or monsters or the ghost who ruled this place.

That wasn't really Tanshu, materializing like magic out of nowhere just as his grip on the bakeneko slipped, sinking careful teeth into the scruff of the cat's neck and beginning to drag her in the wrong direction, not the direction he'd been going, why that way, fine, maybe the dog knew best.

Meirō wasn't really there, following not far behind Tanshu with a strange, straight-bladed sword in hand, looking in six directions at once, silencing him with a hand over his mouth when he tried to ask a question, leading him forward and then stopping him and then leading him through a gate, dodging threats he couldn't even see or hear because his head was full of mud.

And Sekken. Sekken sitting cross-legged in a narrow lane, Sekken leaping to his feet, Sekken flinging his arms around Ryōtora – and that was the moment it stopped feeling like a hallucination. Because his warm, wiry body was *real*. The bony fingers digging into Ryōtora's back were ten conduits of life, bringing him back to the world. Ryōtora was still exhausted, and he could feel Sekken's exhaustion, too… but he wasn't in the dead cell anymore. He'd escaped. And for a moment, there in Sekken's arms, he felt like he was safe at last.

Only for a moment. "We have to find somewhere to hide," Meirō said.

"We have to get Kuzu," Sekken said, sliding one arm around Ryōtora's waist for support. "And get these manacles off Ryōtora. Inn first. We'll think of our next step along the way."

Meirō led them, scouting the way with quick glances around corners, doing her best to keep them out of sight. Even if word of Ryōtora's escape hadn't yet spread from the palace, a man with his hands chained and a woman with a bakeneko draped over her shoulder like an outsized black towel would attract a great deal of attention.

But Ryōtora was *out*. The sheer relief of that would have made Sekken giddy if he couldn't feel the other man's weariness and weakness in every dragging step. What had happened to him in that cell? Now wasn't the time to ask, and Ryōtora was in no state to answer… but if Tōji had appeared in the alley right now, Sekken would gladly have taken Meirō's sword and stabbed her.

He was too occupied with those thoughts to pay much heed to their specific path. But when Meirō left them briefly in a shadowed corner, darted off, then returned with a couple of tools in her hand, the hidden market and the mundane one abruptly connected in his mind. "Are we near the shrine to the Fortune of Chisels?"

"It's not a shrine here," Meirō replied in a low voice, "but yes, that's why I led us this way. I got a hammer, too."

With Sekken's sash to muffle the blows, she was able to strike apart the chain joining Ryōtora's wrists, though not to remove the manacles entirely. Sekken wrapped the damaged fabric back around his waist and helped the other man up again. "Come on, we're almost there. Just a little farther." *And where will we go after that? Where can we find shelter from Tōji?* Ryōtora had been optimistic about his ability to break them out of the market, but that was before his imprisonment.

The ground floor of the inn was deserted save for the meditating tea tsukumogami, but from upstairs came the quiet murmur of voices. Although getting Ryōtora up the steps was hard, Sekken preferred that to leaving the man in the public rooms, where any crockery general who walked through the door could easily grab him. The voices were coming from the room Kuzu and Meirō shared, Kuzu's high, piping tone and another that sounded female – but not, as Sekken had assumed, like Elder Sister Noren.

Meirō heard the difference, too. After a swift glance at Sekken, she laid Sayashi's limp form very gently on the ground before drawing her blade soundlessly from its sheath. Her free hand crept out to grasp the edge of the door, then, in one smooth movement, she yanked it open and threw herself into the gap.

Kuzu squeaked and scuttled backward. Fuguruma Yōhi merely smiled, looking cadaverous in the light of the room's single lamp.

*What is she doing here?* Sekken didn't like that smile at all, and liked even less that the old woman had been alone with Kuzu. He remembered far too well the way she'd urged him to write a letter to Ryōtora; very suddenly, he was grateful that Kuzu was illiterate.

Especially since the old woman's book cart was there with her. If she was indeed the tsukumogami of that cart, she could hardly leave it behind, but the wheeled wooden box somehow managed to seem threatening.

"You didn't wait for dawn," Fuguruma Yōhi reproached Sekken.

"Ryōtora didn't wait for rescue," he said tersely. "How closely bound are you? Will you report us to Tōji?"

Kuzu had recovered from her surprise. The old woman reached out and stroked the girl's hair. "No, no. I'm busy. Little Kuzu here has agreed to write something for my cart. Only… she doesn't know how to write." Her rheumy, yellow eyes flicked up to Meirō, Ryōtora, landing at last on Sekken. "But I'm sure you could take dictation."

Tanshu growled softly. Sekken felt like growling himself. "She's not writing *anything* for you, with or without help."

"I want to," Kuzu said earnestly. "Grandmother here says she keeps all kinds of letters and diaries in her cart – hopeful ones, loving ones, sad ones. Anything people feel strongly about. I want to write a letter to my amo." Her narrow chin wobbled as she drew a wavering breath. "I- I want to tell her how much I miss her."

A thousand disastrous scenarios flashed through Sekken's mind: everything from that letter stripping Kuzu of the memory of her mother to it raising the woman's ghost from her probable grave. Addressing Fuguruma Yōhi instead of Kuzu, he said, "We're not going to play along."

"*Write the damn letter!*" the yōkai snarled, her face twisting in rage. "Her letter, your letter, one from that man you're propping up or the cat you came here for – I don't care who writes it, but this girl goes nowhere until I get one!"

"I'll do it," Ryōtora said in a bloodless whisper.

"Over my broken hands," Sekken shot back. "I'll do it."

Kuzu shot up and stamped her foot. "I said I want to! I'm the only person who cares enough to remember my amo, but if I put a letter about her into Grandmother's cart then at least there will be proof she was alive! She lived and she loved me and I want *somebody* to know that."

Tears traced gleaming lines down her face, and her hands were clenched into fists. Sekken's heart ached. At least when he died, there would be a memorial tablet with his name on it, set in the ancestral altar of Isawa Miyuki's children. He'd be listed among the students of his school, noted as the author of a few unremarkable works and as the man who'd helped stop the Night Parade. How much did an ordinary townswoman live on in memory after her death? Among her friends and family, yes... but Kuzu's amo had been so alone, there was no one to take care of her daughter after she was gone. Just one more commoner, valued only for the work she could do.

Ryōtora eased away from him, sinking down to the mat. Very quietly, Sekken said, "All right."

He wished he had better paper than what he kept tucked into his kimono, better ink than the stuff in his writing kit. But they had no time to go search the market for supplies, so he made do with what he had.

Kuzu tucked herself onto her knees, sitting with her hands clenched tight in her lap. "Amo," she whispered, and he wrote it down. "I miss you."

Her words drifted through the room, scarcely more substantial than the light. "I think about you every day. I wish you hadn't gone to the market that night. I wish stupid Hanbachi hadn't spilled his medicine. I- I told myself that you'd been taken by the market, because it meant I could pretend you were still alive. I told myself that so much, I even started to think it was true. That if I could find you, we'd go someplace together and be happy. I held on to that every day I was at the Reiya, because it meant I wouldn't be there forever. But…"

Her breath wavered. Sekken wet his brush again and waited.

"But it's not true," Kuzu said at last. "Something else happened to you. Maybe I'll never know what. I just know that if you were alive, you would've come back to me by now. So I- I- I'm going to have to be strong on my own. I'll try to do what you would have wanted, amo. But I'll never stop missing you. I love you."

Her words gave way to quiet sobs. After a moment, the broken links of the manacles clinked as Ryōtora shifted across the tatami; when Sekken looked up, he found Kuzu crying into the other man's shoulder. Her letter was done.

He waited until the ink had dried, then folded it and looked at Fuguruma Yōhi. The old woman's face no longer looked demonic in the lamplight. She said softly, "The girl should give it to me herself."

Kuzu roused enough to hold out her hand. Sekken gave her the paper. She presented it to Fuguruma Yōhi with both hands, sliding it forward on the mat.

With a long, shuddering sigh, the yōkai accepted it, then turned toward her cart. Leaning close to the panels, she said, "Well, they're none too bright, and who knows if they'll manage anything useful. But we get so few visitors nowadays, I think we might have to take the chance. It's your choice, though."

She slid open the cart's wooden side. Tanshu came abruptly to his feet – but not in defense. His ears pricked up like they'd caught an unexpected sound.

As Fuguruma Yōhi placed Kuzu's letter in the cart, something else came unfurling out.

A scroll of paper and ink, long and sinuous like a dragon, with more scrolls forming its arms and wrapping around it like a robe. It rose up nearly to the height of the ceiling before subsiding, like a cat stretching after a long sleep.

"At last," it breathed, its voice as dry and papery as its form. "I've been waiting."

Ryōtora didn't have a name for what he was looking at, but its deep spiritual aura told him this was no common tsukumogami. Chains clinking, he placed his hands on the mat and bowed. "Have we freed you from prison?"

"From safety," the old woman said, sounding annoyed. "I put him in my cart to protect him from Tōji. But I can only open it when someone gives me something to put in there, and do you know how rarely anyone comes into this market now with strong enough feelings to be worth me adding them to my treasures? And none of you would oblige! Your stubborn cat friend refused me, and *you* refused me, and even your ink-stained lover there refused me – only this girl was kind enough to help!"

Tiredness assisted Ryōtora in keeping his reply behind his teeth. *If you had told us why you wanted it...* But yōkai behaved according to their own inscrutable logic. Scraping together the dregs of his energy, he said, "Please forgive our ignorance. Who is it that you have been protecting?"

"I am a kyōrinrin," the paper creature replied. "And I am a sutra of the Fortune of Fate."

A shiver chased across Ryōtora's skin. When he looked at Sekken, the other man's eyes were wide. Choosing his words with visible care, Sekken said, "I regret to say that I know nothing of the Fortune of Fate."

"Of course you do not," the kyōrinrin said, sounding tired. "My lord has been held captive for many long years."

Now the shiver became an outright jolt. "Captive?" Ryōtora whispered, horrified. "Who could—"

"Tōji," Meirō said, her voice flat. "I presume."

The kyōrinrin bowed in rustling acknowledgment. "As she calls herself now. Yoshimi is her true name."

Hadn't Ryōtora felt it, when he prayed to the spirits outside the palace? Something binding Sayashi – a power no ghost should be able to wield. It had felt more like a Fortune's hand upon her.

"Tōji did more than just capture your lord, didn't she?" he said to the kyōrinrin. "She somehow usurped his role."

The old woman spat, not just a noise, but an actual gobbet of saliva onto the tatami, making Sekken cringe. "*Lady of the Market.* She usurped more than just that."

Her words apparently helped Sekken forget his disgust. "Wait. This has been bothering me ever since... how do you write *yōhi*?"

What shreds of quick-wittedness remained between the

two of them had clearly gone to Sekken, because Ryōtora couldn't follow his sudden concern with language. "Why does that matter?"

"Chirizuka Kaiō," Sekken said, his finger tracing invisible characters on the straw of the mat. "Strange king of the garbage heap – I saw how Sayashi wrote that one. Fuguruma Yōhi –" He gestured at the old woman. "*Fuguruma* is her book cart. *Yō* could be the same character as in *yōkai*. But the *hi*... is that the character that means 'queen'?"

"It is," the kyōrinrin replied. "I will say what neither she nor her husband can: that they are the rightful rulers of this market. Not Yoshimi."

Proudly, the old woman said, "The things people throw away, and the attachments they can't let go of. That's us."

Those monstrous-seeming creatures? But beauty and ugliness had no bearing on morality, and Ryōtora supposed nothing said the rightful rulers of the market had to be good in the first place. And Chirizuka Kaiō had been helpful to them, after a fashion. No wonder Sayashi had said she wasn't sure if he was loyal to Tōji.

"I love history and linguistic puzzles as much as anyone," Meirō said, sounding utterly insincere, "but we have more immediate concerns. Sayashi needs treatment, you and Ryōtora both need rest, and we all need a safe place to hole up, where Tōji – Yoshimi – can't get at us. I presume these noble yōkai want us to overthrow her and free the Fortune, but none of that's going to happen if we get arrested en masse by General Uebe and his minions."

Far too cheerfully, Fuguruma Yōhi agreed, "You're right about that."

"But where can we go?" Sekken asked. "If Tōji has control of the market, backed by the stolen power of a Fortune… is there anywhere here that's safe?"

Meirō said dryly, "Inside that cart, apparently. But it would be a little cramped for all four of us. Five, if you count the dog. Six, if you count the cat."

Ryōtora turned to the kyōrinrin. "You seem to be free of Tōji's influence. Can you protect us?"

It folded its paper arms in a regretful bow. "So long as she holds my lord, I must obey her. Even more than others in the market must do. I hid in order to keep her from taking advantage of that."

Then, just as Ryōtora's heart was completing its sinking, the creature added, "But it is possible that Enjiki could help you."

"Enjiki?" Sekken echoed, coming alert like Tanshu. "Why do I know that name?"

"It was on the travel permits you got from the shrine," Meirō said. "The 'Keeper of the Threshold.'"

Sekken was practically vibrating. "No, not that – I mean, yes, that, but – the threshold! When I rescued Tanshu and the broom started yelling, that was the name it shouted, warning him that we were escaping!" His rapid volley of words halted; then he blinked and looked at the kyōrinrin. "So why him? Who exactly is Enjiki?"

Fuguruma Yōhi answered. "The one person Tōji can't go near," she said. "The man she loves."

# CHAPTER TWENTY-FOUR

"I'll be fine," Meirō said, for the third time. "It's almost funny, how concerned you are for my safety, when a few days ago you were ready to take me prisoner."

Sekken appreciated the irony, too, but it didn't make him any less worried about sending Meirō out to be a distraction. Yet what other choice did they have? They couldn't afford to wait for the streets to empty at dawn; the odds were too high that someone would come looking for them before then. And their group was far too large and unwieldy to hope they'd make it all the way to Enjiki's house by stealth alone. They needed a diversion, and when Sekken had suggested using Tanshu, Meirō feigned offense. "You'd rather send a dog than a Scorpion? Or do you doubt my skills that much?"

It wasn't her skills Sekken doubted. He was worried about what interpretation Meirō might be placing on the poem that rural oracle had spoken. *A scorpion's fate* – it didn't have to mean death, especially now that they knew the Fortune of Fate was involved in this business. But she'd thrown away her entire career to follow up on that oracle's words; if she made it out of the hidden market alive, she was almost certain to be dismissed from her position, and she might face harsher penalties than that. Even Scorpion were capable of deciding they preferred death to disgrace.

He couldn't put any of that into words, though. All he said was, "How will we know when to move?"

Meirō grinned. "You'll know."

Then she was out the door and into the night. Sekken closed his eyes and drew a deep breath, trying to find some well of unused energy inside his body and mind. He wanted desperately to sleep. There wasn't even any promise of rest once they got to Enjiki's house.

*The man Tōji loves.* Clearly there was a whole tale there, lighting a burning candle of curiosity in Sekken's mind, but they couldn't linger around here for its performance. One thing at a time, and their most pressing need was for safety.

From somewhere outside came an unholy crash, followed by shouting. Sekken wondered what Meirō had done, and hoped he'd get a chance to ask. For now... "Let's go."

An inugami, a scholar carrying an unconscious bakeneko, and a priest propped up on one side by a skinny peasant girl, on the other by an animated sutra. Sekken felt almost like an illustration of the Night Parade of a Hundred Demons – one drawn by an artist who thought the whole thing an amusing jape, rather than a threatening reality. Tanshu was their scout, as good as Meirō at checking to see if the way was clear before leading the others down an alley or across an intersection. The shouting had grown louder, more yōkai hurrying to see what was going on, and was that a *glow* Sekken saw over the rooftops? He prayed to the Fortunes that Meirō hadn't lit the market on fire, deliberately or accidentally. In a city like this, that would be a greater peril than Tōji's stolen power.

They made it to the alley behind the house, and Sekken realized their *other* problem. Someone had moved the crate he'd stood on before to get over the fence, and even with its help, he wasn't sure he had the energy to climb.

"This is it?" Kuzu whispered – the first words she'd spoken since dictating her letter to Sekken. Before Tanshu could do more than square off with the fence like he was preparing to do battle with an old enemy, Kuzu climbed it as nimbly as a monkey. At the top she paused and asked, "What should I say?"

All eloquence had deserted Sekken. *Apologize to the broom for me* – that hardly seemed like a useful answer. The kyōrinrin said, "Tell him we come in the sacred, unspoken name of the Fortune of Fate."

Kuzu vanished over the fence. Sekken sagged against it, wishing he could put Sayashi down, but knowing that if he did, he would never muster the strength to pick her up again. What had Ryōtora done to her? The other man had given a very incomplete and confusing account of what happened in the palace, from which Sekken had mostly gathered that Sayashi *wanted* Ryōtora to attack her. All well and good as far as it went, but now they couldn't wake her. It wasn't good for a human being to be unconscious this long, and Sekken doubted it was good for a bakeneko, either.

A *clack-clack-clack* from around the corner made him haul himself upright. Something was coming.

Something that proved to be a broom, hopping along on its handle end – a broom that stopped dead when it saw their group. "You!" the hahakigami said, looking at Tanshu, and then its gaze went to Sekken. "And *you*!"

"Apologies for my previous intrusion," Sekken said wearily. "And for this one. I – ah – can explain?"

The broom's bristles made for a ferocious scowl, but all it said was, "You'd better explain inside. Come in the front door this time, like a civilized intruder."

It was a relief to finally lay Sayashi on the floor, though not a relief to see her complete lack of response to being hauled around like a sack of rice. Sekken slumped down next to her, Ryōtora following him a moment later. He couldn't even muster the energy to bow when a man entered the room – a man he'd seen asleep upstairs, the day Sekken broke into the house.

"You must be Enjiki," Sekken said. "At least, I hope you are."

"And you," Enjiki said, mouth thin, "are the man who promised me he wasn't going to give one of my charms to a priest."

His words didn't make sense at first. Enjiki seemed no older than forty at most; the man who'd sold the charms had been ancient, shriveled, his features nearly lost amid the deep wrinkles of his face. But when Sekken stared at him, imagining that face crumpling in on itself with age…

"How?" he whispered. "Or – why? Were you disguised, or is *this* a disguise, or–"

Enjiki sighed. "It's a long tale. One that, I think, you shouldn't be forced to sit through right now." He ushered Kuzu forward with one gentle hand and said, "From what this girl tells me, you've all been through a great deal."

Ryōtora roused enough to ask, "If you're the one who let us in here, can you let us out? Back into the ordinary world?"

"We can't leave," Sekken said immediately. "Not without Meirō. And the problems here–"

"Are things we might be able to address better if we regrouped outside," Ryōtora said. "We could talk to Lord Utaku. Find a priest other than Sir Nihei to consult with. Come back when we're ready."

Enjiki had knelt to examine Sayashi. Over his shoulder, he said, "I could let you out, yes. But I was gambling when I sold you those charms, hoping you'd be able to fix matters here. Now that you've caused so much trouble, Tōji's minions would likely be waiting for you the moment you came through the gate." He hesitated. "And... your friend here is in no state to make that journey."

"Are you a physician?" Sekken asked.

"An apothecary," Enjiki murmured. "A long time ago."

Exhaustion had drained Ryōtora's cheeks pale, and now guilt dragged his head down. "I'm responsible for her injuries. At her request, after a fashion, but she's bound to serve Tōji."

"That explains a great deal." Enjiki gathered the bakeneko into his arms and stood. "I will see to her. Give me a moment."

He vanished deeper into the house, leaving the two men and Kuzu with the hahakigami. The broom watched Sekken untrustingly. Sekken was too tired to care. Enjiki had hoped they'd fix the problems in the market? All they'd accomplished so far was nearly getting Ryōtora and Sayashi both killed.

By the time Enjiki came back, Ryōtora had dozed off, right there on the wooden floor. Sekken wanted to join him. Eyeing the sleeping priest, Enjiki said, "I can't carry him up the stairs."

Neither could Sekken. "Come on, Ryōtora," he said, nudging the other man. "Just a little farther."

"You said that last time," Ryōtora mumbled, exhaustion slurring the words almost into unintelligibility.

"Yes, well, this time it's true. I hope."

Maybe he shouldn't have added that last part. But Ryōtora was nothing if not determination on two legs; he forced himself upright, and together they lurched up the stairs to the room whose window Sekken had climbed through before. The futon was narrow, made for only one occupant, and there was only one pillow, but neither of them cared. Sekken gave Ryōtora the pillow, folded his chisel-slashed sash under his own head as a replacement, and squirmed around only enough to move the broken end of a manacle chain from under his hip before he was out.

Ryōtora woke to find that Sekken's usual restlessness had removed him entirely from the futon. He now sprawled across the mat, head pillowed on one arm, still firmly asleep.

The only reason Ryōtora had woken before him was the manacles on his wrists. They and their dangling fragments of chain were irritatingly heavy and cold – and a reminder of the dead cell. Or maybe Ryōtora would have had nightmares of that prison regardless.

Sunlight streamed through the open window, helping to banish the shadows of memory, but Ryōtora couldn't judge the angle. Was it morning? Afternoon? Whatever the answer, the light was reassuring. Dawn had come without Tōji's people finding them; they were likely safe until sunset.

But that didn't leave them much time to find answers.

He tried to rise quietly, but something – the rustle of his clothes; the faint clink of the chains; the shift of his shadow across the floor – woke Sekken. Yawning prodigiously, he said, "The world truly is upside down, when you're up before I am."

"Everything's upside down," Ryōtora said softly. *Ghosts taking on the power of Fortunes...*

Sekken stretched like a cat, then glanced around, frowning. "Where's Tanshu?"

An embarrassingly loud grumble came from Ryōtora's stomach. Sekken grinned, a faint echo of his usual humor. "And where's food? Let's find out."

Ryōtora was still tired as he followed Sekken down the stairs, but not half so exhausted as he'd expected to be. When they got to the ground floor, they found the answer to one of their questions: Tanshu was on his back, paws in the air, submitting to a good belly-rub from their host. *Enjiki,* Ryōtora thought, studying the man. *Keeper of the Threshold. But what does that mean? Who is this man?*

Enjiki had been smiling at Tanshu, but it faded as he glanced up at the two men. Not hostile, just the weight of many cares settling on him again. "Up at last? Good. I didn't want to rouse you, but you've not much time before sunset."

"Thank you for your hospitality," Ryōtora said, bowing. "I should have thanked you last night, but I fear I was in no fit state for it."

"Did anyone else come while we were asleep?" Sekken asked. "A woman, dressed as a peasant – well, she was the last time we saw her, but she might have changed clothes. Likely carrying a sword, and..."

He trailed off, seeing Enjiki shake his head. Meirō

hadn't come. Ryōtora had only the faintest memory of the conversation with her last night, but it was enough to worry him. What if Meirō had been captured? Would she be locked in the dead cell, even though she wasn't a priestess?

Those thoughts must have shown, because Sekken laid a reassuring hand on his arm. "Meirō's resourceful. She may just have gone to ground."

Even in the daytime? Before Ryōtora could say that, his stomach spoke up again, making him flush with embarrassment. Diplomatically, Sekken said to Enjiki, "Tōji had him locked in a special cell, and I'm fairly certain she didn't feed him. Do you have anything he might eat?"

"Unfortunately, no." Enjiki patted Tanshu's belly one last time and straightened. "I don't need food anymore. But if you're willing to send your girl Kuzu out, there's a noodle shop not far away that she could raid."

"Will that be dangerous?" Ryōtora asked.

"In the daytime, probably not. The tsukumogami don't rouse unless provoked."

Sekken rubbed the back of his neck, laughing awkwardly. "Yes, your broom friend. I do apologize for that. Again. Did I remember to say that last night?"

Ryōtora knelt on the wooden floor and said, "I can do without food for now. Answers are more important. Please forgive my rudeness in prying, but… You said you sold the charms in the hopes that we might address matters here. We've been told that Tōji, Yoshimi, has great affection for you, and yet she cannot come near you. We also know that she has usurped the role of a Fortune. But between these things, many pieces are missing."

"Great affection." Enjiki exhaled. "I suppose she saw it that way. Maybe I did, too, once."

"How do you see it now?" Sekken asked, settling at Ryōtora's side.

"Obsession," their host said bluntly. "Possessiveness. Unwillingness to accept change. All of these things and more."

He began to pet Tanshu again, as if to give his hands something to do. "You know Yoshimi is a ghost?" At their nods, he said, "We knew each other in life. Loved each other, I suppose. I was the son of an apothecary; she was the daughter of a sandal-maker. Had things gone well ..."

When the pause stretched out too far, Sekken murmured, "What went wrong?"

"Many things." Enjiki's gaze had gone distant. "But what broke everything was my father falling sick and dying. Ironic, isn't it – an apothecary meeting his end that way? It left us in debt, and I had three younger siblings to care for, my father's business to maintain, his employees and students to look after. I couldn't put Yoshimi ahead of all those other people. I had to marry someone who could help me take care of everyone else – not just with money, but with hard work. Yoshimi was never much for either of those things."

Ryōtora thought back to the woman he'd met in the palace. Yes, he could see the roots of that tree in Enjiki's description.

Their host's voice strengthened, shaking off the mists of that distant past. "I don't know what exactly Yoshimi did. I wasn't there to see all of it. I don't know if she committed suicide and thereby wound up in the market – she threatened to drown herself, when I told her I wouldn't marry her – or if she found her way here and then died, or if her death came later still.

And I don't know how she wound up with the power of a Fortune. But I'm sure that my own passage into the market was her doing. And when we came face to face..."

His hand had gone still on Tanshu's back. The dog huffed softly and laid his head on Enjiki's knee.

"She told me we would never be parted," Enjiki said. "That she would bind us together not only in this life, but in all our lives to come. I- I tried to tell her that would be true anyway, that true lovers always come together again. But I didn't mean it. I was just trying to persuade her to let me go. Maybe she could tell, or maybe she just didn't trust the Fortunes. Either way..."

He shuddered, glancing around. "I ran. I could feel whatever she was doing chasing me. I was here when it caught me, and I've been here ever since. I can't leave. I can't die. The version of me that faces out into the world gets older and older, aging more than any human ever should; the version of me that's here never changes. There is no Fortune here, only me. I'm the Keeper of the Threshold because that's where I'm trapped: on the threshold between the ordinary world and this one, between life and death."

The flat resignation of that statement was almost as awful as the dead cell. *How long has he been caught here?* Ryōtora wondered, shuddering at the idea. Though the number hardly mattered. From the sound of it, Enjiki had more than lived out an ordinary lifespan. His soul should long since have gone to its judgment in the underworld and returned to face a new rebirth.

As should Yoshimi's. But if she could trap Enjiki here, Ryōtora doubted his own prayers would be able to banish her like an ordinary ghost.

Sekken's mind had already gone to work on the problem. "Why can't Tōji come here? Is it that she's *incapable* of it, or that she fears to do so?"

"We've never tested it," Enjiki said. "Kanbōki – the broom you met – thinks there's a risk that if she approaches the threshold, we'll go over it together. She'll likely haunt me for lifetimes to come, but at least she would be out of the hidden market. Maybe she would even leave her stolen power behind; Kanbōki hopes so. If you ask me, though, I think she just doesn't want to see me. She knows I don't love her anymore, and she can't bring herself to face it."

"Any chance we could trick Tōji into entering this place?" Sekken asked. "Put your broom friend's theory to the test?" When Enjiki shook his head, Sekken sighed. "I thought not. But I had to ask."

There was only one answer – one that unfortunately came with a great many questions attached. "Yoshimi has committed profound blasphemy," Ryōtora said. "And all her control hinges on a power that should not be hers. We have to take that power back."

From behind him came the papery voice of the kyōrinrin. "You have to free my lord."

The scrolling body of the sutra rustled into the room like a snake, followed by the broom spirit. Tanshu growled very softly at Kanbōki, and Sekken said, "If you don't mind my asking, Enjiki – why did you imprison my inugami, anyway? You weren't mistreating him, I know, so why lock him up?"

Enjiki looked at the broom, whose bristles scowled. "All right," Kanbōki said. "It was my idea. I thought, if we could convince the dog to help us, it might sneak into the palace and steal the thing Tōji has the Fortune trapped in. But that beast refused to cooperate."

A spark of hope flared inside Ryōtora. "What did she use to trap him?"

"We don't know," Enjiki admitted. "We hoped the dog would be able to tell."

That made the plan even longer of a shot than it would have been in the first place… but in Enjiki's shoes, Ryōtora might have been just as willing to grasp at straws. When he glanced at Sekken, the other man was busy thinking. "Boxes," he said. "A paper inscription, maybe. There's a story of a malevolent kitsune whose soul got trapped in a rock, but that took a priest's doing. I don't suppose Tōji has the gift of speaking to the spirits?"

Nausea twisted in Ryōtora's gut. "She doesn't," he said, before Enjiki could respond. "But that's what she wanted from me. She offered to free me, if I would trade my ability to her."

All the blood drained from Sekken's face. He didn't even erupt in curses or protest; Ryōtora's words had left him speechless. Softly, Ryōtora added, "I was going to refuse. Knowing what I do now… under no circumstances will I help her gain more power."

The kyōrinrin said, "She would need to have my lord's prison close at hand when she makes her deals."

Ryōtora tried to remember what Tōji had with her when they met. But he'd just come out of the dead cell then; he hadn't been at his most alert. And Tōji might very well keep the object hidden until she was ready to use it. Which meant…

"*Sayashi*," Sekken said, and popped to his feet with enviable vigor. "Is she awake? Can we talk to her?"

"She is… resting," Enjiki said cautiously. "I have her in the room where your inugami was kept, in case she felt compelled to return to Tōji. But since it seems she's under no such orders, you should be able to speak with her."

They found the bakeneko in her cat form, small at first, but growing to larger size as soon as they entered. Ryōtora sank to his knees before she was done shifting. "I am so sorry for hurting you. I should never have gotten myself imprisoned in the first place, then you would not have had to take such a risk."

Sayashi's lip peeled back from her formidable teeth. "No, you shouldn't have." Her tail lashed, then, grudgingly, she added, "But I shouldn't have gotten myself trapped, either. So we're both stupid."

It wasn't forgiveness – but Ryōtora neither expected nor wanted that. Instead he said, "We have a thought that might free you from Tōji's service… and do a good deal more."

She listened as they explained the situation and what they sought. At the question of what object might imprison the Fortune, she said, "I didn't see much. Tōji had me facing the floor for most of the time. It could have been something tucked inside her kimono, or on the table next to her – too many possibilities."

Ryōtora's heart sank. That meant falling back on his other, less appealing idea. "If it contains a captive Fortune," he said, "I suspect I'll be able to find it. But doing that will require me to ask the spirits for help."

Sekken tried to look optimistic. "Well, if we destroy the object right afterward, that will break Tōji's control, right? Everybody who's forced to obey her will be free?"

"Perhaps," the kyōrinrin said, sounding far less than sure.

"Even if we aren't that lucky," Ryōtora said, "it's still the only right course of action. The Fortune *must* be released. No mortal soul should hold such a being captive."

Sekken nodded in sober agreement. "In that case… Enjiki, how long until sunset?"

"No more than an hour."

"Then we'd better act quickly," Sekken said. The grin he offered Ryōtora was lopsided. "I hope this won't offend your sensibilities too much, but I think we have to take a cue from our absent Scorpion friend. We need to sneak into the palace."

# CHAPTER TWENTY-FIVE

Ryōtora wasn't happy about breaking into Tōji's palace, but the underhandedness of the approach was the least of his reasons.

He wished they had more daylight left, so they could search for likely candidates for the Fortune's prison by mundane means before he had to resort to prayers. He wished he and Sekken could have rested for longer before attempting this, and that he could have eaten something more than a handful of mochi balls stolen on their way through the streets. He wished Meirō was with them.

He wished Sayashi *weren't* with them.

The bakeneko had insisted, though, scoffing at the notion that "a pure-hearted priest and a scholar with ink for brains" could manage without her help. Ryōtora was worried about lingering effects from what he'd done to her, but he was even more worried about what would happen if Sayashi came anywhere near the Lady of the Market. Whether she wanted to or not, their ally might transform into an enemy without so much as a tail-flick of warning.

But Sayashi had smelled that Tōji was a ghost. She and Tanshu stood a chance of finding the Fortune's prison, and failing that, they would serve as excellent guards. And she was right: he and Sekken needed her help breaking in.

She knew where they could climb the wall, well away from the komainu that guarded the front gate. She knew where in the palace Tōji had her private quarters, the most likely location for the object they sought. She even knew which floorboards and stair steps were liable to squeak, muttering something under her breath about being far more intimately familiar with them than she wanted to be.

They passed very few yōkai. A quiver of arrows leaned next to a door, which Ryōtora no longer assumed was just an object someone had left lying about; he noted with a shiver that it bore the same crest as the saddle-creature Sayashi had torn apart. Sekken was able to slide the door open one silent finger-length at a time, and they crept through with the guard none the wiser. A gong hung on the wall near the stairs, but by avoiding the bottom step they were able to pass it without triggering any creak that might wake it.

At the top of the stairs, though…

Ryōtora grabbed both Sekken and Sayashi by the sleeves. When they turned to look at him – Sekken with concern, Sayashi with a glare – he nodded upward. Draped above the door to Tōji's quarters was a length of cloth he recognized all too well: the jatai that had stood ready to strangle him when he met with the Lady of the Market.

The way the ends of the sash dangled, they couldn't slide the door open without disturbing it.

Sayashi scowled and nodded her head to the right. Together

they went out onto the upstairs veranda, where another door gave access to Tōji's quarters. This one had no guard on it – at least, none they could see. They had no way of knowing if something waited inside, perhaps leaning up against the panel, ready to fall and wake if the door moved.

Or rather, *Ryōtora* had no way of knowing. Sekken looked at Tanshu. They'd wrapped bits of cloth around his paws to muffle the click of his nails against the floorboards; now he padded forward and sniffed carefully at the door. He wagged his tail encouragingly, and Sayashi eased the door open.

No creature began shouting an alarm. Leading the way, Ryōtora stepped into Tōji's quarters.

He waited a moment to let his eyes adjust to the dimness. Like the room he'd met Tōji in before, this one was decorated more with an eye toward ostentatious display than any kind of taste. The folding screens that divided the space were painted with clashing scenes. The chests of drawers were lacquered and fitted with gold, the shelves crowded with precious objects. And, he realized with a sinking heart, not only could any one of those things be the Fortune's prison... any one of them could be a tsukumogami.

Anything they touched in here might betray them.

Not moving from his spot, Ryōtora scanned the room, hoping something might stand out. Too many objects competed for his attention: jade sculptures, porcelain bowls, boxes of precious wood. When he glanced toward a pair of panels at one end of the room, painted with a dragon and a tiger locked in mortal combat, Sayashi placed her hands next to her cheek and mimed sleeping. So Tōji was behind those doors... and with her, quite possibly the Fortune's prison.

Waiting would only increase the danger, as sunset drew ever closer. Would Tōji awake the moment the sun dipped below the horizon? Praying she was a late sleeper – and praying the doors weren't sentient – Ryōtora stepped noiselessly across the floor and slid the panels open.

The room beyond was far more austere than the outer chamber. Just a low chest of drawers, its top littered with cosmetics pots and brushes, and a futon…

…that held no occupant.

Ryōtora froze. Where was Tōji?

*She's a ghost,* he thought, suddenly appalled by his own foolishness. Unlike the tsukumogami, she wouldn't revert to the form of some object during the daytime. She might let her subjects believe she slept, the better for them to forget her dead state, but in truth, she would simply vanish.

If Tōji wasn't here at all…

*Then we're free to act. Even if we wake something, she can't respond.* The general or some other warlike yōkai might, but Ryōtora and his allies should be able to hold such creatures off – at least for the precious few minutes he might need to find and destroy the prison.

But they'd wasted so much time already, creeping about with silent care. Bringing his hands together, Ryōtora began to pray.

Only to hear Sayashi yowl, "My lady! My lady, the humans are here!"

Everything happened too fast.

Every piece of porcelain in the room rattled and flew together, assembling itself into the hateful form of General

Uebe. The folding screens leapt to guard the misty shape coalescing in midair. The door they'd avoided smacked open and the sash shot through like an arrow, heading straight for Ryōtora.

Without thinking, Sekken flung himself on the fabric, knocking it to the ground. The jatai writhed in his hands like a snake, except that both ends seemed equally dangerous; one wrapped around his wrist and yanked his arm behind his back. As Sekken fought to free himself, he heard Sayashi shouting at Tōji. "My lady, they came here to find their Scorpion friend – they meant to threaten you and force you to release her–"

*That's not true,* Sekken thought. It broke his attention for one crucial heartbeat: something struck him across the head, and as fire flashed through his brain, the jatai let him go.

When his vision cleared, he found the battle was over – if it had ever really started. The sash had Ryōtora in its grip now, binding his arms and his mouth, wrapping tightly enough around his throat that Ryōtora's face was turning red. The futon from the unused bedchamber had pinned Tanshu to the floor. And General Uebe himself stood by Sekken, razor-sharp fingers poised like knives to cut him apart.

Tōji had finished manifesting within her protective ring of screens. Sayashi was still babbling lies, a flood of words Sekken realized was designed to keep Tōji from asking questions. All the Lady of the Market had to do was say, *tell me what they intend to do,* and Sayashi would presumably be forced to spill everything. They never should have brought her along... and yet, without her help, would they have even gotten this far?

Ryōtora thrashed helplessly for air. "Let him go!" Sekken shouted. Sheer desperation made him reach out, trying to grab one end of the jatai. General Uebe's hand came down and carved four bloody lines across his arm.

But at a lift of Tōji's hand, the jatai eased its hold. In a high, thin voice, she said, "How noble of you, coming here to free your friend."

Tōji was the Lady of the Market, ruling over all the tsukumogami within its walls. She was clever enough to imprison a Fortune. She was surrounded by allies.

She was not, however, a very good liar.

*Meirō isn't here.* That epiphany doused Sekken in relief. He didn't know where she was, but Tōji didn't have her. Yet he couldn't simply tell Ryōtora: right now, their safety depended on Tōji continuing to believe they'd broken into the palace for the Scorpion. If her attention drifted from that, she might guess far more than they wanted her to.

But her thoughts were on other dangerous things. "I once offered you your freedom in exchange for your connection to the spirits," Tōji said. "I wonder. Would you give it to me for *her* freedom?"

The jatai unclamped from Ryōtora's mouth. In a hoarse voice, the priest said, "For all of us. Promise to let us all go… and yes. I'll give you my gift."

"No!" Sekken cried. An idiotic objection, born of pure reflex, outrunning his common sense. But it served them well, making Ryōtora's offer seem more genuine.

An offer that Sekken, once he had a moment to think, had no doubt was thoroughly calculated. The kyōrinrin had told them Tōji would need the Fortune's prison on hand to make any such deal. Ryōtora was trying to draw that object out into the open.

But then what? Could Ryōtora destroy it before any of the yōkai reacted? Sekken prayed with wordless fervor that he could.

Tōji drifted into her bedchamber and sat down in front of the chest of drawers there, opening pots of rice flour and charcoal to paint her face. "All of you?" she said, making a show of reluctance. "When you've intruded on my quarters like this? Not to mention the damage you did when you broke out before."

"All of us," Ryōtora rasped. "You will grant safe passage out of the hidden market for myself, Asako Sekken, Bayushi Meirō, Kuzu, the inugami Tanshu – and the bakeneko Sayashi."

Sayashi jerked in surprise. Tōji stopped her preparations, expression hardening. "She swore herself to me for a century."

"And you will release her from that oath. When will you have another chance to make a deal like this one? You have a ban against priests in your market; you might wait a century for another one to appear."

Annoyed, Tōji yanked open one of the drawers and took out a polished silver mirror. Holding it up so she could inspect her face, she let the silence stretch out as she considered Ryōtora's terms.

All of Sekken's attention was on the mirror.

There were plenty of stories about such things. That kitsune who'd wound up trapped in a rock had been exposed by a mirror that showed her human form to be a lie. Others were said to reflect the truth in a more subtle way, warping the viewer's appearance to signal their inner virtues and flaws.

But above all, mirrors supposedly had the ability to trap spirits.

He caught Ryōtora's gaze, then directed his own urgently toward the mirror in Tōji's hand.

The other man knew better than to nod or give some other sign of acknowledgment, but his lips began moving soundlessly. Sekken willed his own strength to the priest, not caring if it caused his own collapse, so long as that mirror got destroyed–

But the jatai realized what was happening, and it clamped down on Ryōtora's throat.

Sekken screamed. Before he could move, General Uebe slammed him backward, knocking all the air from him. Sekken saw those knife-like fingers coming down–

–and then he wasn't there. Sekken was abruptly in a different part of the room, pinned underneath a futon that had been lured into complacence by his lack of resistance.

He bit the futon and flung it off himself. In three bounds he was across the room, past the choking Ryōtora to where Tōji sat, mirror in hand. He got the briefest glimpse of Tanshu's furry face before he snapped his jaws shut on the mirror, biting as hard as he could, fighting to dent or scratch its surface and cursing the need for stealth that had wrapped his paws – Tanshu's paws – with cloth.

Tōji shrieked and fought back, trying to wrench the mirror from his mouth. Then her shriek became a snarl of fury, and he felt the silver between his teeth buzz and spark like lightning.

With a snap like breaking bone, the connection broke. Sekken was back in his own body, bleeding where General Uebe had slashed him again, and he couldn't feel Tanshu anymore.

At all.

The loss gutted him – but Tōji, devoting her attention to the severing of that link, had made the wrong choice. Tanshu didn't need Sekken's presence in his mind and body to act. In Tōji's moment of distraction, he dragged the mirror from her grip. With a mighty flick of his neck, he flung the mirror across the room, toward the door the jatai had left open.

Where Bayushi Meirō stepped into the gap, sacred sword in hand, and brought the point stabbing down into the mirror's heart.

# CHAPTER TWENTY-SIX

Air had never felt so precious, not even after Ryōtora escaped the dead cell. He gasped in breath after breath, his pulse thundering so loud in his ears he could hear nothing else, see nothing but red until at last the world came back.

The first thing he saw was Sayashi, in cat form once more, panting almost as hard as he was and standing over the shredded remains of a silken sash.

The second was Bayushi Meirō, materialized as if out of nowhere and holding General Uebe against a wall at the point of a broken sword.

The third was Sekken, bloodstained, arms wrapped tight around Tanshu and tears streaming unchecked down his face.

And then...

Ryōtora's mind couldn't quite encompass what stood in the doorway. It looked like an ordinary man, shaven-headed and wearing a robe as plain as a monk's. He might have passed a hundred such men on the street and never given them a second glance. But like a rock skipping off the surface of a pond, his mind flinched from the depths behind that simple appearance. If he sank into it, he might never come back.

Tōji was wailing, a thin, despairing sound.

The man – the Fortune – picked something up from the floor. The mirror Ryōtora had tried to destroy, now impaled upon the snapped-off point of a sword.

"Yoshimi." The Fortune's voice was like his appearance: a pleasant surface hiding unimaginably more. "You knew this day would come. Yet as with so much else, you refused to accept it."

The Lady of the Market was on her knees amidst a crumpled pool of silks, her robes stretching around her in disarray. For the first time, she resembled the ghost she was, with her hair wild and her face drained of color. "Of all the Fortunes," she whispered bloodlessly, "you are the cruelest."

The Fortune of Fate shook his head. "No, Yoshimi. That is one of many things you fail to understand. Cruelty suggests that I impose suffering where it is not deserved, that I rejoice in subjecting others to pain. Neither is true." He opened his hand and let the ruined mirror drop to the floor. "What I oversee is like the falling of objects. It is the natural consequence of events that have brought them to their current state. You will suffer for what you have done, yes, but not because I wish to punish you. Your own inability to release your desire has created your fate."

"You could change that," she spat, dragging herself across the mat toward him. "You may claim you impose nothing on us, but you have the power to remove it. Yet you don't."

"Should I grant you mercy?" He gazed down upon her, unblinking. "You, who trapped a man on the threshold between life and death… who assumed rulership over this world by means of stolen power… who took pleasure in forcing others into deals that benefitted only you. I should spare you from the consequences of your actions?"

Yoshimi's fingers dug into the mat, trembling. "Yes."

"Why?"

Instead of answering, she began to weep silently. The Fortune of Fate knelt, so that he no longer loomed over her. Softly, he said, "You want me to spare you because you are afraid. But the karma that follows you from one lifetime to the next is not simply a punishment, it is a lesson. One you need to learn, Yoshimi, so that someday your soul can be free. You have hidden from your teacher long enough."

He held out his hand, as if in blessing. And Yoshimi faded: first going translucent, then vanishing entirely, until her robes lay empty upon the mat.

The Fortune inhaled slowly, his eyes closing. Then, opening them, he turned to General Uebe. "Go and find the king and queen of this place, and bring them to me."

Meirō retreated, but didn't lower her broken blade. The crockery general saluted and said, "As you wish."

Once the rattling clatter of his steps had faded, the Fortune turned to those who remained in the room. The screens had retreated to the walls; the futon had folded itself into a neat pile, like the bedding equivalent of a bow. To the tsukumogami, the Fortune said, "You are all now free of Yoshimi's rule. In due course, I think this market will return to what it should be: a place of refuge for those things which humans discard, and a source of life and awareness for those they treasure. But it may take some time."

Then his gaze fell upon Sekken. Ryōtora hadn't dared move to the other man's side; the weight of the Fortune's presence held him pinned. The Fortune said, "You have suffered a wound, I see."

More than one. Sekken's right sleeve was soaked in blood, and more stained his left shoulder. But the way his hands tightened on Tanshu said that that was not the wound the Fortune referred to. In a voice thick with tears, he said, "This inugami is... was... my familiar. Passed down to me by my holy ancestor, Kaimin-nushi. Tōji – Yoshimi – she–" he swallowed convulsively "–she broke that bond."

Ryōtora's own throat closed up. Tanshu, severed from Sekken? A thousand ramifications flickered in his mind, but all of them were pushed to the corners by the descending weight of grief. Sekken lived, and Tanshu lived; he should be grateful for that. He *was* grateful for that. And yet, he knew how much the inugami had come to mean to Sekken – not just as a beloved companion, but as a part of himself. He might never have intended to be a witch, but to lose that now...

The Fortune said, "If you wish that wound healed, it will be. That lies within my power."

After the way he'd spoken to Yoshimi, the offer came as a shock. Ryōtora was too exhausted and battered to keep his reaction from his face, and the Fortune said mildly, "You are surprised?"

Choosing his words with extreme care, Ryōtora said, "I know very little of your nature, august one. From your words, I took you to be a more impersonal overseer, who does not intervene."

"The wound was taken in service of freeing me," the

Fortune said. "Good deeds bring their own consequences, just as evil ones do. And Yoshimi had no right to break this bond."

Sekken stared up at him. "I'm supposed to pass the bond on to my child, so – but we were told you're the Fortune of Fate, not…" His eyes widened. "Ah. I think I see."

Despite everything – or because of it – his reply dragged a wisp of hysterical sound from Ryōtora. It would have been a laugh, had his throat felt capable of any such thing. *Of course: introduce Sekken to a Fortune, and he'll start trying to understand its nature.*

The Fortune was nodding. "Fate is not merely the weight a person carries from one life to the next. It is the circumstances surrounding them in that life, including the people – whether those people are human or not. What binds you and that inugami is a manifestation of karma. Therefore it falls under my power."

Perhaps some of Sekken's intellectual curiosity was bleeding over to Ryōtora, because he couldn't help thinking of Yoshimi's deals. Taking his connection to the spirits… yes, he could see how that would be the transfer of a karmic bond. Even Sayashi's century of servitude, creating a burden of fate that should not have been there.

Sekken looked at Tanshu. The dog responded by licking his face enthusiastically. Half laughing, half crying, Sekken said, "Yes. Please."

Nothing changed that Ryōtora could see. But he felt it, thrumming along the connection between him and Sekken, like the string of a biwa resonating when its neighbor was plucked.

He wasn't surprised when the Fortune turned back to him. "As for the two of you ... the bond between you is most unusual. I have not seen its like in a very long time."

Ryōtora wasn't sure what to say to that. He settled for dragging himself into a proper kneeling position – which he should have done long since – and bowing.

"People think of karma as a burden or a blessing," the Fortune said, "when often it is both. But burden or blessing is in the experience of a thing, not the thing itself. Which is it for you?"

"August one – I–" Lost for words, Ryōtora looked at Sekken.

After a moment's hesitation, Sekken said, "I... I think it's both."

Hearing him say that brought an odd sort of relief. The discovery that they could steady the balance between them had made things immeasurably better, but not perfect; that balance required constant maintenance. Life would be easier if they didn't have to worry about that, if they could just go back to living ordinary lives where each of them could act without consideration for the other's health.

And yet, didn't that consideration bring them closer together? Not to mention how their connection had protected Ryōtora when he was in the dead cell – or the way he was able to share in Sekken's link with Tanshu. Ryōtora suspected they hadn't yet found all the benefits their bond could bring.

But they didn't have to pretend those benefits made the downsides go away. They could acknowledge the latter, without seeming ungrateful for the former.

"Both," Ryōtora agreed.

"Do you wish to keep it?" the Fortune asked. "If not, I can

part you once more. Not as two half men, but each of you whole."

He'd known the Fortune would say that. And he didn't have to look at Sekken to know the answer... but he did anyway, so they could share that moment of certainty before he spoke.

"Thank you, but no," Ryōtora said softly. "Our connection is a consequence of our actions. We will keep it, and learn from it."

No smile touched the Fortune's face, but his serene expression radiated approval. "Very well."

At some point during their conversation, Meirō had unobtrusively knelt, laying the broken sword at her side. Sayashi, Ryōtora realized, had vanished. But she hadn't gone far. The Fortune raised his voice slightly and said, "Bakeneko. You need not hide from me."

Sayashi slunk out from behind one of the bedchamber doors. She was still in cat form, but after a moment, she flickered uncertainly into a human shape, then knelt and made a credible bow. "August one."

"I know of your deal with Yoshimi," he said, almost kindly. "And you aided these others in freeing me. Ask what you will."

She squirmed. "It doesn't matter."

"It mattered enough for you to accept a hundred years of servitude."

"Not just for that," she protested. "I'd gotten in trouble from trying to steal–" Then her gaze, sliding uneasily away from the Fortune, landed on the hilt at Meirō's side. Sayashi jerked. "*That* sword! Why do you have it?"

Either Meirō was the only person in the room not fazed by the presence of a Fortune, or she was better than the rest of them at hiding it. She said, "Because I needed a weapon."

"Why did *you* need it?" Sekken asked Sayashi. He hadn't let go of Tanshu – Ryōtora suspected he wouldn't for some time yet – but the inugami had settled down, mostly in his lap. "You never told us why you came here in the first place. What is all of this about?"

Red crept up Sayashi's neck. Hunting for some place to look that wasn't at Meirō, Sekken, or the Fortune, she arrived at Ryōtora. Like a held breath, the tension finally breathed out of her. She said, "It's all your fault. The two of you, and your stupid dog, and – you made me *think*. About all those years ago, when I saved a man's life and prevented a war, and because of that, the Fortune of Death offered me a chance to reincarnate as a human. Which I turned down, of course. But…"

Her *of course* lacked the self-assurance it had held in the past, and the *but* trailed off with a note of longing. Sayashi ducked her chin. "I decided to look for him. The man I saved. He's long dead, of course, but I wanted to know where he was now. *Who* he was now." She nodded at the sword. "That used to be his. It turns out his family remembered the story of how I saved him, even hundreds of years later. I waved at him as he was riding along the road, and because of that he avoided an ambush, helped stop a war. That's why they donated the sword to the shrine to the Fortune of Roads, when his family line eventually died out. Because of *me*."

Meirō picked up the blade, slid its remains into the sheath, and presented it to Sayashi with both hands. "I did not know. This should be yours, then."

"I don't want the *sword*," Sayashi snapped. "I wanted it because it would help me find *him*. Fukiau Otondo, whoever he is in this lifetime. Tōji promised she would find him for me, if I served her for a hundred years."

In a hundred years, that man would have died and been born again. But Ryōtora supposed one incarnation was as good as the next, when it was the soul itself she sought.

Sayashi gave the Fortune a furious, embarrassed look. "So there. That's what I wanted to know. It's stupid and it doesn't matter, but I was curious. Where is he?"

This time the Fortune did smile, ever so faintly. "He is offering you his broken sword."

Meirō froze. Then, with the exaggerated care of someone who would drop her burden if she moved too fast, she laid the sheathed blade on the mat.

Sayashi gaped at her. "*You?*"

The Fortune spoke, since Meirō seemed incapable. "Trapped in that mirror, I could do very little to affect the world. Fate continued on its way, but without oversight, without maintenance. I could, however, lean ever so slightly on the karmic bonds that exist. Such as those between you and these two men… and you and the reincarnation of the man you saved."

*The oracle's prophecy,* Ryōtora thought. *A Scorpion's fate –* the karma that had brought Meirō into contact with them, and through that, to Brittle Flower City, where she used her own ancestral sword to free the Fortune.

Almost inaudibly, Meirō said, "It felt so comfortable in my hand, even though it's an old style. And you… you looked familiar to me. And I've always liked that shrine. I visit it every time I pass through Brittle Flower City." Her laugh was a stuttering thing. "I keep a lucky cat figurine in my baggage, a little thing waving its paw. Botan makes fun of me for it."

She finally looked up and met Sayashi's eyes. "I guess you've found me. What now?"

Sayashi shrank in on herself, more uncertain than Ryōtora had ever seen her. "I... I wanted to ask you what I should do. I don't know why I thought you'd know, or even care that I asked, when you've lived so many lives since we last saw each other."

"Who can say if that's true?" Meirō said. "Maybe we've encountered each other over and over again."

That suggestion robbed Sayashi of speech. Hesitant to intrude, but suspecting that Sayashi herself would never say it, Ryōtora spoke up. "When you say you wanted to know what you should do... are you talking about your own reincarnation?"

"Yes." Sayashi muttered it into her own lap, a grudging surrender.

Sekken shifted, posture straightening. "You've been thinking about what I said to you. About how being human means having people to help you."

Sayashi drew a deep breath, hands curling inward. "Not just what you said. What you've *done*. You even came all the way here, the two of you – and–" when her head came up, her eyes were bright with tears "–Ryōtora, you bargained with Tōji for my release. You didn't have to do that."

"Yes, I did," Ryōtora said simply.

Meirō hummed in understanding. "You want to know whether you should be reborn as a human."

"I doubt I even can," Sayashi said, with a defensive veneer of unconcern. "Not any time soon, anyway. I haven't been as good as I once was."

Ryōtora looked at the Fortune of Fate. "What have her deeds earned her?"

The Fortune shook his head. "That is for her to discover, when she goes before the Fortune of Death."

Something about how he said it chilled Ryōtora. "But, she's not dead."

Very quietly, Sayashi said, "I think I sort of am."

He whirled to face her. Sayashi tried to smile, but it came out thin and wavering. "My deal with Tōji. That I'd serve her for a hundred years. I think …"

The moment outside the dead cell, when Ryōtora had prayed in desperate confusion for the spirits to do something, *anything*, to stop Sayashi from attacking him and shoving him back into the cell. And she'd dropped like a stone.

But not died – not quite – because her oath of servitude wouldn't let her escape so easily.

Sickness overwhelmed him. And then Sayashi was there, hugging him, saying fiercely into his ear, "Damn it, you're not allowed to feel guilty! I knew what I was doing. Seeing you dying in that cell, when the only reason you'd come to this city was because of me – and it wasn't just you who would suffer because of that, it was Sekken, too – if I'd let that happen, I wouldn't *want* to find Otondo after that, because I wouldn't be able to look him in the eye. So what if I'm dead? You've died only the Heavens know how many times. All you humans have. You got over it."

That was the worst description of reincarnation Ryōtora had ever heard, but it cracked the ice encasing his heart. He gave a broken laugh and returned Sayashi's hug, knowing this first embrace was also the last.

"I will pray to the Fortune of Death to be generous," he said, letting her go. "And to the Fortune of Fate."

Sekken eased Tanshu off his lap and embraced Sayashi as well. "I will do the same."

"You're getting blood on me."

Tears were slipping down his face again as he pulled back, but they caught against the edges of his smile. "I will know you in any lifetime, Sayashi, because you will always find some way to deflate me."

Then, hesitantly, Sayashi looked at Meirō.

Who wore an expression of mixed shock, bafflement, wonder, and warmth. "What do I know of the underworld and reincarnation?" Meirō said. "I don't even know what my own karma will look like, after my errors this time around. But if you want to know what I think…"

Conviction flared in her eyes. "Yes," Meirō said. "Try to become human. If not in your next life, then in the one after that, and on and on until you pass through mortality and attain the Heavens. We'll find each other again, I'm sure."

Sayashi reached out. For just a moment, Meirō gripped her hand. Then Sayashi's body blurred, and not only because of Ryōtora's tears. She flowed from human to enormous black cat, to small black cat, to a tiny shadow on the mat… to nothing. He whispered a prayer, and she was gone.

# CHAPTER TWENTY-SEVEN

The broom spirit, Kanbōki, was the only one left in the house at the threshold of the market. Sekken wished they could have said goodbye to Enjiki, thanked him for his assistance and wished him well in his next life, but he understood why the man hadn't waited. *If I'd spent centuries trapped and unable to move on, I'd take the first chance I got, too.*

"What will become of the threshold?" he asked Kanbōki, gesturing at the barred door. "Without Enjiki here?"

The hahakigami rattled its bristles in irritation. "What do you think I am, an ordinary bundle of twigs? We brooms do more than just sweep floors. We sweep evil spirits out of places, babies out of their mothers..." It narrowed its eyes at Sekken. "Guests who have overstayed their welcome out onto the road."

Sekken bowed, hiding his smile. "You will have your chance soon enough. There are only a few things we must do before we go."

He'd obtained better paper and ink, and brushes for the others to use. So far as he knew, none of those items were sentient. They each sat in their separate corners, him, Ryōtora, and Meirō, while Kuzu played with Tanshu out behind the house, and they wrote their own letters.

Sekken didn't know what the other two were writing about, but his was a message to Sayashi's future incarnation. Although the reborn bakeneko might well never see it, he understood what Kuzu had meant, about wanting there to be some record of her mother's existence. Sekken fully intended to write other accounts of Sayashi... but he wanted this one to stay here. The tale of the cat spirit he'd met in Seibo Mura, who had in turn been a peasant, a geisha, a slave, and always – in her own prickly, sideways fashion – a friend.

The creaking of wooden wheels heralded the approach of Fuguruma Yōhi, with Chirizuka Kaiō at her heels. Sekken had reflexively expected them to appear grander now that they were restored to their positions as rulers of the market, but they were unchanged: still untrustworthy-looking, ogreish creatures, gathering up the detritus of human lives and hearts. *The things people throw away, and the attachments they can't let go of.*

Attachments they were supposed to free themselves from, in order to escape the cycle of rebirth. But that was always a work in progress.

Sekken gave Fuguruma Yōhi his letter, and Ryōtora followed suit. Meirō was last. Nothing came out of the cart as the letters went in, and Sekken wondered just how many missives and diaries and other documents lay hidden within that unassuming box. Hidden, but not forgotten: he had no doubt that Yōhi remembered them all.

Chirizuka Kaiō set down a lacquered box with a carrying handle. "I suppose we owe you some thanks," he said, sounding not particularly gracious. Sekken doubted he was capable of graciousness. "So as a favor to you, we're letting a few of our subjects leave."

Mystified, Sekken opened the top of the box – then jerked back in surprise when the bowl inside sat up.

"We feel we've gotten to know you and Lord Isao rather well," the bowl said, gesturing at its fellow implements: the kettle, the whisk, all the accouterments of the way of tea, packed neatly inside the box. "And it is more satisfying to fulfill our purpose than to sit here in the market, alone. We would like to go with you when you leave."

Sekken stared at Ryōtora, trying desperately not to laugh. Not because the offer was funny – in fact, it was deeply touching – but because he couldn't imagine how they were supposed to explain a box full of animated tea utensils to everyone back home.

Diplomatically, Ryōtora said, "You might attract a great deal of attention – not all of it good. And I was recently given an heirloom tea bowl by an important lord, in recognition of the service I rendered him. I would not want to insult him by setting that aside, but neither would I want to insult *you* by failing to enjoy your company."

"We won't be like this outside the market," the whisk said, also sitting up. "I mean, we might be from time to time, if there's need. But it takes effort, being fully alive out there."

The bowl nodded. "And I would be glad to make the acquaintance of this heirloom you mentioned. If it is not yet properly awake, I look forward to guiding it along that path."

A tiny headache was forming between Sekken's eyes as he tried to think through the ramifications of that. What *was* the difference between a nemuranai and a tsukumogami, a spiritually awakened item and one that had taken on a life of its own? He might have the chance to investigate that question first-hand.

Ryōtora's eyes were still bloodshot from his near-strangling, but he seemed amused as he nodded to Sekken. Bowing to the bowl, the whisk, and everything else inside the box, Sekken said, "We would be honored by your company. And you have our profound gratitude for the aid you've rendered us."

The implements lay down again. He closed the box, Meirō called Kuzu and Tanshu in, and the hahakigami unbarred the door that led to the street. When Chirizuka Kaiō and Fuguruma Yōhi had entered, it opened onto the hidden market, populated with barrels and lanterns and sandals and carts with their own hands and legs and eyes, but now the dawn street was nearly deserted. Only a few yawning humans wandered past, getting ready to open their shops for the day.

Sekken bowed the others through: Meirō, Kuzu, Tanshu, Ryōtora. Then he followed them, Kanbōki sweeping vigorously at his heels, and the door closed behind them forever.

Ishi was the first to spot them, from his station at the gateway to the Emerald Magistrate's headquarters. His wordless shout brought Tarō running, and for a few minutes, everything was chaotic questions and answers and exclamations of surprise.

Sekken had been half afraid they'd emerge from the market to find that a year had passed for every day there – or longer. Instead, it seemed time had continued at its usual pace. They'd been gone four days, which was more than enough time for worry to set in.

*Lord Utaku thought the Scorpion had killed you all,* Ishi signed to Sekken, while Ryōtora apologized to Tarō for inadvertently leaving him behind.

Meirō snorted and signed back, *I don't know whether to be insulted or flattered. I think these two are indestructible.*

It made Ishi jerk in surprise, because Meirō hadn't shown any particular facility with sign language before. She grinned. Her face was no longer bare, but in place of the masks she'd worn before, she'd tied a tattered strip of embroidered silk across her face, with holes cut for the eyes. Sekken recognized that silk; he'd wrestled briefly with it when he tried to stop it from attacking Ryōtora. It seemed faintly morbid for her to wear what amounted to the flesh of the dead jatai, but in the end, it was fabric, not skin. And he suspected she'd chosen it as a memento of Sayashi, who'd killed the jatai to save Ryōtora.

Utaku Teruo came striding out from the main building and jerked to a halt at the sight of them. Meirō wasted no time in kneeling and placing the chokutō she'd stolen on the ground. The point remained in the hidden market, stabbed into the heart of the mirror; Sekken didn't know what the Fortune of Fate or Chirizuka Kaiō had done with that relic. What lay inside the sheath was broken. "I surrender myself to the Emerald Magistrates," Meirō said.

"Before you make any decisions," Sekken said to Teruo, "you should hear the whole story. It's not what any of us thought."

Ryōtora nodded in agreement. "While I understand that there must be consequences for Lady Bayushi's disobedience, those consequences should also take into account her other actions. She has freed a captive Fortune."

"A captive *F*–" Utaku Teruo swallowed the rest of that exclamation and said, "You'd better come inside."

Inside there was food, which Sekken and Ryōtora both fell upon ravenously, and tea from cups that didn't talk to them, and a physician who bandaged Sekken's wounds more effectively than Ryōtora had been able to do. Sekken also wanted to sleep for three days, but he'd passed through exhaustion to a kind of gliding, unreal state where he could keep going as long as there was something for him to do.

Which mostly consisted of a lot of talking. Teruo listened to their explanations, and at the end he said, "So you believe Bayushi Meirō's actions were justified."

Ryōtora, of course, was capable of discussing moral philosophy even when his eyes were crossing with weariness. "Is it right to judge her deeds by their eventual outcome, when she herself did not know where they were leading her? That is not for myself or Asako to decide. Her choices were well-intentioned, though, and we are deeply grateful to her. If we have any latitude to make requests of the Emerald Magistrates–" Teruo's quiet huff answered that question "– then I ask that she be treated kindly."

Teruo sat cross-legged and cross-armed, like a statue. "She'll have to answer to the shrine authorities as well, for her theft. Even if the sword was hers in another lifetime, once dedicated to a shrine, it's not supposed to be taken back. As for the rest..." He fell silent for a moment, then nodded. "Demotion is likely, at a minimum. But if I can arrange for her to remain within the Emerald Magistrates, I will."

They both bowed to him. In the quiet, sound came through from outside the room: a high-pitched giggle, followed by a brief bark.

Sekken glanced at Ryōtora, then at Teruo. "If I can ask one

other favor from you, magistrate… I have a legal question you might be able to answer."

Kuzu was playing with Tanshu again outside. If her antics with the dog had the faintly determined air of a girl trying to distract herself, Sekken could hardly blame her; Kuzu had been through ordeals of her own.

He whistled Tanshu back to his side, and he and Ryōtora led Kuzu over to sit on the edge of the veranda. Sekken could see the vitality seeping out of the girl as she braced herself for what was coming.

Ryōtora asked, "Kuzu, do you have anywhere in Brittle Flower City you could go other than the Reiya?"

She clamped her jaw and shook her head. Sekken doubted she could even go back to the Reiya, after the way she'd left, but Kuzu was too proud to say it. Or too ashamed. Or too resigned: she'd been abandoned once before, and believed such things were now her fate.

"We've spoken to Lord Utaku Teruo," Sekken said. "And we've arranged two alternate possibilities for you. One is that you can stay here in the city and work for the Emerald Magistrates. Lord Utaku will take you on as a maid."

Shock widened Kuzu's eyes. It was a windfall as unlooked-for as a purse found lying in the street – but Sekken held up his hand before she could accept. "Or," he said.

"Or," Ryōtora said, "you can come with us."

Kuzu turned to stare at him. "Come with you…"

"To Dragon lands. Which are a very long way to the north, and they'll be unlike what you're used to. Colder. More mountainous. We won't be living in a city like this one. But…"

Ryōtora's austere face softened into a tentative smile. "Asako and I are to be married. And we would adopt you as our daughter."

Kuzu didn't answer. Sekken didn't think she was capable of sound.

Ryōtora had been similarly speechless, when Sekken asked Teruo about the laws around adoption. But not for long; once he regained his tongue, he'd given unhesitating support to the idea. They'd been through too much with Kuzu to simply leave her behind now that their business in Crane lands was done.

Sekken said, "You helped us here, Kuzu, at no small risk to yourself. If you hadn't been brave in writing that letter for your amo, we might never have known what was going on in the hidden market."

Ryōtora gave Sekken a warning look. "But, Kuzu, don't think this is something you had to earn – much less that you have to go on earning it. We're offering this because we want to make sure you're taken care of. I know going to an unknown land might be frightening, though… and it can be hard, living in a samurai family when you were born a peasant. I speak from experience. So we won't be offended at all if you'd rather stay here."

Kuzu seemed to have stopped breathing, and she stared at Ryōtora when he mentioned his own birth. Then her eyes jerked away, as if afraid she would give offense. Tanshu, who'd flopped panting on the ground at their feet, got up and licked her hand in encouragement.

She whispered, "Tanshu's going with you?"

Sekken scratched vigorously behind the inugami's ears. Tanshu leaned into it with a blissful expression. "Of course. I would never leave my dog behind." *Not even when a vengeful ghost tries to take him from me.*

An enormous, wet sniff came from Kuzu. "Then – yes, my lords."

Ryōtora laid a gentle hand on her underfed shoulder. "Not 'my lords,' Kuzu, not anymore. I am Ryōtora, and he is Sekken. And perhaps, once you have been settled in Dragon lands for a while… you might think of us as your fathers."

Then it was the long road north, with no certainty of what awaited them at the end.

Ryōtora felt that uncertainty like a weight on his shoulders. Meirō wasn't the only one who'd turned aside from her duty, and who hoped the results of her deeds might buy her lenience. Kuzu wasn't the only one journeying to a new and unfamiliar home. He could tell Sekken didn't want to lay his own nervousness on Ryōtora, but it came through whenever they sat and shared tea, using implements that always felt the slightest bit warm, even when first lifted from their box.

At least they had proper travel papers, issued free and clear by Utaku Teruo after he released them from their nominal positions as yoriki. He advised them to travel through the Lion city of Rugashi, then across the river to the lands of the Dragonfly Clan, the traditional gateway to the mountains of the Dragon. They sent messages ahead from there, so by the time they reached Shiro Agasha, not only were they expected, but their story was known.

At least in its broad strokes, and to the people who needed to hear it. Ryōtora scarcely had time to see to it that Sekken, Tanshu, and Kuzu were settled into temporary quarters before he was whisked away to speak with his daimyō at great length. He reported honestly, holding nothing back – not even the self-serving logic by which they'd accepted Meirō's offer of appointment as yoriki, as if that excuse would justify their dereliction of duty. "In the end it turned out for the best," he said, "because it brought Lady Bayushi to where she needed to be. But I cannot justify my actions on those grounds. I should have been forthright in my intentions, rather than evading the matter when I spoke to Mirumoto Otoyu."

The Agasha daimyō had chosen to meet with him in her dry garden, rather than a formal reception room, which he hoped was an encouraging sign. She said, "The Fortune of Fate seems to have laid a rather heavy hand on your life, so I can hardly fault you for the unexpected turns your path has taken. But yes, you should have been more forthright. After all the service you have rendered to this clan and to the empire, Isao, you have earned the benefit of the doubt. If you told me you needed to go to Brittle Flower City, I would have granted you permission."

It would have taken additional time, sending a message to her or asking in person, and who knew what the effects of that might have been. For one, Meirō would likely not have gotten involved. But the daimyō's comment was rebuke and kindness in one, and Ryōtora accepted both with a bow.

"Here is your punishment," she said, in a light tone that made it clear she wasn't particularly serious. At a lift of her hand, an attendant hurried forward and handed her a small scroll, which she passed on to Ryōtora.

Once he'd read it, he said, "My lady... it was my intent to ask for permission to build a shrine to the Fortune of Fate." He grimaced. "Permission and, ah, funds."

"You can do both," she said, nodding at the letter. "And you'll have both. Now go, I have other business to attend to. Share that message with your husband-to-be."

Ryōtora went out into the steep streets of Shiro Agasha, bathed in the golden light of late afternoon. The castle itself was perched atop a rocky crag, easily defensible should enemy forces ever penetrate this deeply into Dragon territory, but the castle town clung to a series of terraces cut into the slope. The sight had made Kuzu gape when she first arrived, and now he found her, Tanshu, and Sekken outside their inn, standing by one of the low walls that prevented erosion.

They weren't alone. And when Ryōtora saw who was with them, he ran forward with a glad cry.

His adoptive father, Sir Keijun, pulled him up out of his bow and into a hug. "I knew I would be a grandfather soon," he said gruffly, "but not *this* soon." He nodded at Kuzu, who blushed and crouched to pet Tanshu.

"We've already had all the introductions," Sekken told Ryōtora, "so you can skip that part. Your daimyō left you in one piece? You seem to still have all your limbs."

Ryōtora laughed. "I do. In truth, it could have been far worse."

"Hard to shout at a man who freed a Fortune," Keijun said. "Not to mention everything else you've done." His craggy face was bright with pride.

Sekken peered at the scroll in Ryōtora's hand. "What's that?"

"Our fate," Ryōtora said, and handed it over.

Sekken unrolled it, eyebrows climbing skyward as he read. "Who's Agasha Riwaka?"

"She was one of my teachers."

"And she thinks *we* can teach *her* something?"

Her message phrased it that way, but purely out of politeness. "In the same way that a butterfly caught in a net can teach the one who caught it," Ryōtora said wryly. "She wants to study your bond with Tanshu, and the bond between us. She once spent several years with the Isawa, debating all manner of theological mysteries, and when she came back, she started talking about building a small school here for the study of such things. I suspect she intends to use us as her foundation stone – metaphorically speaking, of course."

Sekken rolled up the scroll. "I thought our plan was to build a shrine, not a school. But… no reason it can't be both."

Already his eyes were alive with light, considering the possibilities. Ryōtora felt the same light in his own heart. A shrine to the Fortune who oversaw all such karmic bonds, where priests, monks, and scholars could come to study and discuss the links of fate that bound actions to consequences, witches to familiars, lovers to each other, across the gulf of lifetimes.

Answering such questions might take more than one incarnation. Standing with Sekken in the afternoon sun, with the mountains of the Dragon spreading out before them like the folds of an embroidered robe, Ryōtora said, "Then let's get started."

# ACKNOWLEDGMENTS

Once again, I owe a significant debt of gratitude to Matthew Meyer, whose series of books on yōkai (*The Night Parade of 100 Demons, The Hour of Meeting Evil Spirits, The Book of the Hakutaku,* and *The Fox's Wedding*) have been indispensable to my research. Many of the tsukumogami who appear in this novel are drawn, via his work, from real Japanese sources – but not quite all.

The real ones include: the kutsutsura (boot), hasamidachi (scissors), osakōburi (hat), kosode no te (short-sleeved kimono), bakezōri (straw sandals), karakasa kozō (umbrella; not to be confused with the more sinister bone umbrella, the hone karakasa), chōchin obake (lantern), kameosa (jug), narigama (flaming kettle), hahakigami (broom), waniguchi (shrine bell), biwa bokuboku (biwa, a stringed instrument), furu-ōgi (folding fan), yama oroshi (grater), komainu (guardian lions, called shīsā in Okinawa and shishi in China), kura yarō (saddle), byōbu nozoki (folding screen peeping tom), kaichigo (small box, specifically one for holding decorative shells), jatai (obi), kyōrinrin (sutra), furuutsubo (quiver of arrows), and shōgorō (gong).

The mirror used to trap the Fortune is inspired by the ungaikyō from Japanese folklore. General Uebe is based on Seto Taishō/General Seto; since the name of the original apparently refers to a well-known pottery-making area in Japan, I chose to name his Rokugani analogue after the Uebe Marshes in Crane lands, on the theory that there might be good clay there. Chirizuka Kaiō and Fuguruma Yōhi are likewise drawn from real folklore, though not linked as a married couple; Chirizuka Kaiō is sometimes called the king of the tsukumogami. Plus, of course, the bakeneko Sayashi and the inugami Tanshu are based on real yōkai!

Why did I go the route of inventing some yōkai, when in the past I've stuck to those attested in Japanese folklore and L5R canon? Mostly it's because I wanted to populate the hidden market with many ordinary objects, and of the list of tsukumogami available to me, some are sufficiently arcane to the Anglophone reader that I would spend more time explaining the object than its role in the story merited. In order to keep the market focused on the types of things that would be found within its walls, I invented the barrel tsukumogami seen briefly at the gate, the carts described as being on the streets (though there is an oboroguruma, a type of oxcart carriage for aristocrats), the tall lacquered sandals that attend Tōji (okobo, the style of geta worn by maiko), the futon that pins Tanshu down, and Elder Sister Noren. To the best of my knowledge, I also invented the tea ceremony tsukumogami – the tea caddy, whisk, bowl, cloth, scoop, kettle, and incense box – though I'm startled not to have found any references to such things in my reading, given how tea utensils are treasured as heirlooms! I hope my additions are within the spirit (no pun intended) of yōkai nature, and that they added some color to the tale.

One thing I did not invent, though I renamed it: the Brittle Flower City Pigeon. Books like this existed in the Edo Period, and some of them were called Sparrows, evoking the idea of getting a "bird's eye view" of the city. Since Rokugan has a Sparrow Clan, though, I decided to avoid that echo by naming them for a different urban bird. I owe thanks to Nishiyama Matsunosuke and his translator Gerald Groemer for *Edo Culture: Daily Life and Diversions in Urban Japan, 1600-1868*, and Mary Elizabeth Barry for *Japan in Print: Information and Nation in the Early Modern Period*; they helped me evoke the mercantile feeling of Brittle Flower City, which is very much based on Edo and Osaka during the Edo Period.

My thanks also to my editor, Charlotte Llewelyn-Wells, and my agent, Eddie Schneider!

# ABOUT THE AUTHOR

MARIE BRENNAN is a former anthropologist and folklorist who shamelessly pillages her academic fields for inspiration. She recently misapplied her professors' hard work to *The Night Parade of 100 Demons* and the short novel *Driftwood*. She is the author of the Hugo Award-nominated Victorian adventure series The Memoirs of Lady Trent along with several other series, over seventy short stories, and the New Worlds series of worldbuilding guides; as half of M A Carrick, she has written the epic Rook and Rose trilogy, beginning with *The Mask of Mirrors*.

*swantower.com*
*twitter.com/swan_tower*

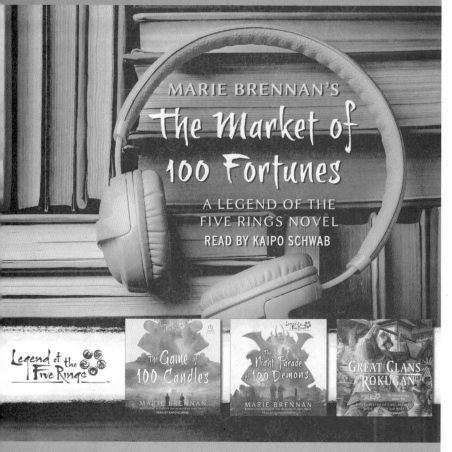